A RECKONING OF STORM AND SHADOW

SHADOW

BOOK THREE OF HEIRS OF WAR

JAMIE EDMUNDSON

Rarn Publishing

BY JAMIE EDMUNDSON

A RECKONING OF STORM AND SHADOW

Book Three of Heirs of War

Author website jamieedmundson.com

Cover: Bastien Jez

Visit the Heirs of War page which includes downloadable colour maps of key locations:

For David, Holly, Grace & Joseph

DRAMATIS PERSONAE

DALRIYA

Guivergne
    Esterel, King of Guivergne
    Liesel, Queen of Guivergne
    Peyre, Esterel's brother, Duke of Morbaine
    Sanc, Esterel's younger brother
    Rab, Sanc's dog
    Loysse, Esterel's sister
    Auberi, Duke of Famiens, Loysse's husband
    Alienor, Loysse's daughter
    Syele, Loysse's bodyguard
    Cebelia, Loysse's lady maid
    Brayda, a maid
    Brancat, castellan of the Bastion
    Lord Russell, steward of Morbaine
    Umbert, son of Russell, Peyre's friend
    Domard, Duke of Martras
    Ragonde, Domard's man
    Gosse, Lord of the March

Sul, Gosse's man
Caisin, Lord Chancellor of Guivergne
Ernst & Gernot, Caisin's thugs
Sacha, Lord Courion, Royal Steward
Coleta, Sacha's sister
Florent, Lord of Auriac
Robert, son of Raymon, the former Lord of Auriac
Arnoul, Lord of Saliers
Benoit, Arnoul's son
Jehan, a guardsman in The Bastion
Inhan, a warrior of Morbaine
Firmin, a trader

Empire of Brasingia
Idris, Prince of Atrabia & Duke of Luderia
Tegyn, Idris's sister
Bron, Idris's mother
Emlyn, Idris's uncle
Ilar & Macsen, Idris's cousins
Inge the witch, adviser to the emperor
Teuchenberg & Wechlitz, Luderian noblemen
Jeremias, Duke of Rotelegen
Katrina, Duchess of Rotelegen, sister of Liesel
Friedrich, Duke of Thesse
Otto, Friedrich's chamberlain
Emmett, Archbishop of Gotbeck

Magnia
King Ida
Elfled, his mother
Brictwin, Ida's bodyguard
Morlin, Elfled's bodyguard
Herin, a warrior
Belwynn Godslayer

The Midder Steppe
    Cuenin, a chieftain
    Jorath, a chieftain
    Frayne, a chieftain
    Brock, a chieftain

The Confederacy
    Gethin, King of Ritherys
    Rhain, King of Corieltes

Others in Dalriya
    Ezenachi, Lord of the Avakaba
    Jesper, a Halvian
    Maragin, a Krykker chieftain
    Stenk, a Krykker chieftain
    Lorant, King of the Blood Caladri
    Hajna, Queen of the Blood Caladri
    Theron, King of Kalinth
    Leontios, Grand Master of the Knights of Kalinth
    Zared, King of Persala
    Gansukh, Khan of the Jalakh Empire
    Bolormaa, Gansukh's mother
    Oisin, King of the Orias (Giants)

SILB

Scorgians
    Lenzo, Prince of Scorgia
    Gaida, Lenzo's lieutenant
    Atto, Duke of Sinto
    Amelia the Widow, merchant of Arvena
    Dag, Amelia's agent
    Nolf Money Bags, merchant of Arvena

Kassites

Holt Slender Legged, chieftain
Mildrith, Kassite champion

Nerisians and Gadenzians
Lothar, King of Nerisia
Temyl, Nerisian champion
Guntram, Gadenzian champion

Rasidi, Telds and Egers
Ordono, King of the Rasidi
Mergildo, Rasidi champion
Kepa, Teld champion
Haritz, King of the Telds
The Eger Khan, ruler of the Egers
Hamzat, brother of the Eger Khan
Kursuk, Eger general

THE STORY SO FAR

There's been a considerable gap between books 2 & 3, longer than I originally wanted. But that's often the way when writing & publishing, especially epic fantasy!

So if you're not rereading books 1 & 2, here is the bare bones summary. I hope you enjoy the last instalment of this series.

Finally, a big thank you for supporting my career. Writing books was a long held dream of mine, and I couldn't continue to do it without your support. It means the world to me.

Jamie

Yarm, November 2023

Summary: An Inheritance of Ash and Blood, Book One of Heirs of War

The events of Book One are set in the world of Dalriya.

Sanc, born with red eyes, is the fourth child of Duke Bastien of Morbaine. When he and his dog, Rab, are attacked near his home, his sorcerous powers emerge. Jesper, a forester who looks out for him, invites his old friend, Rimmon, to Arbeost. Rimmon begins to train Sanc in the use of magic.

When Sanc's brother, Peyre, defends him against a group of older bullies, Peyre is exiled to the Empire of Brasingia. He accompanies Duke Walter of Barissia to Essenberg, in the duchy of Kelland. Peyre meets Liesel, Duke Leopold's sister, and tries to defend her against Inge and Salvinus, Leopold's dangerous ministers. When he confronts Leopold about her treatment, Leopold cuts him across the face. Walter is forced to intervene, and has Liesel taken to safety in Atrabia.

The death of the king of Guivergne leads to a war of succession. Bastien, the rightful heir, is opposed by Auberi, Duke of Famiens. Sanc and Peyre help their father to defeat his enemies and claim the throne. Sanc's sister, Loysse, is married to Auberi as part of a peace deal. Once peace is restored, Rimmon leaves Guivergne for the south.

Liesel befriends Tegyn and Idris, the children of the Prince of Atrabia. She joins the army of Atrabia when it heads to the empire's border with Cordence, a kingdom that has been invaded by the Turned. The Turned are the enslaved followers of Ezenachi, a god who has made his home in Dalriya. When the imperial army tries to stand against him, Ezenachi demonstrates his power. He immobilises the army of thousands and kills the emperor. When the Atrabians return home, Liesel and Idris are captured by Inge and Salvinus, and taken to Essenberg.

When Rimmon returns to Guivergne, he asks Sanc to accompany him south. Along with Jesper and Rab, Sanc accompanies Rimmon to Magnia, a kingdom besieged by Ezenachi's Turned. Sanc finds a way to release Herin, an old friend of Rimmon and Jesper's, from Ezenachi's enslavement. They help the Magnians against Ezenachi's invasion. But Sanc and Rimmon cannot withstand the god's power. Sanc is persuaded by Rimmon to travel to another world, to seek a being powerful enough to withstand Ezenachi. Herin volunteers to go with Sanc. When the teleportation begins, Rab leaps into Sanc's arms.

In Guivergne, the death of Bastien means his oldest son, Esterel, is made king. Esterel makes Peyre Duke of Morbaine. When Jesper asks for Peyre's help in Magnia, he leads an army south, only to find Sanc has gone. Peyre fights alongside the Magnians. But again, Ezenachi is too powerful, and kills the king of Magnia. When he captures Rimmon, with the intention of enslaving him, Jesper kills his old friend. Ezenachi imposes a peace on the Magnians, adding the southern half of the kingdom to his realm.

With the fighting over, Peyre vows to rescue Liesel from Essenberg.

Summary: A Crucible of Fire and Steel, Book Two of Heirs of War

The events of Book Two are set in the worlds of Dalriya and Silb.

Sanc arrives in the world of Silb, with Rab as his only companion. Here he meets Lenzo, Prince of Scorgia. He accompanies the Scorgians on their retreat from the invading Nerisian army, to the island city of Arvena.

Meanwhile, in Dalriya, the Empire of Brasingia slides towards civil war. Peyre arrives in Essenberg to agree a marriage between Liesel and Esterel, while hiding his own feelings for her. He takes Liesel to Valennes; where she marries Esterel, and becomes Queen of Guivergne.

Maragin, the Krykker chieftain, arrives in Valennes. She reveals that she has two sacred weapons, a dagger and sword, that can be used to kill Ezenachi. She also reveals that Belwynn Godslayer is in Magnia. Jesper travels with the Krykker to Magnia. They find Belwynn and convince her to help them gather the other five weapons of Madria.

Prince Lenzo and Sanc agree to build a coalition against Lothar of Nerisia. Sanc travels to the lands of the Kassites, where he meets their champion, Mildrith, and five chieftains. He joins them in a campaign to eject the Nerisians from Kassite lands. But when they march against Lothar's army, they are defeated, and the Kassite lands are lost.

The murder of Duke Walter of Barissia prompts Esterel to launch an invasion of Brasingia, with the aim of stopping Liesel's brother, Leopold, from becoming emperor. The Guivergnais army invests Coldeberg. Liesel brings Cordentine exiles to Valennes, while Peyre neutralises an attack by the Middians. After a long siege, Coldeberg is taken, and Esterel is made Duke of Barissia. But in an act of revenge, Leopold has Duke Auberi and his captured soldiers blinded.

Jesper travels to Halvia and persuades Oisin the Giant to return to Dalriya with the spear. King Lorant of the Blood Caladri brings the staff, and the Persaleians provide the shield. Finally, in a deal with Khan Gansukh, Belwynn takes possession of the Jalakh Bow. With six of the seven weapons of Madria in their possession, Belwynn leads this new group of champions south, to Magnia.

When Emlyn refuses to supply them with his Atrabian troops, Leopold and Inge decide to use Idris. In the company of Gervase Salvinus and an invading army, he sets off for Atrabia. But instead of aiding Salvinus, he leads his force into a trap. Salvinus is captured and killed, and Idris becomes Prince of Atrabia. He leads his army into Luderia. At Witmar, the nobles of the duchy agree to transfer their allegiance to him and make him duke.

Sanc and Mildrith escape the lands of the Kassites. In the company of Prince Lenzo, they sail to the lands of the Rasidi, where Lenzo concludes a treaty of alliance with King Ordono. But Sanc discovers it is a trap. As they escape, Sanc meets Herin, who has been living with the Telds since Sanc's arrival in Silb. The Teld champion, Kepa, flies them to her homeland. With options running out, Sanc, Mildrith & Herin enter the lands of the dangerous, lizard riding Egers, in the hope they can form an alliance. They find the Eger Khan, who is still a boy.

When Inge recaptures Coldeberg and kills its defenders, Esterel resolves to conquer the Brasingian Empire for good. Leopold's Kellish army retreats before the Guivergnais and withdraws to Essenberg. It transpires that Idris has led his own army to the capital. With no options left, Inge meets with Esterel and transfers her allegiance to him. Despite Liesel's protests, Esterel has Leopold executed.

In Magnia, Belwynn finds that Queen Elfled has become an Asrai and wears the Cloak. With seven weapons and seven champions, they travel into Lipper lands, to find and kill Ezenachi. When he arrives, the god easily subdues and turns them, making them his champions.

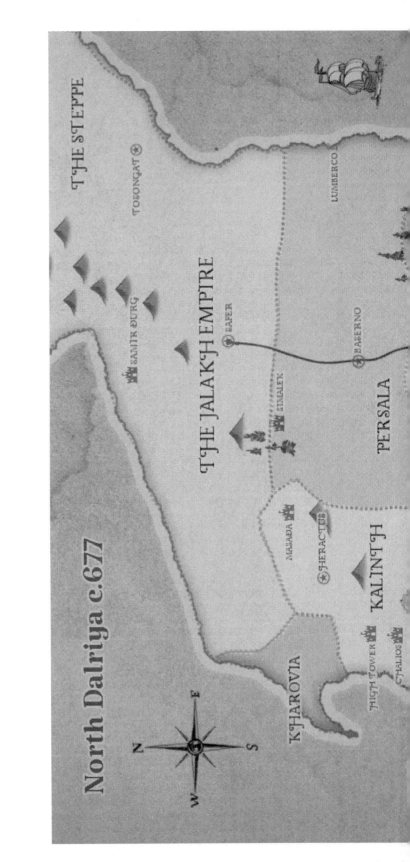

North Dalriya c.677

THE STEPPE

TOSONGAT ⊛

SANIK BURG 🏰

THE JALAKH EMPIRE

SAFER ⊛

SIMALEK 🏰

LUMBERCO

BAERNO ⊛

PERSALA

MAGADA 🏰

HERACTUS ⊛

KALINTH

KHAROVIA

HIGH TOWER 🏰   CHALLOS 🏰

N W E S

TO HALVIA
GRENDAL
SWARTEN
EDELENY
GRAND CALADRI
GREAT RO
GRIENNA
BLOOD CALADRI
BARBARIANS
BEARMEN
LANTINEN SEA
VALENNES
GUSLAR
ROTELEGEN
GUIVERGNE
RIVER COUSEL
BURKHARD CASTLE
WITMAR
TREGIAN
ATRABIA
ITAINEN SEA
ESSENBERG
LUDERIA
KELLAND
ARBEOST
BARISSIA
MORBAINE
MIDDER STEPPE
BRASINGIAN EMPIRE
CONFEDERACY

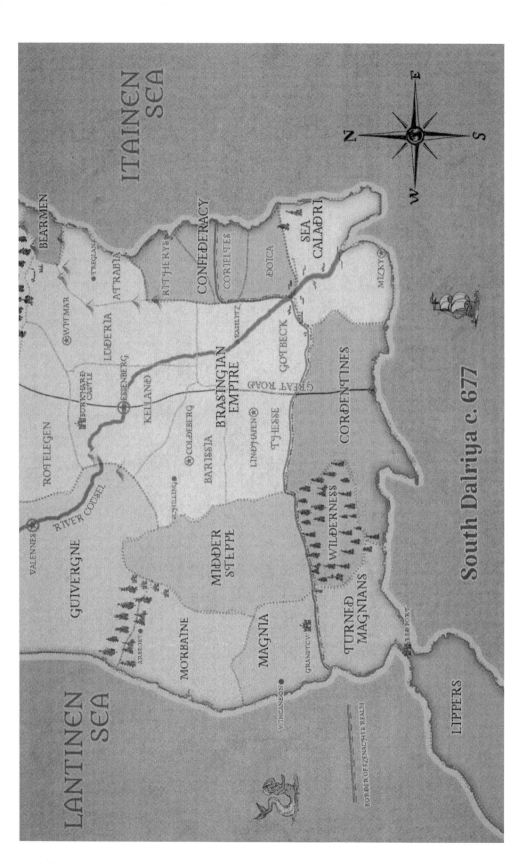

South Dalriya c. 677

LANTINEN SEA

ITAINEN SEA

BEARMEN

CONFEDERACY

SEA CALADRI

GUIVERGNE

ROTELEGEN

BRASINGIAN EMPIRE

LUDERIA

ATRABIA

RITTHERYS

CORIELTES

DOICA

MICKY

WTTMAR

TREGLAN

BURCHARD CASTLE

ESENBERG

KELLAND

COLDEBERG

BARISSIA

LINDHAFEN

THESSE

GOTBECK

GASEITZ

GREAT ROAD

CORDENTINES

MORBAINE

MIDDER STEPPE

MAGNIA

WILDERNESS

TURNED MAGNIANS

CORDENTINES

GRANSTCYF

RED FORT

WINCANEON

VALENNES

RIVER COUSEL

ARBENE

RSTLLING

LIPPERS

BORDER OF ZNACHTE REALM

N

E

S

W

PART I
STORM

677

The Lands of Silb c.677

SANC

LANDS OF THE EGERS

Sanc and Mildrith led the Eger Khan to a spot sheltered by some boulders and a few trees. It was nothing like the forest clearing where Rimmon had taught Sanc to control his magic. The land of the Egers reminded him more of the Midder Steppe—empty and open, usually as far as the eye could see.

The khan had mastered defence against most attacks. Today, he had to defend against magic. Mildrith sent her attacks against him, while Sanc stayed by his side, instructing him—and ready to intervene if needed. If their khan was singed by a blast of magic, the Egers' tolerance of the foreigners in their midst would soon evaporate.

He and Mildrith swapped roles. Sanc fired at the khan from several angles, exposing him to his array of different looking blasts. For his final task, the khan had to defend against both of them at once.

The experience made Sanc even more thankful for Rimmon's tutoring. It felt strange that he was now passing on his teacher's lessons to someone else. He missed the Haskan sorcerer. The amount of time he was taking in Silb; the slow progress towards achieving his mission; such things were never far from his mind.

'I am most grateful for your efforts,' the Eger Khan told them at the end. The boy—for, despite his position as leader of his people, he was still a few years away from adulthood—always seemed to have a serious face, with arresting brown eyes that commanded attention. Like all Egers, he had a fearsome appearance. Their heads, shaped from birth, were elongated.

'Thank you, Your Majesty,' Mildrith said.

Sanc smiled. 'I'm trying to recall how often I thanked my teacher for my lessons. Not enough, I think.'

'You will get a chance to pass on your gratitude,' said the khan.

'True. Soon, I hope.'

* * *

SANC, Mildrith, and Herin were surrounded.

A hundred Egers stood around the roped off area, eager to watch what transpired. Six giant lizards, of various shapes and sizes, were led inside by their handlers, who gripped leather reins or metal chains. The creatures seemed docile enough. But it was hard to ignore their sharp teeth or their huge mouths, capable of stretching open so wide that Sanc could easily imagine being swallowed whole.

Hamzat, older brother of the khan, folded his arms and raised his chin as he looked at the three of them. 'If you go to war with the Egers, you must learn to ride a lizard.'

'No way,' Herin said. 'Get me a horse.'

'No horse would travel with an Eger horde,' Hamzat said. 'And for good reason. Our lizards are well trained, but they are still predators. If they decide they're hungry, it is difficult to change their mind.'

'That's not reassuring me,' Herin complained.

Sanc was in two minds about it. He had what he considered a healthy fear of the creatures. But the thought of riding one had an undeniable appeal.

'Alright,' Mildrith said. 'I'll try. Which one?'

'Approach the one that attracts you,' Hamzat said. 'But understand, a mount chooses its rider as much as a rider chooses its mount. If a lizard decides he doesn't want you on his back, it is wise to respect that.'

Mildrith's choice was the smallest of the options. Lean, with a long tail, and long legs that sprawled out to the sides. Its scales were a mix of reds, oranges, and yellows that reflected the sunlight. Unlike some others, Sanc had not caught sight of its teeth, but its claws were long and sharp. He held his breath as she approached.

The handler passed her the leather reins, which ran up to a bit in the creature's mouth. The saddle set up on this lizard was minimalist: two straps that ran around its trunk, securing the seat.

The handler went down on one knee and Mildrith put a booted foot onto his thigh. She sprang into the saddle. The lizard didn't move; not even a twitch of its head.

'See how easy it is!' Hamzat cried, as the Egers murmured their appreciation.

It was enough to give Sanc the confidence to go next. He approached a green lizard that looked like it might be the comfiest option. One of the largest of the choices, all of its features were thick: head, neck, trunk, and legs; even its tail, a stubby muscle which projected out behind, instead of falling to the ground like Mildrith's mount. Yes, it had sharp teeth protruding from its mouth that undeniably put Sanc off a little. But they were a long way from the saddle. This was secured onto a flat back that would surely give a smooth ride.

When he neared, the lizard turned its neck to him, opened its mouth, and bared its teeth. It emitted a low growl. A close inspection of those fangs was enough to change Sanc's mind. 'I think I'll try this one instead,' he announced, turning to an alternative.

His second choice was cobalt blue, with a yellow underbelly. Its back sloped down, front legs longer than the rear ones, ending in a long, spiked tail that curled along the ground. Indeed, it was a rather spiky creature. On the other hand, it wasn't threatening to bite or gore him, and made no sound or movement as he approached.

Sanc placed a hand on one leg as he studied the saddle. Two leather straps dangled from each side, with footrests on the end—

presumably like stirrups in purpose. He placed his foot in one and swung himself into the saddle. It was an easy manoeuvre, and as he took hold of the reins, the lizard showed no signs of distress. His head was slightly higher than his mounts. At the back of the lizard's head, and along its neck, he could see more spikes had been cut and filed down. A necessary modification, since otherwise he would have been in permanent danger of getting impaled.

'Well?' he called over to Herin.

With a shake of the head, Herin walked over to select his mount. He went straight for the green lizard that had warned Sanc away.

'He's not the friendliest,' Sanc advised.

Sure enough, Herin was growled at, and given a full view of its curved teeth.

'Don't complain to me about it,' Herin said to the beast. 'This isn't my choice.'

At Herin's words, the lizard closed its mouth and turned its neck in the opposite direction.

'Come on,' the Magnian said to its handler. 'Help me up.'

It was quite a distance to the saddle, but the handler gave him a leg up and told him to put his weight on the thick scales that protruded from the side. Herin clambered up and settled into the saddle, then gave Sanc a superior look. 'Don't take no for an answer,' he said.

'I'll have to give you that one,' Sanc admitted. 'What are you going to call yours?'

'Don't be ridiculous.'

'Mine's called Red,' Mildrith said.

'Mine's Spike,' said Sanc.

'Don't get cocky,' Hamzat called over. 'You haven't learned to ride them yet.'

* * *

BY THE TIME the Eger army was ready to march, all three of them were reasonably proficient at handling their mounts.

Battle was another matter entirely. There was no choice but to use a spear when fighting from the back of a giant lizard. Swords simply didn't have the required reach.

Sanc had never enjoyed spear work, feeling clumsy with the weapon. With some training from Hamzat, however, he soon got to grips with the basic moves. He even found he could hold and thrust one-handed while holding Spike's reins.

With a glance at his muscled right arm, he realised he was a different physical specimen than fourteen-year-old Sanc, who had scrabbled ineffectually in the mud of Arbeost's training grounds. He was battle hardened—a warrior. He still didn't think of himself in that way. But if that was what others saw when they looked at him, perhaps it was time to embrace it.

There was one remaining problem. Rab wasn't having it. He barked at Sanc and Spike relentlessly, refusing to accept the new arrangement. The Egers looked on, bemused, as the dog's antics threatened to hold up their departure.

In the end, Sanc deployed his magic. It was no bad thing to remind the Egers of his powers. He knew it was the only thing that had stopped the Egers from killing them when they first entered their lands.

As soon as Rab rose into the air, he stopped barking. The Egers gasped at what they saw. Sanc thought his dog looked decidedly dopey, as his limbs flopped, and Sanc transported him over, depositing him onto the front of his saddle. Rab sniffed about a little before curling up into a ball. 'I think we're ready to leave now,' Sanc announced.

They journeyed north. There were Egers on foot, and Egers mounted on lizards. Having lived with them for a few weeks, Sanc had got used to the elongated heads of the southernmost people of Silb. He had even got used to their lizard mounts. But he still knew they made a fearsome-looking army. Their physical presence alone would trouble their enemies.

They headed for the land of the Gadenzians. It was the only region of Silb that Sanc had yet to set foot on. Sometimes, he would reflect on his efforts and see only failure. He had fought his way across the continent and got no closer to fulfilling his mission. As time passed, his chances of saving Dalriya receded. But there was something about travelling that brought renewed hope. Perhaps this time, his allies would make a breakthrough.

'The borderlands with the Gadenzians have long been contested,' Mildrith explained as they rode along. She sat at the same height as Sanc, while Herin was significantly higher. 'The Gadenzians created three margravates to defend the border. Each margrave has significant resources and warriors to defend their territory and will support one another.'

'But they won't be expecting an attack?' Sanc asked.

'They won't,' Hamzat answered, who rode alongside them. Despite his young age, the Eger had taken on responsibility for managing the foreign sorcerers who had arrived in his people's lands. 'Lothar will still believe he has time before he needs to deal with us.'

It took Sanc a few moments to work out what Hamzat meant by that. He glanced across to the Eger Khan, riding with an honour guard of six of the best Eger warriors. Ruler and champion combined, Hamzat's younger brother was only twelve years old, and yet the weight of his people's wellbeing rested on his shoulders. Sanc knew something of what that was like. He had been the same age when his magic had first manifested. But he had not been required to rule.

'You mean Lothar knows the age of the Eger Khan?' Sanc asked Hamzat.

'Of course he does. When our last khan died, Lothar knew he had more than a decade of freedom to turn his attentions to the rest of Silb.'

'But he won't leave the khan alone forever?'

'No. Soon he will send Temyl and Guntram to kill my brother and neutralise us again.'

'So that's why it took so little persuasion for you to join with us?' Herin asked. 'The khan needs Sanc and Mildrith's protection as much as we need his army.'

Hamzat shrugged. 'In many ways, it is too early for us to act. My brother does not have the power to challenge Lothar's champions. But the longer we wait, the more likely it is they come for him. With two champions, we become a match for them. It is a risk for us. I hope you don't let us down.'

'I don't intend to,' Sanc said. 'But what about our strategy? We attack the Gadenzians and expect Lothar and his champions to come and drive us out?'

'I hope so,' Herin said. 'The Telds are facing a double invasion. They need some relief.'

Hamzat sneered. 'Who cares about the Telds?'

Sanc made a face at Herin, pleading with him not to rise to the bait.

Hamzat returned his gaze to Sanc. 'You have fought the Nerisian. You know better than me what Lothar will do. Whatever it is, we must be ready. Above all, our khan's safety must be guaranteed.'

Sanc nodded his agreement. But he knew there were no such guarantees. For any of them.

* * *

THE NERISIANS and Gadenzians had cut no corners when it came to defending their southern border. Stone forts stood at regular intervals; the land cleared around them to give the defenders sight lines of the territory they controlled. Between them were watchtowers, designed to pass warning of attack along the chain of fortifications.

In the twilight, they met with the Eger generals and looked across the intervening space at the nearest fort. The Eger Khan was with them, but he remained silent. He was learning the ways of war and had nothing to contribute. But the pretence that he was in charge had to be maintained.

'Surely there are not many soldiers in each fort?' Mildrith asked. 'You said yourself that Lothar isn't expecting a serious Eger attack. He has taken his armies across Silb in the last few years. He must have depleted the garrisons here.'

'That's a reasonable view,' said Kursuk, a prominent general. 'We could comfortably take out more than one fort at once, in my opinion.'

This statement was debated by the Egers until they agreed a compromise. They would capture two forts and three watchtowers first. Apart from the minimal numbers needed to take the towers, that meant dividing their army in two, each division focused on taking a fort. Kursuk would lead a larger force. The Eger Khan's would be smaller but would include Sanc and Mildrith.

'A night time attack?' Herin asked.

The Egers looked at the Magnian as if he had gone mad. Sanc was glad it was Herin who had suggested it because he couldn't see anything wrong with the proposal.

'The lizards sleep at night,' Hamzat explained.

'Then we do it without them,' Herin said.

Kursuk frowned. 'How would you get inside?'

Now it was Herin's turn to look confused. 'Build ladders and other equipment.'

The general shook his head. 'That is not the Eger way.'

THEY HAD to wait until the sun was high in the sky before the giant lizards were ready to move. Eger riders approached the Gadenzian fort. The defenders shouted a warning, and the Egers came under arrow fire. As Mildrith predicted, the numbers on the walls suggested the garrison was well below capacity.

The Egers made for the stone walls, cutting the time the Gadenzians had to pick them off. Sanc used his magic to protect those around him, arrows rebounding from his shield.

Then Sanc saw what the Egers had been trying to tell them, and his jaw dropped. Lizards ran up the vertical walls of the fort, their riders clinging on. Within moments, the Eger riders were clashing with the Gadenzians at the top. Lizards scrabbled over, and the walls were breached.

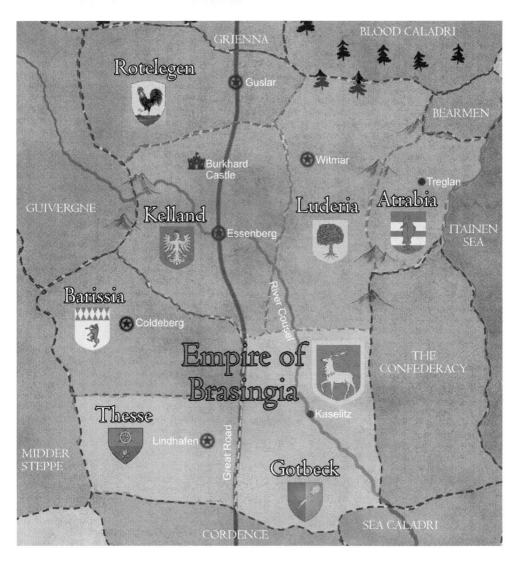

LIESEL

GUSLAR, DUCHY OF ROTELEGEN

The chicken soup smelled delicious, steam rising from Liesel's bowl. She was famished after days of riding. Still, as she blew to cool it, then spooned it into her mouth, she struggled to find pleasure in the meal.

She was in her brother-in-law's hall, in Guslar castle. Her niece and nephew, whom she adored, were only a table away. She should have been happy. But she had a tough conversation ahead, one that she had put off long enough.

And then, there was the anger that had stayed with her for days. Red hot and raw. Her husband had killed her brother, after promising he wouldn't. And Inge, the woman behind the conflict, was now his adviser. The value of her sorcerous powers to him meant she would escape justice for her crimes.

Her fights with Esterel had been so bitter he had sent her away. She had travelled north, with Peyre's army of Morbaine, and her arbalests. They had helped Jeremias push the Griennese and Trevenzans out of Rotelegen, and carried out reprisals beyond the border.

The army of Rotelegen had revenge on its mind, and their duke was keen to discourage any further aggression from his troublesome neighbours. They had spent days wasting the countryside of south

Grienna until Jeremias declared himself satisfied. Such was the price paid by those who had allied with Leopold.

Now they were back to the comfort of the castle and the facade of civilisation it offered. All talk had been about the campaign. It was time to steer the conversation to other matters.

Liesel studied Jeremias, Katrina, and Peyre as she took her soup. The oldest by a few years, Jeremias was lean and fit. Reserved, usually in control of his emotions, Liesel had learned to detect the signs of stress and strain which lay under the surface. He was a survivor in a brutal world. Her sister was like her—tall and curvy, and after having two children, looked more like their mother every day. Since becoming a mother herself, Katrina tended to favour the safest course of action. Peyre, the youngest of the group, was all muscle. Back in Valennes, he'd had Brancat work on his fitness, and his physicality was a match for anyone. Liesel had always seen him as one of her closest allies. But he could be distant. Since Leopold's death, it had got worse.

Liesel knew she was the one who would have to make a start.

'You know you will need to return with us to Essenberg?' she asked Jeremias. 'There will be the vote and then the coronation.'

'Aye. I know.'

'And how do you feel about that?'

'What do you mean, Liesel?' Katrina asked, a nervous look in her eyes.

'What else can I mean?' Liesel said, impatient. 'Jeremias was elected emperor two years ago. Now there is to be another election, which Esterel will win.' She looked at Jeremias. 'How does that sit with you?'

Jeremias put his spoon on the table. 'Things have changed since then, Liesel. Making me emperor was Walter's plan to stop the title going to Leopold. Now Walter and Leopold are both dead. Esterel holds Barissia and Kelland. Idris holds Atrabia and Luderia. Your husband will be emperor.'

'I know all that,' Liesel said. 'I was asking how you felt about it.'

'What do you expect him to say, Liesel?' Peyre asked her, sounding as exasperated as she felt. Their relationship was tense now. She could tell he disapproved of her recent actions, even if he would not come out and say it.

'No one is prepared to say how they feel,' Liesel said. 'We're family. It's a reasonable question to ask.'

Jeremias raised a hand. 'Alright, Liesel. I have mixed feelings. Part of me feels that something has been taken from me. On the other hand, I could do without the responsibility of the title. Katrina and I are happy here in Guslar. I worry about the power your husband will now wield. But I recognise we need his strength to stand against Ezenachi. Is that a satisfactory response?'

'Yes,' Liesel said. 'Thank you.'

'And how do you feel about it, Liesel?' Katrina asked her in a gentle voice. 'You would be empress of Brasingia as well as queen of Guivergne. I know everyone else imagines you are delighted. But I'm sure you have reservations.'

'I didn't, before,' Liesel said. 'I wanted Leopold and Inge gone, and I wanted Esterel to be emperor. For the sake of the people as much as myself. But when I witnessed Leopold's trial, I saw how unfair it was. That he should carry the blame, while Inge retains all her status and power. He was only a boy when she got her claws in him. He didn't stand a chance. Now I am supposed to tolerate her, make small talk with her as if nothing has happened?'

'No one likes it,' Peyre said. 'No one thinks it's fair, least of all, Esterel. But we must tolerate Inge, because Ezenachi is worse. You know that as much as anyone.'

'If we don't do what's fair and what's right, then what's the point?' Liesel retorted. 'What do we have power for? To defeat our enemies and live in luxury,' she said, waving her arms about the hall, 'while most of the people live hand to mouth, in squalor? By what right do we rule if we see evil and ignore it? If we reward it?'

'You're talking like a child,' Peyre let out.

'Peyre!' Katrina said, shocked. 'You are talking to your queen!'

'No!' Liesel said. 'I appreciate it, Peyre. I appreciate some honest talk at last. I'm sick of people holding their tongue around me.'

'Liesel,' Jeremias said. 'When I was a boy, my father and all my brothers were killed in one day. There was only me and my mother left after that. We didn't have the strength to defend Rotelegen from the Isharites. No one helped us. We had to abandon this city. Abandon our family's duchy and take our people south. There, we waited at Burkhard Castle for the Isharites to come and finish us.

'My right to rule hung by a thread. A boy who couldn't defend his people. Do you think I worried about fairness, justice, and right-eousness? I had to fight just to survive—to make my way, one step at a time, back to this castle. To claw back the inheritance that my fore-bears had left me and that I had nearly lost. With all respect, your talk of right and wrong, your questions about how I feel—these are matters for those with the privilege of time and wealth to worry about. Esterel will be emperor. Inge will be his adviser. I suggest your time is better spent on matters you can control.'

'At last,' Liesel said, trying to keep bitterness from her voice. 'I understand what everyone thinks. I am an over-privileged child.'

'No, Liesel—' Katrina began.

'—It's fine. I happen to disagree. I happen to believe that right and wrong matters to everyone, especially the vulnerable. I believe there is nothing in the world that requires me to shrug and say, "oh, it can't be changed. I must accept it." But it seems I am the only one who thinks like that.'

* * *

THEY LEFT Guslar in the company of Peyre's army of Morbaine, taking the Great Road south.

They passed Burkhard Castle on the second day of the journey. It was a monument of pain for Liesel. Her father had spent his last days there, in a doomed attempt to hold back the forces of Ishari. It was where her brother had committed his first atrocity, the blinding of Auberi and his soldiers. Had it been Leopold or Inge who had given those orders? *I would dearly like to know.*

They arrived in Essenberg with the preparations for Esterel's inauguration as Duke of Kelland in full swing. It was planned to be the first in a schedule of formalities that would cement her husband's unprecedented accumulation of power. The leading magnates of Brasingia and Guivergne walked the corridors of Essenberg Castle and ate together in its great hall. Both sides were learning where they stood in relation to one another. Domard, Duke of Martras, was insistent that a duke of Guivergne equalled a duke of Brasingia. The Brasingians were less sure. But no one could doubt that Esterel stood head and shoulders above all others.

When it came to becoming duke, however, Esterel was reliant on Liesel. The Kellish were the proudest of all peoples and disliked the idea of a foreigner becoming their duke. If it wasn't for his marriage to Liesel, he would have struggled to gain acceptance. As soon as Liesel returned to the capital, he pressed her to meet with the noble families of the duchy and the citizens of the great city.

She and Katrina embarked on an endless round of lunches and dinner parties, reassuring those with concerns that little would change. Their family had ruled Kelland for over two hundred years, and in those years the empire had risen to prominence in Dalriya, with Kelland usually the dominant player. Liesel spoke of having a son, and how she wished her father, Emperor Baldwin, could still be here to see it. That never failed to warm her audience to the idea of Esterel ruling them. Nothing was said of Leopold. His reign was fast becoming a topic not fit for polite conversation.

She achieved enough for the Kellish to accept the direction in which things were going. The people of the duchy acknowledged Esterel's possession of the title in a ceremony in Essenberg cathedral. The bishop of Essenberg declared Esterel duke, explaining to those gathered how the title had come to him through Liesel. The prelate made no mention of the huge Guivergnais army that was still camped outside the city; or of the execution of the previous duke. No one objected.

A hot brand of anger still burned in Liesel. She had known, for a long time, how things had to be. Her birthright was valuable to Esterel and he would have been a fool not to exploit it. It didn't stop her from feeling used. Since their father had died, his children had been used by anyone who could grab the reins. Today was the culmination of that struggle, and it was hardly an outcome he would have wanted.

Outside the grand building, Esterel was swamped by well-wishers who waited for a chance to speak with him and shake his hand. Her husband had a natural charisma. Allied to his good looks—clear blue eyes, long blond hair—he had a way of making everyone feel special.

Stood to one side, Liesel was relieved to see Idris and Tegyn approach. Her Atrabian friends were an antidote to the world of Essenberg. One lanky, the other petite, the siblings shared the pale skin and dark hair that was typical of their people.

'Well, you are Duchess of Kelland,' Idris said. 'After fleeing this place all those years ago, that must feel good?'

'You would think so,' Liesel said. 'But there are things that stick in my throat.'

'Inge?' said the Prince of Atrabia. 'She'll get hers. Don't worry about that. We'll give it some time. Let her relax. Then, a knife in the back, just when she believes the threat has gone.'

Liesel looked around, expecting to see the witch staring at them. 'That's music to my ears. But your loose tongue will get you into serious trouble one day.'

Idris waved away her concerns.

'I don't understand how either of you can have complaints,' Tegyn said.

'What do you mean?' Liesel asked her.

Tegyn jabbed a finger at her brother. 'You're Prince of Atrabia and Duke of Luderia.' She turned on Liesel. 'You have Duchess of Kelland to add to your title of Queen of Guivergne. And yet you grumble and plot. When will you stop and give thanks for the way things have turned out?'

Before Liesel could reply, her friend turned on her heels and stomped away.

'What, by Gerhold, was that about?' Idris asked, staring after his sister with a bemused expression. 'It was her father they killed as well as mine, was it not?'

'I'm not sure. But I know Tegyn has long dreamed of a good marriage. Perhaps she sees us with these titles and feels left out.'

Idris grunted. 'Perhaps she doesn't realise what torment comes with them? How I'd love for my principal concern to be about finding a wife.'

'The apples on the other side of the wall are always the sweetest. I should have done more to help her. She is my best friend, after all.' Liesel studied Idris. 'And you need to be thinking along the same lines.'

'What?' Idris said. 'I'm far from giving up on you, Liesel. Every night in that cell, I remembered a stolen kiss on a river bank. How I was half frozen, and then I had a taste of your warm lips. I didn't feel the cold after that. You were the one reason I had to live. You still are.'

Liesel took an involuntary step backwards and looked about them a second time. 'I've already warned you once,' she hissed. 'You say such words about the wife of the man who will be made emperor? You have lost your sense!'

'Oh, I have,' Idris agreed with a grin. 'I am quite mad.'

'Perhaps you are, at that. In which case, you need to do a better job of hiding it.'

* * *

WITH THE DUCHY of Kelland now his, there was every reason for Esterel to press on. The very next day, the great and the good returned to Essenberg Cathedral for the imperial election.

Precedent said the ceremony should have taken place in Guslar, but the rules that governed the empire were bending with the strain of recent events. Everyone, it seemed, was determined to forget the election of two years ago, which had come close to ending in bloodshed.

This time, Esterel was the only one of the eligible dukes who put themselves forward. He received the votes of all the electors, the first time that had happened in the empire's history. As those gathered left the building in record time, a sense of calm had returned to Brasingia, something that had been missing since Ezenachi's execution of Emperor Coen. The empire had a new leader. It was ready, once more, to defend itself.

Liesel left the cathedral with her arm through Esterel's. 'The coronation can wait,' he was saying to the men who had made him emperor. 'We all have troops in the field who need to be sent home. I know all of you have borders to defend. But rest assured, I will stay here for the time being, and I will maintain a standing army. As soon as you need my help, you will get it.'

Idris, Jeremias, Friedrich, and Emmett. They all gave Esterel the same look of gratitude. Since his conquest of Cordence, Ezenachi's lands ran along the entire southern border of the empire. Now, after his forces had annexed half of the Confederacy, he threatened their eastern border as well. That situation would have been even worse if Idris hadn't intervened. But even Idris, with all his self-belief and boastfulness, wasn't pretending that he didn't need Esterel's strength to keep the enemy out.

Liesel left them to it and walked through the crowd that had gathered outside, looking for her sister. She spotted her, surrounded by the Kellish aristocracy. Their enthusiasm for Esterel had risen another notch now that he had regained the imperial title for Kelland. Liesel headed over, but stopped when a figure stepped into her path.

Inge. Liesel hadn't seen her in the cathedral. They had avoided one another in the weeks after Leopold's trial and execution. But it seemed the witch now wanted to change that.

'Most satisfactory,' Inge said to her, as if continuing a recent conversation. 'Brasingia and Guivergne are stronger now than ever.'

Liesel stared at her. After the havoc she had wrecked, to bask in the outcome seemed too much even for her. But the days when Liesel would stand like a lost child with nothing to say were long gone. 'You say it as if this was your plan all along.'

'Oh, but it was, darling,' Inge said, using her cloying voice. Stick thin and child faced, she always looked the picture of innocence. 'I planted the idea of your marriage with Esterel years ago. The union of Guivergne and Brasingia couldn't have happened without some sacrifice and war. Nothing truly changes without conflict. Six years ago, no one else would have thought it possible. They would have laughed if I had even suggested it.

'But look at what happened today. Thousands of warriors, millions of people, united under you and Esterel. Dalriya has a ruler strong enough to stand up to Ezenachi. I don't expect gratitude. But I thought you, if anyone, would recognise what I have achieved.'

Liesel was aghast. But she was ruthless with herself, keeping any emotion from her face.

The worst of it was that Inge seemed to believe every word she said. She had been nothing but a menace, causing pain and war when there hadn't needed to be any. So many had suffered. And Inge—Inge hadn't suffered at all. If Esterel was so powerful, then she, as his adviser—as the only sorcerer in this new realm—was as well. But to pretend to Liesel that this outcome was the culmination of some master plan meant she was as mad as she was powerful. And that made her dangerous.

'I suppose I never thought about it,' Liesel made herself say. 'But I see it now. Everything you did led to this moment. Without you, Brasingia wouldn't have stood a chance.'

'There you go,' Inge said, a pleased look on her face. 'You were always the smartest of Baldwin's children. The bravest. It would have been so much easier if you were the son and Leopold the daughter. But I did what I had to with the resources he left me. I think he would be pleased. All you need to do now, Liesel, is give your husband children. Lots of children. And the future is secure.'

'I certainly will,' Liesel heard herself say, as if it was some other person speaking.

They parted, and Liesel continued on her way to her sister. She felt dizzy and her vision blurred, making two Katrinas. But her mind was clear. *If Idris doesn't do it,* she told herself, *then I shall have to kill her myself.*

SANC

LANDS OF THE GADENZIANS

The Egers took more forts, the local garrisons too reduced to stop them.

Evidence of Gadenzian leadership soon appeared, however. Some forts were abandoned, while mounted patrols intercepted Eger forces, raiding and harassing. The Gadenzians hit them after dusk, while the lizards slept. They knew the weaknesses of the Egers, and they made life uncomfortable.

Meanwhile, the Egers behaved just as Sanc had been told they would. They killed all captured adults. Children who looked young enough were sent south into Eger lands. Their heads would be bound and their identities altered. The cruelty of it repelled Sanc, and he shared more than one look with Mildrith and Herin, none of them happy. But they had been under no illusions when they came to seek the Egers as allies, and didn't interfere.

Instead, they mounted their lizards and scouted to the northwest. The Gadenzians would have wasted no time in alerting Lothar to the Eger invasion. Sanc could see no reason why he wouldn't suspend his invasion of Teld lands and come to defend his own.

He certainly hoped so. They had left Kepa, the Teld champion, and whatever warriors could support her, against both Lothar's army and

23

the Rasidi. The Telds would retreat into their mountain fastnesses, but they couldn't hold out forever.

At last, they spotted the signs of a large force on the march. At the core of Lothar's army were his Nerisian infantry, with more iron armour and weaponry than the rest of the seven peoples put together. Complementing them were the Gadenzian cavalry. In addition, he now had Scorgian and Kassite units. Their leaders defeated and their lands taken, these warriors had switched their allegiance to the man crowned emperor. In exchange, they would win the rewards he could offer them.

Of equal importance to the warriors Lothar commanded were his champions. Attuned to their power, Sanc knew Temyl and Guntram travelled with Lothar. Lothar's army was superior to the Egers, but Sanc and Mildrith could match his champions. The Eger Khan's magic powers were undeveloped and he would stand no chance in a contest. But might his presence help them?

'I think we need your tactical thinking,' Sanc told Herin as they watched the dust clouds that travelled with the thousands strong army that came for them. 'What will Lothar do and how can we stop him?'

Herin gave the matter some silent thought. 'Wizards can sense each other's presence?' he asked at last.

'It varies. But anyway, I can mask myself. I hid from Mergildo in Aguilas, and I can do that again.'

'Good. That might give us a chance. Lothar's champions will expect the two of you. Sure of his superiority, Lothar will come for the Egers, wanting an engagement. Temyl and Guntram will accompany him to provide support. They'll expect two champions with the Eger army. But what if those champions are the khan and Mildrith? They won't be watching out for you. When the fighting starts, you and I get to Lothar and kill him.'

'Maybe. Temyl and Guntram have always attacked in the past.' Sanc turned to Mildrith. 'What do you think? Could you hold the two of them off for long enough? They'd have the advantage in magic and in numbers. It could be a massacre.'

'We could use the captured forts,' she suggested. 'We'd need to persuade the Egers to defend rather than fight in the open. Even for Temyl and Guntram, it would take time to break through. But you'd need to come back and help. Whether or not you succeed in getting to Lothar.'

'Of course. I promise.'

* * *

SANC AND HERIN waited in a captured watchtower. The room at the top was tiny, only big enough to hold a dozen warriors, but comfortable for two. It was one in a chain of towers and forts taken by the Egers, and now defended against the approaching imperial army.

They had a clear view of Lothar's force as it passed from west to east, only a few miles to the north. The emperor had not underestimated the Egers. It looked like he had abandoned his invasion of Teld lands, taking his entire army with him. As well he might, Sanc supposed. The Egers were a threat, while the Telds were an irritant that he could deal with another time.

'What is he waiting for?' Sanc asked Herin the next morning. They had taken it in turns to keep watch through the night and he was feeling sleep deprived and grumpy. He was anxious, too, to get on with things.

'He'll be meeting with local leaders. These margraves. They know our numbers and deployment.'

Sanc's stomach churned. Between the margraves and Lothar's champions, they would know which fort Mildrith and the Eger Khan occupied. He hated this part of their plan, leaving Mildrith exposed. Even though he knew she was strong enough to defend herself.

At last, they saw the Nerisian units approach. Thousands marched for the forts to either side, while about a hundred came for their position. Those at the front of the column wore chain mail and carried shields, while those in the rear carried ladders. In the middle were a dozen archers. Certainly, a strong enough force to take a tower of this size.

Sanc and Herin lit a fire and sent smoke up into the sky as a warning. They wanted their tower to seem just like any other. Sanc could see smoke rising from the other Eger controlled fortifications. He was using his magic to mask his presence in the tower. It was the most subtle of spells, like throwing a flimsy veil over himself. If he didn't take care and his magic was too obvious, he would be detected.

Herin shot an arrow at the approaching soldiers. They reacted quickly, shouting to one another, and soon arrows were flying up at their viewing platform, forcing Herin to retreat out of the way.

So far, so normal, Sanc told himself. The Nerisians had no reason to doubt they were about to take a lightly defended tower. While the enemy covered the north side with their archers, he could risk peeking to the east and west, at the neighbouring forts. It was a similar picture. The Nerisian forces were approaching the walls. The Egers didn't have enough archers to stop them. Soon, ladders would be propped up, and rams would batter the gates. The fighting, Sanc knew, would be ferocious.

His attention returned to his own tower. He and Herin had retracted the stairs leading up to the tall tower and there was no easy way for the Nerisians to get in. Instead, they leaned their ladders against all sides of the tower. Sanc could hear the soldiers climbing towards their position. It was time to act.

Sanc left the safety of their tower room and moved into the open. It didn't take long for the archers to draw and release their arrows. He returned the missiles whence they came, turning defence to offence just as Rimmon had taught him in the Forest of Morbaine. With the archers temporarily neutralised, Herin rushed to his side.

Sanc gestured to the top of the nearest ladder. 'Grab on.'

Herin didn't hesitate. Sanc joined him and pushed away from the tower. The ladder swung out, held still in an upright position for a heart-stopping moment or two, and then began its fall.

'Toric save me!' Herin bellowed, as he clung tightly to the wooden pole while the ground below seemed to rise to meet them.

Sanc cushioned the ladder's fall, and they stepped off onto solid ground. So, too, did three soldiers who had begun climbing the thing.

Sanc blasted them with magic, then produced a magical shield that covered himself and Herin, as the archers fired again.

A good half of the enemy were climbing the remaining ladders, into what they were yet to realise was an empty tower. That left the armoured soldiers and archers, spread out around the base of the building.

Sanc and Herin drew swords and attacked. Another warrior may have hesitated, but Herin had assured him that his friend Soren had used similar magic to Sanc's shield. The Magnian struck out with his blade, confident that the Nerisian fighters wouldn't be able to hit him back. It made things easier for Sanc, who had to concentrate on two spells while swinging his own sword. They left a trail of corpses as they performed a loop around the tower.

'That'll do,' Herin decided, looking at the remnants of the force that had come for them, most now climbing into the empty tower.

Sanc agreed. They made their way north, aiming to find Lothar's camp.

BEHIND THEM, the Nerisian army attacked the Egers. Sanc had to put that from his mind. Instead, he had a target. Lothar. Killing him would end this war that raged across Silb. That, he had to hope, would put him one step closer to achieving his goal of saving Dalriya.

Herin pointed. 'Could this be him?'

A unit of cavalry, about a mile from the chain of fortifications. Sanc used his magic to hide himself and Herin as they moved closer. There were a few hundred at rest. It didn't look like they were expecting to get involved in the fighting any time soon. He knew they were Gadenzians, and he knew horsemen would be little help in the initial attack on the forts. They would chase down the Egers should they retreat.

Was Lothar one of these riders? He thought it likely. The emperor had been described to him, but his appearance—tall, light brown hair grown long, blue eyes—hardly distinguished him from the other warriors gathered here.

'I think I need to get closer,' Sanc whispered to Herin. Perhaps Lothar's mount and accoutrements would help identify him.

'Wait,' Herin hissed, and pointed in a different direction.

A lone rider was approaching from the south. Most likely a scout, come to report on progress. Sanc waited as the rider neared the cavalry and slowed. Then, movement from amongst the Gadenzians. Flanked by two riders, a figure manoeuvred his mount forward to meet the scout. Everything in the encounter told Sanc it was Lothar. The way he held himself; the opulence of his horse's barding and the way his own armour had been scrubbed so hard it shone; the way the other riders deferred to him; the way the scout bowed his head before passing on his news.

'That's him,' Sanc whispered, his mouth suddenly dry.

'Aye, lad,' Herin confirmed. 'Time to do it.'

Sanc hesitated, as disparate thoughts invaded his mind. Doubts assailed him, telling him it was a trap. At the same time, he told himself how easy it would be to destroy his enemy. He became acutely aware of his own body: the beat of his heart, the twitch of muscles, the tingle of skin. For those first moments, he didn't even realise what he was doing.

When he looked up, he saw Lothar had left his horse and was rising into the sky. He was shouting, looking about wildly, while his men panicked, barking instructions at one another. As soon as Sanc realised what he was doing, his attention transferred from his own body to Lothar's. He felt the man struggling, futilely, against the magic that had him in its grip. He could feel the beat of Lothar's heart and thought how easy it would be to grab hold of that muscle and squeeze the life from him.

How easy, but how cowardly, too. That wouldn't do. Sanc removed the spell that made him invisible. It took Lothar a few struggling breaths before he set eyes on Sanc and his outstretched arm. Their eyes met. It was only right that Lothar should know who his killer was. The emperor seemed to calm as he looked down, accepting what was to come. Sanc reached for his heart.

It was only then he realised this was how Ezenachi had killed

Emperor Coen. *Am I become Ezenachi?* The implications hit him like a hammer blow. At last, the question he had wanted to ask himself escaped and burst into his consciousness.

Is this right?

Sanc didn't know the answer.

'Sanc,' came a warning voice.

Herin. He looked across. Of course, the Gadenzian riders were heading straight for them—spears, axes, and hammers in their gloved hands.

Is this right?

He only had moments to decide. How was he supposed to know the answer?

The last person he expected to see came to help him. She appeared in ethereal form, impossibly beautiful, hovering above him.

Mother?

'This isn't right,' she answered him. 'There is another way.'

Relief flooded him. Sanc lowered Lothar, returning him to his mount. As the thunder of the Gadenzian horsemen bore down, he grabbed hold of Herin. He teleported them away.

When they stopped, Sanc's head was spinning. He put his hands to his knees, but the world continued to roll and whirl, as if he was standing on deck in a storm.

'Why?' Herin asked him. Confused. Disappointed. 'Why didn't you do it?'

Sanc looked at him. He opened his mouth to explain. He would tell Herin about Ezenachi and his mother. But when he tried to speak, the words wouldn't come. Instead, a pain grew in his head. He stared at the blades of grass on which he stood. He didn't even realise he was falling before he hit the ground.

PEYRE

ESSENBERG, DUCHY OF KELLAND

Esterel had given his orders to his generals. The victorious army of Guivergne would be divided up and, Peyre supposed, this was how things would be from now on. With a huge empire to defend, stretching from the Lantinen coast all the way to the Itainen, Esterel needed commanders everywhere.

The king himself would stay in Essenberg with the royal army and his closest friends, Sacha and Florent. Since the death of Miles, those three had got even closer. In his more charitable moments, Peyre understood why.

Duke Domard would take the forces of Martras south-west, to Coldeberg, and govern Barissia on Esterel's behalf. Coldeberg was where Leopold had committed his final outrage, with the murder of Miles, Elger, and many other loyal warriors. It did not surprise Peyre that his brother wanted little to do with the place. Peyre had loved his time in Barissia, staying with Duke Walter. But that seemed so long ago, and he too was happy for someone else to deal with the duchy.

That left himself; Arnoul, Lord of Saliers; and Gosse, Lord of the March. Peyre would take the army of Morbaine home. It was the first line of defence should Ezenachi restart his conquests in the south-west. He firmly believed that was only a matter of time. Arnoul and

Gosse would return to their estates and be ready to defend Guivergne. The kingdom had been stripped of its warriors, save for those who served Auberi, Peyre's brother-in-law.

With all farewells said, Peyre left in the company of Arnoul and Gosse. Umbert was with them, and Benoit, Arnoul's son, whom Peyre had nicknamed the Viper. Peyre decided it wasn't a bad group of travelling companions. He'd done his bit to build friendships with the Brasingians, but he wasn't sad to be leaving the empire behind. Idris made him uncomfortable. His only regret would be not seeing Liesel for a while. He was sorry she had taken Leopold's death so hard. But he had struggled to offer her comfort when that was the precise outcome he had wanted.

Still. Offering Liesel comfort wasn't his job. Esterel was her husband; Tegyn and Idris, her friends. He'd had enough time to get used to that.

Two days of travel and they had left the empire of Brasingia for the kingdom of Guivergne. Yet it was all one realm now. They all felt the novelty of it.

'Our role has always been to defend the border,' Gosse said. 'Now there is no border.' He spat on the ground, to emphasise his disquiet.

'Don't worry,' Peyre said. 'There'll still be plenty of fighting to do.'

'I suppose so, Your Grace,' the big man said, looking slightly more cheerful.

PEYRE'S WORDS turned out to be prophetic. He had Benoit directing the scouts, out of habit rather than expectation. But when the heir of Saliers returned in the company of a dozen Middian horsemen, Peyre knew something was up.

'Hail, Duke Peyre,' hollered one of the Middian riders as he pulled up. It was Cuenin, chieftain of the Black Horse tribe, through whose lands Peyre had once marched his army. Like most of his countrymen, Cuenin wore his jet black hair in a ponytail. 'I am relieved to find you.'

'You have news?' Peyre replied. 'We have come from Essenberg and have heard nothing.'

'It's happened at last. I've had word from Brock and Frayne. Ezenachi's army has invaded. The vossi, as well as Lippers and Cordentines. But it's even worse. They report the army is led by a Giant. They say it must be Oisin Dragon-Killer, because he wields the Giants' Spear. With him is a man who has slaughtered many of our horses with the Jalakh Bow.'

Peyre frowned, struggling to make sense of the account. Jesper had travelled to Halvia in search of Oisin. He knew there were plans, led by the Krykker, Maragin, to find the other weapons. But that didn't explain how the spear and bow had ended up in the Midder Steppe. *Perhaps Ezenachi has been busier than I feared.*

His companions looked similarly baffled. The only difference was, they looked to him for answers.

'Even if only a part of this account is true, we are in trouble,' he said. He considered the men at his disposal. 'Benoit, return with all haste to Essenberg. The king must be warned, and I will need his orders. Umbert, the same, to Valennes. Tell my sister to put whatever forces she has on alert.'

'And you?' Cuenin asked him. 'Now is your chance to prove you are a man of your word, Duke Peyre. Bring your army south and fight alongside us.'

'We agreed to an alliance,' Peyre admitted. 'The sharing of information and plans. And it included my right to take my forces across Steppe lands. Allow me to send units through the Steppe to Morbaine, where I must hear their news without delay. If Ezenachi has sent a force into the Steppe, Magnia may also be under threat.'

'You have that right,' Cuenin acknowledged. 'But what of helping us to fight Ezenachi? You will leave us to defend our lands alone? We will be crushed.'

'This is King Esterel's army, not mine,' Peyre answered him. 'He decides if and when we go to war.'

'While you wait and think over your options, Middians die,' Cuenin said, a sneer coming to his face.

'Then I suggest you gather all your warriors and hurry south to help your people. When I am free to act, I won't hesitate.'

'Come,' Cuenin said to his followers, turning his horse about. 'We have talked and begged all we can. It's time to fight.' He led his warriors south and for a while Peyre stared after him, wishing he could fix his gaze on the peril coming their way.

* * *

PEYRE WONDERED if something had changed in him. Two years ago, he had hardly hesitated to bring the army of Morbaine into Magnia against Ezenachi's forces. Now, he felt constrained—unsure of how to act. *Perhaps this is what happens as you age,* he wondered. *Have I grown less brave? Or maybe I learned some lessons in that encounter with Ezenachi. The god came close to killing me. He did kill Edgar and Rimmon. If I oppose him again, he will not spare me a second time.*

Then again, it was only sensible to wait for more information. He needed to know Esterel's response to the news; and he would prefer to wait for Umbert's return from Valennes. He had sent Gosse, with his force of fur-clad warriors, across the Steppe to Morbaine, with instructions to assess the situation in Magnia. Without the full picture, he might make a hasty error. And yet, there was a sense of dishonour in sitting tight with his army, while he knew the Middians were in a desperate battle for survival.

For advice, he was stuck with Arnoul. Saliers had kept his own recruits in the field with Peyre's, giving no suggestion that he wished to return home. For a long time, Peyre had judged him to be a snake. And maybe he was. But he had a mind for strategy.

'I believe we should wait, even if it's uncomfortable to do so,' the Lord of Saliers said. 'Think of how many days it took for the news of Ezenachi's invasion to reach us here. Who knows what the situation is now? Marching south into the Steppe may not help at all. We need to hear the news from Morbaine, and from your brother, at the very least.'

Reassured, Peyre waited. It was two days after Cuenin's visit that the next messenger arrived, though it wasn't anyone he had been expecting.

It was Inhan, one of the few survivors from Peyre's Barissian Guard. Peyre had asked him to stay in Morbaine, as an aid to Lord Russell. Leopold had taken the young man's hand in the massacre at Coldeberg. Taking him to war in Brasingia had seemed too much, too soon.

Inhan hadn't complained about being left behind. He probably needed the time. Now, he came to Peyre's tent and Peyre couldn't stop his eyes from drifting to where the hand used to be. In its place, Inhan had a metal one, strapped to his arm. The fingers of the hand were bent, creating a grip.

'Your Grace,' Inhan said. 'My Lord of Saliers,' he added, with a brief nod. He held the hand up for Peyre and Arnoul to examine. There was no sign of the misery on his face that had once been there.

'Remarkable,' Arnoul murmured.

'It can hold a shield tight, no problem. Or the reins of my horse.'

'It is good to see you back in action,' Peyre said. 'You must return to my side when you are ready. But you are come from Morbaine?'

'Lord Russell sent me as soon as we received the messenger from King Ida. Ezenachi's forces have invaded Magnia. When I left, they had already taken several castles, and this was a week ago.'

'Probably attacked the same day they invaded the Steppe,' Peyre suggested.

'I haven't heard that news.'

'You didn't see Gosse and his force? I sent him across the Steppe to Morbaine.'

'No. I travelled through Morbaine, probably passing farther north than he did.'

'Well, I'm glad you came. No doubt Ida asked for our aid?'

'He did. I bring his message, and one from Lord Russell.' Inhan retrieved the two bound parchments from inside his cloak, handing them over. 'The King of Magnia is at pains to warn that he cannot hold the enemy for long. What is the plan, do you think, Your Grace?'

'That is hard to say. The enemy gets ever closer to our border. But the king must decide what is best. You will rest here, Inhan, and then I would ask you to ride to Essenberg. You are best placed to tell my brother the situation.'

'I don't need to rest. Fresh provisions and a new mount, and I will leave immediately.'

Peyre smiled. It was good to see Inhan had recovered his strength in so short a space of time. It was something positive amidst the grim tidings.

* * *

TWO MORE DAYS of waiting with no more news, and then there was a surfeit. Benoit returned from Essenberg. Umbert was back from Valennes, and Syele had come with him. She delivered news of a more personal nature. Loysse had given birth, and Peyre was an uncle of a little girl. It was joyous to hear. But he wished he could have been told in different circumstances, and been given the opportunity to celebrate with his sister.

Finally, as evening came, chieftains Frayne and Jorath rode into camp with a small entourage. Their very presence, not to mention their bedraggled appearance and Jorath's arm wound, made it clear how the war went in the Steppe.

Peyre invited everyone to a late dinner in his tent. 'It's only right that we all share our knowledge and devise a plan. First, I have my orders from Emperor Esterel. I am not permitted to bring soldiers into Middian or Magnian territory. Instead, I am tasked with defending the Guivergnais border.'

'What of our alliance?' Frayne demanded. 'The Emperor is the one man who can stop this terror. Too many of my people have died already. Not least, my old friend Brock, whose folk are either dead or Turned to do Ezenachi's bidding. The longer Esterel delays, the more Ezenachi's army grows.'

'Ezenachi's forces have invaded the remnants of the Confederacy in the east,' Peyre told him. 'As well as Magnia. The emperor has much to consider.'

'I understand that,' Frayne pursued. 'But I have been forced to take my people north, away from their lands. We have lost everything. Surely you can see a line must be drawn? Your realms will be next.'

Peyre shared a look with Benoit. The young man had made it clear that the lack of action had been Inge's advice. She had assured Esterel that Ezenachi wouldn't take the war into Brasingia or Guivergne. Whatever his reasons, Esterel had sided with her against other voices.

'I don't doubt you are right. But it is my brother's right to decide when he will fight. Arguing with me about that will not get us anywhere. I want everyone to hear from Syele, who speaks on behalf of the Duchess of Famiens. She has some information that will help us understand what is happening.'

The Middians fumed. Syele waited for everyone in Peyre's tent to give her their full attention. The Barissian wore her blonde hair loose, and sword and dagger on her belt. Peyre knew she had more knives hidden elsewhere. 'Oisin Dragon-Killer came to Valennes only weeks ago. He was in a group that held six of the seven weapons of Madria. With him were Lorant, King of the Blood Caladri, and Maragin, a chieftain of the Krykkers. Jesper, a Halvian known to many here, had the Jalakh Bow.'

'Then he is the one who fights with Oisin,' Frayne said.

'I'm sure,' Syele agreed. 'There was one other with them. Belwynn Godslayer had the dagger with her. They passed through on their way to Magnia. They had hopes of getting the weapon that had eluded them, the Cloak of the Asrai. From there, they intended to find Ezenachi and kill him.'

Peyre observed as his guests digested all that news, piecing together the implications.

'So, we are to assume they failed?' Saliers asked. 'Not only that, but some were turned by Ezenachi? I presume no one has heard of them since?'

'Not that I know of,' said Peyre. 'It would seem they are all dead, or turned. And I would suggest turned is more likely.'

'With what reasoning?' Frayne asked him.

'From what you tell me, Ezenachi sent only two into the Steppe, to lead the invasion.'

'Aye. Two only. I would have heard if there were more. But that could mean the others are dead.'

'It could. But Ezenachi divided his forces into three and attacked simultaneously. Most likely, he divided the weapons and their wielders, too. Benoit?'

'An Atrabian came to King Esterel's court on the same day I did,' Benoit explained. 'She warned that the Turned of the east coast had new leaders. A Caladri sorcerer with a magic staff, protected by a Krykker with a sword.'

'I think we can infer that the other weapons—dagger and shield, if not cloak—are in Magnia,' Syele said.

'So what?' Frayne asked. 'How does this change things?'

'The threat from Ezenachi was bad enough,' Peyre said. 'But if he now has powerful champions who can do his bidding, we are in trouble. Who do we have with the power to stand against Oisin and all those others? My brother does not have a single individual, except perhaps Inge the witch. Even if she could match one, I doubt she can hold back two. Nor can she be in three places at once.'

'So you will not help us at all?'

'I give you an offer. Evacuate the Steppe. Take all your people with you into Guivergne, where we will give you refuge. It is an offer I strongly advise you to accept.'

LIESEL

ESSENBERG, DUCHY OF KELLAND

Liesel knew her isolation was growing day by day. *Is it something about Essenberg? Can a place do that to a person?*

In Guivergne, she thought she had escaped this feeling. For a while, she had. Now, she was Empress of Brasingia, inheriting the title her mother once had. Surely, she wasn't meant to be this friendless. Had her mother experienced the same thing? Did that explain her vile relationship with Salvinus?

Tegyn had left with Idris for Atrabia. Liesel could hardly object to her wanting to support her brother, now he was prince. But Liesel missed her desperately—missed both of them. And she knew there was a wall between her and Tegyn these days. She had let her friend down in some way.

Meanwhile, her sister was in Guslar, no doubt content to let the politics of empire pass her by. Peyre had gone to Guivergne and who knew when she would see him again?

For Esterel seemed to have no desire to return to Valennes. Brasingia was his new toy, and he was still having too much fun with it. She avoided him now. In the daytime, he wanted to discuss his coronation as emperor, the final ceremony that would confirm his powers. At night, he wanted to make Liesel pregnant. His touch began to repulse her. She dreaded the day he put her aside for failing to give him children, and yet longed for it, too.

And then, of course, there was Inge. How much of what she felt was down to the witch, it was hard to say. But sharing the castle with her once again was like a poison, stealing any happiness she might have felt. The private meetings with Esterel; the whispers in his ear. Inge enjoyed revealing how she had shared a bed with Liesel's father. Would she ensnare her husband, too? She made Liesel feel powerless, just like she had felt as a child.

WHEN SHE HEARD Tegyn had returned to the city, it was like someone had thrown her a line.

She rushed down the castle corridors to the Great Hall. When she saw her friend, she broke out into her first smile for a while.

They met eyes. Tegyn gave her a dark look and her smile disappeared. *Does she hate me now? She wants me gone? But it's too late to turn around and leave.*

'Tegyn?' she said hesitantly.

'Liesel.' It was said with warmth. Tegyn reached for her and they embraced.

It was such a relief that Liesel had to fight away tears. 'What is it? You have such a sombre look that I know something bad has happened.'

'They're back. Ezenachi's Turned. They've forced their way through Corieltes and have struck Ritherys. They could be at the border with Atrabia by now.'

Liesel's heart gave a heavy beat. 'Idris?'

'He's raising our army. Sent Ilar and Macsen to Witmar, to raise the Luderians. And sent me here.'

'You must speak with Esterel.'

'Aye. Is he about?'

'I think so. Come, let's go together.'

. . .

39

'THE KING ASKED NOT to be disturbed,' said the guard outside Esterel's new council room. It was said respectfully, as if he was asking her to decide.

'Who's in there with him?' Liesel asked. She nearly asked if it was Inge, but she stopped herself.

'Benoit of Saliers, Your Majesty.'

Liesel and Tegyn shared a look.

'Saliers left with Peyre,' Liesel said. 'I wonder why else they would send Benoit back if there wasn't trouble?'

'Quite,' Tegyn confirmed.

'I'm afraid you'll have to let us in,' Liesel told the guard.

Esterel sat at his table while Benoit stood to one side. Her husband gave Liesel a look of irritation at first, but when he saw Tegyn was with her, he waved them in. 'Benoit has come with dire news. I hope you're not intending to join him, Lady Tegyn.'

'Hope all you like, Your Majesty. The Turned are back. They've cut through the Corieltes defences and entered Ritherys.' She glanced at Benoit. 'There is bad news elsewhere?'

Esterel gestured at Benoit to speak.

'The Midder Steppe, my lady. Duke Peyre sent me as soon as he heard. But the first reports sounded serious.'

'Then we must do something,' Liesel said.

Esterel sighed. 'I will call a council meeting.'

ESTEREL'S COUNCIL was much smaller than it had been a few weeks ago, when the rulers of two great realms had gathered in Essenberg. As well as Liesel, Tegyn, and Benoit, Sacha and Florent joined them. Also, of course, there was Inge. Only now did it occur to Liesel how few Kellish officials met with Esterel personally. Between them, Sacha and Inge controlled almost every part of government.

Tegyn and Benoit told their stories once more. Most frightening was when Benoit shared the Middians' account of a Giant leading the Turned into the Steppe, along with a host of vossi from the Wilderness. Tegyn added that the Turned invading Cordence were led by a

Krykker and a Caladri sorcerer, wielding magical weapons. It brought home the brutality of what was occurring this very moment in both locations, even if they were miles away.

'This is not unexpected,' Inge said when they were done. 'Ezenachi has had his sights on such an expansion for a while.'

'But what of this Giant?' Liesel asked her. 'The Middians say he wields the Giants' Spear. And his companion uses a weapon that sounds like the Jalakh Bow.' *Surely even you didn't expect that.* 'Maragin and Jesper left for the north to find the weapons of Madria. This sounds like they met with disaster.'

Inge waved a dismissive hand. 'Such details will need to be verified. There are often wild tales told in situations such as this.'

'Sometimes those tales are true. You know that as much as anyone here.'

'Indeed, my queen,' Inge replied, an exasperated tone coming to her voice. She turned to Esterel. 'My point, Your Majesty, is that we should not overreact to this. We have a treaty with Ezenachi, that he will respect your borders. None of this breaks that deal. It is not ideal, of course. But I would strongly counsel against getting drawn into a war over it.'

'That's crazy talk,' Tegyn said. 'Prince Idris is raising his armies to meet this threat. That's the only reasonable response. If we don't do it now, it will be too late.'

Esterel extended his arm, fingers pointing to Tegyn. 'Raising his armies is perfectly reasonable. I shall advise all my lords to do the same. But he must not cross into Ritherys, Tegyn, do you understand? Such a move will break the terms of the deal with Ezenachi.'

'What, he's supposed to wait and watch them get slaughtered? Or turned? And only act when they attack Atrabia? Not likely.'

'That's exactly what he must do,' Esterel thundered, losing his cool. 'And that's an order.'

Tegyn said nothing, though Liesel knew very well that didn't signify her compliance. That was a decision Idris would make, whatever Esterel said.

'Esterel,' Liesel said. 'Can't you see that if we let Ezenachi do this, he will only come for us next? And he'll be stronger when he does. Fighting outside the empire is an infinitely better choice than waiting for his forces to enter our lands.'

'Perhaps he will break his word with us,' Esterel said. 'At that point, we will have to fight him. But I don't intend to lead my people into such a conflict until I must. Surely you understand that, Liesel?'

Liesel turned to Sacha and Florent, looking for their support. Neither met eyes with her.

She caught Inge's expression. She had a gloating smile, pleased she had got her way. But what good would that be when Ezenachi came to finish them all?

'Your Majesty,' Liesel said, 'let me be as clear as I can. I urge you to order your dukes to raise their armies and fight this menace. Honour and sense demand it.'

She saw the bitterness that came to her husband's face. It had first come when she had begged for her brother to be spared. Now it seemed to appear all the time, because they had agreed on little else since.

'Let *me* be clear. To everyone. The armies of Brasingia and Guivergne will be mustered. Every inch of our border must be defended.' He jabbed his finger, first at Tegyn, then Benoit. 'And you will tell Dukes Idris and Peyre that under no circumstances will they engage the enemy unless my territories are invaded, or unless I give them a precise order. Is that clear?'

* * *

TEGYN AND BENOIT left the next day, and Liesel was alone again. All anyone in Essenberg could do was wait for news from elsewhere. Esterel sent his orders out for his lords to raise their retinues. But otherwise, he seemed content to cede the initiative to others. It was so unlike him, and Liesel knew there was no one to blame but Inge.

Another day passed, and they heard Idris was in Luderia, no doubt encouraging the warriors of that duchy to play their part. The Prince of Atrabia had his orders from Esterel, but Liesel doubted he would refrain from intervening in the Confederate kingdoms.

Then, another messenger from Peyre was attending a royal council. This time it was Inhan, the survivor of Peyre's Barissian Guard. He had a metal hand in place of his real one. If such a sight didn't cause Esterel to reassess his faith in Inge, then nothing would. Inhan told them that Magnia, too, had been invaded. King Ida had sent a warning that his people couldn't keep the enemy at bay.

'The destruction of Magnia would put Ezenachi's forces at the border of Morbaine,' Florent warned when Inhan was done.

'You think I don't know that, Florent?' Esterel asked his friend. 'Or care? It was my family home. Ezenachi's realm will reach every part of our southern border. That much is clear. What we can't know is what will happen next.'

'You could leave Idris to hold the eastern border,' Liesel said. 'Take your main forces west, and hit Ezenachi's forces in the Steppe. They won't be able to resist us.'

'Maybe that would work for a while,' Inge said. 'But then Ezenachi will come, and what do you propose we do about him, my queen?'

'If Ezenachi chooses to come, he will come. We can't stop him, whatever we do.'

'We can do our best,' Inge said. 'We can keep our word. And we can make ourselves strong enough that he will refrain from attacking us. Esterel commands an empire with vast resources. If Ezenachi brings war, he will suffer as much as we do. His empire, patiently built for many years, will be wrecked by our armies. Think of everything we have achieved to get Esterel to this position. Think of the sacrifices. Why throw that away?'

Liesel looked around the room. At Esterel; his friends and ministers. Did no one else see through the witch's words? *How dare she talk of sacrifices made?* For all Liesel knew, Inge was working for Ezenachi, keeping Brasingia and Guivergne from the fight. But she had no allies here, and she decided more words from her would only make things worse.

One thing is clear. I can't rely on Idris or anyone else to deal with Inge. I shall have to do it myself.

* * *

INGE WASN'T easy to track down. She seemed to move about the castle like a ghost, appearing in a corridor when least expected or wanted. Recently, she was never far from Esterel's side. No one, it seemed, had ever been inside her private suite of rooms.

But she had her habits. She was wont to take walks in the royal gardens, at least once a day. Liesel had found the best position in the castle to watch her. There was a window, the highest in one of the corner towers, overlooking the gardens. Few people ever bothered to climb so high. Liesel had taken the precaution of walking through the gardens herself and looking up at the window. It was in shadow most of the day—no one could see movement from up there.

Liesel found she could kneel at the window and aim her crossbow quite comfortably. Her sight was well above the hedges that divided up the garden, giving her a wide field of vision. Anyone who walked along the crushed stone paths could be targeted. It was really only a matter of bravery to pull the trigger. Well, bravery and accuracy. She wished she was a better shot. For she was quite certain she would only get one chance at it. If she missed, Inge would be warned and it would all be over.

What will my punishment be, I wonder? But I must do it. I have a responsibility.

She readied herself, waiting for the witch to appear. The advantage of the weapon, an advantage Liesel had been quick to see when she first witnessed their use, was that she could wait like this for as long as she needed to.

But, of course, she was foiled. Footsteps on the tower's wooden stairs below her—stairs that barely anyone used except her. She had no time to hide her crossbow, and her guilt was therefore plain to see.

It could have been worse. It was Florent.

'Your Majesty,' he said politely, taking in the weapon by her side.

44

'Lord Florent,' she replied. Of Esterel's friends, she knew him the least. He was the quietest. Perhaps the cleverest. And everything she knew suggested he was the most ferociously loyal to Esterel. 'Did my husband have you spy on me?'

He had a slim, boyish face, and he gave her a pained look that seemed genuine. 'He asked me to look out for you. Suspected you might get it in your head to do something foolish.'

'And what will you tell him?'

'I hope to tell him I dissuaded you to act on your impulses. Killing a minister of the king would be a great crime, Your Majesty.'

'What makes you think that is my intent?'

Florent gave her a look. 'I am not the cleverest of men. But neither am I stupid.'

Liesel let out a sigh. 'I am the only one who sees her for what she is.'

'Perhaps. Perhaps not. In most circumstances, I would happily take that shot myself. Were it not for the fact there is a rogue god with an army of thousands on our border. Were it not that Inge is the only person of magic in our realm. Were it not that Esterel has decided to trust her, and that this realm would soon descend into chaos if I—and even you, Liesel—were free to disobey him whenever we dislike his decisions.'

Liesel bowed her head. 'I know. I would never have gone through with it. It is, I suppose, a fantasy I am acting out. Imagining a world where I was free to do as I wished. I know you must tell Esterel what you saw. But you could also pass on my words, couldn't you?'

Florent smiled. It was a charming smile, and Liesel thought he must be an excellent actor if it wasn't genuine.

'Of course I will tell him. You know you are the most important person in the world to him, Liesel? We tend not to say these things enough, if at all. But I know that is how he feels.'

She smiled and nodded. 'Thank you, Florent.'

He left, the stairs creaking on his way down.

Perhaps Liesel would have given up on her plan if she hadn't caught sight of Inge's blonde locks, down in the garden below.

She reached for her stave, cradling it in both hands. She had time for some regret for Florent. He would get into a lot of trouble for this. Nearly as much as her.

She aimed, her finger close to the trigger that would release the cocked string. Inge came into view, walking at a steady pace along the path.

Liesel released. She had time to see the quarrel strike the back of the witch's head. Time to see her body collapse before it landed, out of view, behind a hedge. But she was sure Inge was dead.

After all. It is not very difficult to kill someone. Even a witch.

SANC

LANDS OF THE EGERS

Sanc woke and wished he was still asleep. His head pounded, his mouth so dry he could barely swallow, and he felt like he would lose the contents of his stomach at any moment. He could hear a rumble and felt the sensation of moving. Wondering where he was, he made himself sit up.

He was in a cart, trundling through open countryside. His head spun, and he used all his strength to grip the side and lean over. He vomited, then sat back down, exhausted. But his stomach felt better.

He studied his travelling companions. A giant lizard pulled the cart, and around it rode Egers, mounted on lizards. One of the creatures approached the cart. It was green and burly, and carried Herin.

'You're awake,' he commented.

'Water,' Sanc got out, and Herin passed him a waterskin. He gulped at it until his immediate thirst was quenched.

Herin was studying him, and Sanc's memories returned in a flash. He'd had Lothar in the air—could have killed him. At the last moment, he'd changed his mind. He and Herin had teleported away just before the Gadenzian riders got to them. Then he'd collapsed. Now here he was and Herin was staring at him. Demanding answers.

'Where's Mildrith?' Sanc asked.

'The Egers retreated from the forts, mostly in good order. Mildrith agreed she would accompany the khan and protect him. The main army is travelling due south. We're accompanying Kursuk and a small force of riders south east. We thought it would be a good idea to split up. But Lothar's wizards may be chasing us.'

Sanc's heart beat faster as he realised the danger he had left everyone in. Unconscious, he hadn't been using his magic. Temyl and Guntram might be close. He called on his magic. First, throwing a veil over his whereabouts. Next, searching for other magic users. He located two pairs, one to the northwest; presumably Temyl and Guntram. To the southwest, Mildrith and the Eger Khan.

'They are not very close to us, or to Mildrith.'

Herin nodded. 'I guessed, after our run in with Lothar, he would be keen to keep them by his side. But it is a relief to know for sure.'

Sanc digested Herin's other words. *I've forced Mildrith to travel separately. The Egers are retreating. Yet another defeat to Lothar.* And the Egers had been their last chance. Not only that, but it was his fault. He'd been presented with a chance to kill Lothar and hadn't taken it.

'Have you told anyone else what happened?'

'Not the truth, no. I didn't think that would go down very well. I told them we couldn't get to Lothar, that his cavalry chased us off.'

'Did they believe you?'

'The Egers, maybe. Mildrith didn't look convinced.'

Sanc smiled despite feeling so miserable. It did not surprise him to hear Mildrith didn't believe a word. He owed Herin an explanation, but what to say? He couldn't share everything. Certainly not the appearance of his mother. He didn't think anyone would understand that. He didn't understand it himself. 'I realised it was the wrong move,' he said at last, hearing the uncertainty in his own words.

'How so?'

'We didn't come to Silb to kill Lothar. We came to find help against Ezenachi.'

Herin appeared to chew on these words. 'And you think Lothar is the one to help us? With his two champions? Where does that leave our allies?'

'I'm not suggesting we desert one group for another.'

'Then what are you saying, Sanc? We've been here over a year and I'm feeling as lost as ever about what exactly we are supposed to be doing.'

'I feel like I'm gaining some clarity. But I don't claim to have a full picture in my head. I want to go to Peramo.'

'Peramo?'

'It's a holy place, in Scorgia. Where the gods of the seven peoples lie at rest.'

'Ah,' Herin murmured, a look of relief on his face. 'Gods. Now you're making sense. If we can revive these gods, they can defeat Ezenachi?'

'Maybe. The legends of Silb say it was these seven gods who defeated Ezenachi, driving him out. That was why he went looking for a new world.'

Sanc put a hand to his head, which was throbbing badly. The pain prevented him from thinking clearly. He hoped he was making some kind of sense.

Herin noticed. 'I'll get you food and drink. And I'll talk with Kursuk about getting to Scorgia. You rest up. We need you fit and healthy.'

* * *

KURSUK AGREED to take them east, to Scorgia. After a day in the cart, Sanc recovered enough to ride. He transferred from the cart to Spike. While the creature showed no sign of being pleased to see him again, neither did it try to eat him. Sanc was willing to accept such a relationship.

The grassland they travelled through was as featureless as the rest of the Eger lands Sanc had seen. It was a monotonous journey of several days to reach the border with Scorgian lands. Alone with his thoughts, Sanc's mood dipped. *Perhaps we should just return to Dalriya. Admit that we've failed.*

Herin seemed to sense Sanc's gloom. He made him eat and drink, and insisted he went straight to bed as soon as they stopped for the night. Slowly, Sanc escaped his demons and focused on what needed to be done.

He spoke with Kursuk. The Eger general explained he didn't mind the detour. 'We need to patrol our borders from time to time. Especially now we are at war.'

'You don't have garrisons on the border?' Sanc asked him.

'No. Neither did the Scorgians. But Lothar rules now. Better to see with my own eyes whether anything has changed.'

THEY SAW some old fortifications on the Scorgian side of the border, but they were run down, probably not used for generations. Sanc did his best to explain his purpose in heading to Peramo, and Kursuk agreed to pass his message on to the khan and Mildrith.

'I will contact you soon,' Sanc promised. 'This war isn't over.'

'See that you do. The Egers have been sleeping a long time. Now we are awakened, we shall shake Silb once more.'

'I know we drew the Nerisians south and probably saved the Telds,' Herin commented as the two of them continued east on foot. They'd left their lizard mounts with the Egers—they would not have helped them blend in amongst the Scorgians. 'But it feels like we've created yet another problem with those lizard riding dolts.'

'Maybe it was a mistake to wake the Egers,' Sanc agreed. 'But at the time, that was the only option we had.' He sighed. 'You know, Rimmon sent me to a location only a few miles from Peramo. Feels like I've been everywhere else in Silb except there.'

Herin grunted. 'And what if you had visited Peramo first, and found the tombs of these seven gods? Would that have meant anything to you at the time? Don't be hard on yourself. We do what we think is best in the moment. Trust me, it's all too easy to blame oneself for past actions. It only makes you bitter.'

Sanc knew the warrior was referring to his own role in the Isharite Wars. He wondered if one day he would be an old man, looking back on these years and judging himself for what he did right and wrong. It was an unnerving thought, and he determined to take Herin's advice and stay in the present.

* * *

THE SCORGIAN SETTLEMENTS they passed through were small and remote. Many they spoke with were not even aware their ruler had been replaced. Some coins now bore the mark of Lothar instead of Domizio, but neither name meant much to those who lived so independently.

They had the darker features and slighter frames of the natives of Silb—those people who had once worshipped Ezenachi, or at least been ruled by him. Sanc couldn't help wondering what this world had been like in those days. Ezenachi was probably the only one who could tell him that. But the nature of gods and champions continued to nag at his mind, as if there was some puzzle or riddle he must solve. *That is just the way my mind works,* he told himself, looking across at his companion, Herin. *It must be easier to have a warrior's mind, whose solution to everything is killing someone or other.*

To Sanc's left the plains continued, while to his right was highland, the sides of hills carpeted by trees.

It was from this region that the horsemen issued, no doubt having spied the two pedestrians from a vantage point. There were a score of them. They divided into two columns and approached from each side.

'Who are these oafs?' Herin wondered, checking the weapons at his belt and the bow slung over one shoulder.

'If I've got my geography right, that land is called Sinto. The Scorgians who live there fought off the Nerisians.'

Herin sighed. 'Bully for them. Can't they just leave us alone?'

'Hail!' one rider called as he and his companions pulled up. 'Where are you headed, travellers?' he asked, peering at Sanc's red eyes.

'We are going to Peramo,' Sanc told him.

The man's eyes widened. 'You serve Lothar the Nerisian?'

'No,' Sanc answered, wondering what was best to say. 'We work for Prince Lenzo of Arvena.'

The riders of Sinto looked at one another, unsure what to make of their find.

'We are merely passing through these lands,' Herin said. 'We're no trouble to you.'

Sanc supposed he did his best to make his voice sound friendly, but he was out of practice.

'Duke Atto decides who passes through these lands,' the man warned him. 'You can explain your business to him.'

Sanc and Herin shared a look. If he had to, Sanc could probably send these warriors flying. They could grab a horse each and be on their way. But it wasn't an ideal solution.

'Is he close?' Sanc asked the man. 'Only we're in a terrible hurry.'

The man studied Sanc. Sanc and Herin weren't reacting as he might have expected. Neither had shown any concern at being surrounded by twenty warriors and were behaving as if visiting with Atto was an offer they could decline.

'We can give you horses. He's only a brief ride from here. If you are who you say, talking with my lord would benefit you.'

Sanc looked at Herin. 'This Duke Atto might be a helpful ally to have.'

The Magnian shrugged. 'Whatever you decide.'

SANC WAS quick to see why the Scorgians had held onto this territory —or at least, why the Nerisians had made little attempt to take it. The terrain was difficult and easy to get lost in. Steep-sided valleys, streams and rivers broke the land. Defensible points and places ideal for ambush abounded. Fortunately, the warrior who led the horsemen had been honest, and they stopped a couple of miles into the rough terrain. He left them with half of his men and carried on to fetch his lord.

The sun still shone when Duke Atto arrived with the scouting party and half a dozen well-armed warriors. He dismounted and approached Sanc and Herin, who had found a flat rock to sit on while they cared for their weapons.

Sanc stood as the man approached. Atto had a cleft lip, whether from birth or injury, it wasn't possible to know. It meant he could see the man's teeth through the gap in his top lip. He felt a sympathy and some sort of connection, given his own looks had weighed on him for a long time. He offered his hand. 'Your Grace.'

The duke took it. 'Your name?'

'Sanc.'

'I hear I owe you thanks for deigning to stop and speak with me,' the duke said, an ironic tone to his voice.

Sanc smiled. 'It is true we are in a hurry. We have just come from the lands of the Egers and I am keen to reach Peramo as quickly as possible.'

'The Egers?' Atto repeated. 'No one is welcomed in their lands. Ordinarily, I would call you a liar. But I suspect you are telling the truth. I heard rumours of a new champion in Arvena. The stories say you burst into General Wacho's house and killed him and his soldiers.'

Herin turned to Sanc, one eyebrow raised.

'Not entirely true,' Sanc said. 'But I was in Arvena, and I have been to many places in Silb besides.'

'Then you would do me a great honour in telling me your story. Perhaps, in return, there is some way I can help with your journey.'

* * *

ATTO PROVIDED mounts and led them due north for Peramo. He took only four bodyguards. They wanted to travel fast and unobtrusively, not get noticed by any Nerisian units left behind in Scorgia.

'You've told me you have the powers of a champion,' he said to Sanc as they rode. 'Why not use your magic to get to Peramo as you have done in the past? Why were you walking?'

'When teleporting, you need to have a good idea about your destination, otherwise it can be dangerous. I haven't been to Peramo before. The closest I got was the lake to the north. Then there's the toll that using magic takes. If I have all my reserves left, I can teleport wherever I need to go afterwards.'

'I see. And where's that?'

'It feels like I must go everywhere at once. Lothar's enemies have only ever fought him one at a time. It's about time they coordinate and make his life difficult.'

'That's asking a lot. Lenzo and I haven't even coordinated attacks in Scorgia properly.'

'What's stopping you?'

'I don't know. Trust, I suppose. I know Lenzo of old. Wastrel comes to mind.'

'I think you'll find he's changed.'

'If what you have recounted is true, then I have to acknowledge that. It seems the Scorgians are better placed than most peoples to fight. Mine and Lenzo's forces are small. But if we can raise our people against the occupiers, we can cause the enemy some trouble.'

SANC HAD BEEN EXPECTING something grander, but Peramo was a relatively small settlement.

'It is run by priests,' Atto explained. 'Their creed restricts them to spiritual matters. They are not meant to interfere in the world of politics.'

'That didn't stop them crowning Lothar emperor,' Herin reminded him.

'The abbot had little choice in the matter when Lothar marched here with his army. Peramo has been allowed to keep its independence, but the brethren paid a price for it.'

They left their horses with one of the duke's warriors, telling him to wait for their imminent return.

At the town gate, Atto was recognised.

'I must ask your business here, Your Grace,' a guard said. He was dressed in a fine-looking uniform of yellow and blue.

'I am visiting the temple for purely personal reasons.'

The guard gazed at Sanc. These days, he was more at peace with his eyes than ever. But they still made him stand out. Perhaps even identified him. 'Then you are welcome,' the guard said at last. 'But I advise discretion. The emperor has eyes and ears inside these walls.'

'If I am about anything, it is discretion,' Atto replied. 'Thank you for yours,' he said, placing a coin into the guard's palm.

The duke led them into town, quietly pointing out the highlights to Sanc and Herin. There were two buildings of great significance. The residence of the abbot and his staff was palatial, dominating the centre of town. Then, to the south, was the Temple of Peramo. The resting place of the gods of Silb. Atto wasted no time in leading them in that direction, and Sanc felt a flutter in his chest at the prospect of finally observing the place for himself.

The space around the temple had been left untouched, so that it felt like they were entering a small piece of wilderness inside the town walls. Trees grew tall, and in their branches, birds and mammals lived their lives, oblivious of the holiness of the site. Rocks and boulders lay strewn about. Perhaps, Sanc contemplated, the building was originally sited here because of the availability of building materials. Then he recalled the islanders of Ram had told Mildrith that it was the worshippers of Ezenachi who had first founded this site. A shiver ran down his back as the structure came into view.

The temple was rectangular and stone built. On either side of the entrance were seven pillars. Each had a carved effigy. Sanc stopped to examine them. He soon knew who he was looking at, recognising them from his visits to the Temple of Salacus in Arvena. That was where he had first learned about the peoples of Silb and their gods.

Some he was familiar with. Salacus stood on the sinewy forms of his servants, Hasha and Ibil. The Kassite god Ymer was depicted as part tree, part man. Anada, goddess of the Egers, had scaly skin and a tail. Others, he was less sure of. A giant figure stood amongst the clouds and Sanc couldn't tell if he was the god of the Telds, or of the Gadenzians.

They passed the pillars and entered the temple. The atmosphere inside was reverential. A few priests stood watch over the seven stone sarcophagi. Otherwise, only a handful of lay visitors were paying their respects. Most gathered around the tomb of Salacus, the Scorgian deity. Sanc wondered if they were quietly asking him to rid their kingdom of the Nerisians, or simply to keep their families safe in these worrisome times.

He realised he was being stared at. Herin, Atto, and the duke's three companions were waiting on his lead.

'What is the plan?' Atto asked him.

'You can revive these gods?' Herin said, a healthy amount of doubt in his voice. 'I have never heard of such a thing before.'

Now he was here, Sanc wasn't sure what he should do. But he knew the peoples of Silb shared the same legend, that these seven gods had defeated Ezenachi. Maybe they had died a long time ago. Perhaps they only slept—like Oisin, King of the Giants, had done. Whatever they had once been; whatever they were now; he needed to learn the truth.

'We must remove the tombstones,' Sanc said, gesturing at the heavy lids that sealed each god inside.

Wide eyes stared at him in disbelief.

Atto looked around at those who shared the temple with them. 'These priests will complain instantly. They'll fetch the town guards. Did you not hear me at the gate? I am about discretion, not blundering about and creating a scene.'

'Your men have weapons. They can pen them in the temple while we do our work.'

'Maybe. But only for so long. People outside will notice. The whole town will turn on us. The authorities will bring the Nerisians. Let us go see the abbot and ask his permission to work in the temple alone.'

'How likely is he to grant such a request?' Sanc asked. 'And won't that get people talking? I say do it now, while we have the chance. It won't take long to look inside. When the deed is done, I can teleport us outside the town walls. We'll be long gone before they can find where we went.'

Atto still looked doubtful, but Herin nodded his support. 'He can carry us back to our mounts in moments. I have experienced it myself.'

Atto chewed at what there was of his top lip. It was a strange sight, and he stopped himself, self-conscious. 'I should have asked you to demonstrate your magic to me. But I have heard enough to believe you have the power. Very well. We shall gather the priests and bring them to the tomb of Salacus.'

They did as the duke suggested, gathering the dozen people in the temple together, where two of Atto's bodyguards drew bare steel and threatened the group, telling them not to move.

With Salacus' tomb surrounded by their captives, Sanc opted for an alternative. 'This one,' he said.

The resting place of Ymer. *May Mildrith forgive me*, he said to himself. But he had long wanted to know the truth about the god of the Kassites. Mildrith's people had insisted Ymer lived at the top of the Irgasil, until the great tree was toppled by Temyl, the Nerisian champion. When the Kassites had needed him, Ymer hadn't come.

Sanc wasted no time in pushing at the heavy stone lid, decorated with a likeness of the Kassite god that matched his pillar outside. Herin joined him and, with more reluctance, Atto and his remaining retainer gripped the opposite side and pulled. Sanc used his magic to help ease the lid off, the grinding sound echoing around the temple, and no doubt audible by those outside. It was heavy, and they had to take great care to ease the lid onto the temple floor, resting it against the side of the sarcophagus.

Traces of a sweet, scented odour greeted them. Sanc could see jars lining the sides of the tomb. He could smell honey and other fragrances emanating from them.

He turned his attention to the remains of Ymer. Only bones. The body was turned to one side. Sanc scanned him from top to bottom. Ymer's skull faced him. There were empty holes where his eyes once were, seeming to stare back. Sanc put aside such thoughts, just as Atto and his companion gasped and turned away, horrified at what they had done. He could clearly see the ribs, arm and leg bones; the wide slabs of the pelvis. Ymer was human size. There was nothing special about his remains; no sign of the tree-like creature depicted.

Their captives muttered, before Herin told them to stay quiet.

'This is a disgrace,' Atto whispered hoarsely. 'You will not touch the tomb of Salacus.'

'This one next,' Sanc said, barely acknowledging the Duke of Sinto.

Sanc and Herin pushed at the lid of Anada's tomb. Atto shook his head, but he helped once more.

Once the lid was off, Sanc studied the second skeleton. He was searching for specific features that would verify Anada's identity. The bones, noticeably smaller than Ymer's, suggested he was looking at a female human. Then there was the skull—stretched so long, it barely looked human. But it looked Eger. Surely, he was looking at an Eger woman. And only a woman. There were no scales here; no bony tail emerging from her lower spine.

'Well?' Herin said, with a nod towards the temple entrance. 'Sounds like the good people of Peramo are going to storm this place soon.'

So focused on his observations, Sanc only now heard the commotion outside. Atto's warriors looked at him nervously. They would soon be hopelessly outnumbered. He gave a lingering look at the tomb of Salacus.

There was no way he was getting a look inside without a fight. There were four other tombs to inspect. *But do I really think I'll find anything different inside them? The Gadenzian will be tall. The Rasidi and the Teld skeletons will reveal little. But if they still lived, one would have bronzed skin and dark eyes; the other fair hair and violet eyes.*

'Alright,' he conceded. 'I've seen enough.'

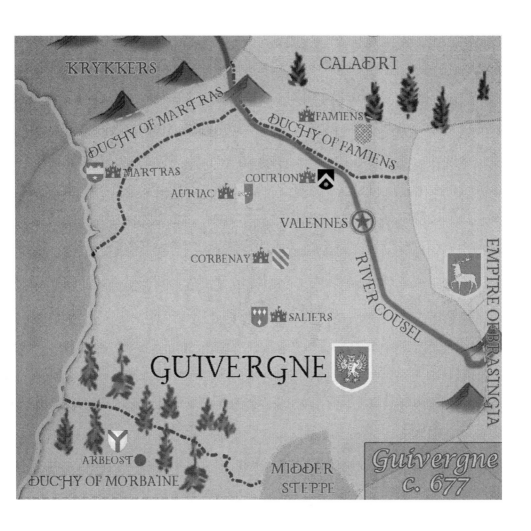

KRYKKERS

CALADRI

DUCHY OF MARTRAS

FAMIENS

DUCHY OF FAMIENS

MARTRAS

COURION

AURIAC

VALENNES

CORBENAY

SALIERS

RIVER COUSEL

GUIVERGNE

EMPIRE OF BRASINGIA

ARBEOST

DUCHY OF MORBAÏNE

MIDDER
STEPPE

Guivergne
c. 677

PEYRE

KINGDOM OF GUIVERGNE

Peyre escaped the boundaries of his encampment. Escaped, for a while, those questioning looks of his soldiers, who wondered how much longer he'd keep them here, in the middle of nowhere.

The sun was bright and warm overhead. The air smelt like the beginning of summer. Time for shearing, and for the hay harvest. It was a day for travelling somewhere.

Peyre recalled what he had done on such a day in previous years. In Arbeost, he would have gone for a ride with Umbert. In Coldeberg, or Valennes, he would have gone into the city.

There were to be no such pleasures today. Instead, another day of waiting in his impromptu camp on the southern edge of Guivergne. It felt like he was tethered to this spot by invisible ropes, caught tight and unable to act. One of these ropes was the order from his brother not to intervene in Ezenachi's conquest of Magnia and the Steppe. It left him feeling useless, while a sense of unease grew within him, and began to feel a lot like dread.

Footsteps made him turn. Umbert and another. It took Peyre a while to recognise the second man. Sul was just as tall as ever, but without the furs Peyre was used to seeing him in, he looked a lot slimmer.

'You said to take any messengers straight to see you,' Umbert said.

'Of course. I'm desperate for news. It's good to see you, Sul,' he said, as they grasped each other in the warrior's grip. 'Gosse sent you?'

'Aye, as soon as we reached the southern border of Morbaine, I turned right back round again. It was already over by then.'

'The Magnians?'

'Retreated into Morbaine. Didn't try to stop the Turned. Said there were too many.'

'King Ida was there?'

'Yes, he led his people. He was pretty cut up, though.'

'I can imagine what he is going through. Having to leave his kingdom behind. The Middians have had to do just the same in the last few days.'

'There's that, yeah. But there was more to it. He saw his mother, you see. She wasn't just one of the Turned, either. She was leading them. Wearing a see-through cloak, she was. Left nothing to the imagination, from what I heard.'

Peyre nodded. So, Maragin and her group had found the Cloak of the Asrai. And just like the other weapons of Madria, its wielder was now under the control of Ezenachi. 'Any other weapon wielders with her?'

'Her bodyguard. Morlin, I think they called him. Said to be carrying a shield that deflects any missile sent against it. Then there was a name that even I have heard of before. Belwynn Godslayer. Carries the same weapon that killed a god all those years ago.'

'The warriors I spoke with said there were too many Turned to fight against. But I have my doubts about that. I think when they spotted those three, the fight went out of 'em. Anyhow. Every Magnian free of Ezenachi's taint is now in your duchy, Your Grace. Lord Russell is doing his best to organise things. But he was keen that I tell you all about it as soon as I could.'

'Thank you, Sul.' Peyre shared a look with Umbert for a while as he weighed his options. He knew he had come to a decision, and that was a relief. 'We're going to Morbaine. I owe that to our men, at least. They have family there, and if Ezenachi intends to continue his conquests, that is where he will strike next. I'll get a message to Loysse. She'll have to defend the rest of Guivergne.'

She had few warriors with which to do so. Most of the Guivergnais army was still in the empire.

But I am Duke of Morbaine, after all. That is where I should be.

* * *

THE ARMY BROKE camp in a hurry, pleased to be returning home. As the final preparations were made, Peyre called his commanders for a meeting. Inhan had reported on his mission to Essenberg, and there were some final decisions to be made.

'The emperor has not changed his mind about our orders,' Peyre explained. 'Or sent any more forces west. It is therefore up to me to prepare the defence of Guivergne. If I am to take the army of Morbaine home, Guivergne is weakened. Arnoul, take your warriors back to Saliers. Put them at the disposal of Famiens and my sister.'

'Of course. Makes sense.'

'My lords of the Steppe,' he said, turning to chieftains Frayne, Cuenin, and Jorath. 'Your people have settled in Guivergne. You, too, should now serve our leadership in Valennes.'

'Thank you, Your Grace,' Frayne said. 'Though I feel we can be of more help than that. Why not base Middian riders in the forts that stretch from Morbaine to Guivergne? We can serve as a quick means of communication between the two.'

'A good idea. One I hadn't thought of,' Peyre admitted.

'I have them from time to time,' Frayne said with a smile.

Peyre grinned at him. 'Turns out those forts my father built have come in very handy.'

'I don't know what makes you think that is a topic for jests,' Jorath snapped, his face implacable.

It didn't bother Peyre. The Middians always looked like they wanted to kill him. Maybe they would. But he sensed he had won a certain amount of respect. When it came to it, he believed they would fight on his side. After all, what alternatives did they have?

. . .

THE MIDDIANS TOOK control of the forts on the way south. That left Peyre with the warriors of Morbaine. As a fighting force, they had proven themselves more than once. Peyre couldn't help feeling stripped of leadership, however. He had Umbert. Benoit, naturally enough, had left with his father. There was Inhan, who was popular amongst the rank and file. But when it came to deciding on strategy, he felt alone.

Gosse and Lord Russell are on the southern border, he reminded himself. *King Ida, as well.* While he did not regret the decision to return to Morbaine, he brooded over what his plan should be. To the south, the Turned were led by Belwynn Godslayer. To the east, by Oisin Dragon-Killer. Every stratagem he concocted seemed destined to lead to defeat.

As they neared the southern border, their numbers swelled. Family members joined the army, eager to see loved ones. Young men—and even the not so young—brought whatever weapons they had. This was different. A threat to their own duchy, not a war fought over the throne of some other realm. Peyre could sense the relief among villagers and townsfolk as they passed through their streets on the way to defend Morbaine. The responsibility weighed on him. These people trusted he would keep them safe, and yet he didn't see how that was possible.

On the last day of marching, they passed rough camps that housed Magnian refugees. They seemed well organised. But the sight sombred his army. This was what Ezenachi had done to a proud people, and Morbaine might be next.

At the border, an attempt had been made to build defences. Wooden watchtowers faced south, placed to give warning of an attack. Basic wooden forts, their palisades made of split timber lashed together, could house a couple of hundred men each. But the border with Magnia hadn't seen war in hundreds of years. It was too late to build stone castles and forts: the structures that might hold back a determined invasion.

Lord Russell greeted Peyre and offered him the best quarters he could provide. But that could wait. Peyre needed to talk over their options before he could think about rest.

Russell invited Ida to the meeting. The king of Magnia had only his bodyguard, Brictwin, for company. But that man was a true warrior, who had fought with Ida's father Edgar in the Isharite Wars. Peyre had with him, Russell, Umbert, and Gosse. They had seen plenty of war in recent years. Between them, surely they could work out the best strategy.

'It's a rough map,' Russell said, spreading a parchment across the table, 'but it has the key locations.'

Peyre had to squint to read the scrawled writing, but the topography looked accurate. 'This is my worry,' he said, jabbing a finger at the Midder Steppe. 'Who knows where this army led by the Giant will strike next? Let's assume an invasion comes. We engage here with the Turned, coming north from Magnia. If the Giant's force from the Steppe comes west into Morbaine, they will cut us off. Not just our military, but the entire population of Morbaine. They can catch us and turn everyone.

'This is the concern with the nature of the enemy we face. It is much more than the deployment of armies a few thousand strong. It is the people who are at risk. They could become our enemies.'

'I fully understand,' Ida said. 'My father faced a similar dilemma. His forts on Magnia's border proved useless when the Turned were able to circumvent them. In fact, it's even worse than you say.' The young king pointed to the coast of Morbaine on Russell's map. 'Somewhere out there is the Sea Caladri fleet. If Ezenachi deploys it in the Lantinen, you could face a three-pronged invasion.'

Peyre let out a breath. 'I hadn't considered that. We are in trouble. And I think I have led my army to the exact place the enemy would want it. They can trap us here.'

They shared glum looks across the map. Gosse looked like he might say something defiant, probably about splitting skulls with axes. But he thought better of it and spat on the ground instead.

'Will you receive any warning of an attack from east or west?' Ida asked Peyre.

'Our Middian allies are positioned on the northeast border with the Steppe. They can relay and give us a fast warning. Lord Russell, what about the coast?'

'We set up a warning system in those years when the Kharovian fleet dominated the Lantinen. It still exists, but it's rudimentary.'

'What about the threat from the south?' Peyre asked.

Ida's youthful face took on a pained expression. 'You know about my mother? Belwynn and Morlin?'

'Sul told me.'

'They make the threat worse than it was the last time. Brictwin, anything else?'

'There are the vossi,' the Magnian warrior said gravely. 'Creatures of the Wilderness, who grow no taller than five feet. Skin hard, like bark. Shrill screams that can sow fear into inexperienced ranks. They lived in tribes in the Wilderness but now they are Turned, they will fight as one with the other people under Ezenachi's command. They have always been aggressive and warlike.' He shrugged. 'Another problem to be aware of.'

Peyre jabbed at the map. 'Then what to do? Anyone?'

He looked at his advisers for help. Gosse shrugged. 'You know my warriors will fight. Whether it be against vossi or any other creature.'

Russell and Umbert shared the same blank expression. 'I wish I could give you a solution, Peyre,' Russell said at last. 'But it might be there simply isn't one. What has King Esterel said?'

Peyre gritted his teeth. 'Now I am here, I wonder if I should have gone to Essenberg myself and had it out with my brother. He simply follows Inge's advice. To stay put and give Ezenachi no reason to attack. But there is a flaw in that argument. If we are attacked here, Esterel will lose his best warriors. Worse, he might find he has to fight them later.'

Russell spread his hands. 'I remember a conversation we had when you first became duke of Morbaine. We agreed you are the one who can make the decisions. The army of Morbaine followed you into

Magnia to fight the Turned. They will follow you again, whatever you decide to do.'

Such comments were all very well. But they weren't answers. Peyre stared at the map, as if it might reveal some hidden key to his dilemma. If there was, he couldn't see it. He turned to Ida and Brictwin. 'Any last thoughts?'

'I would speak with you privately,' Ida said.

Brictwin looked about to say something, then sealed his lips.

'Please, Brictwin,' Peyre said. 'I value your opinion. If you have something to say, I would hear it.'

Ida nodded at his bodyguard and Brictwin spoke. 'I was at Essenberg with the late king when the Drobax came. We thought we could hold the walls against them but they entered the city via the river. I was with him at the Red Fort, too. The Turned came by sea and undid our defences. It was only your brother who saved us that time. I don't have a solution, Your Grace.' He waved a hand. 'But sitting here feels the same as those two occasions.'

Peyre nodded. 'Warning received. Alright. I must get some food inside me and think about this. Your Majesty, you wanted a word?'

Peyre and Ida walked into the trees that surrounded their camp. They were alone—even Brictwin, who followed his master everywhere, stayed behind.

'There is something you need to understand, Peyre. About my mother. She is deeply loved by myself and my people.' The young king had the blond hair of his father and the celebrated looks of his mother. He was handsome—as handsome as Esterel. But it seemed to Peyre it was a boyish sort of face, and he questioned whether he had the steel of his brother.

'Of course.'

'That love is so deep that it is a weakness. If she attacks, my warriors will not strike her. And I will not order them to.'

Peyre frowned. He thought he could understand. He had no genuine memory of his own mother, but he could imagine the strength of such a bond. 'Are you saying the Magnian warriors cannot fight those Turned that Elfled leads? Would they be better off located somewhere else?'

'It is more than that, Peyre. I am saying that I will allow no one to kill her. We must save her. Sanc saved Herin. He freed him from Ezenachi's grip. The same must be done for my mother.'

'But I have no idea where Sanc is now. And I can think of no one else who could do it. I certainly don't trust Inge. And the heroes who might have had such power have themselves been turned by Ezenachi.'

Ida gave him a look of sympathy. 'I know all that. But there it is.'

All Peyre could do was nod. *I am outnumbered. Most likely, I will soon be surrounded. And my allies refuse to fight. I fear I will leave my brother to fight this menace alone. And my other brother—the one who might have saved us—is lost.*

IDRIS

ATRABIA

Idris met eyes with his commanders, judging their courage. The Luderians were his weakest link, of that he was sure. They didn't have the stomach to fight in the Confederacy. The emperor's failures didn't help. Esterel hid in Essenberg while the Turned gathered on every border.

Then there were the Bearmen. Ezenachi had been busy to the north, turning the creatures to his side. Usually solitary, they had become an army. Huge, with powerful limbs and wicked claws, fighting them was a terrifying thought for anyone. Most, it seemed, had gone into the lands of the Blood Caladri. But that could change, and the Luderians seemed unable to shake that thought from their thick heads. He'd put Wechlitz in charge of the Luderian units. He had a certain bloody mindedness about him that lent itself to their situation.

King Gethin of Ritherys led the remnants of the Confederate forces. Accounts suggested Rhain of the Corieltes was dead. Or Turned. Gethin had a grey pallor. If not broken, the man was hanging by a thread, and Idris couldn't rely on the king's warriors to stay staunch.

That left the Atrabians. His uncle, Emlyn, continued to surprise him with his loyalty. His cousins, Ilar and Macsen, were eager to see action. *The great oafs.* Tegyn, his sister, led the archers of Atrabia. She had some kind of point to prove about the pre-eminence of the bow as a weapon. It sounded a lot like madness. But it seemed madness was precisely what was needed.

His mother, Bron, had been persuaded to stay behind in Treglan. She could lead their people if the worst was to happen.

And finally, he asked himself, *how is Idris?* He was aware that he had gone slightly mad during his incarceration in Essenberg. It wasn't normal to look forward to what was to come. But when the warriors of Atrabia looked at him, they saw no fear. Even if he offered them little else, that was a gift.

In the moonlight, everything was black—the hilly ridge to the east, the stand of trees to the south. He gave the signal, and the Atrabians moved. They crossed into Ritherys under the cover of night. He looked across and shared a ferocious grin with Ilar and Macsen. Esterel had ordered him to stay put. But since when did Atrabians take their orders from Essenberg?

Behind his main force, Tegyn followed with her archers. Ahead, Gethin led the warriors of Ritherys. This was their territory, and they traversed the rougher terrain, searching out the enemy. Wechlitz waited at the border, ready to protect a retreat.

Idris wasn't sure if it was a byproduct of his madness, but his strategy came to him with perfect clarity. The Turned weren't expecting an attack. Inge had seen to that, keeping first Leopold, and now Esterel, from confronting Ezenachi. He had an opportunity to strike and must take it. He gave his people his orders, consulting with no one, not even with his family. It added to his aura. Many thought him touched by the gods.

Maybe I am.

They moved in darkness, the excitement they felt tempered by the arduousness of the trek. Idris could feel the tension in his warriors. At times like this, his people became one entity, their minds pooled together. They were pack.

A hiss and a gesture from Gethin's scouts. Ilar and Macsen started to come with Idris, but he held them back with a hand in the air. He trusted his cousins to lead their fighters into battle and hold their nerve. Sneaking up on the enemy unnoticed—not so much.

The scouts led him up a rise. Laid out on the top were Gethin and a few more of his followers. Idris snaked along the ground towards them until he was level with the king, who gestured into the valley below.

The camp was slowly revealed as Idris's eyes turned the dark lumps on the ground into sleeping forms. The valley floor was covered with them. They were thousands strong. It was so unlike a military camp Idris struggled to accept that was what he studied. No soldiers on duty at the edges. No defences. No command centre. Not even a single canvas tent. They slept with no protection from the elements. The idea of luxury seemed meaningless to them.

They simply did as Ezenachi commanded. They would never refuse an order. They were implacable.

If Idris wasn't so cracked in the head, he knew he would share the fear of Gethin and his men. They stank of it.

Idris had the lay of the place inscribed in his mind's eye. But still he searched for more.

'What is it?' Gethin whispered at last, his patience broken.

'The two who carry the sword and staff. Krykker and Caladri, you said.'

'Aye. That's the truth of it.'

'I don't see them.'

'It's impossible to make out individuals in this light. They could be there. If not, they may be over that ridge,' the king said, pointing to the south. 'That is how the Turned have behaved in the past. Their leaders come last.'

'Maybe,' Idris acknowledged. 'I want to get my hands on those weapons. The sword, at least.'

'*That* is what you are worried about?' Gethin hissed, his voice threatening to rise in volume. 'The rest of us see only death in that valley and you see opportunity?'

That's the difference between us, Idris said to himself.

. . .

BACK WITH HIS ATRABIANS, Idris risked taking the time to speak with his commanders. He shot nervous glances at the skyline, knowing the Turned would most likely wake at first light. But in this situation, some preparation would pay dividends. If they could surround that valley, descending from all sides at once, they would have the Turned trapped. It would be a massacre, and the threat to Atrabia would be curtailed. *With any luck, I might grab the sword of the Krykkers as well.*

As soon as he was sure he had got across the basic gist of the plan, he was on the move. He took his own force south at pace, swinging around to the right of the valley. He didn't have the time to take them all the way to the far southern end. Perfection, this was not. But it was a fool who chased perfection when they had their enemy for the taking.

Once they had gone a decent distance, he swung them left. They approached the valley from this new angle. His warriors were not as quiet as he would have liked. But that didn't matter anymore. The Turned were surrounded, more or less. Some might escape. Though he wondered at that. Were they even motivated by self-preservation?

He searched along the edge of the valley for the rest of his army. *I see nothing. I suppose that's a good sign.* But his commanders would be out there. Gethin, Emlyn, Ilar, Macsen, and Tegyn. Each with their own force. Each, if they had any sense amongst them, occupying a different section of the high ground.

'I had the farthest to go,' he muttered to himself, impatient to spring his trap. 'The enemy might be alerted to our presence at any moment.' He nodded to his warriors, then scanned the valley one last time. Drawing in breath, he let out a great war cry and hurled himself down the slope.

The ground was uneven. Idris winced and then grinned as he clattered his shin into a rock. Behind, he could hear his warriors following. Along the edge of the valley, he heard war cries answering his own. Down below, the Turned stirred. They had been given time to react. But the Atrabians would attack together, and that advantage was worth it.

He cursed at the time it took to descend the steep side of the valley. Below, where it levelled out and reached the valley floor, the enemy was already gathering. They seemed an amorphous group, no doubt comprising all the races Ezenachi had turned to his will.

Idris stopped. Turning around, he pointed to the enemy's ranks. 'Shoot!' he shouted. The archers with him stopped their descent and took bows in hand. Idris would have loved to join them, picking out a target and loosing a quiver full of arrows. But that was not his role. He resumed his descent. His archers would soften the enemy up, and he would lead his warriors into their ranks. He drew his short sword from his belt. It was a good weapon for killing.

His judgement was proved correct. His archers punched holes in the enemy ranks. Further, the Turned did not present a line of spears or shields, but each carried whatever weapon was theirs, few armed the same as the one they stood next to. Idris waited only until he had a few warriors to either side. Then he led them in the attack.

A Cordentine, by the look of him, swung a club at him. The strike was easy to avoid. Then Idris stabbed, his own blow not missing. The Cordentine fell, and Idris pressed on, finding his next target. His Atrabians supported him, occupying the Turned warriors who would otherwise have struck from the side.

His blade dealt death again, a mist of blood enveloping him as he pulled it free. The Turned didn't buckle, pressing in to fill the gaps. Wary of pushing too far, Idris retreated. His warriors came with him. It was orderly, and not a single Atrabian had fallen after the first clash.

Only now he had pulled free did Idris hear the shouts and screams. They seemed to come from everywhere: from his archers behind him, and from all over the valley. He looked about, trying to identify what was happening. The shouts were interspersed with the sounds of volleys of arrows. They buzzed through the air, striking metal, and flesh. The Turned didn't utter a word when they were hit. Idris knew the screams were his warriors.

'There, Your Highness,' said the man next to him, gesturing to the sloping side of the valley a hundred feet away.

The sight stunned him. Creatures of the night, it seemed—black, with a green tinge, like seaweed dried out on the beach. They traversed the rocky slope at a frightening pace, moving with strange, jerky motions. In their hands they held spears and tridents, the metal glinting in the moonlight. Then the answer burst through Idris's mind.

'Lizardmen, from the swamps,' he shouted, knowing that once his countrymen knew what they faced, the panic would subside. The Lizardmen had long infested the marshland around the lower reaches of the Cousel, proving impossible to dislodge—by Confederates, Caladri, and imperial troops alike. Given the location, it should have come as no surprise they had been turned by Ezenachi as well. And yet. Even with the knowledge of who he now faced, there was an undeniable kernel of worry at Idris's centre. This was a new, unexpected enemy. One he had not planned for.

'Shoot them!' he shouted at the top of his lungs, wondering why his archers needed to be told what to do.

The Lizardmen were coming for his position, veering towards him. They looked more like vicious animals than humanoids. *I don't like the look of those spears*, he admitted to himself.

'Form up!' he shouted, facing up to the inevitable. They would have to hold their position and treat the new arrivals with respect. At last, a shower of arrows hit the creatures. When they hit, they hurt. The Lizardmen wore only rudimentary armour. But not enough hit to make a difference. The Lizardmen charged, then leapt high into the air, spears held in both hands.

All Idris could do was concentrate on his immediate opponent. The three prongs of the trident were aimed for his chest as the creature fell towards him. He skipped out of the way. The Lizardman adjusted, striking with a two-handed thrust. Idris felt the strike on his side. It didn't penetrate his armour and—what luck!—one prong seemed to be caught in his chain mail.

The Lizardman yanked at his weapon and Idris moved in, his blade punching a hole in the creature's throat. It was a killing blow, and Idris had won precious moments. He sheathed his sword and untangled the spear. A more useful weapon to have right now.

The Lizardmen's attack had been devastating to both sides. Where they had struck, they had killed. Where they had failed, Atrabians had made them pay. Now, Idris would make them pay even more. He struck out, using the spear's length to catch his opponents. He jammed the metal prongs into unprotected legs, disabling the enemy and allowing his comrades to move in for the kill.

Just as he felt on top, and as a vicious grin came to his face, he heard the movement. The ranks of Turned they had retreated from were now coming for them. Idris had time to shout a warning. Then he led his soldiers against the front line. They were outnumbered and isolated from the rest of his army. Only now did he consider the Turned had been better prepared than he had given them credit. Only now did he consider defeat.

CONCERNS over the battlefield melted away. All Idris worried about was a ten-foot space around him. His Atrabians, the Turned unit, and the Lizardmen, had become a chaotic, churning melee. All he had to do was kill and not be killed. There was a simplicity to it—a freedom.

His spear punctured the chest of his latest opponent, but wouldn't pull free. He dropped it, staggering to the side, and pulling free his sword. He found himself a few feet from the scrum, with a chance to look at the battlefield for the first time in a long while. Dawn was breaking, and the picture was clearer than before.

The enemy was winning, but the Atrabians were still fighting. On the other side of the valley, his soldiers had come together to fight off the enemy. A shield wall still held, while behind it arrows rained down on the enemy. It seemed secure enough. But the enemy outnumbered them and they wouldn't hold forever.

Idris looked for his family. He hoped Tegyn still lived, at least.

Then he saw her. Not his sister, but the Krykker warrior. She was directing her units, a battlefield general the Turned had lacked until now. And she held a great sword, two-handed. Idris knew it was Bolivar's Sword. *The gods mean me to have it,* he told himself.

All other concerns forgotten, Idris marched for the Krykker, eyes fixed on the weapon. *You've made a mistake, Ezenachi. Giving me this chance. With that relic, I can lead the resistance against you.*

As he closed on his target, everyone noticed him at once. The noise of battle quietened. A sense of anticipation hung over the valley. The Krykker looked at him, no emotion discernible on her strong features. Idris knew she would not be an easy opponent.

Idris was slow to register the warnings of the Atrabians. Turning too late, he saw the second of Ezenachi's generals. The Caladri sorcerer already had his staff extended in Idris's direction.

He ran, weaving in and out in an effort to avoid the blast. When it came, it lifted him off his feet. Out of control, he landed on the rocky ground.

The nearest cover was a large boulder. Idris pushed himself to his hands and knees, readying himself for a sprint. But when he moved, he collapsed. Only now did he look at his injuries. The blast had hit the right side of his body. Metal armour had disintegrated, and worse —melted onto his skin.

Everything on that side of his body was singed black or red raw.

Idris pushed aside his panic, instead fixing a sardonic grin on his face. If this was how he went out, he wouldn't spend his last moments in self-pity. He made his body move, lurching towards the boulder. A bolt of magic came, and he dove to the ground. The blast struck the boulder, showering him in sharp fragments of rock.

Idris tried to get up once more. His body refused to do what he asked. He let out a roar and pushed himself up. Suddenly, Macsen was there. His cousin's brawny arms were around him. Idris screamed in agony as his burned body was squeezed.

'Sorry,' Macsen said, grabbing Idris's left side. He then half dragged, half walked Idris away.

Up the slope of the valley they went, each step more painful than the last. Idris's focus was on moving his feet. He still heard the arrows of his compatriots flit overhead. Then, a distinct sound—a whoosh of power. He was falling once more, only just putting his hands out to break his fall.

He lifted his head, only to see Macsen's face staring blankly. There was the smell of charred flesh, and he could see steam rising from the gaping wound left by the sorcerer's bolt.

Idris's head dropped. He closed his eyes. He felt tears wet his lashes.

SANC

LANDS OF THE EGERS

Sanc transported himself and Herin across the miles of terrain from Peramo, back to the plains of the Egers. It wasn't easy to locate the army of the Eger Khan; and the teleportation took its toll on his magical reserves. But now was the time to act, and he would push his powers as far as he could over the next few days.

Besides, the closer he got, the more desperate he was to see Mildrith again. It was an unfamiliar experience, wanting to see someone so badly. Part of him liked the feeling. Another part was wary of his own emotions. He remembered, after Tassia's betrayal in Arvena, vowing never to allow himself to get hurt again. *You didn't keep that promise for long*, he chided himself.

The Egers still had hours in the saddle ahead of them. Sanc and Herin's mounts were found, and they joined the column heading south.

Sanc encouraged Spike to speed up, and he pulled alongside Mildrith, who was riding Red. 'I missed you,' he said, and that half smile came to her lips, the closest she ever got to admitting she shared his feelings.

'Thank Ymer you didn't get yourselves killed. I expect an explanation for your absence.'

'Of course.' First, though, he had to do something about Rab. The dog was whining uncontrollably in his desperation to see Sanc again. Sanc had no choice but to teleport the animal up, onto the space in front of his saddle. Rab's tail slammed back and forth in greeting, but he eventually settled. He seemed used to the giant lizards now, and Spike didn't object to the extra rider.

Herin had given them some space to talk, but Sanc called him over. He had words they both needed to hear. Herin came up on Sanc's other side, his great, green—and still nameless—lizard, plodding along.

'It's past time I share everything with the two of you. I have learned much in the last few days and it has finally settled my mind as to what we must do next.' He turned to Mildrith. 'Herin covered for me before. But I must come clean. We got to Lothar. I had him. At the last second, I spared him.'

Mildrith grimaced. 'I thought something was amiss.' She looked at him with her cool blue eyes. There was something dangerous about the Kassite champion. He had always known that. For all their mutual affection, he knew she might turn on him. 'After all his atrocities, why not kill him and end this war?'

'Something in me knew it was wrong, though I couldn't even explain why to myself. I just knew I had to go to Peramo. To see the temple.'

'So that's where you two have been all this time?'

'Yes. We opened some of the tombs there. Finally, I could see the truth for myself.'

Mildrith looked at him warily. He didn't like the look she gave him. Like a cornered animal. But she had to know. Herin, too, was staring at him. For Sanc had yet to share his conclusions with the Magnian.

'I'm sorry,' Sanc said. 'The hope I once had of waking the gods of Silb has gone. They were not sleeping. They were long dead. They cannot stop Ezenachi for us.'

'So what?' Herin asked. 'Coming here has simply been a waste of time?'

'No. Because I learned something else. The men and women who lay in those tombs and have been worshipped as gods were as human as you and I. When I saw that, everything else fell into place.

'Salacus, Ymer, Anada—all of them. They were the champions of their people. Maybe the first, who can say? When they died, new champions were born, just the same as happens now. Their legends as conquerors made them gods to their people. But I believe they had the same powers as the champions do now. Kepa can fly. Temyl can find and manipulate minerals underground. Guntram can summon storms. And you, Mildrith, can make plants move.'

She looked at him, her face impassive, hiding whatever internal struggle she experienced at his words. Sanc had no choice but to continue.

'That truth, I think I have known, at a subconscious level, for some time. It prevented me from killing Lothar. Easier for me, an outlander, to see it than the people born here, where the gods of Silb are universally worshipped. And it gives us hope. Because if Ezenachi, all those years ago, was defeated by the seven champions, then we don't *need* gods to help us. We just need the champions.'

Mildrith remained silent.

Herin grunted. 'I see. So if we want Ezenachi dead, we need Temyl and Guntram to help? It would have been easier resurrecting gods. You think they can be sweet-talked into coming with us to Dalriya?'

'Not sweet-talked, no. In one way, our strategy remains the same. We'll not get anywhere with them unless we can force them to listen.'

'So we fight until we can make them come to a deal?' the warrior asked. He put one hand to his face, stroking his stubble. 'That's not unlike what happened to the Magnians of my father's generation. Two sides who fought in a bloody civil war. They fought each other to a standstill. Had to make a peace, dividing the country into north and south.'

'A bit like that,' Sanc agreed. 'Mildrith?' he said, turning to the Kassite. 'Please say something.'

'I trust you,' she said at last. 'I believe what you say about the gods is true. I'm even willing to swallow my pride and hatred and strike a peace with the Nerisians if it ends this war. And I'll go to Dalriya with you, Sanc. I promised I would. But you can't share this with anyone else. No one will believe you. Because they don't want to. They'll hate you for saying it.'

'She's right,' said Herin.

Sanc nodded slowly. 'Alright, then what?'

'We go to war with Lothar,' Mildrith said. 'When the time is right, we use diplomacy. Only then do we speak of gods and champions.'

* * *

SANC SHARED his war plans with the Eger Khan and his advisers. He didn't refer to his visit to Peramo; didn't mention Adana or any other god. As far as they knew, he still wanted Lothar and his champions dead.

'If you can bait Lothar's army a little longer,' he explained to them, 'we can bring these other forces into the war. When his homeland is threatened, he'll be forced to return. You can turn around and follow, hounding the Nerisians every step of the way.'

The general, Kursuk, nodded along. Hamzat shrugged. 'The Eger Khan will need to deliberate on this plan,' he said, with a glance at his silent brother.

But the Eger Khan raised a hand. 'I have one change to make. I will be safest with another champion at my side. I still have things to learn. Hamzat, Kursuk, and my other generals can direct our army. They don't need me for that.'

The Egers looked deeply unhappy, but their khan had spoken.

'Very well,' Sanc said. 'Then you should go with Mildrith.'

THEY LED the khan a short distance from the rest of the army, where the long grass hid them from sight. It was some responsibility Mildrith had been given. But the boy khan was exerting his authority, and that was how it should be.

First, Sanc and Mildrith pooled their power to send Herin back to the land of the Telds. The Magnian had a smile on his face when he left, no doubt because he was going to see Kepa again.

Then it was time for Mildrith and the khan to go.

Sanc stared at her, trying to remember every feature. *I don't want you to go*, he mouthed at her.

A twitch of the lips. 'We'll meet again soon, Sanc,' she said.

He took one of her hands in his, then took the khan's hand in another. The pair left, teleporting north to her people's lands.

Sanc was tired, but he had one more journey to make. He crouched, giving Rab a pat. 'Just you and me again, boy.'

* * *

WHEN SANC ARRIVED IN ARVENA, he was so exhausted he barely had the energy to make it to Lenzo's house. He spoke with the prince, half delirious, not sure he was making sense, before Lenzo had Gaida take him to a private bedroom.

Sanc woke slowly from a deep sleep. He left his room and made his way, thick-headed, downstairs. Midday sun streamed in through open doors and windows. Lenzo was out, but his servants sat Sanc down and brought him plates of breakfast. Rab pattered in to give him a sniff but then left, preferring the company of the kitchen staff who were probably supplying him with all manner of treats.

Sanc was finishing his meal when Lenzo returned. A small entourage was with him, all of them people Sanc knew, who gave their greetings. One of them was Dag, the ship captain who had shared Sanc and Lenzo's disastrous trip to the lands of the Rasidi. He gave Sanc a grin, and they wordlessly clasped hands.

'I'm glad you're up,' said Lenzo. 'We've made arrangements. What soldiers we have in the city will be mobilised. Our fleet will be commandeered. That will take a little longer.'

'Fleet?' Sanc asked, his head befuddled. He didn't see the need for a fleet.

'I know we're headed for Irpino. But we'll have to get the troops across to the mainland for starters,' Lenzo said, talking to Sanc as if he were still the naïve outlander he had first met. 'After that, it will still have its uses. Dag here will take some of our fighting ships to the Dogne estuary. Maybe sail it up the river. That'll scare the shit out of Lothar. He'll get word the Scorgians are coming to take Mournai. Meanwhile, we'll hit Irpino before he knows we're there.'

The prince looked satisfied with the strategy and it all sounded very convincing to Sanc. He allowed himself a smile. He was surprised at how good it felt to be back in the city. The Scorgians were looking as optimistic as he had ever seen them. *This time*, he told himself, *I will give these people a victory.*

LIESEL

ESSENBERG, DUCHY OF KELLAND

Footsteps, and the murmur of voices, woke Liesel from her daze. Confined in her cell with nothing to do, it was a state of mind she soon fell into.

It would start with looking back over the last year, at all the opportunities she'd had to avoid the very situation she found herself in. Sometimes, in her daydreams, she changed the course of events. Sometimes she didn't, every twist and turn leading to the same outcome. Neither version made her feel any better, and she welcomed the possibility of an interruption to her solitary world.

Sacha appeared, holding a tray of food, while the guard unlocked the cell door. *Always Sacha*, Liesel noted, as he deposited the food on her table. Esterel had not come once. But at least once a day, Sacha would come and make sure she was comfortable. Just as he had always done, taking his role as Esterel's steward with the utmost gravity. Her husband was lucky to have such loyal friends.

She felt an urge to stand and welcome him. Play the role of hostess with the same dedication Sacha had. But that was ridiculous in the circumstances. She remained seated on her bed. 'Thank you,' she said.

'You are well, Your Majesty?' he asked her, taking a seat at the table.

'Yes. But I am always eager for news.'

He seemed to dither for a moment over what to say, then gave her a resigned look. 'We have heard from the east. Your friend, Prince Idris, charged into Ritherys with the warriors of Atrabia and Luderia. A total disaster.'

'He lives?'

'Not sure. All reports say he was badly injured. Some say he was carried out of there, unconscious.'

Liesel's stomach twisted. 'Tegyn?'

Pink came to Sacha's cheeks. *Of course*, Liesel remembered, *they had a fling.* For a moment, she saw the Sacha she had first met, before familiarity had replaced that version. Outrageously handsome, with dark, brooding looks. Somehow, he'd escaped marriage all this time. 'She lives. I made sure to find that out. Anyway, it means an imperial army invaded Ezenachi's territory. Combine that with your execution of Inge, and war seems inevitable now.'

'War was always inevitable.'

He shrugged. 'Maybe. I'm not here to condone or condemn your actions. I do what my king asks of me. Simple as that.'

Liesel understood the rebuke in his words. She supposed, from the point of view of Esterel and Sacha, they would never know if they could have won a peace with Ezenachi. Her actions, and those of Idris, had robbed them of that. She could understand the anger. She just knew they were wrong. Such a peace had always been a fantasy.

'What about the empire?' she asked him. 'The people of Kelland can't be happy that Esterel has put me here.'

Sacha sighed. 'They are not. It makes things very difficult.'

'Then he should release me. This makes no sense.'

Sacha refused even to respond to that.

Well, Liesel thought to herself, *that conversation is exhausted. Things are terrible out there, but Esterel is not doing very much about it.*

'What about Florent? At least release him. Esterel needs his loyal friends around him now. He should take no blame for what I did.'

'Hardly,' Sacha scoffed. 'Esterel, Florent, and I very much agree that the blame is his. He found you in position with the crossbow and left both you and the weapon. Not his finest hour.'

'Only because I persuaded him I wouldn't act. I misled him.'

'Well. Your concern for Florent is a noble thing, Your Majesty. Maybe, over time, Esterel will come to forgive *him*.'

The implication was not lost on Liesel. Esterel would never forgive her. But their personal relationship was hardly what mattered now. They faced a threat which would see the end of both Brasingia and Guivergne—their people turned to become Ezenachi's puppets. Leaving her to languish here served no purpose except to assuage Esterel's fury at what she had done.

Sacha got to his feet. 'Goodbye Liesel. I will check in with you tomorrow.'

I will continue to languish here, Liesel realised. *Until the day Ezenachi comes to Essenberg and it's too late to stop him.*

* * *

THE DAYS MERGED into one another, and Liesel's situation didn't change. Sacha continued to visit. When he did, she tried to pull as much information from him as she could get. Idris, he told her, had survived. But his injuries were severe. Meanwhile, they had received messages from Peyre in the west. He was in Morbaine, ready to defend against Ezenachi's forces, who had conquered the kingdom of Magnia.

Liesel still believed she had done everyone a service in killing Inge. But it had come at some price—confined here on her husband's orders, unable to contribute.

Some days, she decided she had got what she deserved. *I have always been alone, so it's no wonder I have come to end my days like this. There must be something wrong with me.* At other times, she railed against Esterel. She understood him, so why couldn't he understand her? She had not killed Inge to cross him, but to save him from the witch's influence. Even if he disagreed with what she did, what was the purpose of this incarceration? Merely to punish her for going against him? That was a childish reaction, and it lessened him.

No doubt Katrina and Jeremias had heard of her imprisonment by now. What must they be thinking? What must the people of Brasingia be thinking, now their new ruler by conquest had put aside his Brasingian wife?

When the footsteps came this time, she fully expected it to be Sacha again.

Instead, Esterel had come at last. He looked at her through the bars of the cell. Liesel thought she saw some shame in his face. Perhaps seeing for himself what he had done to the Queen of Guivergne and the daughter of the Emperor of Brasingia—to his own wife—he realised the humiliation he had inflicted.

'They have persuaded me to return you to your apartments in the castle.' His eyes kept drifting away from hers.

Is it that sense of shame? Or can he simply not stand to look at me anymore?

'This—' he said, gesturing at her cell, 'isn't doing anyone any good.'

She nodded. 'Agreed.' She had nothing more to say. If he was expecting an apology, or gratitude, he really didn't know her at all.

Esterel's jaw clenched. 'You will still be supervised at all times, however. Until I feel I can trust you again.'

Liesel shook her head in disbelief. But she stopped herself from protesting. 'Very well.'

With a dissatisfied look, Esterel turned on his heels and left.

SACHA MADE ALL THE ARRANGEMENTS. She was returned to her own rooms, but with new maids, who would spy on her and tell him every-thing she did.

'I presume it was you who persuaded Esterel to release me?' she asked him.

He ignored her question. 'You will take your meals here, in your rooms.'

'And not be seen in the hall? I thought the whole point was for the people of Kelland to see me free? I can play the part of the dutiful wife, Sacha. At least in public.'

He had an embarrassed expression. 'You might as well hear it from me, Liesel. You'd have found out for yourself, I am sure. My sister, Coleta, sits with Esterel at the royal table these days.'

'Coleta? But she and Peyre?'

'Had a falling out, it seems. She travelled here from Valennes.'

Liesel stared at him. 'You mean you sent for her?'

He shook his head. 'No doubt you won't believe it. But this is not what I wanted.'

'Not what you wanted? You must have been secretly celebrating Inge's death. Florent and me locked away. You're the only one with Esterel's ear now. Your sister in his bed, giving him the children he's so desperate for. Seems like you've won, Sacha.'

A slew of emotions crossed the steward's face, but he controlled himself. 'Liesel, I know this hurts you. So I will forget your words. But I suggest you don't push away the last remaining friends you have.'

PEYRE

DUCHY OF MORBAINE

P eyre had made his decisions. He had given his orders.
  Even to his own ears, they sounded like madness. But conventional strategy just wouldn't work in the circumstances he found himself in. Ignoring that fact, and carrying on regardless, would have been weak leadership.

Lord Russell would lead the Morbainais north. Not just the army, but the people of the duchy, plus the refugees from Magnia. Yet again, Peyre had given his father's friend the most difficult of tasks. But his people simply weren't safe here. They could make a stand with the people of Guivergne. They might unite with Esterel's army in the empire. Here, they were in danger of being cut off and turned to Ezenachi's side. He simply couldn't allow that to happen.

The real madness lay with his own task. He would enter Magnia with Ida and the king's bodyguard, Brictwin. Peyre had not asked for volunteers to come with them. Only three had taken it upon themselves to ask. Umbert, Gosse, and Inhan. Six of them would go into the conquered kingdom on a fool's errand to rescue Ida's mother.

Most likely, we will fail.

'There is a sliver of opportunity,' he said to his companions as they crossed from Morbaine into enemy territory, trying to explain to them why he was doing something so reckless. 'Ezenachi turned the seven champions who went to kill him. He controls them and their weapons. A huge swing in power towards him. He must be confident that the whole of Dalriya is now his for the taking. So confident, he divided his champions and armies, sending them to different targets at once. It's a move that has put us on the back foot, that's for sure. But his champions are separated. What if, as King Ida wishes, we can capture the three champions in Magnia?'

Peyre noted the dubious expressions of Umbert, Gosse, and Inhan. *They think I've lost the plot. I suppose I should be honoured that they're still following me despite that.*

'Or, at least, what if we can take back a weapon or two? This could be the best chance we'll ever get to retrieve those weapons for our side. And I'm sure I need not remind you that Toric's Dagger has killed gods before. Maybe Ezenachi's overconfidence has put that weapon within reach.'

His friends' expressions changed. Ever so slightly. Maybe his words had at least given them a sense of hope and purpose.

'We can do this,' Ida said, sounding more sure than Peyre had. 'When she was pregnant with me, my mother met the Queen of the Asrai. It's strange to think of it, knowing what my mother has now become. The queen saw my mother's condition and put her hands on my mother's belly. Then she told her I was a boy and that I would become a great king.

'I must believe in that prophecy. Believe that I will not die in this endeavour—that we will succeed and escape.' He studied their reactions and a small smile came to his lips. 'I sense you don't believe in prophecies.'

They were quiet for a while. Then Umbert spoke up. 'I very much wish to believe in that one, Your Majesty.'

'Then let's all agree to believe it. Our families are heading north to safety if it turns out we are wrong. Knowing that, let us believe in prophecy; in heroism; in the possibility that this god has made a mistake. Put aside your doubts. Let us have faith in something, even if it is only in each other. For that is how great deeds are accomplished.'

. . .

BRICTWIN TOOK ON SCOUTING DUTIES. He knew the terrain, and he knew their enemy.

The Turned were unlike a regular army. They didn't carry out the duties one would usually associate with a successful armed force. They didn't scout or defend their positions. They relied on the weight of numbers. It had worked; the Magnians fleeing their own country rather than attempting to stop their advance. But Peyre was glad they had. Ezenachi had failed to recruit as many Magnians into his force as he had managed elsewhere in Dalriya.

Ida's bodyguard reported back after finding the enemy's forward forces. 'They are gathered in the town of Radstock. Little effort has been made to set up a perimeter. While the main gates are shut and the walls are defended, I could get in through a side gate the towns-folk use to fetch water from the local beck. I didn't dare explore much further. I estimate they are thousands strong. Lippers, Cordentines, and Magnians mix inside the town walls. Their supplies must be inside. The vossi have a separate camp outside the town.'

'No sign of my mother?' Ida asked him.

'I didn't see her. Nor did I see Morlin or Belwynn. But there are many occupied buildings where they could be. I think they must be inside the town. They led this army here.'

'So they're just waiting in this town?' Gosse asked.

'Waiting until Ezenachi orders them elsewhere,' Peyre suggested. 'Which may be in concert with the force that occupies the Midder Steppe. Brictwin, how would the Turned respond to any of us approaching them? You said you didn't dare explore further.'

'That is a good question and one we learned the hard way. They can tell the difference between Turned and non-Turned, that's for sure. They're programmed to attack and capture humans. Some among their number have the power to turn humans. We never worked out for sure how they could tell the difference. Perhaps there is more than one thing at work. But I prefer the simplest answer to that. By sight.'

'By sight? How are the Turned so different looking to us?' Peyre cast his mind back to his only interaction with the Turned before now. It had been on the battlefield in Magnia, where he had fought against them from horseback. The only difference he had noticed that day was how eerily quiet they had been.

'It's in the eyes,' Brictwin answered. 'They are dead. Lifeless.' He shrugged. 'Like I say, perhaps there is more to it. Some other sense they have been imbued with. But my feeling is they cannot tell the difference from a distance. They cannot sense those who are hiding. Not that I have witnessed, at least.'

Peyre rubbed at the stubble on his chin. 'So we enter via this side gate. With hoods covering our faces? Would that work?'

Brictwin shrugged. 'I would be wary of the six of us wandering around like that. Maybe if we split up, we would draw less attention.'

'Hmm.' Peyre didn't like the sound of splitting up. 'What if we entered Radstock at night?'

Umbert's eyebrows raised. 'Stumbling around in the dark amongst them? How will we find Lady Elfled like that?'

'We could move about more freely, though,' Peyre persisted. 'The Turned sleep. We know they bother little with posting guards and all the usual measures armies take. I think it would be the best time to act.'

'Let's say we get inside under cover of darkness,' Gosse said. 'What if, instead of going searching house by house, we draw them out?' he suggested, a sly look on his face.

'Draw them out how?'

'By fire. We find their supplies and torch them.'

Peyre looked around his small group for support. No one disagreed with the idea.

'Their supplies are vital,' he agreed. 'If they're threatened, any competent commander would have to act.'

'Alright,' Ida said. 'That will be our chance.' He gave Peyre a look. 'I understand, from your perspective, Belwynn is the most important target. I would also like to see her freed. But just so we are clear.

When we get inside Radstock, all Brictwin and I can focus on is rescuing my mother. I hope you understand.'

* * *

THEY APPROACHED the side gate in the town's west wall. It was a cloudy night, but Radstock's walls were not tall and Peyre felt vulnerable as they hunched against the timbers.

Now was the first moment of truth. Brictwin had closed the gate from the outside, using a wooden wedge to keep it tight. With any luck, the Turned hadn't noticed. If they were out of luck, the Turned had locked it from the inside, securing it against intruders. That would make breaking in a lot more troublesome.

Peyre and Gosse squatted, shoving their fingers under the bottom of the gate. They lifted, forearms straining with the weight. Brictwin took care removing his wedge, then guided them forwards. Peyre shuffled his feet, mere inches at a time, while holding the gate up. When Brictwin could squeeze past Gosse and lift the gate from the side, it got easier. They swung it open, avoiding a single scrape against the flagstones. They were inside the town, and had barely made a sound to alert the defenders.

Are they even defenders? Peyre asked himself, as Brictwin led them along a narrow street. If he was holding this town, he would have given someone the job of looking after that gate, and punished them if he'd found it unlocked at night. He found the laxity of the Turned astonishing. Perhaps, with the retreat of the Magnians, the enemy simply couldn't imagine anyone returning here. If that was the case, it increased their chances of success, which he had originally put as very low.

Remember, he warned himself. *Belwynn, Elfled, and Morlin lead the Turned here. Don't underestimate them.*

Brictwin stopped outside a workshop. It was the length of four normal houses. There was a good chance they could break in and take the place without the neighbours hearing them. On the other hand, a larger building might house more Turned. Still, on balance, Peyre liked the choice and nodded his approval to Ida's bodyguard.

The rest of them drew weapons, while Brictwin carefully pushed and pulled at the wide wooden door positioned in the middle of the wall that faced the street. He shook his head. It didn't open—secured somehow from the inside.

Peyre thought it best to try a different location. After all, the laxity of the Turned suggested they'd find somewhere else easily enough. But Brictwin had other ideas. He drew his sword, then poked it towards the slim gap between door and jamb.

Peyre winced, nervously looking up and down the street. In one direction was the side gate they had entered through. In the other, the street opened to the town square. Along each side ran houses and other buildings, presumably full of sleeping Turned. If Brictwin got this wrong, they would be swarmed in moments.

The tip of Brictwin's blade passed through the gap into the workshop. Bending his knees slightly, he raised the blade up. He nodded, indicating he had the weight of something on his sword, most likely a wooden bar.

Peyre edged closer, gripping his own sword that much tighter.

Brictwin lowered his blade a few inches and then flicked it upwards. He didn't wait to see if it had worked, pushing at the door with hip and shoulder. It opened. The Magnian disappeared into the interior gloom. Gosse was next, then Peyre.

It was much darker inside the workshop and Peyre could make very little out. Hoping his eyes would adjust, he crept forward, allowing Umbert to follow him in, but trying to avoid knocking into any obstacles. He cursed inwardly as Gosse barged into a table; the legs scraping along the floor.

Peyre moved to the right. He caught a shape moving on the floor. Probably a Turned sitting up after being woken by Gosse's clumsiness. Peyre hoped so because he had to strike first.

He moved with small steps, careful to keep his balance. Just as the figure rose, he thrust forward with his sword, holding it on hilt and edge, to ensure he kept as much control and power as possible. He felt his blade cut through clothes and flesh, then grate against bone. On instinct, he raised one leg and kicked out, sending his target sprawling backwards and freeing his weapon.

Desperate moments followed. Peyre hacked wildly at half-seen figures. Fear drove him on—the need to finish the attack before the whole town woke. In the end, two things were in their favour. First, the Turned had been caught by surprise. Second, none of them shouted a warning or cried out when struck.

When they were done, the six of them stood in the workshop, eyeing one another. They stood still, blood dripping from weapons, as they listened for the sounds of fresh enemies coming their way.

Peyre heard nothing. He took in the details of the workshop. It was a carpenter's place, with a large worktable in the centre that Gosse had walked into.

'Sorry,' the big man mouthed when he saw Peyre eyeing it. At the right end of the workshop, where Peyre and Umbert had fought, was a second table, laid out with the equipment and supplies of a seamstress. Perhaps a husband and wife had once worked here, Peyre mused, before being forced to take the essentials and escape north to Morbaine.

There was still no sign they had disturbed the other Turned. 'Let's move them to this end,' Peyre said.

They dragged the bodies into a pile, a dozen of them. It was gory work, and the smell was awful. Peyre couldn't help looking at the butchered remains of Magnians, Lippers, and Cordentines. Innocent men and women, captured and turned by Ezenachi's forces. Minds subverted, then woken from sleep and slaughtered. Despite everything, he still clung to the notion that war could be a glorious affair. But this wasn't war they were engaged in. It was a calamity fuelled by an evil sorcery. And there seemed to be no end in sight.

Peyre shook himself out of his malaise. They had work to do. Safely ensconced in the workshop, they had some time to enact the next part of the plan. Brictwin and Ida left them to go search for the granary, or wherever else the army's supplies might be kept.

'Let's use this table to get to the roof,' Peyre suggested.

Inhan, his metal hand a hindrance to climbing, and Gosse, whose weight was his hindrance, held the table still. Peyre and Umbert climbed atop. Umbert was the lighter of the two, so Peyre gave him a leg up. 'Come on,' he said irritably, his arms beginning to shake with the effort of holding his friend aloft.

Clinging to a wooden batten, Umbert broke through the thatched roof and hauled himself up. He turned around so that his head covered the hole he had made.

'Well?' Peyre hissed up at him.

'You can see the square from here.'

'Perfect.' Peyre dared to think things were going well. 'We'll get some rope.'

It was not long before they had decent access to the roof of the workshop, from where they could take it in turns to spy on the town square. They would be the first to spot Brictwin and Ida's fire. With any luck, they'd also see Belwynn, Elfled, or Morlin. At that point, they would have to react to circumstances. Plans only took one so far.

'We might as well leave Umbert up there for a while and get some rest,' he suggested to Gosse and Inhan. The young man glanced over to the pile of bodies they had made, as if to say how was he supposed to rest up in here. But he dutifully took a seat and closed his eyes.

Peyre felt the same. While he tried to rest, his blood still pumped from the combat.

He couldn't help imagining Ida and Brictwin creeping through the streets of the town. He wondered how the king must feel, knowing his mother was most likely here. That while he wanted to rescue her, she had been made his enemy. She would see him dead, or worse—turned, like her. These were desperate times. He gave up and told Umbert it was time for them to swap.

He waited for his friend to clamber down the rope, then hauled himself up. Pulling himself through the hole until he was outside, he moved cautiously on his hands and knees, careful not to make a sound or put his weight on the wrong spot and fall through the thatched roof.

Once he was in a good spot, he lay down on his front, spreading his weight. The workshop was taller than most buildings, and he had an unobstructed view to the town square. Two fires, set at opposite ends, shed some light. A few figures huddled around them. Again, a rudimentary attempt, he supposed, to keep the town secure. With more defenders on the walls and at the main gates, he supposed the enemy had no reason to do more.

The square was large and open. Peyre tried to envisage what would happen next. If Ida and Brictwin were successful, he imagined the square filling with Turned warriors quickly, pouring from the houses where they sheltered. It could easily hold hundreds. It would be busy with bodies, but how well organised would the enemy be? He sighed. An archer up here would have been useful. Even if they had taken one of Liesel's crossbows.

Worry over what you can control, he told himself. But he couldn't stop a nagging voice at the back of his mind. *What are you doing here, Peyre? Control? You have no control over this situation.*

He saw the smoke first. Faint at first, he had to squint to assure himself he wasn't seeing things. But the sky over the southeast of the town was a definite grey colour. He returned to the opening in the roof to warn Gosse, Umbert, and Inge to ready themselves. When he returned to his position, the sky in that area had an orange pallor. It didn't surprise him. The weather had been warm and dry, while if the thatched roof he perched on was anything to go by, Radstock would burn quickly.

Like something from a nightmare, Peyre heard doors swing open, the tramp of feet, but not a single voice. The Turned appeared in the streets. Some went to the fire. Others filtered into the square. All without a single order being given out loud. How, Peyre had no idea. But that wasn't his concern now. He had to focus on their objective.

In the square, the Turned settled into ranks. But while they faced a dark-haired woman as if she commanded them, he still couldn't see Belwynn, Elfled, or Morlin. *Oh, you fool, Peyre. I forgot.* Syele had warned him. The Belwynn from the stories was long gone. When the Magnian had visited his sister at Valennes, she had the body of a Jalakh woman. That was who he was looking at. It must be.

He slithered to the hole in the roof, trying to regain lost time. He half-climbed, half-fell down the rope, landing on his arse on the carpenter's table.

'She's there, in the square,' he said, scrambling off and onto his feet. 'Remember, all means necessary. Belwynn cannot be killed, so we don't go easy. If capturing her doesn't look possible, then we just take the dagger.'

'Ida and Brictwin?' Inhan asked.

'I don't know where they are. And we have different missions. That was Ida's decision. It's the four of us now. Focus on our task and nothing else.'

Inhan nodded his understanding. Umbert and Gosse hadn't needed telling. Peyre led them out of the workshop, into the street.

THEY RAN DOWN THE STREET, three of them brandishing their weapons —Gosse hands free to keep up. They didn't stop to see whether the Turned they passed recognised them as enemies or not.

Now that it was time to act, a mad delight overcame Peyre. His pent-up tension was released as he sprinted into the square and he had to stop himself from crying out. It was a natural enough thing to do before a battle. But here, where hundreds of Turned gathered, it was still deathly quiet.

He ran for Belwynn, knowing exactly where she was. As he closed on her, she turned his way and he allowed himself a grin. Jalakh features stared at him.

But it was too soon for celebration. Turned warriors closed on him, blocking his route to their new leader. They forced him to stop and defend himself. Blows came from several dead eyed warriors at once, and it was only because Umbert joined him that one didn't connect.

They blocked and parried, surviving the initial onslaught. Inhan joined them. The young warrior caught a spear thrust in his metal hand. With a strong-wristed twist, he ripped the weapon from its owner's grip, allowing Peyre and Umbert to go on the attack.

97

Then Gosse was there, barging his way through the melee. He knocked two Turned to the ground, grunting as he took a heavy blow from a club, then he was free of the scrum.

Peyre pushed the clubman aside and followed his friend. He could see Belwynn's face. She frowned at Gosse's approach, her eyes more alive than the other Turned. She made no attempt to run or defend herself. Toric's Dagger, if she had it, stayed in its sheath.

Gosse didn't hold back. His fist connected with the side of her head and Peyre was sure he heard the snap of a neck. Belwynn fell to the ground.

The big man bent over to scoop her up. Her boot smashed into his face, knocking him over.

She was lithe, quick to get back to her feet. The thin blade of a dagger appeared in her hand.

Peyre grabbed at Gosse, pulling him backwards just in time. Belwynn slashed into the space where the big man's neck had been.

The Turned were on them now, hands grabbing for them, ready to drag them to the ground. Gosse pushed them away, striking out with his fists. Peyre gained the space to swing his blade. Inhan entered the fray. But there were too many, and Peyre couldn't even see Belwynn now.

'This way!' Umbert shouted, gesturing to a street in the northwest corner of the square. Peyre hoped his friend knew what he was doing —that he had checked the route from the roof of the workshop. But he had no choice, as Gosse and Inhan ran for the escape route. Peyre dodged a spear thrust and sliced his blade low, hamstringing his closest opponent. Then he followed his friends, bringing up the rear.

He could see down the street Umbert had selected. It was empty, led back to the west wall, and surely connected to the side gate they had entered through. They were going to make it. The Turned, meanwhile, had been slow to react. He turned around to give the square a final look.

Then he saw them. Elfled and Morlin, the bodyguard by the side of his queen, as he had always been. They were opposite Peyre, in the south-east corner of the square, silhouetted by the orange flames of a fire that had grown out of control. And there, coming from the fire they had started, were Ida and Brictwin. Heading straight for Ezenachi's new champions.

Peyre glanced from that encounter to his friends, disappearing down the street, and back again.

'Shit.'

PEYRE

KINGDOM OF MAGNIA

S hit.'

Peyre gave his friends a last look as they disappeared from view. He wished he could leave with them. But he had seen King Ida and his bodyguard heading for Elfled and Morlin. Two champions supported by a square full of the Turned. *I can't turn my back and run.*

Decision made, Peyre advanced on the confrontation. He ran, avoiding the Turned who moved to intercept him. Even so, he wasn't fast enough to intervene in the scene that played out ahead. He could hear Ida shouting at his mother. His commands went unheeded. They became desperate sounding pleas.

Then Elfled was on him, all nails and sharp teeth. Inevitably, Brictwin intervened, then Morlin. Peyre had nightmares like this, where something terrible plays out before you and you're too slow to stop it.

At last, he reached them. Brictwin was on the ground. Morlin stood over him, raising the Shield of Persala with both hands. Peyre swung his sword, and it clattered into the back of Morlin's head, clanging against his helmet, and sending him staggering away.

Elfled hissed at him. Then she disappeared.

Oh gods. The Cloak of the Asrai.

He knew the stories about how the cloak made its wearer invisible. But he hadn't been prepared for it. He wafted his sword in the air and backed away from where he thought she might be. Then a chill ran down his spine. He turned around, thrusting his sword out. Into empty space.

'Ida,' he said, not hiding the fear in his voice. 'Some help?'

His words seemed to cut through the king's stupor, who grabbed Brictwin and got him to his feet. Then Morlin was on them. Ida swung his blade and Morlin met it with his shield. There was a pulse of energy and the king went flying backwards through the air.

Screw this, Peyre said to himself. *If she gets me, she gets me.*

He moved for Morlin, who was circling with Brictwin. The king's bodyguard refrained from using his sword, a commendable tactic. As Peyre approached, Morlin readied his shield, expecting another sword blow. But Peyre dived below the shield. As he struck, he wrapped both arms around Morlin's legs. It was enough to knock the bodyguard to the ground. Then there was a desperate struggle, as Peyre grabbed the shield and tried to pull it from Morlin's grasp.

Peyre yanked, getting desperate, fearful that at any moment he would feel teeth at his exposed neck. Either that, or the Turned would get there and overpower him. Getting nowhere, he tried another tactic. He launched himself onto Morlin, driving down with all his weight. As Morlin tried to push him off, he butted down, cracking into Morlin's face with his forehead. Not giving him a moment to recover, he pulled at the shield with all his strength, until it came free from Morlin's grasp. Just as Morlin lurched upwards to retrieve it, Peyre rammed the shield downward. It cracked onto the top of his head.

Peyre just had the time to wonder whether the blow had killed him, when a scream made him turn. Brictwin had both hands clenched to one side of his head. It was such a strange position that Peyre couldn't process what he was seeing. Then, he saw the gash in Brictwin's neck and realisation hit him.

Elfled, still invisible, had him. He rushed over, reaching them as

Brictwin slid to the ground. He lunged, shield out, and felt the connection. He heard Elfled's body go flying and land somewhere.

He got to his knees to see to Brictwin. But it was too late, blood pumping from the open wound.

'Look out!'

Ida's voice. Looking up, Peyre saw the Turned had reached him. They converged on him, weapons drawn. He got to his feet as the first blows came. He used the shield to defend himself and his opponents went flying away. He spun around to face a new threat, but it was Ida. The king looked down at Brictwin, face aghast.

'My mother?' he got out.

'I don't know. I flung her away. Invisible, and probably still alive.'

'Morlin?'

Peyre pointed to the prone body. It wasn't moving. Perhaps the Magnian was only unconscious. But the power he felt from the Shield of Persala made Peyre think otherwise.

More Turned came at them. And somewhere out there was Elfled.

'Come on,' Peyre said. 'We need to go.'

Ida didn't argue. He defended Peyre's back, while Peyre barrelled his way through the crowd of Turned, towards Umbert's exit. Any Turned who took a swing were sent flying by the Persaleian Shield. The closest thing it felt like was reaping wheat at harvest time. *I could get used to this.*

Peyre cleared them a path to the street Umbert had taken. They got to the far end, took a right, and left via Brictwin's gate. They kept going. Any time Ida tried to stop, or even turn around, Peyre silently dragged him on.

They ran into the night. Even when Radstock was so far behind them, they could barely see the smoke in the sky, Peyre kept going. He could feel a chill down his spine, and imagined sharp teeth at his neck.

* * *

WHEN THEY REACHED A DESERTED FARMHOUSE, it was too tempting to ignore. Exhausted, they stumbled inside. Peyre was too tired to worry about food, but he found them a blanket each. They sat at the kitchen table, signs of a hasty departure around them, with unwanted items scattered on the floor. Peyre doubted the woman of the house would have left her home so untidy. More likely, other Magnians had passed through on their way north, searching for food or items of value.

'A few hours' sleep and we'll have the energy to get back to Morbaine,' he suggested.

'Did the others get out alright?' Ida asked him.

'Yes.'

'They'll wait for us at the meeting point?'

In their initial, desperate flight, Peyre and Ida had gone off track—far from the meeting place they had agreed on. Peyre didn't know where they were, and Ida seemed to know no better. 'Aye. They'll wait.'

'How long for, do you think?'

'We agreed until first light.'

'I know that's what we agreed,' Ida said. His face was serious. 'But your men are extremely loyal. You think they won't wait for you, or even go looking?'

'I suppose they *are* loyal. They are more than my retainers. They are friends. But they also know how angry I would be if they did something so stupid.'

Ida nodded, though Peyre could tell he wasn't convinced. Peyre hoped the king was wrong. He had been clear about the dangers of their mission. It was always likely they wouldn't all escape. Their duty was to return north.

A melancholy look had come over Ida. He had inherited the good looks of his parents, and his sadness moved Peyre. He reminded him of Sanc. There was a vulnerability there, even though he was a king. Their eyes met.

'You are thinking of Brictwin?' Peyre asked him.

'I have been a fool. All my talk of the Asrai prophecy. Reassuring myself that I was invincible. Not caring enough about those around me.'

'Don't punish yourself,' Peyre advised him. 'We had good reasons for going in. Brictwin understood that. He wouldn't like to think you blamed yourself.'

Ida shook his head. 'It wasn't fair to risk his life in the hope we would rescue my mother.'

'That was a trade he would have been happy with, I am sure,' Peyre said. 'And we came close to getting her. As it is, we achieved something.' He knocked his knuckles on the shield that lay on the tabletop and it gave an answering metallic ring. The shield was in a leather sleeve. The design was faded, but Peyre could still see the face of a bearded man, with two horns protruding from his forehead. He placed his left arm into the grip. He felt an attachment to the great weapon. A desire to hold it, or at least keep it by his side at all times.

He gave a quick glance towards Ida, suddenly wary that the King of Magnia would claim the weapon for himself. After all, they were still in Magnia. But he didn't detect such a desire in his companion, only a look of mild interest. Peyre suddenly felt a pang of guilt at where his thoughts had taken him. He was dealing with a weapon of magic, made by the goddess Madria. *I need to be careful of it,* he told himself, withdrawing his arm and laying it back down.

'The stories I was told say the Magnian warrior, Clarin, wielded the Shield in battle against the Isharites,' Peyre said. 'Maybe a Magnian should wield it again?'

He surprised himself with the offer. Perhaps a part of him wanted rid of the responsibility.

Ida smiled at him. 'A most gracious offer, Your Grace. There is a part of me that feels I should accept, since Brictwin gave his life for us to take the weapon from Ezenachi's control. But I think it suits you more. A shield is for defence and you are a defender of others, Peyre. Not just your own duchy. You have come to my people's defence more than once. You have looked after the refugees of the Steppe. You are the defender of Dalriya.'

* * *

PEYRE FORCED himself to rise early. He'd slept a little, at least. Now he was hungry, and he took some time to explore the farmstead. There were no quick meals to be had. In one barn, he found a few bags of grain. He took some. If they found nothing else all day, it could at least be used to make a pottage for supper.

He returned to the farmhouse to find Ida up and ready to leave.

'Any more idea where we are in the light of day?' Peyre asked him.

'None. All we can do is head north and hope to get our bearings.'

They walked, keen to use the daylight to travel as far as they could. Ida had a good walking pace that matched Peyre's. The terrain was gentle enough, though settlements were few and far between. By mid-morning they had spied a hamlet and they detoured towards it, both tired of hearing how hungry the other was.

The houses were gathered by a brook, and a rough path that ran northeast crossed the water over a timber bridge. A search of the houses was disappointing: they had been cleared—again, probably by a combination of their owners and then other refugees heading north.

'We should try the stream,' Ida suggested, leading Peyre down to the bank by the bridge.

Peyre's spirits rose. 'That was a good idea,' he complimented the king. Several traps lay in the water and, with the settlement deserted for days, surely there would be something in them.

They waded into the brook and were rewarded with a catch of half a dozen fish.

'I say we eat one each now,' Ida suggested.

'Raw?'

'Aye. I could eat it raw. But we can make a fire if you wish.'

'No. Raw is fine.'

'Good. Just don't share the story with my subjects. Kings are not supposed to eat raw fish with their hands.'

'Your secret is safe with me. Meanwhile, I suppose we should follow this path. It will surely lead us somewhere.'

'Agreed.'

With some food in their bellies and a path to walk on, their spirits rose. They carried on into the afternoon, barely stopping for a rest.

Peyre didn't want to give the impression he was tired to the King of Magnia, and he fancied Ida was just the same.

A background noise slowly, almost imperceptibly, registered.

Peyre stopped, cocking his head.

'I hear it too,' Ida said. 'What do you think it is?'

'I'm not sure. But realistically, how many things can it be?'

'The Turned,' Ida said, his voice as forlorn as Peyre felt.

Peyre looked about. There was a hillock to the northwest that would afford them a decent view. He pointed it out. 'Let's get up there and look.'

They made for the location, moving with even more purpose than they had been. Peyre's mind spun, envisaging one threat after another. But there was nothing he could do until he got his chance to lookout. They climbed the hillock, steeper than it had looked at a distance. Peyre resisted the urge to look behind him. He needed to hurry and avoid being seen.

A squadron of ash trees provided them with cover at the top of the rise. Both breathless, they looked out. They pointed simultaneously. Out to the east, in the direction they had been heading, an army marched. It stretched as far north and south as Peyre could see. There were thousands marching on foot, and a few units of cavalry, too.

'The Turned from the Steppe,' Ida muttered.

'Aye. They're so damn quiet, we nearly walked into them. But that's not all,' Peyre said, pointing to the south.

'Damn,' Ida said.

More Turned were coming in their direction. 'It must be the Turned of Radstock,' Peyre muttered.

'You think they're coming after us?' Ida asked.

'Who knows? They're obviously coordinating with the Turned of the Steppe, so maybe it was planned long before we turned up.'

'You were right about the invasion of Morbaine, then. Thank Toric we sent our people north.' Ida sighed, staring south. 'My mother is amongst them,' he said, his voice monosyllabic.

Peyre didn't like it when he got fixated on his mother. 'Aye. And that Giant could be amongst those from the Steppe. Or Jesper, with the Jalakh Bow trained on us.' He gestured to the other side of the hillock. 'I suggest we get moving.'

He turned to go, when he heard a noise that made his blood run cold. Screams. But unlike anything he had heard before. 'What the—'

'The vossi,' Ida said. 'Only they make such a noise.' He gestured, and Peyre could just distinguish the smaller forms of the creatures, moving ahead of the humans who had come from Radstock.

'But the Turned don't make a noise,' Peyre said, feeling bewildered.

'Seems like the vossi ones do. Who knows why? They have ever been more animal than human, anyway.'

'Why are they screaming now? Do you think they are hunting us?'

'That's an unpleasant thought,' Ida said. 'They are fearsome trackers. And they never give up on their prey.'

'Then come, Ida. We need to get moving.'

THEY DESCENDED THE HILLOCK, trying to find that delicate balance between moving fast and not losing one's balance. A sprained ankle would be the end of them.

All the time, the screams of the vossi continued. That Peyre had never seen one up close only made them more terrifying. His imagination ran riot, showing him foul creatures lumbering up the other side of the hill.

As the ground flattened, they ran faster. Peyre looked about, desperate for some landmark to guide him. There was nothing. Worse, they were heading towards woodland. 'Not sure we should go in there,' he said.

'Aye. They'll be faster in there than us,' Ida agreed, already sounding breathless. 'But where else can we go?'

The irony wasn't lost on Peyre. They were somewhere in the borders between Magnia and Morbaine. They were the rulers of each realm. And yet, they didn't have a clue where they were. Peyre wished he had taken a couple of local guides with them. In hindsight, it was a grave mistake. But there was no benefit in dwelling on that.

He tried to think as they continued to run for the trees. They were being chased from the south. More Turned were coming from the east. Veering to the west therefore made sense.

Screams of triumph interrupted his thoughts. Peyre couldn't help it. He stopped and turned around to look. A dozen of the vossi had already crested the top of the hillock. They'd been seen. He studied them. Small and wiry, they wore and carried little. Meanwhile, he was lugging a sword and shield with him, and wearing chain mail. He didn't stand a chance in a foot race.

'Come on,' Ida called.

Peyre resumed his flight, but a sense of doom hung over him, sapping his energy. Anger crept upon him. Anger that having taken the risk and won the Shield of Persala, he would fall here, in the middle of nowhere. His body would lie in the dirt and no one would know his fate. The anger fed him, giving him renewed energy. He would resist that outcome with all his might.

He tried to regain his thoughts. If they got far enough heading northwest, they would reach the coast. Maybe there, they could find a seaworthy vessel and escape by sea. He ignored the critical part of his mind, telling him such a plan didn't deserve the name. It was all he had.

He steered Ida in the direction he wanted. As they reached the first trees, he could hear whistling noises from behind him. Something clattered into his back.

'Throwing darts,' Ida warned him. 'At least the trees will give us some cover.'

They continued into the relative safety of the woodland. But the darts kept coming for them. Then Peyre felt a sharp pain in the back of his leg. He reached down and removed the dart. It was a primitive, wooden design. But that didn't stop the thing from hurting like hell— and, he supposed, explained why the vossi had so many to throw. There was also the question of poison. He tried not to think about that.

The vossi were gaining on them. That was the unavoidable truth. Soon, Peyre knew, they would have to turn and fight. When that happened, they would be outnumbered and killed.

'This way!' Ida shouted, veering to the left. 'A river!'

Hope gave Peyre a fresh burst of energy. If it really was a river and not just a stream, it was the Peronne, which headed west to the sea. Maybe it would save them.

'Can they swim?' he shouted.

'There are no rivers to speak of in the Wilderness,' Ida shouted back to Peyre. 'So I doubt it.'

Then Peyre saw the river bank ahead of them. He saw the grey water, deep and wide. It was the Peronne. He tried to keep up with the Magnian king, but he was struggling now. He set his eyes on the water and ran.

The darts were coming with greater frequency, and several struck him. Peyre had no choice but to turn and put the Shield of Persala in front of him. When the next dart came, he pushed at it with the shield. Incredibly, the dart changed direction, flying back to the vossi who had thrown it. *I should have used it earlier,* Peyre reprimanded himself.

A few more examples of this, and the vossi stopped throwing their missiles. All the while, Peyre was backing away towards the river. But he wasn't close enough.

More and more of the creatures arrived, some of them moving to the side to cut him off from the water. He could see them up close now. Their skin was brown and rough, like tree bark. Their eyes were small and black, with the ferocity of wild animals.

Peyre tried to speed up, but he felt clumsy. Seeing it, the closest vossi moved in for the kill. Spears, clubs, and knives threatened him. He used the shield to defend himself, not trusting his sword arm. When the shield connected properly, it sent the vossi flying backwards. But a spear strike got past the shield and struck him on the chest. Peyre staggered backwards, only just maintaining his feet.

Ida swept past him. The king laid into the vossi, his sword swirling about him. Peyre knew this was his one chance. He turned and ran for the river. He felt like he was running through a bog. He was hot and pouring with sweat. He was loath to drop a weapon, but in the end knew he had no choice. He discarded his sword and grasped the shield in both hands, forcing his body to move—demanding it not betray him.

He heard someone calling his name. But it sounded more like his friend Umbert than Ida. He lifted his head and was so taken aback by the sight that greeted him, he wondered if it was real. A raft in the centre of the river carried Umbert and Inhan. Meanwhile, a great beast of a man was swimming towards him. Gosse.

Relief flooded Peyre, and he charged into the river. The cold water shocked his body, but he kept going until it got so deep he had to swim. He struggled now, holding the shield flat while he desperately pulled water with his other arm. His mail wanted to drown him, pulling him down to the riverbed. He was surprised how quickly his energy gave out.

Gosse reached him, tugging him along. Peyre's head went under and he swallowed water. He surfaced again, choking. The world was upside down, and he couldn't tell where the sky was. But Gosse still tugged him and Peyre held tight onto the shield, like a dog with a bone. Then, hands were on him, and he was pulled up and laid down on his back onto the raft. He spluttered, like a fish out of water. 'Ida?' he got out.

'He's coming,' Umbert assured him. 'Not far behind you. And he's a better swimmer than you.'

Peyre tried to laugh at that, but he could hardly move his lips. They were rigid and unyielding. Only then did Peyre realise what was happening. He tried to warn Umbert, but all he got out was a throaty growl.

'What was that?' Umbert said, putting an ear to Peyre's mouth.

Peyre concentrated. 'Poison,' he got out. 'Darts. Poison.'

'He said he's been poisoned!' Umbert said, sounding panicky.

But Peyre felt his body retreating from the world. The heat inside him and the cold on his skin retreated. He could see Umbert's lips moving, but could no longer hear him. Then the last of his senses left him.

SANC

KINGDOM OF SCORGIA

Ship by ship, Prince Lenzo had built an armada in the port city of Arvena. One grumbling merchant after another had relented to his demands and allowed their vessels to be used for war instead of trade. They listened to his promises of victory with polite faces and sceptical eyes.

The Scorgian army was transported across the narrow stretch of sea separating Arvena from the mainland. Sanc, Rab, and Lenzo had places in the last ship. Upon reaching shore, Sanc waited on the dock while Dag received his final instructions.

'The fleet is strong enough for our purposes,' Lenzo told him. 'There's no point waiting forever for perfection. When you're provisioned, set sail.'

'Aye, Your Highness.'

'And don't let any of those high and mighty men of business tell you what to do. Especially that Nolf Money Bags. You're following *my* orders, alright? And I'll reward you far more when this war ends than any bribes he might throw your way.'

'I don't do this for money, Your Highness,' Dag said simply.

Lenzo gave him a rather surprised look before patting the man on the shoulder. 'Of course. Our people will soon be liberated.'

'Besides,' Dag added. 'Amelia the Widow pays me a stipend much higher than anything you or Nolf would cough up.'

Lenzo's lips pursed. 'Just get going, Dag. And if you lose my fleet, I'll have your head on a pole.'

'Aye, Your Highness,' said Dag, a grin on his face. 'All the best!'

'Come, Sanc,' Lenzo said. 'On to the main event.'

A short distance inland, Gaida was readying the Scorgian troops. All told, the army stood at around three thousand souls. A core of these were trained soldiers, those men they had collected from the Breath Forts two years ago. The rest were a mix of volunteers and conscripts, of questionable use should it come to a battle.

Lenzo noticed Sanc's appraising gaze. 'The hope is we pick up more volunteers as we march south.'

Sanc raised an eyebrow at that.

'Alright. The hope is there isn't much left of Lothar's army to stop us.'

'We'll be fine,' Sanc reassured him. 'He has a huge army in the land of the Egers. He'll have left a large force in the north to keep the Kassites held down. He can't have left many here.'

THEY MARCHED FOR THE CAPITAL. It wasn't the same route they had taken two years ago, when Sanc had first arrived in Silb. But still, his mind returned to that episode.

He had known nothing of the world Rimmon had sent him to. He had met Lenzo and Gaida by chance. Before he knew it, he and Rab were in a boat with them, sailing across a great lake. Then, to the border with Nerisia, where Lenzo had persuaded Wacho to leave the forts. On to the north coast, and the safety of Arvena.

Not for the first time, he wondered what would have happened if he had met Lothar first. Would he have been convinced that the King of the Nerisians was in the right? Would he have applauded as he was crowned emperor? Would he have even cared, so long as he got the help he needed for Dalriya? He'd never know. What he did know was that he had become invested in the people he had met. He needed

Lenzo and Mildrith to—to what? If not to win this war outright, he needed to know they would survive and prosper.

They were soon out of the marshland and out in the open. Each settlement they came to had to be properly scouted. Only the larger towns had Nerisian garrisons, and these retreated rather than try to hold out against Lenzo's force.

The people they spoke with shared what little news they had. There were always a few, in every settlement—however small—who joined the prince's army. Sanc found there was no single reason. Lenzo promised victory, of course. Some had scores to settle with the Nerisian invaders, or simply wanted the foreigners gone. Some wanted to escape their lives, if only for a short while. Others hoped for some advantage in loot or the like.

The truth was, many men needed little convincing to join in a fight. *It's in our blood,* Sanc decided. *Whether in Silb or Dalriya, men fight and kill as if it's the most natural thing in the world.*

The days passed. This part of Scorgia was flat and dry, with decent roads, and they made good time. As the Nerisians retreated before them, the campaign headed towards an inevitable conclusion. There would be no battle out in the open. The Nerisians would shut themselves behind the walls of Irpino and aim to hold out against Lenzo until Lothar sent relief.

'Irpino,' Lenzo declared as the walls of the capital came into view. 'What do you think, Sanc?'

'Very impressive,' Sanc said. Thick stone walls encircled the city, easily as formidable as those of Valennes back home. He could see why the Nerisians had decided it was wisest to shelter here. 'It's strange. I arrived in Silb only a few miles north of here. And yet I've seen almost all the continent before this city.'

Lenzo looked at him, his green eyes as perceptive as ever. 'Your journey has come full circle.' He stared across the flat fields that surrounded Irpino. 'I see no sign of the Duke of Sinto.'

'He'll come,' Sanc assured him.

This was perhaps the one part of the plan Sanc was most worried about. He believed Atto would come—that wasn't the issue. He hadn't got to know the duke very well, but he'd learned enough to realise the two men were not cut from the same cloth. Lenzo made much of his appearance and liked to talk. Atto was blunt and straightforward. They were unlikely to become fast friends. But all Sanc needed was for them to unite against their enemy and not turn on one another.

The Scorgians established a rough camp, far enough from the city walls to get warning of an attack from the Nerisians. The weather behaved, but it was a nervous night and no one got much sleep. Irpino had to be watched. Further, they couldn't be sure there wasn't a Nerisian army loose in the countryside.

Sanc was more confident about that than most. But he had other worries. Temyl and Guntram were still in the Eger lands. He didn't think Lothar would send them away after Sanc had come so close to killing him. But if they did come, Sanc would be outnumbered two to one. He could sense their approach, so long as he stayed awake. Despite the slight chance, he resisted the temptation of sleep. *I'm not risking my plans now, when we're so close*, he told himself.

With nothing better to do, Sanc closed his eyes and searched with his magic. It was a power he had first learned in Magnia when Rimmon had asked for his help to free Herin. It worked best at night, while people slept. This second sight allowed him to rise into the sky, from where he looked down on their camp. Each person's mind was visible as a light in the darkness, brighter when people slept.

He rose higher and moved his vision until he could see into Irpino. Here there were thousands of lights, many times more than in their own camp. Of course, that told him little about the fighting strength of the enemy. Most of these people were citizens of Irpino, and Scorgians at that. He couldn't be certain where their loyalties would lie in the battle to come.

Sanc expanded his vision further. It was an impulse—suddenly, he wanted to find out how far he could see. Never mind he should preserve his energy for tomorrow. The region around the city came into view as he was given a bird's eye view. He rose so high that individual lights were lost to him. Now, he could only see where people gathered—towns and villages that held enough souls to shine.

He didn't stop. A map of Scorgia was revealed to him, with only the largest settlements still visible. Then, the map expanded westward, taking in Nerisia, Gadenzia, and the land of the Egers. Sanc didn't want to stop there. He channelled his magic into the vision, until the lands of the Telds, Rasidi, and Kassites were added—the whole of Silb. At this scale, only the greatest cities were visible—Irpino, Arvena, Mournai, Aguilas, and a half dozen others.

Lights, with a brighter intensity, drew his attention. Two were in the lands of the Egers. Another four were in the north—two in the lands of the Kassites, one amongst the mountains of the Telds, the last close by in the kingdom of the Rasidi. The six champions of Silb.

He stopped the spell, and the vision disappeared. He was gasping for breath. He scanned the surrounding space, but no one had noticed —except Rab, whose tail gave a few lazy wags before he went back to sleep.

* * *

WHEN DAWN CAME, the Scorgians rose bleary eyed, and a degree of vigour came to the camp. The Scorgians lacked the discipline Sanc had witnessed in the armies led by his father and Lord Russell. But they were good enough for what he needed.

Lenzo called him for a meeting over breakfast. 'What's the plan? Do I ready the soldiers yet? What about Atto?'

'He's coming.'

'How do you know?'

'I've seen him.'

Lenzo studied Sanc. A question seemed to form on the prince's lips, but he then thought better of it. 'Very well.'

'With your leave, I'll meet them. Bring them here.'

'*With my leave,*' Lenzo repeated sarcastically. 'As if *you* are the one taking orders from *me*. Fine. Fetch the warriors of Sinto. The sooner they get here, the sooner we start. I hate all this waiting. It interferes with my digestion.'

. . .

SANC BROUGHT Duke Atto and his force of a thousand warriors to Lenzo's camp. The duke dismounted and told his followers to wait, trusting Sanc to lead him over. Lenzo approached them, only Gaida at his side.

'Duke Atto,' Lenzo said as they closed on one another. 'I knew you would come. It is past time we worked together. Gaida,' he said, turning to his lieutenant.

Gaida produced an object. It was a drinking horn. He passed it to Lenzo, who presented it to Atto. 'From the Temple of Salacus in Arvena. It is said to be the drinking cup of Salacus.'

Atto thanked Lenzo and took the horn. He cast a sideways glance at Sanc. No doubt, Sanc thought, the duke was also recalling their visit to the Temple of Peramo. Atto had objected to Sanc's attempt to inspect the tomb of Salacus, though Sanc was sure the duke knew as well as him what they would have found. An ordinary set of bones, just like the other tombs Sanc had inspected.

'A most gracious gift, Your Highness,' Atto said. 'I shall display it with pride in the Temple of Sinto. As you say, it is high time we fought together. Time to drive the enemy from our homeland. Time also, I believe, for you to take your true title.' To everyone's surprise, Atto got to his knees. 'You are the rightful king of Scorgia, Lenzo. It is time that I and everyone else address you as Your Majesty. We must take Irpino and have you crowned in our capital to remove Lothar's taint from our realm.'

Sanc found Lenzo's feline smile amusing.

'Please, sir,' Lenzo said, holding out his hands, 'on your feet.' He helped Atto to stand. 'If that is your will and the will of our people, then indeed I will finally claim my father's title. First things first, though. We must reclaim our capital. Sanc, I feel we are reliant on you to explain how we might accomplish such a feat, given our limited resources.'

Sanc couldn't have been more satisfied with the way the meeting had gone. He turned to gaze across at the walls of Irpino. 'Have your soldiers arranged in their ranks facing the gatehouse. I will do the rest.'

. . .

SANC LIFTED himself into the air, above the level of the city walls, and advanced towards his target. He heard the shouted warnings coming from Irpino's battlements. The first arrows fizzed towards him. The closer he got, the more missiles came, and the more he had to deflect them with his magic. *Just like Rimmon taught me,* he thought, surprising himself with a nostalgic pang for his lessons in the forest of Morbaine.

As he passed over the outer wall, it occurred to him just how much he was thwarting the city's defences. They were built to stop attackers from breaking through or climbing up. Apart from the arrows, most of which sailed well wide, the Nerisian garrison simply had nothing to stop his progress.

He lowered himself into the open space behind the gatehouse. Rocks, arrows, and other missiles came thick now, and it was time to fully shield himself with a protective orb of magic. It cost him far more in energy, but he would not risk a missile escaping his attention and taking him out.

When he felt his feet settle on secure ground, he gathered his magic. Before him were the stone walls, metal portcullis, traps, murder holes, and other defences of the gatehouse. He let loose his magic, giving it a golden streak, as if it were a beam of sunshine. The stone fell apart. The portcullis buckled and fell to the ground as rubble dropped around it.

Once the dust had settled, a gaping hole had appeared. It ran through the gatehouse, wide enough for half a dozen men to march side by side. The stone roof was still intact, though it looked a little precarious.

Sanc left through the mess he had made, pleased with his work. He had deployed relatively little magic. The Scorgians had a route into the city. The Nerisians might still resist, in which case, Sanc would have to use more of his energy. But he didn't expect the enemy to hold out for long.

SANC

IRPINO, KINGDOM OF SCORGIA

The Nerisian garrison in Irpino surrendered shortly after Sanc's attack. They couldn't prevent Lenzo and Atto's forces from entering the city. They couldn't stop Sanc. In the end, they had to be protected from the citizens of the capital, who were quick to turn on their conquerors.

The prince soon had the city in the palm of his hand, delivering a speech that struck the right tone of nationalism and humility. He referenced Sanc, briefly and vaguely, as the champion of Scorgia. But most people didn't care too much about exactly who Sanc was. There was a new regime in charge and it had the support of the people. No doubt it wouldn't be long before Lenzo was crowned king.

Afterwards, Sanc met with Lenzo and Atto. 'It is time for me to leave,' he told them. 'There is still much that needs to be done.'

'Leaving us to it, eh?' Lenzo said with a rueful smile. 'We're defenceless without you.'

'The Eger army is still in the field,' Sanc told him. 'Your fleet is sailing up the Dogne towards Mournai. I expect Mildrith will have risen the Kassites by now. Lothar won't know where to turn first. There's a chance he'll come here, but only a small one.'

'I know,' Lenzo agreed. 'Besides, we're ready to take his ire and defend this place if we have to. Right, Atto?'

'Aye. Soon as we fix that gatehouse.'

Sanc smiled. 'Sorry about that.'

'Look after yourself, Sanc,' Lenzo said.

Sanc was surprised to see emotion on the prince's face—equally surprised when he got a lump in his own throat. He gave the man a farewell hug. Sanc couldn't quite put a finger on what their relationship was. Father figure? Older brother? Close uncle, perhaps. But despite Lenzo's sharp tongue, a genuine bond of affection had grown between them.

Sanc nodded a farewell to Atto. 'Come on, Rab,' he said, turning away. 'We've still got work to do.'

Teleporting all the way to the lands of the Kassites would be a big drain on his magic. But he was helped by his vision from the other night. Knowing precisely where Mildrith and the Eger Khan were, allowed him to pick a suitable destination.

He took Rab in his arms and began. As always happened, his senses blurred and left him, and time was hard to measure. He was deposited at his destination feeling groggy and ill. He put Rab down and bent over, taking a few moments to gather himself.

When he was recovered, he used his magic once more, bringing up his mental map of the surrounding terrain. It wasn't as effective at night, or when people were awake. But the distinctive lights of Mildrith and the Eger Khan were easy to find, only a short walk away. With them were about a thousand other individuals—no doubt the Kassite rebels she had persuaded to join her.

Sanc and Rab walked east, through the edge of the White Forest, where the trees became sparser and gave way to an uneven terrain of rock and grassland.

'I know you,' said a voice. A Kassite warrior—long-haired, with a bow in her hands, sidled out from behind a tree. 'You fought with us against the Nerisians.'

'Yes,' Sanc said. It was good, he supposed, to see the Kassite force had scouts operating in the vicinity of their camp. 'I've come to fight again. Do you know where Mildrith is?'

'I'll take you,' the Kassite agreed.

The Kassites had never been the most organised fighters, but the force Sanc found was an especially crude affair. No horses or transport, just a few hundred warriors who had brought whatever weapons and armour they had. In most cases, very little.

I shouldn't be surprised, he told himself. *They've been occupied by the Nerisians ever since I left.* The only resistance they could offer were quick raids, carried out from the safety of the White Forest. Still, it made him wonder what they could achieve against the Nerisian occupiers with so little.

Rab sprinted off, and Sanc knew what that meant.

Mildrith strode towards him and he felt a stupid smile form on his face. She looked even more beautiful than he remembered. But as they stood before one another, he knew she wouldn't appreciate such sentiments. Instead, he stood there awkwardly, unsure what to say.

'I've missed you,' she said. He breathed in her scent as she leaned in and kissed him. She laughed at his bemused expression. 'Come,' she said, leading him towards the centre of the camp. 'How has it gone in Scorgia?'

'Success. We took Irpino. And I was surprised by how well Lenzo and Atto got on.'

'Huh. I'm surprised anyone can get on with that swaggering arsehole. But that's good news. You got here sooner than I thought you would. How are your reserves?'

'I'm depleted and exhausted.'

'Then rest and let me handle things here.'

Sanc didn't argue. Mildrith brought him to the leaders of this ragged band. To one side stood the Eger Khan.

'Your Majesty,' Sanc said in greeting.

The boy nodded solemnly back.

'Sanc! Good to see you! And your little friend, too.' A Kassite warrior, a good head taller than Sanc, held out an arm in greeting.

'Holt Slender Legged!' Sanc said with a smile as he took his arm, genuinely pleased to see him. 'I was hoping you'd still be running the Nerisians ragged.'

'O' course. Last chieftain standing, though,' he said, with more sorrow than pride. 'In truth, we've been harassed and chased and squeezed near as far as you can do to a man or woman without breaking 'em. When Mildrith arrived here, with His Majesty the Khan in tow, I thought maybe Ymer is watching over us after all. And now you're here, too.'

'Indeed,' Sanc said, 'with some good news from Scorgia. But what is the plan here?' he asked, gesturing at the force they had gathered.

'A bit farther east and we can hit Listshold,' Holt said.

Sanc shared a look with Mildrith, recalling the last time they were at the settlement. Chased north from Jackdaw Hill by the Gadenzian cavalry, they had thought to find shelter there. Instead, the Gadenzians had got there before them, and had captured List. The man's screams returned to Sanc's mind. A horrible, broken noise. He wasn't grateful for the return of those memories.

Mildrith gave him a sympathetic look, as if she hadn't experienced it with him. 'If we take that place, it will send a message. To Kassite and Nerisian alike.' She waved a hand about their camp. 'With a victory, we'll get the numbers and supplies we need.'

THEY ATTACKED LATE, as oranges and purples painted the sky overhead. It was the time of day when a warrior has eaten his evening meal and is contentedly thinking about bed. The defenders were totally surprised.

They were also ill-equipped to fend off the Kassite assault. The beginnings of a stone castle had been constructed on the site of List's wooden fort, with the obvious intention of dominating this territory for good. But it wasn't ready, and offered the defenders only the barest refuge. The Kassites went in hard and quick, arrows, stones, and spears flying. Any attempt to form a shield wall was immediately broken by Mildrith, who blasted the rows of shields apart.

Sanc was content to fight with sword and shield. He fought side by side with the Eger Khan, who practised his defence and attack magic in an encounter that was about as safe as real combat could be. Sanc was ready to intervene with his own sorcery, but his sword-work was good enough.

Rab joined them. His growls certainly gave the enemy pause, especially since they had never seen such a creature before. He was also more sensible than in his younger days, avoiding putting himself in danger. When the last of the Nerisians either turned and ran, or surrendered, the attack had been a success by any measure.

Sanc met with Mildrith and Holt by the foundations of the Nerisians' stone fort. 'What will you do with this?' Sanc asked.

'List would have wanted it torn down,' Holt said. 'But I don't know. If we finish it, a strong fort here would be very useful as a base to expand from.'

'I think you're right,' Sanc agreed. 'But either way, you'll have to do that without us. Our destination must be the land of the Telds now.'

'You can't be serious?' Holt demanded, face aghast. 'Look at us. We're barely surviving. Leave us now and the Nerisians will just undo all we've achieved.'

'You can get more people behind you now,' Mildrith told him. 'Besides. The Nerisians we've faced have been weak and leaderless.'

'This is the strategy,' Sanc explained. 'Lothar has the Egers to deal with. The Scorgians are taking back their kingdom. If we can make progress to the west as well, Lothar will be in serious trouble. His last priority will be Kassite lands. All you need to do is hold on. Don't over commit. Don't take risks. Just wear them down, like you've been doing. We'll do the rest.'

'Just leave Mildrith with us,' Holt said. It was somewhere between a plea and a demand. 'You belong here anyway,' he said, turning to her. 'You're our champion and we need you.'

Sanc shook his head. 'I can't spare her.'

'Why do you get to decide? An outlander? When did that happen?'

'Because he's the one who's going to end this war,' Mildrith said. 'I trust him. So should you.'

* * *

SANC, Mildrith, and the Eger Khan sat on the ground holding hands, while Rab nestled in Mildrith's lap. Mildrith lent her power to Sanc as they teleported away from Listshold.

He couldn't know for sure, but Sanc had reason to hope Herin's mission amongst the Telds had born fruit. When he sought the best location to travel to, he could see that Kepa, the Teld champion, was in the far northwest of the kingdom. Close by, only just across the border, was the Rasidi champion, Mergildo. Was a meeting between the two sides imminent? *Either that or they're about to do battle.*

They arrived at a village high in the mountains. It was where Kepa had taken them on their escape from Aguilas. Sanc had less than fond memories of that journey, flying across the sky on nothing but a rug. He didn't feel good now, either. The magic he had used in the last few days had left him weak, and the mountain air didn't help. When he tried to get to his feet, he felt light-headed and close to fainting. He sat back down, then lay on his side, waiting for his body to recover. His breaths were ragged.

'Can I do anything?' Mildrith asked, while Rab licked his face.

'I'm not trying to be melodramatic,' Sanc said. 'But I'm struggling to move. I don't want you expending any more magic, either.'

'I'm not sure I have anything left. You said Kepa was nearby?'

'Yes. In the village, I presume.'

'Then we will look for her. Come, Your Majesty.'

Rab looked torn as Mildrith and the Eger Khan left Sanc on the ground. Sanc thought he was going to leave with them, but he lay down next to Sanc.

'Good boy,' Sanc said, and received some more licking. He tried to regulate his breathing. He knew he was exhausted, and that some rest would more than likely sort him out. He and Rab had travelled virtually the length of the continent in a few days. He remembered Rimmon's constant warnings about overusing his magic and imagined his stern face at ignoring them. *It's all been necessary, though,* he told his teacher, as if he was with him.

'What's this?'

A pair of leather boots appeared in Sanc's vision. He looked up. It was Herin.

'I know the Morbainais are soft, but this is taking things a step too far.'

Sanc was simply too tired to offer a response to Herin's ribbing.

Seeing this, the Magnian bent over and lifted Sanc to his feet. His warrior's strength kept Sanc on his feet and he half-walked, half-carried him back towards the village.

There was something about being held up by Herin that relaxed Sanc. After being responsible for the fates of two worlds for so long, he allowed himself to be led about, barely conscious of where he was taken. He was deposited in a bed, and finally, allowed to sleep.

LIESEL

ESSENBERG, DUCHY OF KELLAND

Liesel opened the door to her apartment. Sacha had been knocking. He looked serious.

'Esterel is about to speak in the main hall. You have the right to come and listen.'

'Very well.' She studied his face, trying to guess. 'Is it about Coleta?' Anger scarred his handsome features.

She raised her hands. 'Obviously not. Apologies. Did Esterel invite me?'

'No, but he didn't specifically exclude you, either. If you're coming, come.' He strode away, not looking back.

Liesel scurried after him. Sacha radiated powerful emotion—not just anger. She began to wonder—to worry—what Esterel was about to say.

When they reached the main hall, it was already full. Sacha approached the dais on which Esterel stood, alone. Liesel stopped well before it, standing amongst the throng. Esterel's eyes flickered over them both, but didn't linger on Liesel long enough for her to detect any emotion there. *He's simply no longer interested in me,* she realised.

She looked about the room for familiar faces. There were few. Coleta joined her brother. But Sacha was the only one of Esterel's friends there. Florent was still in his cell, and Miles was dead. None of Esterel's family was here. He was in a foreign land. When she thought about it, it was shocking how isolated he had become in such a short time. She looked at the dais, the same dais on which her father and brother had once stood, and knew it for the curse it was. *And it's my fault he's here.*

'Friends,' Esterel began, but the word chimed false. Usually the life and soul of any event, her husband sounded distant. 'The moment has come. Ezenachi's forces have crossed into the empire. Gotbeck has been invaded. It is time for Brasingia to stand against this menace. Agents will be sent to every corner of the empire, asking for soldiers. My army will fight to keep the enemy out. *I* will fight.' Then there was a smile, and something of the old Esterel had returned. 'And I've never lost a battle yet. So, who will stand and fight with me?'

The hall erupted in shouts of defiance and support. Liesel joined them. Because what else could she do? This was her homeland, after all. She pushed through to the dais. Close to Coleta. Beautiful Coleta. An hour ago, she had hated her. She didn't hate her any more. Now she felt she and Esterel had belonged together all along, and it was a shame she had got in the way.

'Esterel!' she called up.

Her husband looked down, a look of pain on his face. He seemed to think twice about responding. 'Liesel?' he said, relenting.

'Let me join the army. Give me the arbalests to command. The Brasingians will fight better with me there.'

She knew it was the truth. Esterel was emperor, but he was still a foreigner. The Kellish needed one of their own to fight for. Liesel was all they had.

It wasn't what Esterel had been expecting her to say, and he paused, thinking about her request. 'Very well,' he said. 'I will give the orders.'

* * *

THE ARMIES of Guivergne and Kelland marched south along the Great Road, knowing the Turned came north on the same highway. News from Gotbeck arrived regularly. The enemy had crossed both its southern and eastern borders—miles and miles of territory, impossible to defend.

Archbishop Emmett had pulled his forces back to Kaselitz, on the Cousel, not so far from the border with Kelland. The fighting there was fierce, but it had given time for refugees to escape north.

Esterel stopped when he reached Kelland's southern border. The army he controlled was thousands strong, containing most of the fighting men of Guivergne, and those of Kelland, the strongest of the seven duchies that made up the empire. Liesel's arbalests—well supplied with bolts, and trained in Valennes by Cordentine experts— added a cutting edge. But the enemy, if less skilled, was more numerous. It made sense to wait for reinforcements.

The first to arrive was Domard. He brought with him the fighting men of his own duchy of Martras in Guivergne, and the duchy of Barissia. Arriving from Coldeberg, this force was the second largest in the empire.

Sacha had informed Liesel she should attend the war council, and so she was present in the royal tent when Domard gave his report. Grateful that Esterel had allowed her there, she resolved to pay him back by keeping quiet. She was one of a select few. Liesel felt the absence of key figures, like Peyre, or Farred, or even Saliers, who would have contributed to the discussion. Miles had been the royal marshal, and Esterel was yet to replace him. Domard, too, appeared to look about the tent, as if expecting more arrivals.

'I knew the bastards would invade sooner or later,' the duke said, oblivious to the tensions amongst those in the tent. Liesel had argued the same, while Esterel had clung to the belief they wouldn't.

Esterel gave his duke a dark look. 'No Friedrich?'

'He's staying put,' Domard said. 'He has the Turned on his east flank. Wants to stop them invading Thesse.'

'I ordered him here,' Esterel said, his voice brittle.

Domard gave his king a look, only now sensing the stress in his voice. 'True, and I did make that point, Your Majesty. On the other hand, we also have the Turned in the Steppe to the west of us. Friedrich's Thessians could protect our flank should they try to join the Turned in Gotbeck.' He looked about the tent. 'I didn't think it was such a poor decision.'

Esterel said nothing.

'What news to the west?' Sacha asked him.

'The Steppe is taken, but the border is quiet. I have been sending scouts to track their movements. It's not an easy task. But it looks like their forces have gone west.'

'Into Morbaine?' Sacha asked.

'I suppose so. I can't be sure of anything. But with a force in Magnia, it would make sense for them to link up and invade Morbaine. Just the same as they've done in Gotbeck, if you think about it.'

'Then I will pray to Gerhold that Duke Peyre can hold them off,' Sacha said, sounding like he meant it.

'It's not such a bad thing,' Esterel said. 'Peyre has a good core of soldiers with him. And the fact the Turned have split their forces in two makes our lives a little easier here. Perhaps we will get a chance to take them on in the field and win a victory.'

Everyone agreed. It sounded like Esterel was trying to stir himself for the battle to come. But Liesel knew him well, and there was something unconvincing in the way he said it.

* * *

THEY WAITED A FEW DAYS MORE. Liesel wondered if crossing into Gotbeck wouldn't be better, but kept her opinions to herself.

The news from Gotbeck got steadily worse until they spoke with survivors of Kaselitz. The town had fallen to the Turned, and it was rumoured Emmett had been killed in the fighting. Gotbeckers still poured north, escaping the devastation. Liesel knew others would now be turned, joining the ranks of their enemy. *Gods, we need to fight them*, she kept telling herself. *We should have done so a long time ago.*

At last, the armies from the rest of Brasingia joined them. Jeremias brought the warriors of Rotelegen. Katrina and the children had stayed in Guslar, but Liesel still found comfort in talking to her brother-in-law about them.

Idris arrived with the armies of Luderia and Atrabia. He caused an immediate stir. He already had the habit of revealing the scars from his captivity in Essenberg. Now, he came bare-chested. The only armour above his waist were his gauntlets and a vambrace on his left forearm. This revealed the burned, puckered flesh on the right side of his torso.

'I was so close to getting to the Krykker,' he explained to Liesel. 'I didn't see the Caladri sorcerer before it was too late. One blast and he did this to me. We've taken out sorcerers before, but this one was different. Must be that staff. Anyway, I could barely move after that. Thought it was all over. Then Macsen came, carried me away. Before the Caladri bastard got him.'

'Is he alright?' Liesel asked him.

'No. He died on the spot. No suffering. Our archers gave me enough cover to crawl out of there. It was excruciating, I can tell you that. Still feels like I'm on fire. I've not worn clothes over it since. Thought I would die. But the gods must still have some purpose for me. Maybe to kill that Caladri. Or the Krykker. Or both.'

She had thought him a bit of a fool, but Liesel grieved over Macsen's death. These wars were taking too many young lives. After Idris had visited with her, Liesel spent some time with Tegyn.

'Was it awful?'

'It wasn't a massacre,' her friend told her. 'We retreated in good order. The Luderians supported us. We lost Gethin and most of his soldiers. And, of course, Macsen.' She grimaced at a memory. 'As well as that Caladri sorcerer, there were Lizardmen. We hadn't expected that. Ferocious creatures. They'll be coming this way, Liesel. You need to prepare your warriors for that.'

'And Idris? He seems—'

'Worse? He is. I fear he's mad. Most of the Atrabians like it. Even the Luderians still do what he asks, despite what happened. Perhaps, now he's joined Esterel's army, his more impulsive ideas will be reined in.'

'Your uncle?'

'Says Macsen was a hero. I don't know what he says in private. But Idris has the complete loyalty of the Atrabians, so he has no choice but to follow.' She shook her head. 'And you, Liesel? News still reaches Atrabia, you know. You killed Inge?'

'Aye. With my crossbow.'

'Tell me you didn't do it to prove crossbows are superior to proper bows, Liesel?'

Liesel grinned. 'No. I did it...for Esterel, as much as anyone. She had him under her spell. Convinced it was best to avoid a confrontation with Ezenachi. He wasn't grateful for my intervention. Had me locked up.'

'But you're here now.'

'True.'

'So he must also be furious with Idris for attacking the Turned? Even more than he was with you?'

'I suppose so. But his anger is dissipated now. His choices are gone. The war is here.'

'And you think he should be grateful?' Tegyn shook her head. 'You and Idris. You're just the same.'

'Would you have done any different, Tegyn?'

Her friend sighed. 'Honestly, I don't know. I'm not in charge, and I have no wish to be. But like you say, the war is here. There's no point in quarrelling over the past.'

THE NEW ARRIVALS expanded Esterel's war council. Idris lost little time in saying his piece. 'I failed in the attempt, but I don't think I was wrong. If we can get that sword and staff from the Krykker and Caladri, we will neutralise their threat, and take it for our own.'

Liesel could tell Esterel was unimpressed with Idris, but trying to keep hold of his emotions.

'No one here can use the staff,' Esterel said, with a glare at Liesel.

I get it, she said to herself. *Inge could have used it.* But she kept her mouth shut. There was nothing to gain from that argument, and she didn't want to be removed from the council.

Idris looked from one to the other, obviously picking up on the tension. 'The sword, then.' He raised his hands. 'I wouldn't object to you wielding it, Your Majesty. By all accounts, you're a better swordsman than I.'

It was said with good humour, but it got the barest of responses from Esterel.

Where has your sense of fun gone, husband? Liesel wondered. *I hope it's not down to my actions. That's not what I wanted.*

'What of these Lizardmen I have heard about?' Jeremias asked. 'How best to prepare against them?'

'They are physically powerful and terrible to look upon,' Idris told him. 'They leapt over our shield wall and fought with spear and trident. But they can be killed, like any creature. After facing the Drobax, I doubt the men of Rotelegen will blanch before their assault.'

Jeremias nodded. 'I will warn my soldiers. The way you describe them, they sound most like the Dog-men who I fought against all those years ago. A breaking force, but vulnerable to missiles and less disciplined than trained warriors.'

'Agreed,' Idris said. 'My archers will watch out for them. Liesel's arbalests would also decimate their ranks, I am sure.'

Liesel inclined her head in agreement.

'And the route?' Domard asked, prodding at a map of imperial territory. 'The Cousel divides Gotbeck in two. Makes things awkward. Do we split our force? Don't want the vermin to outmanoeuvre us.'

'I'd rather not,' Esterel said. 'History tells us the Turned offer little in terms of strategy. If we come at them, they will fight us. I want to fight at full strength.'

'I would have agreed, until recently,' Idris said. 'We have seen them divide their forces this year, strategically and tactically. It might make sense for me to lead a small force on the east side of the river. Otherwise Luderia is open to them.'

'They can already enter Luderia from Confederate lands,' Esterel answered him. 'I don't want another defeat. By sticking together, we're better able to deal with whatever is thrown at us.'

Most eyes turned to Idris. It sounded like there was criticism in Esterel's words.

But Idris smiled it away. 'You're the emperor. So long as we get revenge, I will be happy.'

LIESEL

KELLAND/GOTBECK BORDER

Numerically, the latest additions to Esterel's army made little difference. But Liesel could tell morale had improved. Five of the seven imperial duchies had come together—plus hundreds of warriors who had fled Gotbeck, hastily incorporated into the army of Rotelegen. This balanced the importance of the warriors of Guivergne, who were still the core of Esterel's force. There was a sense of unity. When the order to advance was given, they seemed ready for what was to come.

As soon as they crossed into Gotbeck, scouts were sent ahead, and everyone was on full alert. They knew the enemy had taken Kaselitz. They were probably even closer. A confrontation felt imminent. Liesel prepared her arbalests as best she could. This would be different to fighting Brasingians. She made sure they knew about the Turned, and the Lizardmen.

It was still morning when the scouts returned with their news. A great army of Turned was headed their way. The army stopped, Esterel deciding their current location was as good as any to set up his forces. Liesel could barely focus when he went through the battle plan with his generals. It didn't seem real.

Her arbalests were divided into units and spread across the front of the army's position, ready to shower an enemy approach with missiles. When the enemy closed, they would retreat through the gaps between the main divisions.

Liesel's unit was near the centre of the line. Behind her was Esterel with the army of Guivergne, the cavalry tucked in behind the lines of infantry. To his left was Domard, with the Barissians and warriors of Martras. To Esterel's right, Sacha led the army of Kelland. Beyond him was Idris, with the Luderians and Atrabians. Jeremias had the men of Rotelegen and Gotbeck in reserve. It was a huge force. Liesel supposed in all the recent years of war, it might be the largest ever raised. The Turned that came to break through their lines might be greater.

But surely, they can't match us, Liesel told herself. *Even with those Lizardmen. Even with Maragin and Prince Lorant leading them. Even with the sword and staff, they are just two people.*

Warning shouts came. Liesel squinted into the distance. She saw the first line of Turned, marching steadily towards her position. It all happened so quickly, she felt lost. A legion of thoughts threatened to steal her focus. *How had it got to this? What would become of Brasingia—of Dalriya?*

No, she told herself. *None of that is my concern now. Now I must lead by example.* She took a deep breath, calming herself. 'Ready cross-bows!' she called out, putting as much composure and authority into her voice as she could. Those under her immediate command prepared their weapons, and the order was passed left and right to the other units, until hundreds of arbalests had loaded their first bolt into their weapons. 'And no releasing until the order is given!' she added. She could not afford to lose control of her soldiers. It would only take a few to panic for more to follow, loosing their bolts in a frenzy. They had been trained to follow orders; to maximise their capabilities. But training could never replicate reality.

The long line of Turned came closer, and behind them was another line, and another, and more—as far as the eye could see. Ezenachi must have stripped the southern lands of all their people. Man or woman, old or young, all had been sent into the empire. Liesel realised this was the god's most important moment. If he broke them here, the rest of Dalriya would open before him. He'd have won. A snarl of defiance came to her face. Her people and their allies would stop them. They had the weaponry and discipline to see off this horde.

'Hold!' she shouted, aware the temptation to shoot would be there. The first Turned were in range of the most powerful crossbows. But releasing now would be wasteful. Too many bolts would miss completely or strike harmlessly. Every bolt counted. They had to soften up the enemy. The warriors who would have to fight in the shield wall relied on them.

The lines of the enemy kept coming. A few missiles came from their ranks now, but most fell short. She felt the stares of her arbalests on her, willing her to give the order.

She strode a few paces ahead, so everyone could see her. A Cordentine woman she had taken to Valennes accompanied her, holding a huge shield that protected them from arrows. Liesel held one arm aloft. She knew all her arbalests would be trained on her now, ignoring the advancing Turned. She wondered if Esterel could see her, and what he thought. Once, he had been overly protective of his wife, wishing she would stay behind in safety. Now, he allowed her to stand in the front line and hadn't sent even one of his soldiers to protect her.

It was time. Liesel dropped her arm. The click and twang of pulled triggers and released strings could be heard all around her. It was a deadly hail of bolts they sent into the first ranks of the enemy. They should have screamed in pain. Instead, they fell dead or dying, or clutched at cruel wounds in soundless contortions.

'Load!' she shouted needlessly. Only a simpleton needed such an instruction. The Turned moved faster now, intent on closing the deadly gap between themselves and the army of Brasingia and Guivergne. Liesel retreated to the ranks of her unit. 'Fire freely!' she shouted. A second wave of bolts flew from the crossbows, bringing down any Turned who got close.

Liesel doubted any normal soldier would willingly run at her arbalests. The Turned only did so because they had no choice. She wondered whether, somewhere inside, these slaves knew what they did and tried in vain to release themselves from Ezenachi's grip. It was a horrible idea, and she tried to rid herself of it.

Her arbalests loaded their third bolts, as more Turned came to replace those who had fallen.

Then a familiar sensation struck her. Despair came with it. A ripple of energy, rising from the ground to shake her bones and squeeze her guts.

'I gave Brasingia a final chance,' came a voice, dry as dust. It echoed, as if they stood, not outside, but in a deep cavern underground. 'You have broken your contract. Your realm is terminated, and your people are mine.'

Ezenachi approached, walking past the foremost of his Turned. To each side strode Maragin and Lorant, sword and staff in their hands.

Liesel's teeth and tongue fizzed as he unleashed his magic, holding her to the spot. His Turned were protected from her arbalests, and try as she might, Liesel could not grab her crossbow, never mind aim at Ezenachi. She raged at the unfairness of it, tears streaming down her cheeks.

'Your armies invaded my lands. You killed the one champion you had,' he said, a tone of bewilderment in his voice, as if he couldn't understand their stupidity.

That was me, Liesel told herself. *And I have been stupid*, she added, as guilt and self-loathing settled on her. *How did I fool myself that this moment would not come?*

'Who is your leader now? The one who must submit to me?' Ezenachi's voice was relentless, confident the final humiliation of the Brasingian Empire would play out just as he wanted it to.

Liesel felt the magical hold on her relax somewhat.

And then a voice called out. 'That would be me.'

Esterel rode forward. He was seated on his finest stallion, horse and rider bedecked in all their finery. The sun glinted off Esterel's armour, and Liesel thought he looked like the great monarch he had always wanted to be. A legend, even if he had no way of stopping the menace that had come for him.

But Liesel didn't want him to go out like this—to ride willingly to his death. He could run, or—she didn't know what. But not this.

She ran to him. She wasn't the only one. Sacha, on horseback, was faster, placing his mount in front of his friend's. Domard was there, and Idris, and Liesel joined them. They all said the same, in their own way. *Don't go. Please.*

Esterel dismounted and gave them a good-natured smile. 'I knew this moment would come. Don't mourn me. I made Guivergne and Brasingia into something stronger. I ask you to keep my legacy alive.'

He turned to Liesel, and a hand went to her cheek. He wiped away a tear with a thumb, while a look of melancholy came to his face. 'You were right, Liesel. I was trying to avoid this fate. I thought, at least if I had an heir to follow me, my death would be more bearable. That was the foolish side of me. I'm sorry.'

Liesel shook her head. 'No. *I* was wrong. I lied to myself, that this wouldn't happen.'

Esterel gave her his last smile. Then his hand was gone. He left them, walking past the arbalests, towards Ezenachi. Liesel and the others stood watching him. He was their king and emperor, after all, and he had given them an order.

Esterel stopped. He spoke and his voice was loud, carrying across the battlefield. This was his farewell to his people, and it was the confident, heroic Esterel who they would remember.

'I am Esterel, King of Guivergne and Emperor of Brasingia. You have invaded the lands of my people. Know this, Ezenachi, you have the power to kill me. But I have instructed my lieutenants to continue the fight against you. My army will stand against you after I am dead, and neither you nor your army has the power to turn so many aside.'

Esterel's words were said with absolute certainty, and Liesel found she believed them. After all, had Ezenachi ever defeated such a great army? He could keep every one of them immobile. But for how long? Had anyone really tested this god's powers? *I was there when Coen was killed,* she reminded herself, *and what did we all do? Retreat. What if we had fought?*

'You speak nobly, Emperor Esterel,' Ezenachi replied, his words sounding like they were both inside Liesel's head and passing through her body. 'If only your lieutenants had obeyed you and kept the bargain between us. I do not wish to slaughter so many brave and blameless individuals. I hope you don't force me to give such an order.'

'Ah. In that case, I have a solution to propose,' Esterel said. He drew his sword, pointing the tip in Maragin's direction. 'A duel with your champion. Whichever of us loses, their army will retreat.'

Liesel found a bitter smile had come to her face. Only Esterel would dare play such games with a god.

They waited for Ezenachi to respond, but he was silent, as if Esterel's proposal had broken him. Finally, he spoke. 'My champion holds Bolivar's Sword. You cannot win.'

'Then I die. My army retreats. But you respect this new border. You stop your conquests with Gotbeck.'

'Very well,' Ezenachi answered. 'It seems an honourable solution.'

Maragin stepped forward mechanically, her face expressionless. Even before she was turned, the Krykker had been a formidable figure. Now she seemed invincible. But Esterel twirled his wrist, his sword spinning in his grasp, and Liesel knew his warriors believed. Would that make the outcome even more cruel?

There was no more preamble. The two fighters closed on each other, and the swords clashed for the first time. It was Esterel who pulled away. Liesel didn't think the Krykker was stronger, but her sword was, and Esterel was right to avoid Madria's weapon where possible. He moved swiftly, his blade flashing in and out, looking for a weakness. He was faster, both feet and hands. Maragin responded to everything with dogged defence, not giving an inch. She was relentless, incapable of making a mistake.

Liesel watched as Esterel took more risks. He chopped high, then low, but Maragin was ready. Esterel swung his blade at shoulder height. Maragin blocked it, and Esterel's sword spun away. Like everyone around her, Liesel gasped, expecting the end.

But Esterel now grappled with the Krykker for control of Bolivar's Sword. As the Krykker pushed forward with her weight, Esterel toppled backwards, dragging her with him. Maragin lost her footing, and she was sent flying head over heels.

Esterel ripped the sword from her grasp. With a cry of delight, he cracked her with the side of Bolivar's Sword, sending her to the ground. He raised the weapon in the air.

'I win!' he declared. 'And I will keep this weapon as my own.' His soldiers cheered their approval as he strode back to his ranks. Liesel could see his grin from to ear to ear. He turned back to Ezenachi. 'And you must retreat your army.'

'No,' Ezenachi snarled, and Liesel felt the fizz of his magic as she was locked in place once more. The god made a fist, pulled it towards his chest, and Esterel was pulled off his feet, flying through the air, until Ezenachi had him by the neck. With his other hand, he ripped Bolivar's Sword from Esterel's grip, before throwing Esterel to his knees.

Ezenachi held the sword aloft. 'You want your reward for defeating my champion?' he asked. He plunged Bolivar's Sword through Esterel's breastplate as if it wasn't there. The tip of the blade burst through the other side. He ripped it out, and Esterel fell to the ground.

Liesel struggled in the god's grasp. She couldn't move or cry out. He held an army of thousands in place, forcing them to watch.

Ezenachi glared in her direction. Liesel felt his sorcerous grip relax. 'Who is the new leader of this army?' he demanded.

'I am, you bastard!' she cried out. 'I am Liesel, daughter of Emperor Baldwin, wife of Emperor Esterel, Queen of Guivergne. And I will never submit to you. No Brasingian or Guivergnais ever will!'

With a small twist of his wrist, Ezenachi regained complete control over her. He pulled her to the ground—her face shoved into the dirt. He was suffocating her, and she couldn't move or speak. *So be it*, she told herself, scared but defiant. *Esterel and I will show our people the way. He can't do this to all of us.*

'Stop!' came a shout. Idris. 'She is not the new leader. I am Esterel's heir, in Guivergne, Kelland, and Barissia. He swore this to me, before many witnesses. With four duchies, I am already emperor.'

Ezenachi lifted Liesel's face from the dirt. *Is this true?* he asked her. The question was asked in her mind, not out loud. He ripped the truth from her, not allowing her to hide anything.

Yes, she admitted, recalling the pair's first meeting, in Esterel's camp outside Essenberg. She showed Ezenachi how they had argued, until Idris had demanded he become Esterel's heir, in return for his support of Esterel's claim to the imperial title. When he had the information he needed, Ezenachi dropped her. Forgotten. Unimportant now.

'You will respect my dominion over Dalriya,' Ezenachi intoned. 'You will withdraw this army. In return, I will end my conquest with Gotbeck. You shall keep the rest of the empire.'

'No!' Liesel shouted.

She was ignored.

'I, Emperor Idris, accede to your terms, Ezenachi. By this declaration, I submit to your authority.'

PART II
SHADOW

677

LOYSSE

VALENNES, KINGDOM OF GUIVERGNE

Loysse left the Bastion, with Cebelia in attendance, and Syele for protection. Their trips into the city had the familiarity of routine now. They would take the horses to The Royal Oak, stable them, and pace along the streets, stopping at most every shop on the way. Cebelia would complain her feet were tired, and Syele would scowl at the passersby, muttering about the dark atmosphere in the city.

Not that the Barissian was wrong. News of the war to the south had filtered into Valennes, and none of it was good. Magnia was conquered, and there were fears that Morbaine would soon follow. Peyre was stationed on the border, and Loysse worried for him. Meanwhile, Ezenachi's forces had also taken the Midder Steppe, and the rumours said the Empire would be next.

Esterel had been in Brasingia for months now. The citizens of Valennes felt his absence keenly. They were used to having their king resident in the city. Now, when Dalriya was under threat, and the enemy appeared to be heading relentlessly for Guivergne, he was gone. Loysse heard all the fears and accusations spreading amongst the people. It was said her brother favoured his new conquest over his home. Liesel, it was claimed, had poisoned him against Guivergne.

So it was that Loysse came into the city every day. Talking with the citizens; reassuring; doing her best to counter the dark rumours. It helped her, too. Full of nervous energy, wishing she could do more. At least she could do this.

Every moment spent away from Alienor gave her a pain which she swore was physical. Her babe was eight weeks old now. Healthy, hungry, and vocal. She had been blessed; she knew. With her maid Brayda able to nurse, she was left in the best of hands. Auberi doted on his daughter as well, her arrival giving him a focus that helped him forget his own troubles.

Loysse just wished her family could meet her. Syele had given Peyre her news. She had written to Esterel, but heard nothing back. Of course, she understood he was busy. But she wondered if he even knew he had become an uncle.

Then there was Sanc. *He would have loved to meet her.*

I am blessed, she insisted to herself. *But how I wish this war, with all its misery, had never happened.*

The sound of horses clopping along the road drew her attention. There were about thirty mounted warriors, bearing the familiar design of four silver diamonds on crimson, and she spotted Arnoul of Saliers at their head. Apart from the warriors of Famiens under her husband's command, and the small number of Bastion guards who took their orders from Brancat, Saliers' was the only military force left in the kingdom. Should the Turned cross the border into Guivergne, his force of a thousand was all that stood between the capital and the enemy.

Saliers spotted her and drew his men to a halt. Only then did Loysse recognise one of the other men who rode near the front. 'Lord Russell! You have come from Morbaine?'

He made himself smile at her, but Loysse could see he was exhausted. 'Aye, Your Grace. I have led the people out of the duchy. I know your next question, and I must tell you, Duke Peyre is not with us.' He looked about him, judging what was best to say in the current company. 'He and Umbert both stayed behind.'

'I would hear about it all. My Lord of Saliers, our horses are only at The Royal Oak. I assume you are heading to the Bastion. May we accompany you?'

'Of course, my lady.'

After a quick detour back to the inn, they resumed their journey. Loysse rode next to Lord Russell. Syele took her other side, a dour grimace sufficient to discourage anyone else from joining the conversation.

'Peyre ordered a complete evacuation,' Lord Russell told her, speaking with the dull voice of someone in desperate need of sleep. 'It's not just the people of Morbaine I've led north. It's the Magnians, too, and what is left of the Middian tribes.' He gestured at the man who rode behind them. 'Chieftain Frayne has accompanied me. His riders have helped to evacuate people across the border.'

Frayne gave her a little bow and a tired smile of his own.

'Thank you,' Loysse said to him. 'Your people are welcome here. But Lord Russell, there is no real border between Morbaine and Guivergne. It is one realm. Is there any reason to think the Turned will stop there?'

He shrugged. 'I don't know.'

'That is how they have operated so far,' Frayne piped up. 'They invade one region at a time. They may well stop and consolidate once they reach the border of Guivergne proper.'

Loysse nodded to acknowledge his words. 'And Peyre?' she asked Lord Russell.

Her father's friend rubbed at his face. 'King Ida returned to Magnia to rescue his mother. Peyre went with him. He hoped to win back the weapons of Madria.'

Loysse recalled her meeting with Belwynn and the other champions, all wielding a weapon of Madria. They had seemed sure, in their own ways, of their purpose. How quickly Ezenachi had turned them to his bidding. *Peyre thinks he can steal into the enemy camp and take those weapons?* It sounded like madness to Loysse. *And, of course, Umbert joined him in it.*

She gave Lord Russell a sympathetic look and decided not to bother him with further questions for now. But while Peyre had saved a great many people, he had also left them a very great mess to take care of.

* * *

THEY STILL MET in the royal council chamber, even though they lacked the great lords who had once attended on Esterel in Valennes. As well as Loysse and Auberi, there was Caisin, the Lord Chancellor, who had been the one constant figure in government over recent years; Lord Russell; and Arnoul of Saliers. It didn't seem nearly enough to cope with the challenge they faced.

'I admire Duke Peyre,' Arnoul said, 'but on this matter, he has made a very great mistake. He has simply moved a problem from one border to another, when it would have been better to stand and fight where he was.'

'The risk,' Russell said, 'was that all those thousands would have been turned, and become soldiers in Ezenachi's army.'

'And what you have done instead, Lord Russell,' Saliers said, his dark eyes emotionless, 'is lead an invasion of Guivergne yourself. You have done Ezenachi's work for him.'

Russell's mouth set in a thin line. Loysse could tell he struggled to control his anger.

'Come, Saliers,' Auberi said. 'Such language. Most of those people are our countrymen.'

'Whatever words we choose to use,' Saliers replied, 'won't change the basic facts. We have no hope of feeding them. Caisin, if I am wrong about that, please correct me.'

'You are not wrong, my lord. With so many men still absent in Brasingia, we have struggled with the harvests as it is. I'm afraid we don't have the resources to support so many.'

'And so,' Saliers continued, implacable, 'we face a famine, and then disease. Thousands of desperate, starving people, who will do anything to get their hands on some food. The inevitable outcome is bloodshed. The people are scared. We've already had incidents with those Cordentines Queen Liesel brought into the city.'

'Those Cordentines helped us defeat Leopold,' Loysse reminded him.

Saliers nodded at her. 'I know that, Your Grace. I still command a company of them myself. But there are tensions in the city between these immigrants and the locals. Imagine if we have Middians, and Magnians, added to that. Up and down Guivergne. We'll have riots. Massacres.'

'Then we must speak to the mayors and councillors of every town,' Loysse said. 'Explain the situation. Take greater control of food production and ensure we take enough to feed these people. It is hard work, but it is possible.'

'It isn't,' Saliers said. 'There are simply too many.'

'Then what?' she asked him. 'What alternative is there?'

'They need to be moved on. Before it's too late.'

'Could we get some to take refuge in the empire?' Caisin suggested. 'The Middians and Magnians, let's say. Try to integrate the Morbainais here. It would only be fair and reasonable. What do you think, Lord Russell?'

'It's tricky. Peyre promised these people shelter in Guivergne. The Magnian king is absent. These people may not take well to being told to move on.'

'They can take it how they like,' Saliers said. 'These people need to go and fight for the lands they have lost. Running away has solved nothing. They can't expect so many to be housed and fed. I'm sorry, but they've been promised something that just isn't possible.'

* * *

LOYSSE WORKED day and night with Lord Caisin to source supplies for the thousands of refugees who had arrived in Guivergne. She sent a letter to Esterel detailing the problems they faced. She sent Russell and Frayne back to their people, urging them to stay patient, and ration their own supplies while she came up with a solution.

But events moved out of control. Saliers had to use force to put down a revolt in Valennes, the anger and fear that had been building in the city stoked further by the arrival of the refugees in Guivergne.

Then it got worse. A report that Frayne, the Middian chieftain, had led a raid in the countryside, taking food from farms and villages to feed his people. Loysse hated to admit that Saliers had been proved right.

As soon as news of the attack spread, Guivergnais of all rank and station inundated the government with demands that they remove the foreigners. They came to the Bastion, demanding to be heard.

In the end, Auberi said he would meet with the petitioners. 'They are less aggressive when they come before a blind man,' he had said, with a hint of a smile.

Syele accompanied Loysse along the corridors of the Bastion, from Caisin's office to her private rooms. All she wanted to do was spend time with Alienor. She felt guilt at being away from her daughter for so long, and guilt that she was failing to govern Guivergne properly.

'I wonder what will come of all this,' she admitted. 'I just hope and pray Peyre returns soon. That would be something. The worst possible outcome would be sending our own troops against the Morbainais.'

'True enough,' Syele said. 'The Morbainais and their allies would be more than a match for any force we can raise.'

Loysse sighed, feeling even worse. As they approached her rooms, Loysse saw two young men loitering outside. One was Benoit, Arnoul's son. The second she recognised as Robert, the exiled heir of Auriac.

Robert had lived with her in Arbeost. But his father Raymon's rebellions had irrevocably broken his relationship with her family. His estate had been given to Florent, and he had been sent away to Martras, under the watchful eye of Duke Domard. *What is he doing in the Bastion?*

'Lady Loysse,' Benoit said pleasantly.

'Benoit. You have come to see me?'

'He was just showing me your rooms,' Robert said. 'I heard you have a baby. I would love to meet her.'

Loysse stared coldly at him, not quite believing his cheek. All he did was smirk back at her. 'I am too busy for your tomfoolery. Go and learn some manners before you speak to me again.'

'Off with you,' Syele added, placing a hand on the hilt of her sword.

Robert raised an eyebrow at this, then with a smile, put a hand to his own weapon.

'Come on,' Benoit finally intervened, giving his companion a shove. 'Let's get going.'

Loysse watched them go before entering her rooms. 'I don't like it. He has a very great animosity for my family, and he is asking to see my daughter? Was it meant as a threat? I will speak to Saliers about this.'

'Saliers himself is acting like he is running Valennes,' Syele warned her. 'Whatever he says to your face, watch out for that one.'

Loysse put a hand to her head, reminded of the recurring dream she kept having. She was hanging over the edge of a cliff, clutching a rope with both hands, the only thing stopping her from falling. As she hung there in her dream, she could see the threads snap, one by one, and knew the rope would soon break.

SANC

LANDS OF THE TELDS

Sanc woke to find Mildrith leaning over him. She had a hand on his shoulder.

'I could get used to you being the first thing I see when I wake,' he mumbled.

He got the Mildrith response—the smallest of smiles. Clearly, the enthusiasm of their reunion in the Kassite lands, when he had received a kiss, was over.

'We're meeting with Mergildo shortly. Thought you'd want to come.'

Reality—unwelcome but insistent—returned to his thoughts. 'Of course I do,' he said, sitting up.

SANC SPOKE with Kepa as they made their way down a mountain trail towards the agreed meeting place with the Rasidi. He was pleased they walked, and that no mention was made of flying on rugs.

'How have things been since I was last here?'

'It was touch and go for a while,' answered the Teld, her violet eyes sparking in the morning sunshine. 'We had Ordono's invasion from the west and Lothar's from the east. They weren't far from meeting and cutting our realm in two. That would have been the end. Bringing the Egers into the war saved us,' she said, with a brief glance at the Eger Khan. 'Thank you.'

The presence of the Eger Khan in Teld lands was a shock that not even the experienced champion, Kepa, had quite got over. Sanc knew the enmity between the two peoples was generations old. But they had treated the Eger leader with the utmost respect. He wondered if it was too much to hope his presence here might heal at least some of the animosity.

'King Haritz?' Sanc asked.

'He is ill. A result of the stress he was under, I am sure. I am keeping him informed of developments, but the doctors say he shouldn't be moved unless it's of the utmost importance. It might kill him.'

'I'm sorry,' Sanc said. 'Does he have a son and heir?'

'He has a daughter and a grandson. But the Teld crown does not necessarily go to the oldest child of the king.'

'Who does it go to?'

'We like to say the new king "emerges". The best candidate is chosen.'

'*You* should take the crown,' the Eger Khan said to Kepa. 'That is how the Egers do it. The most powerful should be khan.'

There were a few exchanged glances at that. Sanc didn't think the khan had meant to be rude. But the Eger's belief in their own superiority was deeply ingrained. The young man didn't even question whether the way his people did things was the only acceptable way.

Sanc watched as Kepa opened her mouth to respond and struggled to find the right words. She knew a rebuttal and defence of her people's traditions might be misinterpreted by the khan as a criticism of his. Finally, she settled on an answer. 'The peoples of Silb can all learn from one another.'

Sanc thought it a good answer. He looked at the slight frown on the khan's face. *Perhaps he is thinking about it. That's probably all we can expect.*

. . .

THEY MET the Rasidi delegation on the border. There were only two men Sanc recognised. The champion, Mergildo, was tall and aged. The last time Sanc had seen him, he had been following him through the streets of Aguilas, only to find him meeting with Temyl and Guntram in an inn in the city. Outnumbered, he and Mildrith would have been in serious trouble if Sanc hadn't acted on his suspicions.

Now, it was Mergildo who was outnumbered. Sanc knew that for a fact. His ability to track the other champions meant he could never be caught by surprise again.

With Mergildo was one of King Ordono's right-hand men, whom he had met briefly in the royal garden of the palace. When the introductions were made, he was reminded of the man's name—Guillen, Mayor of the Palace. When the Eger Khan was introduced, the man's eyes widened. 'I had no idea His Majesty the khan would be here.'

'Neither did I,' Kepa assured him, then gestured at Sanc and Mildrith. 'They only arrived yesterday.'

'This changes things,' Guillen said. 'I am not authorised to speak for King Ordono in negotiations with the Egers.'

'What, then?' Kepa asked him.

'The king waits nearby. I will speak with him. I think it likely he will wish to come and meet the khan himself.'

'Very well,' Kepa said. 'We'll be waiting.'

'Mergildo?' Guillen said to the Rasidi sorcerer as he turned to go.

'I will wait here.'

The mayor shrugged and departed in haste.

Mergildo looked at Sanc, his dark eyes revealing little, except an inner confidence. He was tall, old to Sanc's eyes—no doubt at the height of his powers, with a lifetime's experience of using magic. 'I hope there are no hard feelings about Aguilas. It was political, not personal.'

Sanc felt himself rile up. 'If it was political, it was a misjudgement. Siding with Lothar made no sense, for whatever reason.'

'My king had to make a choice. At the same time he was in communication with Prince Lenzo on Ram, he was in talks with Lothar. What did we know about you at that point?' He flipped a hand at Mildrith and Sanc. 'You're both young. The Kassites had lost to the Nerisians—badly. Lenzo had a fleet but no army. Really, what could we say, except advise him not to take such a risk? There was nothing you could have done once you arrived at the palace. The decision had already been made.'

That damn campaign with the Kassites, Sanc thought. *We let ourselves be talked into taking Lothar's army on and paid a heavy price. But I'll not make that mistake again. I may not be a natural strategist like my brothers. But I'm learning.*

'If you'd had any guts,' Mildrith said to him, 'you'd have joined our side and this war would be over.'

'Maybe so,' Mergildo acknowledged, not showing any offence. 'The Rasidi are not so interested in displaying guts, champion of the Kassites. We are more interested in winning. Certainly, though, the introduction of the Egers into the war has changed things,' he said, with a respectful nod towards the Eger Khan. 'You showed guts and guile in equal measure when you achieved that. You have won the respect of my king.'

Ordono soon arrived, with Guillen and other members of his entourage. But it was the king who needed to be convinced now, after they had failed to do so before. He nodded brusquely at Sanc and the others, before bowing before the Eger Khan. 'Your Majesty. It is an honour to meet you.'

'Likewise, King Ordono,' the young man said. 'Thank you for coming to see me in person.'

'Of course. Well, this is something,' the king said, gesturing around. 'Teld, Rasidi, Kassite, and Eger, in one place. It feels momentous.'

'It is,' the khan said, with that certainty that still surprised Sanc. 'But you should hear the words of one who is not from Silb at all,' and he nodded at Sanc to speak.

'Very well,' Ordono said, though he didn't look happy about it.

'I don't believe I need to warn anyone here of the power and ambition Lothar has displayed in recent years,' Sanc said, 'or convince you of the need to stop his expansion before it's too late. We are close to doing that. Three days ago, I helped the Scorgians retake Irpino. Their fleet is currently in the Dogne, sailing to Mournai.'

He could see the surprised reaction amongst the Rasidi to his news. But Ordono looked less than happy. He didn't want to be called a fool for siding with Lothar over Lenzo.

Sanc struggled with what to say next. He wanted to tell these people about his discoveries at the Temple of Peramo. He glanced at Mildrith. She had warned him against revealing the truth, arguing no one wanted to hear it. He suspected she was right.

'The world I came from is under attack by a god named Ezenachi. It wasn't until I arrived on the Isle of Ram that I discovered Ezenachi came from Silb. He was defeated when the seven peoples took this continent from him. That is why he left and invaded Dalriya.'

He looked at his audience. They were listening, and no one seemed to think he was making it up. It was hard to know what these individuals believed, or how much of their history each people had conserved. He wondered if the Rasidi, with their culture, art, and fine palaces, might have retained more than most.

'Ezenachi is close to conquering my world. We have no gods left to defend us. And you might think, "good", let him have it. But I don't believe he will rest there. He travelled from Silb to Dalriya, and that means he can travel back again. And he could bring his army of slaves —whom we call the Turned—with him. He can return to Silb, looking for revenge. If he gets here and finds the seven peoples divided—at war—it will be that much easier for him to defeat you.'

Sanc studied Mergildo's reaction carefully. He knew if anyone knew about Ezenachi, it would be him. The Rasidi champion gave little away. But he didn't sneer in disbelief.

'You came to our world to save your own?' Ordono asked him.

'I was sent here to look for help. I can't force you to help me, that's true. But at the very least, I can warn you that Silb is in danger. I can ask you to bring some peace and unity to this land before it's too late. And I can try to persuade you that saving my world also means saving yours.'

Ordono turned to his champion. 'Mergildo?'

'We need to talk, Your Majesty.'

The Rasidi delegation excused themselves.

Sanc watched them go as a light flickered in his chest. *I think I've done it*, he dared tell himself. *I think I've persuaded them.*

* * *

THEY MET with Lothar at a fortress owned by one of his margraves, in Gadenzia. The Nerisian army, withdrawn from the lands of the Egers, was camped a mile away.

It was still the greatest army in Silb. It was still undefeated. It was the same army that had conquered the Scorgians and the Kassites. Yet things had changed, and Lothar knew it.

Lenzo had undone most of his work in Scorgia. The Egers had been awakened and had their own army in the field. The Telds and Rasidi had come to an arrangement, detaching his one ally, King Ordono, from him. Even the Kassites, beaten and bloody, were rebelling once more.

All the peoples of Silb were represented in the peace talks. All had their own views on what peace should look like. Lothar made it plain that he could not give up all his conquests—his people wouldn't accept it. He also demanded the return of the Gadenzians abducted by the Egers. Lenzo was accommodating. Kepa was difficult, insisting that Teld lands should be restored.

The diplomacy went back and forth. None of it concerned Sanc who, having successfully gathered these people together, was now a spare part.

He was surprised, therefore, when Lothar approached him in the main hall. The king was flanked by his champions, Temyl and Guntram. It was strange to be in such proximity to the two men who had been his greatest enemies in Silb. The older, Temyl, still had hostile eyes, and visibly seethed during the negotiations. Guntram, who towered above them, was more placid. But both were still highly dangerous, and Sanc could see Mildrith staring over, ready to defend him if needed.

'I would like to speak with you alone for a moment, outlander,' Lothar said. 'My champions will stay here.' He gestured at Mildrith. 'The other champions can keep an eye on them. Ensure they don't try anything.'

Temyl's mouth twitched. 'I advise against trusting him, Your Majesty.'

A look of frustration came to Lothar's face. 'If he wanted to kill me, he could have. That's the whole point.'

With Temyl silenced, Lothar led Sanc from the hall into the open air. Servants and soldiers crossed the courtyard, but there was enough space for some privacy. Sanc took another look at Lothar. Tall and athletic, light brown hair grown long, blue eyes—he looked princely enough, and yet Sanc expected more.

'You *could* have killed me,' Lothar said, referencing his comments to Temyl. He waved a hand at their surroundings. 'Why choose this instead? Why not finish the war, hunt me down, kill me and my champions? You have four champions against two, not even counting the khan. You could have done that, and then Lenzo and those others could have taken whatever lands they wished.'

'I nearly did,' Sanc admitted. 'When I had you in the air, I was so close to doing it.' He recalled the moment his mother had come to him, and frowned. He had still not reconciled that vision; had not shared it with anyone else.

'I thought so, at the time. Then I began to wonder, were you scaring me into submitting to you? Because it was just like—' The king paused, and looked at Sanc for a while, as if debating whether to say more. 'Five years ago, Ezenachi came to me.'

Only seven words, but everything Sanc understood about the world was undone and flung into the air. 'What?' It was all he could say.

'He came to Mournai in secret. He demonstrated that his power was greater than Temyl and Guntram's.' A scornful grin came to his face. 'They fled. Later, Temyl justified their actions, but I knew from that moment on, no one could protect me from Ezenachi.

'He raised me into the air, just like you did. Explained how easy it would be to kill me. Then, his demands. I had to conquer Silb for him. If I failed, he would kill me and my champions, and give Silb to a more worthy ruler. Ordono, or Domizio. When he left, and Temyl returned, we agreed I had no choice. The Egers would be quiet for years. We had an opportunity to do it, if we were careful. If we hid our ultimate goal, we might get to a point where it was too late for the other kingdoms to stop us.

'After the invasion of Scorgia, I thought we were there. I made myself emperor. There were still three champions left, but the Kassite, Rasidi, and Teld would never work together. Then you arrived. And slowly, things unraveled.'

Sanc nodded, slowly processing Lothar's story. 'I realised, at the last moment, that it was far better to unite the peoples of Silb than to kill you. If you have met Ezenachi yourself, then you must support my plan to defeat him.'

'Of course I do,' Lothar agreed. 'And I will say as much to the other rulers. I look back now and wonder why I didn't do what you have done. I could have warned the other rulers and tried to unite Silb against him. I won't deny the thought of conquering Silb held an appeal. I was young and ambitious. But even when the Abbot of Peramo placed the imperial crown on my head, I couldn't really enjoy it. At the back of my mind, I knew I was doing it for someone else.'

'I appreciate your honesty,' Sanc said. 'I've often wondered something. When I first came to Silb, I arrived close to Irpino. I could easily have met you first, instead of Lenzo. What would you have done if I had come to your court, asking for help against Ezenachi?'

'You admire honesty, outlander?' Lothar pursed his lips. 'Temyl would probably have killed you. We were already set on our course. And if he had killed you, maybe Silb would be ours. So be grateful you met Lenzo first.'

Sanc nodded, unsure what to say. But he felt a sense of relief at the king's words.

'Now I have a question for you,' Lothar said. 'What is your relationship with Ezenachi? You behave like him. You share his powers.'

'Share his powers?' Sanc demanded.

'So Temyl says. When you lifted me from my horse, and I felt your grip on my heart, it was just the same. You can travel between worlds. You have a second sight. Why are you so similar?'

'I'm not similar,' Sanc said. 'I want to destroy him.'

Lothar shrugged at Sanc's words. But he didn't look convinced.

PEYRE

DUCHY OF MORBAINE

Opening his eyes felt like a monumental effort. Gradually, Peyre's senses returned, and he noticed his surroundings. He sat with his back against a tree. He faced into a small glade, where sunlight dappled down through the leaves and a refreshing breeze came and went.

He flexed, pulling at tight pieces of skin dotted over his body. Many of them ached. He put a hand to the most painful, on his back. A bandage had been placed over it, but he could tell it was a wound that had been sealed with hot metal. He recalled being struck by vossi darts. His wounds had been cleaned of poison. He owed his friends thanks. They may well have saved his life.

In the centre of the glade, Umbert and Gosse, bare-chested, knelt over a carcass, using their knives to butcher it. When the breeze blew in his direction, he caught the stink of their work.

Peyre allowed his mind to process the events he could remember. He and Ida had been running from the vossi of the Turned army, their damned screams filling his ears. He hadn't even realised their darts had poisoned him at first, though he had become slow and clumsy, forced to turn and fight them before they reached the river. Ida had intervened, and he had run into the river, where, miraculously, Umbert and the others were passing on a raft.

Ida? Umbert had said the king was right behind him, but as soon as Peyre had been dragged onto the raft, he had fainted.

'Where is Ida?' he asked, his voice a horrible croak.

Both men stopped what they were doing and turned, giving him a surprised look. With grins of relief, they got to their feet and headed over. Umbert put a waterskin to Peyre's lips, and he drank thirstily.

'Well?' he said.

'Ida and Inhan have gone west, to the coast,' Gosse said. 'If they can find a vessel, they will return for us.'

'You sent them alone?' Peyre asked.

'They are the fastest,' Umbert said. 'And we had you to look after.'

That was true. Peyre felt chastened. 'Of course. And thank you, it can't have been easy with me like this. The vossi?'

'We travelled a long way north by river. It's hard to say how far behind they are. That said, every stray sound has me on edge.'

'I'm sure. Here, help me get to my feet, will you?'

'If you're sure.'

Umbert and Gosse took a hand each and raised Peyre up. He walked about the glade, getting his blood circulating.

'The poison has worn off?' Umbert asked.

'Seems like it. Everything went rigid. Now I just feel stiff and sore. The Shield is safe?' he asked.

'Aye,' Gosse rumbled. 'Ida told us the story.'

'I couldn't leave them,' Peyre said, almost apologetically. 'It's just a shame about Brictwin.'

'If you hadn't gone back, they would likely both be dead,' the big warrior said.

Peyre was happy to believe that was true. Besides, they wouldn't have the Shield otherwise. 'I have to admit, you've both done well the last few days. Starting with getting me onto that raft.'

'You're welcome,' Gosse drawled. 'And now you're back in charge to screw everything up again.'

* * *

WHEN UMBERT and Gosse finally served up dinner, Peyre realised he was famished. They insisted he slept while they shared watch, and when he woke the next morning, he felt fully recovered.

It was another warm day, but there was little to do except wait. Peyre began to understand Umbert's nerves. He kept imagining a horde of screaming vossi coming for them, running through the trees, and throwing their darts. The thing was, the longer they waited, the more likely it was the Turned *would* appear.

It was therefore a relief when Ida and Inhan returned, with only half the morning gone. Unfortunately, their expressions killed any joy Peyre felt.

'It is good to see you awake, Your Grace,' Inhan said.

'Just spit the news out,' Peyre replied.

'We got to the coast,' Ida said. 'It's occupied. We could see Caladri ships pulled up along a beach. They're heading inland, in this direction. They'll be here soon.'

'Then we need to go,' Peyre said, hiding his disappointment.

They set off, heading north. With the Turned approaching from west, south, and east, they had no other options. 'The Peronne?' Peyre asked, wondering if the river was still open to them.

'We travelled as far as we could,' Umbert said. 'The river shallowed and the current was against us.'

Peyre thought as much. That placed them roughly in the middle of his duchy. He kept thinking as he walked. His legs and back soon burned with the effort, but he welcomed the pain. The enemy's strategy was clear enough. They had sought to surround Morbaine, trapping his army and the people of his duchy. They would have been a useful addition to Ezenachi's forces. It reassured him he had done the right thing in evacuating everyone north.

But none of that helped their current situation. If only they had horses, they might still escape. The Turned coming from the Steppe were mounted—he'd seen them with his own eyes. The vossi to the south moved faster than they could. Meanwhile, up and down the long coast, the Caladri would be disembarking thousands more. The chances of escaping the three-pronged invasion were slim. But Peyre had no solutions. All they could do was try.

They stopped for a brief rest and to eat. At least they had plenty of supplies. Their waterskins had been filled from the river. They had fish, meat, and a potage made from the grains Peyre had scavenged in Magnia. Surely, Peyre considered, that gave them some advantage over the enemy? *Even an army like the Turned can only travel as fast as its supplies.* Then he considered the Caladri fleet, each vessel potentially packed with victuals, and he doubted all over again.

Morbaine was a land of worn paths, made by frequent use, rather than straight roads. Peyre, Umbert, and Inhan had travelled them often enough to choose the best route north. It gave them another edge over the enemy. Despite that, it wasn't long into the afternoon when they heard the first signs of the Turned.

Unsurprisingly, it was the vossi. Their screams seemed to echo around the countryside. It was a useful warning, and they still sounded some distance behind. But soon, they had a second problem. Caladri were moving ever eastwards. Hearing their approach, they knew they were in trouble.

'Who knows how far north they landed?' Umbert hissed. 'They'll be ahead of us soon.'

Peyre knew his friend was right, and began leading the group northeast, to keep some distance from the advancing Caladri. But that could only work for so long. The inevitable happened. They began to hear noise from the east, too. They were probably already surrounded.

Peyre led them uphill. The beginnings of a plan had been forming in his mind, but it required a heavy dose of luck. He drove them up a steep slope, past trees and through bracken. Gosse was panting. Peyre knew the warrior would sink to his knees before he'd utter a word of complaint. At the top of the slope, Peyre looked east. His eyes flitted wildly across the terrain, and he forced himself to calm; to breathe. He regained an icy control and scanned the area once more.

Hope dared to burst in his chest. He had suspected the Turned from the Steppe would send their riders ahead. There they were. As he watched them approach, he reckoned it was a troop of about thirty horsemen in all. *Too many. Far too many for us to handle. But this is our one chance.*

He turned to his companions and studied their faces. They hadn't given up yet. 'Here's what we'll do.'

PEYRE WAITED ALONE. He'd found a large tree to hide behind. His plan was already in motion. There was nothing to do now but wait and play his part when the time came.

He heard the horses. Thirty of the beasts, urged into a canter, pushing their way through the forest scrub. He peered around his hiding place and saw Ida and Inhan. They were running at full pelt past his position, jumping over and swerving around obstacles, maintaining enough speed to stay ahead of the riders. Behind them, the Turned were only gradually gaining, the terrain preventing them from letting their horses go at a full gallop. Close up, Peyre could see the riders were all Middians, captured and turned in Ezenachi's invasion. It had given the god yet another class of warrior with which to make his conquests.

He emerged, moving to intercept the riders, while counting how many went past after his friends. At half way, he launched himself into the path of the remaining horsemen, the Shield of Persala held before him. They rode at him, confident they could swat him aside.

But as they connected with the Shield, they were sent flying away. Horses went tumbling, crashing into those behind them. Riders were launched from their mounts, sailing through the air. It was carnage, only a few Middians pulling up in time to avoid it. They looked at Peyre, wary of his weapon, and unsure how to respond.

It allowed Peyre a chance to glance behind him. He couldn't make out Ida or Inhan, suggesting they had escaped their pursuers. What he could see were the Middians milling about, pulling at their horses' reins. A riderless horse bolted back in Peyre's direction. Gosse and Umbert had strung ropes across from one tree to the next. Ida and

Inhan had led the Middians into a trap and there was no way out of it except back the way they had come. Realising this, they had turned and were urging their horses back towards Peyre. Now, his friends emerged from behind trees, grabbing at soldiers and mounts.

Peyre moved in to finish the job. The retreating Middians rode straight for him, intent on knocking him down. They hadn't seen what Peyre's Shield could do. He launched himself at them; the Shield protecting him from the incredible force of a horse at gallop, and instead knocking them away.

Some lost their footing; others threw their riders; some both. Shouts and screams seemed to come from everywhere, humans and horses running in every direction to escape. A Middian on foot came for Peyre with a hammer. Peyre put his shield in the way, but the Middian's strike had been a feint. Peyre skipped aside, just avoiding the next blow. On the back foot, he tried to avoid the deadly weapon, while pulling a dagger from his belt.

Then Umbert was there, his sword coming down on the Middian's head from behind, knocking him to the ground. Behind Umbert was Gosse, leading a group of horses.

Peyre didn't waste time. He grabbed the reins Gosse offered him and leapt into the saddle. He turned his horse left and right, looking for trouble. The Middians still on their feet avoided him, running away or melting into the trees.

Peyre looked for his friends. Umbert and Gosse were mounted. Ida joined them. 'Inhan?' he called.

'Here!' the young man responded, kneading his mount towards them through the trees. He held the reins in his metal hand.

Peyre couldn't quite believe they'd done it. 'Let's ride!' he shouted, a grin of triumph appearing on his face as they escaped through the trees.

LOYSSE

VALENNES, KINGDOM OF GUIVERGNE

Loysse had faced tough experiences in her life. *The only woman in my family since my mother died. Father's decision to marry me to Auberi. My husband's blinding. Childbirth, a mere two months ago, when I feared I would suffer the same fate as my mother. I've had my fair share.*

But she felt this meeting of the royal council might be the worst of the lot. She prayed, something she didn't do very often. *Sibylla, give me the strength to get through it.*

She took Auberi's hand and led him to the council chamber. In Esterel's absence, they had ruled Guivergne from here. That authority he had given them was slipping away. *Those threads are breaking*, she told herself, *and I can't find a way to stop it.*

Four men waited for them. Caisin, Lord Chancellor, the only one she considered an ally. But she knew, in the current circumstances, she could rely on no one. Arnoul, Lord of Saliers, the man who had positioned himself as her rival.

Then there were the two newest members. The citizens of Valennes had been whipped into a frenzy, demanding fresh blood on the council. Law and order had broken down, six Cordentine women murdered in four days, one still a child in Loysse's eyes. She'd had no

165

choice but to concede to their demands, knowing all the time that Saliers was pulling the strings.

So it was that Benoit, Saliers' son, had been sworn onto the council. He was much like his father, respectful on the outside, his real thoughts unreadable. Firmin, the trader who had riled up the people of Valennes, was different. A man of no pedigree, who shouldn't even have been allowed inside the Bastion, was now a councillor of the realm. His smug smile; his fat finger, jabbing at Loysse and Auberi as he threatened more violence if he didn't get his way—it took all of Loysse's resolve not to scream and shout and slap him across the face.

'Gentlemen, please sit,' Auberi said.

Her husband kept his temper so easily and was unfailingly polite. *He doesn't have to look at them*, Loysse reminded herself.

'We have this offer from Lord Russell to consider,' Auberi began.

'First, if you don't mind,' Arnoul said. 'A plea on behalf of Lord Robert. In the circumstances, I think it a common sense proposal. We should return his family's lordship of Auriac to him.'

Loysse couldn't believe what she had heard, struggling to keep her emotions in check. 'King Esterel deprived his family of those lands for rebellion. They belong to Lord Florent.'

'I know, Your Grace,' Arnoul replied. 'But we have a foreign army in our lands and Lord Florent isn't here. There are many estates in the kingdom which lie ungoverned. As well as Auriac, there is the great duchy of Martras. We need to put men in charge of them, who can raise soldiers and supplies. Robert would have the loyalty of the people of Auriac. As I say, it is mere common sense to restore the estate to him.'

'Agreed,' Firmin said.

'I can't accept that,' Loysse replied.

'Then we put it to a vote?' Arnoul suggested.

Loysse's stomach fluttered at that. She needed Caisin to support her position, and she didn't know if he would.

'I don't think that's necessary,' Auberi said. 'Let me think about your request, Arnoul, before I decide.'

Loysse watched Arnoul study her husband with his dark eyes—

assessing; measuring. Auberi wasn't easy to read these days. A green band of cloth across his eyes, Loysse knew he was far more inscrutable than she was. The relationship between the two men was a complicated one. Saliers had once fought to make Auberi king. Former allies, each had submitted to her father. Loysse knew she couldn't be sure what game they played now.

'Very well, Your Grace,' Arnoul said at last. 'Have some time to decide. But it is a matter that must be decided with urgency.'

'Understood. Now, Lord Russell's message. A meeting with him, and this Middian, Frayne, would be beneficial. Calm things down.'

'The only thing that would calm things down is those barbarous Middians returning to the Steppe,' Firmin said. 'Roll your eyes all you like, Your Grace,' the trader said to Loysse.

His finger was out. Jab, jab, jab. *How I'd like to lop that digit off. No doubt he'd continue to shove the bloody stump in my face.*

'But the people of Guivergne will never trust him after what he did. That's the plain truth.'

'Then tell him that, by all means,' Auberi said. 'But without a meeting, we get nowhere.'

'I still think ushering them into the empire would be the best option,' Caisin said.

Saliers shook his head. 'The Magnians and Middians are allied with the Morbainais. They won't leave their protectors. The only option is to send them south.' He sighed. 'Maybe a meeting is necessary. But it can't be in Valennes. I can't control the citizens. My soldiers are outnumbered. They'd likely lynch the Middians as soon as they walked through the city gates.'

A barefaced lie, Loysse thought. *You've stoked every base instinct of these people.* She disliked the idea of leaving the Bastion. She knew Brancat, the castellan, wouldn't give the place up. But she felt the need to stay here and defend it, nonetheless.

'Where, then?' she asked him.

He shrugged. 'My estate is close enough to their camps. No doubt they're eyeing up my villages as we speak.'

'We have a country to run,' Loysse objected. 'Taking the court all that way is a luxury we can't afford.'

'I will go with Arnoul,' Auberi said. 'You stay in the Bastion with Alienor and keep things ticking over. Caisin, I think you should stay, too.'

Suspicious looks passed across the table, while Auberi simply sat there, apparently oblivious and above such things. Loysse didn't even know who had won the latest skirmish. *But the rope still holds, Loysse,* she told herself. *You haven't fallen yet.*

* * *

LOYSSE HAD her days with Alienor. It still surprised her how much time such a small, sweet thing could steal.

But even when with her daughter, the worries never truly went away. *Ezenachi has taken Morbaine. When will he turn his attention to the rest of Guivergne? Where is Peyre? When will I get news from Brasingia? What will come of my husband's and Saliers' meeting with the refugees? Why must a woman's role always be to stay home and wait for the men? I am sick of being left behind.*

Finally, Caisin sent word that her husband's force had returned to Valennes. She left Alienor with Brayda, and she and Syele made their way to the battlements of the Bastion. It was a clear day with a blue sky and the city looked most beautiful from this vantage point. But that kernel of apprehension lay deep within her. She had made sure the gates to the fortress were closed, and she wanted to see their arrival for herself.

'There,' Syele said.

The soldiers came into view, marching up the road to the Bastion. The standards of Famiens and Saliers were both held aloft. But as they neared, Loysse saw something was wrong. The leaders of the force rode at the front. She could see Arnoul, Benoit, Firmin, even that blackguard Robert of Auriac. But no Auberi. Among the standards was a long pole, topped by a decapitated head. Loysse gasped. 'Who—'

'It is Frayne, the Middian chieftain,' Syele said.

Relief flooded her, quickly followed by shame. 'Go fetch Brancat,'

Loysse said immediately.

Something was wrong. Very wrong. She watched as the force halted, the Bastion's moat a barrier between them and the fortress. She saw the looks of consternation and anger amongst her enemies. They gazed up at the walls, from where defenders armed with bows looked down.

Syele returned with Brancat.

'No Auberi?' he asked.

Loysse immediately felt stronger for his presence. A faithful servant to her family, she knew she could trust the man who had trained her brothers since they were children.

'No. I will demand an explanation.'

Brancat frowned. Loysse knew he was a little uncomfortable with her. Esterel had put her in charge, but to the castellan, she was just a young girl. He struggled to know his place. 'I am the castellan, Lady Loysse. I think it much better if I speak with him on your behalf.'

Syele gave Loysse a brief nod, and she relented. 'Very well.'

'Your orders?'

'Arnoul and his cronies are not getting in,' Loysse told him. 'And I need to know about my husband.'

'Of course.' Brancat made his way to the battlements directly above the spot where Saliers waited. Loysse stood close by, out of sight.

'Lord Saliers,' Brancat shouted down. He still had that training yard voice, and the soldiers gathered below quietened. 'The Bastion is sealed. I cannot permit entry to your force.'

'On whose orders?' Saliers shouted up.

'My orders, my lord.'

'You govern Guivergne now, do you?' Saliers asked, the surrounding men guffawing at the jibe.

'No. I am castellan of the Bastion, appointed by King Esterel.'

'Very well, Brancat. I will not argue with you on that score. But let's cut to the chase here. I claim lordship over Valennes and the Bastion. I am the only one in the kingdom ready to defend it. I have here the head of Frayne, an enemy of Guivergne. Know that if these gates are not opened forthwith, I shall bring another enemy here and have him executed. Lord Russell will be beheaded before these walls. You know the man, Brancat. Don't make me do it. And tell Lord Caisin and Duchess Loysse of my demands. Tell them I won't be leaving.'

'I understand,' Brancat said. 'And I ask you for the whereabouts of Duke Auberi.'

'Duke Auberi is safe,' Saliers replied. 'For now. But I cannot guarantee that forever.'

A chill ran down Loysse's spine at the words.

Brancat left the walls and approached Loysse. 'The bastard,' he hissed. 'I am sorry, Loysse. But whatever he threatens, I advise you do not open these gates. All could be lost if you do that.'

Loysse knew she was in shock. Her mind wouldn't think clearly, and she didn't know what to say. 'I don't understand how it has come to this,' she said at last.

'Agreed,' Syele said. 'To threaten Auberi with his soldiers there? Something has happened. Have the soldiers of Famiens given their loyalty to Saliers? Or at least, some of them? It is the only explanation I can see.'

'But Lord Russell—' Loysse said. 'I can't allow that. And he'll do it, you know. The bastard will do it.' She saw Syele and Brancat share a look.

'I think we should speak with Lord Caisin,' Syele suggested.

THERE HAD BEEN A LONG SILENCE. Caisin was rubbing the top of his head, as if encouraging his intellect to bear down on the problem. Loysse had a respect for the man's cleverness. She had never been completely sure about his loyalty. But as she studied him, she only saw concern, and when he lifted his head to look at her, there were tears in his eyes.

'I am sorry,' he said to her. 'But this is my thinking. Why on earth would Saliers dare to behave like this, when Esterel could return from Brasingia and destroy him? There is only one logical answer, and believe me, the man plays by cold logic. Nothing else. It must be something has happened to Esterel. Something serious. I fear your brother is dead, and Arnoul is making a play for the throne.'

Loysse stared at him. The world no longer made sense. Saliers was trying to get into the Bastion, and Caisin was telling her Esterel was dead.

'I don't want to believe it,' Caisin said, realising she wasn't going to say anything. 'I always thought, from the first moment I met him, that Esterel would be a great king. But he has faced a threat no mere king could stop.'

'But we would know,' Loysse said, trying desperately to find the lie. 'Messengers would have been sent to Valennes—'

'Yes. Then I realised. Saliers was given the town of Schilling and the land about it. He controls the road out of Barissia to Guivergne. If the message came via Coldeberg, he could have suppressed it. Used the knowledge to steal a march on us. He might have known your brother's fate for days.'

Loysse shook her head. 'Why would it have come from Coldeberg, not Essenberg?'

'Any answer to that would be a guess. But if the Turned invaded the empire, Esterel may have fought them in the south. The messengers would be sent from there.'

It made sense. It was an explanation for Saliers' behaviour. 'The snake,' she said. 'Pardoned by my father. And all this time, just waiting to pounce on us. Do you think he will have turned on Auberi?'

'It's hard to say. He may have won Auberi's soldiers over with his talk of foreign enemies. If Auberi was aware it was happening, he may have confronted Saliers, or gone along with it. You know him better than me.'

'He is vulnerable. He can't pick up on all the subtleties any longer. He needs me for that.' Loysse shivered. 'Gods, why did I let him go alone?'

'I recall he suggested that, Your Grace. But we must focus on what to do now.' He glanced up at Brancat, who had refused a chair and stood to attention by the table. 'Is there to be a siege? How long can we hold out? Can we trust those in the Bastion to stay loyal?'

'In theory, the Bastion can hold out for weeks,' Brancat said. 'When the enemy is our own people, the danger of betrayal is much higher. It would only take a few determined individuals to let them in.'

'We can't hold out,' Loysse said. 'He will kill Lord Russell. And then Auberi.'

'Russell wouldn't want you to open the gates for him,' Brancat said. 'Besides, he might be dead already.'

'No,' Loysse shook her head. 'Saliers wouldn't lie in front of his soldiers. He made a promise in front of them and he will carry it out.' She looked from the chancellor to the castellan. 'What is there to gain in holding out here? Saliers has the army. The Bastion will fall eventually.'

Brancat looked at her. 'If Saliers aims to be king, and Caisin's suppositions are correct, your life and that of your daughter are in grave danger. We can't let them take you.'

It was said with such simple sincerity that Loysse couldn't help but smile at him. But Loysse had lived all her life the daughter of a duke, then of a king, then the king's sister. She had always been a political misstep, a lost battle, away from an executioner's axe.

'If we turn this into a siege, Saliers will surround the Bastion, and he'll take it in the end. Then Alienor and I will be taken.'

'Agreed,' Caisin said. 'I'm sure you know there was a similar situation not so long ago. I escaped the Bastion with your brothers. It seems we must do something similar. Decide who goes, who stays, and act fast.'

'I agree,' Loysse said. 'I just hope I can trust you.'

'You can,' Caisin said.

'If not, I will give him justice,' Brancat declared.

'I will come or stay, as you wish,' Caisin said. 'But I suggest we tell no one else the plan until it is enacted. The fewer people who know, the less chance of information leaking.' He grimaced at Brancat. 'Or the more chance of knowing who leaked it.'

'Even if you escape the Bastion, what chance is there of making it out of the city?' the castellan asked, clearly concerned with the idea.

'The duchess will wear the cheapest clothes I can find, and a ragged cloak,' Caisin said. 'By the time she gets out of the moat, she'll smell just like she looks. People believe what they see, in my experience.'

THEY AGREED that Brancat and Caisin would stay and talk to Saliers from the battlements, stalling him while Loysse escaped. She had Alienor strapped to her chest. She sniffed the top of her head. 'Please be quiet, dear,' she asked her babe, almost pleading. Alienor tended not to complain while Loysse was moving. That gave her a sliver of hope.

Syele would be her companion. Brayda had her own family to care for. And Cebelia would struggle with literally every aspect of the escape. Brancat promised to explain it to them after Loysse had fled.

Only two men accompanied them. Loysse knew them by sight— the Lord Chancellor's enforcers, who carried out his dirty work. Ernst and Gernot, he named them. They had fled Valennes with Esterel and Peyre, and that reassured her. Thoughts of her brothers made her emotional, and she pushed them aside. She had a daughter to look out for now. That had to be her focus.

The four of them looked out from the tower door, on the opposite side of the fortress to where Saliers' force waited. The bank was clear. Part of her couldn't believe Saliers hadn't posted soldiers here yet. *Unless he has them hidden somewhere, spying on us. He doesn't,* she tried to convince herself. *His first instinct is to threaten people. And he assumes that will work.* She feared for Guivergne under his rule. But she knew she had to take this one chance at escape and worry about the rest of the world once she was safe.

'Time to go,' one of the men muttered. Ernst or Gernot, she didn't know the difference yet.

They opened the door and walked, in broad daylight, across the kill zone to the moat. Syele helped Loysse to lower herself in. She had to stop herself from crying out. It was freezing, and it stank so badly it made her eyes water. 'I'll never complain about your business again,' she whispered to Alienor.

LIESEL

ESSENBERG, DUCHY OF KELLAND

P lease, sit,' Idris said, offering her a chair.

He stood, a ball of barely contained energy, his torso uncovered as it always was these days.

The Atrabian had taken it upon himself to occupy the ducal apartments of Essenberg Castle. The apartments once inhabited by her father, brother, and husband. Now he invited her in and offered her a chair.

Liesel took it. She had so little fight left in her. They had buried Esterel in the crypt beneath the castle, where her father and the other dukes of Kelland had their tombs. It seemed wrong to Liesel. Everything about the situation was wrong, of course. But Liesel believed Esterel should have been laid to rest in Valennes, not here.

Esterel had become emperor of Brasingia and duke of Kelland. He had died on imperial soil, resisting an invasion. The people wanted to see him laid to rest, and Liesel accepted it all.

She had worn the widow's black and cried at her husband's casket. Yet it had all happened in a fog-like dream, in which one merely observes the events playing out. She was a spectator, one step removed from the action, with no control over what came next.

Now the funeral was over, all minds were on the election of Esterel's replacement. That was how the empire worked, and Liesel knew it as well as anyone. It was why she was here. Nothing surprised her anymore.

'Liesel. I love you.'

Alright. That surprised her. 'What?' she asked, as if being woken from the dream-like state of the last few days.

'I didn't think it would be such a surprise for you to hear. I've not hidden it, have I?'

Liesel looked at Idris's dark eyes, so deep that she felt she could never really know everything he was thinking. They sparkled now, as they did whenever he was up to mischief. 'I've only just buried Esterel,' she heard herself say, as if speaking the lines of a character in a fireside story. She felt like that was all she was capable of. She didn't really know what Liesel thought about anything.

'I know. And I am truly sorry. Do you believe me? I did genuinely like him. He would have made a great emperor. But this is where we are, Liesel. I intend to become emperor and I want you to be my empress. I want us to marry.'

Liesel shook her head. 'This is...wrong. To talk about such things.'

Idris frowned. 'What else should we be talking about?'

'Ezenachi. Brasingia. Dalriya. We need to save our world, Idris. And we have little time.'

'Agreed. And how do I do that? First, I must become emperor and unite Brasingia. With you by my side, that task will be so much easier. You are loved by so many, Liesel. Outside of Atrabia, I am thought a dangerous madman.'

'I don't—I can't. Marry you.'

A small sneer came to his face. 'Of course.' He gestured at his scarred and burned flesh. 'Because of this.'

'Not those physical things,' Liesel said. 'But because of who you have become.'

'Is it any wonder what I have become?' he asked her. There was passion in his voice now, the self-mockery gone. 'I was locked in a cell in this very castle for months. Beaten and tortured. My father was killed here. You remember that, don't you, Liesel? It was who gave me the news, after all.'

'Of course I remember,' Liesel said, pained that he could even ask.

'I survived. And they're dead. Your brother; Salvinus; and Inge—all dead. I rule where they once did. You wonder that I have become this strange monster?'

'You are not a monster, Idris. And I don't wonder at it. But I don't love you. Maybe I did when we were younger. But I don't want to marry you. I don't want to become your empress. I never made such a promise to you.'

'I could make you marry me,' he said. 'Many men would.'

'Perhaps. You want my gratitude that you wouldn't force me?'

Idris sighed. 'No. But I would know where you stand. You support your sister's husband over me?'

Jeremias had wasted no time in leaving for Rotelegen. There was an argument, among some, that he should be duke of Kelland. Katrina was the oldest child of Baldwin, and they had children. Jeremias was also easier to stomach for many than Idris.

'No,' Liesel said. 'And I don't think you need worry about him. You have four duchies, Idris, and with Gotbeck gone, it is four out of six. You are the one who spoke with Ezenachi and agreed a peace. I don't see anyone disputing your election.'

'Then what, Liesel? What else will you do? You have as much right to rule Brasingia as I do. It is what the people want. I wouldn't force you into my bed or any such. If you really care about Dalriya, you would do this.'

'It's hard to explain, Idris. You would think less of me.'

Idris groaned. 'Gods, nanny. Just spit it out.'

Liesel stared at her hands resting on her lap. 'After watching what that creature did to Esterel, I feel like I am locked in my own prison cell. The world around me is grey. Nearly invisible. My—' She swallowed and forced away tears. 'My flame has sputtered out, Idris. I feel like I am no use to you or anyone.' She looked up at him, fearful of his mockery or anger.

Idris had gone still. When he spoke, his voice was quiet, not like

Idris at all. 'I understand, Liesel. Every night I return to that cell.' He allowed himself a smile. 'Some nights you visit me, and bring colour to my world. I am sorry I can't do that for you. But I think someone, or something, will. Give it time.'

Liesel stood and walked over to her old friend. Neither had any more words, and they just clung to one another.

* * *

TEGYN VISITED HER.

'Idris told you about our conversation.'

Tegyn looked at her, her eyes so like her brother's. 'I got the gist. The man's version. Yours is probably ten times as long.'

Liesel smiled. She was still wary with Tegyn, worrying her loyalty was to Idris over her. But she didn't really think that was true. Tegyn had come as her friend.

They talked, and it helped. Liesel felt a bit more like herself. Yet there was still a hole inside her. She didn't know what to do or where to go. She was purposeless, and she hated herself for that, when the world needed people of purpose so desperately.

There was a knock at the door.

Tegyn was swift to go over. 'Florent,' she said.

'Let him in.'

Auriac entered the room. 'My lady,' he nodded at Liesel.

Released from his prison cell after Esterel's death, Liesel had done her best to avoid Florent. He wore a haunted look that said the death of his great friend and king was all his fault. Liesel couldn't stand to look at him, because of course that meant everything was her fault, as well.

His eyes flicked to Tegyn and back to Liesel. 'I request some words in private.'

'Tegyn is my friend. She can stay,' Liesel said.

'I understand. But I have been asked to speak to you without the presence of Lady Tegyn.'

'Why?' Tegyn demanded. 'It is unseemly to talk to Lady Liesel without another lady present.'

'It is alright, Tegyn,' Liesel said. 'I will find you afterwards.'

'It isn't alright,' Tegyn huffed.

'Tegyn,' Liesel repeated.

With great reluctance, her friend left and closed the door behind her. Liesel couldn't be sure she wasn't listening on the other side.

'I come with a message from Sacha, Lord of Courion,' Florent said.

All rather formal, Liesel thought. 'I see.'

'He has asked me to extend to you a formal offer of matrimony.'

'He what?'

'Sacha would like to marry you, Liesel. He has a great affection for you. What is more, he feels a duty to care for you after Esterel's death.'

Sacha? Liesel asked herself. *Her head spun. What is his game? Is this a play for the throne of Guivergne? Surely not when there is Peyre, Loysse, and her child? Is there anyone else going to propose to me today?*

Florent was studying her reaction. 'Sacha wanted me to make it plain that he doesn't want an immediate response. If, once you have considered it, you wish to decline, you can tell me. Sacha will never speak of it again, and there will be no awkwardness between you.'

'Florent, please thank Sacha for the offer. But tell him I do not wish to marry him, and I won't change my mind about that. I hope he will continue to be a good friend.'

'Of course he will. There is no need to even ask. Good day, my lady.'

Florent left, and Liesel took a few moments to process the visit. Was this her future now? A pawn in every ambitious man's plans?

She knew, as soon as she thought it, she was being unfair and self-centred. There were many people in worse situations than her. *Your husband is dead, Liesel*, she told herself. *Partly down to you. You have lost your titles. But your people are in danger. Time to stop wallowing and deal with it.*

* * *

178

THE SOLDIERS of Guivergne were restless. They had followed their great king and war leader into the empire, and won glory. Then watched, helpless, when Ezenachi killed him.

There were fights and unruly behaviour every day in the streets of the city until they were forbidden entry. But that wasn't a proper solution. Tegyn told Liesel about the conversations Idris had with Sacha, Domard, and the other lords of Guivergne. The soldiers wanted to return home, and no one saw the value in opposing their wishes.

Even Idris. According to his agreement with Esterel, he had inherited the kingdom of Guivergne as well as the duchies of Kelland and Barissia. He hadn't renounced his claim—that wasn't his style. But Idris was more capable of recognising reality than he let on, and agreed that the conquering army of Guivergne should leave Brasingia, even if that stripped the empire of its best fighting force. As a concession, Domard agreed to remain in Coldeberg with his force, and govern Barissia on Idris's behalf.

Liesel and Tegyn took their horses outside the city walls to watch the army leave. Sacha and Florent led them on the march northwest. It was a wrench to watch her arbalests go. She had created them— built the crossbows, trained the men and women, and there was a mutual bond of respect and affection. Still. From what she had heard about the Turned's invasion of Magnia and the Midder Steppe, Liesel knew they would be needed.

'Liesel, you are crying!' Tegyn said.

Liesel put a hand to her cheek and felt the wetness. 'I'm sorry. It hurts to see them leave without me.' She cast a glance back to Essenberg. 'And I have never had a love for this city.'

'So, you think you might go north, to Guslar?' Tegyn asked.

Liesel nodded, though she had little enthusiasm for that, either. Katrina and Jeremias would welcome her. She had no doubts about that. She had a niece and nephew to dote on. But what role would she have there? The sorry widow of Emperor Esterel, reliant on her family's goodwill? She repressed a shudder.

Tegyn was staring at her. 'Liesel?'

'What?'

'You don't want to stay in Brasingia. You want to return to Guivergne.'

'Of course I do,' Liesel said, only realising it was true as she said the words. 'But that's not possible. I am nothing but the foreign widow of the old king to them.'

'Nonsense,' Tegyn said firmly. 'Peyre and Loysse would be delighted to see you. Your arbalests—' Tegyn couldn't help a small look of distaste. 'You are their commander. Valennes is where you made your home. Esterel is gone, I know. But it was more than just him, wasn't it?'

Liesel bit her lip. 'Maybe. But I can't—'

'Yes, you can. You know very well you can ride and join them right this moment. I will tell Idris. At least then he won't be tempted to make you marry him.'

'I could. I suppose. But what about you?'

Tegyn sighed. 'I wish I could come with you, but not this time. Idris is about to be made emperor. He needs some help.'

'I understand.' Liesel reached over and they embraced. 'You're right. This is what I want. I must try, I suppose.'

'Of course,' Tegyn said.

Now it was her friend's turn to look tearful, and Liesel decided she wouldn't prolong the agony any longer. She nudged her mount until it was cantering after the army of Guivergne. She caught up with the lines of marching soldiers, feeling embarrassed and stupid at her appearance. But all she got were smiles and cheers of approval. *I do have a bond with these people*, she admitted, *more than I have with my own.*

With more confidence, she sped up, heading for the very front of the long column. She passed Florent, leading the warriors of Auriac. She saw him turn his head towards her and she looked away, pretending she hadn't seen him.

At the front, she found the army of Courion, the black and gold of their standard drawing her eye to where Sacha and Coleta rode. She approached brother and sister. They both turned to her, each of them offensively attractive. They even shared the same sorrowful look, the loss they had suffered etched on their faces. *Why does it make them look even more handsome, while I am puffy-eyed and ugly?*

Liesel fell in next to Coleta. 'I decided I wanted to return to Valennes. Even though Esterel is no longer there.'

They both nodded. There was no judgement, or hostility. Just understanding. At times, she had thought of them both as her enemies. But Esterel had loved them, and she should have known better.

'Esterel has left a hole in all our hearts,' Coleta said softly. 'But he would want us to carry on and do our best for Guivergne. The people need our help. I know there is very little I can do compared to you, Liesel. But I will do whatever I can.'

Liesel reached out a hand, and Coleta took it. 'Thank you, Coleta. I agree, we must all pull together.'

I think, she said to herself, *you loved my husband more than I ever did.*

PEYRE

DUCHY OF MORBAINE

They rode north, putting distance between themselves and the encounter with the Turned Middians. The mounts they had taken gave them a chance at escape. But they had also drawn attention, revealing themselves to the Caladri from the coast and the vossi coming from the south.

The Middian mounts were well-bred horses, and they navigated the rough terrain of northern Morbaine with ease. Peyre knew they had to make use of their new speed, because they hadn't escaped yet.

That became all too clear when he saw a line of soldiers spread out amongst the trees ahead of them. He shouted a warning, stopping his mount. 'Sea Caladri. They've got ahead of us.' He glanced at his friends. The hope generated by grabbing the horses had evaporated.

'They have bows,' Umbert warned.

His friend was right. Peyre could see the Caladri archers fixing arrows to their strings. Riding at them would be suicide. But the same could be said about going in any direction.

'So we're surrounded?' Inhan asked. The others already knew the answer to that.

Peyre looked at the young man. He'd already lost his hand in service to Peyre. *Why did I drag them into Magnia?* he asked himself. *The*

Shield. He took the relic, fixing the straps to his left arm. Then he drew his sword. 'Ride behind me. Let the Shield deflect their missiles.' He looked each one in the eye. 'Do you understand me?'

They nodded. Each knew the risk they took. But they would follow him.

Peyre pushed his Middian mount, encouraging it to charge towards the Caladri. It was reluctant, and he had to give it a kick and a slap to get it going. Even then, it wasn't as fast as he had hoped. He raised the Shield, hoping its radius of power would cover himself, the horse, and those who rode behind. It wasn't something he'd yet had time to test.

The Caladri targeted him, arrows flying in from left and right, as well as ahead. The Shield repelled most, sending them flying back towards the archers. Others got through. One skittered off his thigh; another embedded itself in his side. It felt more like a bruise than a deep wound. His mount was hit, and suddenly she was flying ahead, straight for the Caladri, who tried to stop them. Peyre parried one strike with his sword; stopped a second with his shield. His horse buffeted a third Caladri and broke through the line.

'Go on,' he encouraged, relieved to have got through. With some luck, it was a big enough gap for his friends to follow. He kept going, encouraging his mount to find a route through the trees, until he was sure there were no more Caladri lying in wait. Only then did he dare look behind him. He smiled as he saw four mounted figures following him, all clear of the Caladri.

Then his smile disappeared.

'Gosse!' he shouted, frantically trying to gesture while he gripped sword and shield. 'Umbert!'

Gosse turned around and just in time grabbed Umbert by the arm, supporting him. Umbert had gone white and had nearly toppled from his horse.

Ida was quick to dismount. He clambered onto Umbert's mount, while Gosse helped Umbert shift backwards. Once Ida was settled in the saddle, Umbert wrapped his arms around him.

Inhan checked behind them for danger.

Peyre nudged closer. An arrow protruded from Umbert's back. The bastard Caladri had got him as he escaped, probably at close range. The head of the arrow could have gone deep. 'Can you ride?' Peyre asked him.

Umbert looked at him. He was still pale, and his eyes weren't focused properly as he looked at Peyre. 'Yes,' he said.

'Alright,' Peyre said, unconvinced. 'We'll have to try. Gosse, please stay by their side.'

'Aye,' Gosse said. 'Anywhere we can stop nearby?'

If it wasn't for his concern for his friend, Peyre would have allowed himself a grim smile. 'Yes. We're not far from Arbeost. We just need to pray the way is clear.'

* * *

PEYRE LED THEM NORTH. They couldn't ride as hard as he would have liked for fear that Umbert would fall. Nevertheless, their progress was steady, and there were no more Turned waiting for them. Peyre reckoned they remained ahead of the enemy.

But then what? His mind kept circling around the problem. If they reached Arbeost with no more incident, there was still no reprieve waiting. Peyre recognised the childish part of him that believed, *if I can just get home, it'll be alright.* But no one was in Arbeost. It was deserted, just like the rest of Morbaine. There were no friends or family waiting to lend their strength and fight with him. His father had passed; his brother was in Brasingia; Brancat was in Valennes. Sanc, who might have saved him with some sorcerous spell, was in some other world.

Arbeost was no stronghold. His family's chateau was constructed with defence in mind, but the five of them stood no chance against the thousands chasing them.

That left the Forest of Morbaine. Dense and dangerous, the forest was no haven. From what Ida had told him, the vossi would be more at home there than they were.

The only sliver of hope Peyre could find was that if they entered the forest, maybe the Turned wouldn't follow. They had respected borders in the past. Once they'd taken Magnia, they stopped before moving on to Morbaine. What if Ezenachi's orders were to conquer Morbaine, and in their slave-like bewitchment, they simply stopped once they reached the border with Guivergne?

Is that truly all you have? he demanded of himself, a wretched feeling overwhelming him.

'Peyre,' Gosse called over.

The warrior had Umbert in his arms. Peyre steered his mount over and helped him get a hold of his friend. Umbert was mumbling incoherently, close to losing consciousness. Between them, they carefully lifted him off Ida's horse and laid him on his stomach in front of Gosse. Peyre snapped the arrow sticking out of his back, making it less likely to get caught.

Everyone looked at him.

'We're close to Arbeost now,' he told them. 'When we get there, we can treat him and allow him to rest.'

It was a lie, and a bad one at that. But they kept moving, picking up the pace a little. The noise of the vossi could still be heard behind them. Peyre hated their mindless screams, but it had the advantage of telling him how far behind the enemy were.

The tracks Peyre followed became more familiar, reminding him of the rides he and Umbert had enjoyed as young men. His friend was suffering now. Peyre wasn't sure if he would make it, even if they were granted some rest. Which was impossible.

Then he heard a new sound. He looked to the right. There, among the trees, a hundred yards away. Half a dozen Middian horsemen. They were tracking his band's progress, keeping their distance for now. Peyre kept an eye on them as he connected with the path that led to his old home. After a while, one of them rode off, disappearing southeast. *Reporting on our whereabouts. We're screwed.*

At last, Arbeost came into view. It hadn't changed at all, as if held in time. Apart from the fact it was deserted. They passed the fields on each side of the path, then came to the houses. On the east side lay the church and paddocks—emptied, of course. On the west, the mill, the stream, and Brancat's training grounds. Ahead, the path ended at his old home.

Peyre dismounted, then helped with Umbert. He got him to the ground, then had to wrestle with him to stop him from lying on his back.

'No, Umbert, on your front. Or at least on your side.'

He looked at the wound. The arrow had pierced through the chain mail and padding Umbert was wearing, leaving a mangled mess. It would be an ordeal to remove the arrowhead, and he doubted that was a good idea.

'What do you think?' Gosse asked him.

'To slice through the mail like that, I'm guessing it's a bodkin. In which case, we might pull it out relatively easily. But we don't have the resources to treat him. He'd likely bleed out. If I'm wrong, and it's a broadhead, we might kill him getting the thing out.'

'Then we'll fetch what we can find from this house and bandage him,' Gosse suggested.

Peyre stood, looking at his companions. 'It will take time to sort this out. Time we don't have. The Turned know we are here and will soon have numbers enough to take us. I will take Umbert inside and stay with him. We'll hold out for as long as possible. You three need to take the Shield. Cross through the forest into Guivergne.'

'You're here because I wanted to return to Magnia,' Ida said. 'I'll not desert you.'

'I'm staying,' Gosse said, so firmly Peyre knew he had no chance of dissuading him.

'Me too,' said Inhan.

'No, Inhan,' Peyre said. 'One of us needs to escape this mess. It has to be you. Take two horses. Tell my sister what happened here.'

'But—'

'That's an order, Inhan.'

'I refuse it.'

Peyre stared at him, disbelieving.

'Peyre,' Gosse said quietly. 'You can't send a man on their own through the forest. He likely won't make it, anyway. He has earned the right to stay and fight with the rest of us.'

'Gods!' Peyre hissed. He knew the anger boiling within him wasn't Inhan's fault. 'I'm sorry, Inhan. We'll all stay.'

'It's all academic, anyway,' Ida said, gesturing down the path they had taken to the chateau.

Two dozen Turned riders walked their horses towards them. The screams of the vossi were growing in volume. Soon they would be here as well.

Peyre shook his head. The miraculous escape on the river. The capture of the Middian horses. All for nothing. He had taken the Shield of Persala. For nothing.

Then there were the other parts of his life. Things left undone and unsaid. Unbidden, a roar of pain and anguish erupted from within him. He tilted his head to the sky and let it out, the sound so loud and disturbing that his companions had to grab the reins of the skittish Middian horses they had taken.

'Alright,' he said when he was done. 'Let's get Umbert inside. The horses, as well. We can hold out for a little while.'

They wasted no time in following Peyre's orders, getting Umbert settled comfortably on furs in the main hall. Peyre rushed to make the chateau defensible. He raised the drawbridge, preventing the enemy from getting easy access to the only entrance. Made from stone and wood, the building had been built with a mix of comfort and defence in mind. It certainly couldn't withstand a prolonged siege. If the Turned used fire, they would be in trouble. But the defences gave them some time to gather themselves.

Gosse and Ida worked together on bandaging Umbert's wound, while Inhan made a small fire to keep him warm.

Something made Peyre leave them to it. He wondered what stopped him from settling for a few brief moments and helping his best friend. *There's something wrong with me*, he told himself. *I can't accept when I'm beaten. I always thought I was meant for greatness. It hurts to stop and look reality in the face.*

He made his way up to the first floor of his chateau. From here, he could look out from an embrasure on the enemy. In the short time since entering the chateau, a significant force had gathered outside. He could see and hear the vossi, who had run all the way here. More kept coming, in ones and twos—surely exhausted from their efforts. There were more horsemen, perhaps a hundred now. As he watched, a unit of Caladri appeared.

Soon, there would be thousands of Turned, ready to take the last piece of Morbaine from him. For now, they stood about aimlessly, the different peoples joining together with no apparent thought given to where they might position themselves or how to break in. No leadership.

If it was me out there, I'd be demolishing the houses and making ladders, or firebrands. How is it that an enemy with such obvious weaknesses is beating us? He studied them, eyes straining. He knew himself well enough to know why. He was still searching for a way out, even when they were cornered. *Even when we've lost.*

Then he saw something that made his mouth hang open, his mind unable to process it. Plodding around the chateau from his left, and heading for the Turned, was a great, brown and grey-coloured monster. It walked on all fours, with clawed feet and a long tail. Peyre could feel his heart beat faster and his body prepare for fight or flight, even though he was safe behind the walls. Most curious of all, though, was the boy who sat atop the thing in a saddle.

He couldn't help but stare at the sight, which meant it took a few moments before he noticed the others. Three more of the creatures, one red, one blue, and one green—each with a single rider—followed the first. In the sky, he saw what looked like a woman. She was flying, standing atop a rug. Then, some distance behind the monsters, three more figures followed. Two rode horses, while the third rode a creature significantly larger that moved differently to either horse or monster.

A red blast lanced across the scene. The woman had sent a missile into the vossi, sending half a dozen sprawling to the ground. The vossi screamed in defiance and threw their darts into the sky.

They're attacking the Turned, Peyre realised. He tried to shout at his friends, telling them to come and see. But no words came. He was too intent on watching what was unfolding before his eyes.

The Turned held their ground. It made them so different from any other armed force, which would surely have broken and fled by now. But as the four giant monsters lumbered towards them, the horses took it upon themselves to flee. They turned and bolted, racing away in all directions, their riders unable to control them. More than one rider pulled too hard on the reins and was rewarded with being bucked off and dumped onto the ground.

Those infantry that remained moved to meet the newcomers in battle. But more magic lanced into their ranks, and then the great monsters were on them, hitting out with their claws and snapping down with their sharp teeth.

Peyre watched the Turned get eviscerated and, at last, the sight woke him from his stupor. He left his spot and ran down the spiral staircase to the hall. Everyone looked up at his wild entrance, save Umbert, who had given in to sleep.

'I need to go out there,' Peyre said. He grabbed the Shield of Persala from the floor, strapping it to his left arm. 'The Turned have been driven away!'

'By who?' Gosse asked.

'I don't know.' Peyre wasted no time in getting to the front of the chateau and pulling on the drawbridge mechanism. He felt a hand on his arm.

'Are you sure?' Gosse asked him, looking concerned.

'Yes.' Peyre considered explaining what he had seen, but thought that might make his companions even more doubtful.

Gosse helped him lower the drawbridge, while Ida removed the locking bars from the gate. The three of them pushed it open and his two friends gasped. Approaching them was the largest of the creatures. It was a lizard—green, covered in scales, with thick limbs.

The rider peered down at them, frowning. 'We thought we heard someone shouting.' He looked at Peyre. 'You look familiar. And that shield I know very well.' He glanced to Peyre's left and nodded. 'Prince Ida.'

'*King* Ida,' the Magnian replied.

'Ah. I'm sorry. Forgive me. We have only just returned to Dalriya, and we're ignorant of what has happened the last couple of years. We didn't know what to expect.' He glanced behind him, to where he had helped destroy the Turned. 'Seems things aren't so good.'

Peyre put together the man's words. 'You're Herin?'

'Alas, that's true.'

'Is my brother here? Sanc?'

'Aye. He's on the blue, spiked one. Insists on giving it a name—'

But Peyre heard no more. He sped past Herin, not even considering how close he was to those huge lizard fangs until after he'd run past. The rest of Herin's group had dismounted and were examining the bloody remains of the Turned they had killed.

'Sanc!' Peyre cried.

A man turned at his call. It wasn't Sanc, though. It was a burly, bearded, long-haired warrior. And yet. His eyes were red. 'You came back?' Peyre asked.

Sanc smiled. 'Peyre!' He strode over and they embraced. Peyre fought away tears as they separated.

'I'm back,' Sanc said. 'I'm sorry it's taken us so long. I hope I'm not too late?'

Peyre stared at him, hardly believing what was in front of him.

As for his brother's question, he wasn't sure how to answer that.

LOYSSE

VALENNES, KINGDOM OF GUIVERGNE

Alienor fussed and fretted. Loysse put her to her breast again. It was the only thing that kept her quiet. It was impossible to keep her silent all day. And wrong. But they were in a precarious position and Loysse had little choice.

Ernst and Gernot had got them out of the Bastion, and past Saliers' guards, who manned the walls of the city. But they had only gone as far as East Valennes, and the first safe house. It was Loysse's first time in the east side of the city. It was a sprawling jumble of a place. But that made hiding easier. Even so, Caisin's agents had already moved them once. Loysse's face was well known amongst the people. They had to be cautious.

Meanwhile, Saliers had let it be known he was looking for mother and baby, with a large reward for any information. Any sound of a baby crying would alert those who worked and lived nearby. Any of them might decide they wanted the coin Saliers was offering. Loysse couldn't help feeling paranoid and fearful. She did her best to keep her emotions at bay, knowing they would transfer to Alienor.

Footsteps. Syele appeared. Her one companion in all of this. The warrior kept lookout; kept her fed; kept her sane. Loysse thanked Peyre daily for putting Syele at her service. She couldn't imagine how much worse it would have been alone. But Syele's face was grim, and Loysse felt her heart flutter.

'There's a patrol,' the Barissian said.

Another one. Loysse glanced at the rickety ladder that led up to the loft space. 'Do we have to?'

Syele nodded. Sighing, Loysse stood and gently rocked her babe. The fat little piglet was so full of milk, surely she would sleep? Slowly, she detached Alienor, still rocking her back and forth. Syele had already clambered up to the loft.

Loysse carried Alienor to the ladder and took the first step. She hated this. The ladder was so spindly, she was sure it would break every time she put her weight on it. Second step, cradling Alienor in one arm. Then, the worst bit. Taking the babe in both arms, she raised her up, while Syele leaned down and took Alienor under the arms, lifting her up to the loft space. Relieved, Loysse quickly followed them up.

Syele returned Alienor to her, then pulled up the ladder, before placing a wooden board over the hole. It was dark, cramped, and stuffy in the little space. Loysse hated it. She was convinced there were mice or rats living up here. She sat with Alienor in her lap, waiting for her eyes to adjust to the sudden lack of light. Syele's form moved to the gap in the roof where she could look down on the street below.

'You think they know we're here?' Loysse asked her.

'No. They're carrying out door-to-door searches. Well, look who it is.'

'Who?'

'Benoit, Arnoul's brat. They're certainly taking it seriously.'

Of course they were. Saliers wanted to be king, and that meant he wanted Loysse and Alienor dead.

Yet again, she questioned whether she had been right to run when she did. Saliers was now master of the Bastion, Caisin and Brancat deciding it was better to surrender the fortress than face a siege. If she had stayed, she might have been in Arnoul's clutches by now. But would he have dared have her murdered under the noses of the Guivergnais nobility? Out here, in the lawless east of the city, they could be slain, then dumped somewhere, and no one would ever know.

'We need to get out of the city. Head north, for Famiens.'

Syele grunted. 'They'll be expecting that. He'll have people out on the roads, asking at every town and village. The same if we were to try to head south. If we can hold out here a bit longer, they'll tire of looking.'

Such arguments were convincing, and Loysse always bowed to them. Until the next patrol came looking for them, and she was convinced they were fools to stay. The truth was, anything they did carried a risk.

Three loud bangs on the front door downstairs. Benoit's soldiers had reached their little house. It was one in a row of terraced buildings, crammed together. The only reason this one didn't collapse was because its neighbours leaned on it from both sides.

They waited, looking at one another. Their breathing sounded too loud in the silence. Another three knocks, someone giving the door a good pounding. It was liable to fall off its hinges. Alienor stirred. Loysse began to rock her. The floorboards she sat upon creaked. Syele stared at her, eyes wide. *What am I supposed to do?* Loysse wondered. *Creak the boards, or let her cry?*

They waited, each moment that passed feeling like an age. Then the sound Loysse was dreading. They were kicking the door down.

'Move,' Syele hissed, the sound of panic in the woman's voice flooding Loysse with fear.

This was their plan of last resort, but Loysse knew she had no choice but to follow it. Getting off her feet into a crouch, wary of banging her head against the rafters, she retreated into the darker confines of the loft. Holding Alienor tight, she squeezed through the small gap into next door's loft. With no light here, she put a hand down and felt her way along a wooden beam. Putting her weight to either side of it might result in her crashing through the ceiling of next door's house. When she walked into a cobweb, the strands sticking to her face and hair, she decided she had gone far enough.

'Here,' Syele whispered.

Loysse reached out a hand, clutching at empty air until her fingers closed on cold steel. She took the warrior's knife—one of many Syele carried about her person—and tucked it into a boot.

Then, Syele closed the gap between lofts with a wooden board. Loysse thought it had been dark before, but she supposed she must invent a new word for this. She shivered. Alienor didn't stir. Perhaps the darkness had its benefits.

All Loysse could do now was listen. Although faint, she could hear men's voices. She wracked her brain. Had they left signs of habitation? Probably. They'd had little time to react to the patrol's arrival. Her mind turned to the wooden board covering the way into the loft. It wasn't hard to miss. If Benoit's soldiers saw it, would they look up here? If they did, what would happen? She knew Syele wouldn't go without a fight.

She realised she was holding her breath and took in some air, trying to stay calm. It was strange how quickly time became impossible to measure in the darkness. Her ears were tuned to the neighbouring loft space where Syele waited. Would she hear the scrape of wood that told her their hiding place had been discovered?

When she did, she nearly leapt to her feet in shock. She needed all her control to stay still. She could hear a man's voice, alarmingly close. It sounded like he was muttering down to his fellows. A series of male grunts suggested they were heaving him into the loft space. Loysse heard him scrabbling up. A few moments of silence. Then, a horrible, throaty rasp.

Sound exploded. Men shouting. Thuds. A crash. A scream of pain. *A man's scream*, Loysse tried to assure herself. *It was a man's scream.*

Alienor made a cry of complaint.

No, darling. Not now. Loysse fumbled at her top and gave her baby her breast.

Downstairs, it had gone silent. Alienor's feeding sounded deafening in the small space. *It's not*, Loysse tried to convince herself. What had happened to Syele? She waited for the sounds of discovery, of soldiers clambering up to capture her. She heard nothing.

· · ·

LOYSSE STIRRED and took a few panicky moments to remember where she was. *I fell asleep?* She felt Alienor still clamped to her breast. She moved her hand to detach her when she realised why she had woken. On the other side of the slim wooden partition, there was light. *A lantern,* she suspected. *Someone is searching.*

She froze, not daring to move. Her eyes fixed on the piece of wood separating the two spaces. *Can they see me through it? No, or else I could see them.*

There was no sound coming from the other loft space, but she could sense someone was there. Only a few feet away from where she sat, feeling more vulnerable than she ever had in her life. It was unnerving, and worse—somehow she knew who it was. Benoit. If he'd sent a soldier up to do the looking, there would be conversation back and forth. But that wasn't his style. If his men had captured Syele, or killed her, or even if she had escaped and left her victims behind—he would want to come and see for himself. Some sense told her she was right.

The light moved, flickered, and receded. She heard him clambering down the steps. She thought she caught the muted sound of conversation, but couldn't be sure. Silence returned. Loysse didn't dare move. She sat still, her back aching after being in the same position for so long, her arms aching from holding Alienor. She didn't know how long she waited. Finally, Alienor began to cry, and the noise shook Loysse into action. She lifted her daughter and gave her a sniff.

'I'm surprised no one smelt you,' she told her.

I can't stay here forever.

She pushed herself along the beam to the wooden board, doing her best to slide it away without making a noise. She clambered through the gap, emerging into the other loft. Too late, she realised she had dragged herself through a pool of blood. She looked down into the house below, knowing that if anyone had been stationed there, they would have found her. Satisfied it was empty, she looked around for the ladder. She saw it, propped against a wall. Relief flooded her.

'Wait here, darling,' she said, putting her down, as far from the blood as she could. Alienor was nowhere near capable of rolling about yet. Loysse sat on the edge of the hole, dangling her legs. She peered down. It wasn't such a large drop. She turned over on to her stomach, hands grasping at the loft floor, and inched her way farther out, until her stomach was over the drop. She moved her hands to the edge of the drop and let herself down. For a moment, she hung there, then she lost her grip and fell. Her feet hit the floor first, then she fell backwards onto her bottom.

She sat there for a moment, checking for any injuries. There was no harm done. Her eyes caught sight of the ladder and she got herself to her feet.

Behind her, the door of the house burst open.

LOYSSE

VALENNES, KINGDOM OF GUIVERGNE

The door of the house burst open.

Loysse turned to see two leather clad soldiers coming for her, weapons drawn. She had no time to review her options before they were on her, one of them grabbing both arms while the second held a short sword to her neck. They were whooping with delight, a sound that terrified her.

'He was right!' the swordsman crowed, while the other began dragging Loysse out of the house. 'And you said it was a waste of time,' he added to his friend, as they took her into the street.

'I didn't say that,' said the second soldier moodily.

'It doesn't matter,' his colleague continued joyfully, as they led Loysse past the terraced houses.

It was evening, the summer sun shedding the last of its rays across the sky. Loysse had a leaden feeling in her stomach. She yanked at the man who held her, hoping a sudden show of strength might surprise him, but he held her tight.

His colleague frowned and gave Loysse a slap across her face. She stumbled from the force of it. No one had ever struck her like that before. What was worse, the offender wasn't even looking at her anymore, totally disinterested. He had turned back to his friend.

'Doesn't matter, because we're going to get more coin in one go than everything we've earned up to now.'

Loysse's head was spinning. She had to accept that they could kill her at any moment. Then, there was Alienor. She was still in the house's loft. She had to do what was best for her daughter.

'That's true,' said the man holding her, brightening. A thought seemed to cross his mind. 'Where's your daughter?' he asked Loysse.

'Syele took her.' Loysse hadn't been sure what she would say before she was asked—it just came out. Somehow, she managed to sound convincing. Now she just had to hope that was the right decision.

'Syele? That bitch who killed Greg and Os?'

'Aye, well. We'll track her down before too long.'

So, Syele had escaped. And they hadn't caught her. Loysse grabbed on to the hope that provided. Maybe Syele would return to the house and find Alienor.

They led Loysse to a building much larger than the one she had been hiding in. Her captors didn't knock, simply walking her in. The aroma of beer told her it was an inn. She took in a bar and tables. Armed soldiers had taken over one area, perhaps a dozen in all. The patrons turned to stare as she was guided in and propelled towards this area.

Loysse's heart sank. A man stood, a smile of delight on his face. Robert, son of Raymon. She would have preferred Benoit, or even Arnoul. She would have preferred anyone.

'Take her to my room,' Robert said, a chilling, hungry look on his face.

Loysse allowed them to lead her to a set of stairs that led up. She wanted to fight, but what could she do? Instead, dark thoughts entered her mind. It was no longer about whether Robert would kill her. It was about how he would do it, and she wondered whether she had the strength to take what was coming.

They took her to a room above the lounge. She was guided in, and finally the soldiers released her arms.

Robert stared at her as if he couldn't believe his luck. 'She was in the house?'

'Aye. Heard her before we saw her. How did you know she'd be there, my lord?'

'In fairness, it was Benoit's idea to keep an eye on the place. His cleverness is our reward, eh, lads? And the babe?'

'Wasn't there. Just her. She says the Barissian woman has the daughter.'

Robert frowned at that. 'I doubt it. Did you do a search?'

'Well. The babe wasn't with her—' said the first soldier, looking uncomfortable.

'And we thought you'd want her brung as soon as,' the second added.

'Go back and search that damned house!' Robert ordered, his chummy demeanour vanishing.

The two soldiers left, and Loysse found herself alone with Robert. He shut the door and turned to her with his hungry smile. 'I've waited a long time for my chance at revenge on your family. I'll never get to punish Esterel, who had my father killed and stole my inheritance.'

So, it was true. Esterel was dead.

He looked at her reaction. 'You didn't know?'

'Not for sure.'

He studied her for a while. Loysse sensed his emotions were torn. *Is he deciding what to do with me?*

'It surprises me,' he said, 'but I actually feel sorry for you. You know, growing up in Arbeost, I always liked you. More than the rest of your family. Sometimes I even imagined marrying you. Taking you to live in Auriac. Stupid, maybe,' he said, with a quick look at her, as if hoping it hadn't been so stupid.

Your life is on the line, Loysse. Play this well. 'Not so stupid,' she made herself say, her voice barely above a whisper.

'Yet you married Famiens, while I had my lands taken from me.' Suddenly he was angry; accusatory. Dangerous.

'My father made me marry Duke Auberi.' There was no lie there.

'That's true enough. You know Saliers will kill you?'

'I'm not surprised to hear it.'

'I'd rather you were kept alive. Funny how your brother Peyre became bosom friends with Arnoul and Benoit while I was cast out. Yet they're the ones who want to see you and your daughter dead.'

Loysse struggled to know what to say. 'You think Auberi will stand to have his daughter killed?'

'Auberi will never know about it. He's basically a captive now. He only knows what we tell him.'

Loysse felt close to panic, which might rob her of the chance to talk her way out of this. She had to take a gamble. 'Then you're the only one who can save me,' she said.

Robert's eyes bored into hers, then roved over her body. Loysse desperately tried to hide her revulsion. 'I suppose I am,' he said at last. 'What reward would I receive for saving your life, Loysse?'

'Anything.'

Suddenly, he was striding over, the distance between them closed in a moment. Both hands were on her and his lips were pressing into hers. She took a step backwards, and he followed, pressing her up against the wall. His lips pressed into hers again, his tongue forcing its way into her mouth. She turned her face away, and he nuzzled at her neck.

'My daughter?'

He backed off a little. Annoyed. 'What about her?'

'I need to know she's safe.'

'Is she at the house?'

'Yes. In the loft.'

'Then my men will fetch her.'

'I need to see her.' She tried a winning smile—tried to pretend she wasn't disgusted and terrified.

'See her after.' He grabbed her by the arms, dragging her back into the centre of the room. She resisted, and he pulled all the harder. 'You're ungrateful, Loysse. After I said I would help you.' He threw her onto the bed.

She looked up at him. A stupid, selfish man child. Esterel was dead, killed by Ezenachi. And all Robert could think about was forcing himself on a woman in need. A fiery anger burned away her fear. 'You're right,' she said, patting the bed.

Robert didn't waste any time. He lay down next to her, mouth at her neck, hands on her chest. Oblivious of Loysse reaching into her boot.

She stabbed him in the neck. How many times, she couldn't say. More than was strictly necessary, that was for sure. She stopped, pushed his body off, and got to her feet. Robert and the bed were soaked in blood. She was covered in blood. She was shaking. She wanted to scream, and bit her lip until she tasted blood.

'Get it together,' she muttered.

She had to fetch Alienor. But how would she get through the common room, full of Robert's soldiers, looking like this?

Think, Loysse, she demanded. But her mind didn't want to think. It wanted her to look at Robert, mouth wide open and eyes staring like a gaping fish.

The door swung open. Loysse turned in alarm as someone burst into the room.

It was Syele. The Barissian stopped, looking at Robert laid out on the bed. 'I see you used my knife, then.'

Loysse's jaw was working, but she struggled to get any words out. 'Alienor's still at the house. In the loft. We need to go. Robert's men are headed there.'

'No, she's not,' Syele said. She walked back out of the room, bent down, and picked up a bundle.

Loysse had to stop herself from squealing in relief. She rushed over, grabbing her baby from Syele. Alienor seemed none the worse for wear.

'I got out of the house,' Syele explained. 'I had to run for it. But when I knew I'd lost them, I doubled back to the street. I nearly went back for you, but at the last moment I saw they had the place under surveillance. I decided to wait for night time. Big mistake. They grabbed you. I knew Alienor was still inside, so I figured I ought to get her first.'

'Of course.'

'Then I got a bit of luck when I saw your captors leaving this place without you.'

'Thank you, Syele. We'd better go.' Loysse made to leave the room.

Syele put a hand up, stopping her. 'We can't go out the front door! Robert's men are down there.'

'Oh. I thought—'

'You thought I'd massacred the lot of them? I'm not nearly as bloodthirsty as you, it seems.'

'Don't, Syele. I can't bear to look at him.'

'I came in through a window. We'll leave the same way. First things first, that daughter of yours needs a clean. It's so bad I'm surprised no one smelt me coming.'

SANC

ARBEOST, DUCHY OF MORBAINE

It had been strange enough, returning to his childhood home and finding it deserted. Peyre's appearance felt even more bizarre. But more sombre feelings soon took over, as Peyre delivered a roll call of the people who had fallen since Sanc's absence. Rimmon was the hardest loss to take. Killed by Jesper of all people when the Haskan was captured by Ezenachi. It had happened only days after Sanc had left for Silb.

How he had wanted to see his teacher again. How he had wanted someone else to help him shoulder the burdens he carried.

Herin took the news even worse than Sanc. He walked into the forest, not heeding the warnings about the Turned in the area.

Peyre and Ida told him about King Edgar's death. About how Jesper and Belwynn had gathered the seven weapons of Madria once more, and how those champions were now the slaves of Ezenachi. Including Ida's mother, Elfled. Esterel's friend Miles had been killed in a war with Brasingia. Half the dukes of the empire were dead because of it, and Esterel had made himself emperor.

All the while, Ezenachi had been extending his control. Sanc blamed himself for taking so long to return. But he also wondered at the actions of the rulers of Dalriya. With Rimmon gone, it seemed they had ignored the threat to the south. Perhaps that was unfair. All Sanc could say for sure was that the world he had returned to felt unrecognisable.

They stood in his family's chateau, long deserted, like the rest of Morbaine. Umbert was laid out on the floor of the main hall, unconscious. Sanc was upset to see him laid so low, an arrow still lodged in his back. He turned to Mergildo. The Rasidi champion was the only one who commanded magic that might help. 'Can you do anything?'

'Is he important to our task?' Mergildo asked. 'It would take considerable effort.'

'What's he say?' Peyre asked.

Sanc raised a warning hand to his brother. 'He is.'

Mergildo looked at him sceptically. There was more than a little tension amongst the seven sorcerers who had teleported from Silb to Dalriya. Sanc had gathered them, persuading them, and the rulers of Silb, that intervention here was necessary. To protect Silb from Ezenachi's return. But that didn't make him the leader. Each of them was an equal, and Sanc had no power to command Mergildo to do anything.

With obvious reluctance, Mergildo knelt next to Umbert and examined the wound. He placed a hand on Umbert's back, the protruding arrow between his thumb and forefinger. Sanc watched as the flesh of Umbert's back writhed, weeping fluid that pooled on the floor. With a strangled noise, Peyre turned and walked away. There was a part of Sanc that wanted to do the same.

Instead, he remained transfixed. He watched as the arrow was pushed out by Umbert's own body until Mergildo could simply take the end and remove it with no resistance. Slowly, the flesh settled. Not healed—not at all. It was red, raw and swollen. But the arrow was out, and without the internal damage that such a procedure normally caused.

'It needs to be bandaged and kept moist,' Mergildo said.

Sanc repeated his words.

'I will fetch what we have,' Peyre said. 'And tell him thanks,' he added, a little reluctantly. 'You think he will be alright?'

Again, Sanc had to act as translator.

'He needs to rest,' Mergildo said. 'Moving him will be dangerous.'

'We'll have to come up with a plan,' Sanc replied.

The brothers scoured the chateau for material that could be used as a bandage.

'I've told you about events in Dalriya,' Peyre said. 'No doubt you have your own stories to tell.'

'That's true enough. But we only have time for the essentials. First, I discovered Ezenachi came here from Silb, the continent I travelled to.'

'Came here...?'

'I believe he made the connection between Silb and Dalriya, that allowed me to travel back and forth. He came here because he was defeated in Silb. There are seven peoples who live there, and each has a champion. When they first came to Silb, it was these champions who drove Ezenachi away. My assumption—my hope—is that we can do it again, here in Dalriya.'

'Each champion has sorcery?'

'Yes.'

'And together, they defeated Ezenachi? Took this land called Silb from him.' Peyre thought about it. 'But they didn't kill him?'

It hadn't taken his brother long to find the weakness in Sanc's plan. 'They didn't kill him. It's impossible to know exactly what happened. These events are more legend than history. But I have returned with the only people who have a chance of defeating him.'

'Of course. You've done well, Sanc. I'm just wondering what the next steps should be.'

'I need to get you and your friends out of here. Then the seven of us will face Ezenachi.'

'You'll have a job finding him first.'

'I know where he is.'

Peyre looked at Sanc. 'Magic,' he said, with that same distaste he'd always had. Never mind that magic may have just saved Umbert's life; or that it was the only chance they had of stopping Ezenachi. *Did I really think that would change?* Sanc asked himself. He tried to understand his brother's reaction. He had powers that Peyre didn't—powers that Peyre didn't even comprehend. Perhaps it was only normal, in Peyre's position, to feel threatened.

By the evening, Umbert had recovered consciousness, and it seemed like he was on the mend. He was as pleased to see Sanc as Peyre had been.

When Herin returned, it was time to decide on their next move. They sat at table in the main hall, sharing a meal of whatever provisions they could muster. Peyre's friends looked warily at the champions Sanc had brought from Silb.

Those champions were more wary of one another than they were of the inhabitants of Dalriya. They possessed a confidence, derived from their abilities, which stayed with them even in this foreign world.

Sanc repeated once more the knowledge he had gleaned about Ezenachi, and his belief—a better word than hope—that he and the six sorcerers could defeat him. 'I can see where he is. Last time I looked, he was in the south of the Empire.'

'Actually inside the Empire's borders?' Peyre asked.

'Yes.'

'Then I fear for Esterel and the others. I need to get out of here as soon as possible.'

'Agreed,' Sanc said. 'Herin?'

'I would ask to come with you. I suppose I offer little. Only my sword. But I would dearly like to see Ezenachi dead, and his slaves freed. I'd be happy to lay down my life for it.'

'You offer plenty that no one else does, Herin. Where we go is no place for Rab,' Sanc said, turning to Peyre. 'Could you take him with you?'

'Of course. But I'm not sure how we can escape Arbeost once you leave.'

'I've thought about that, and discussed it with Kepa,' he said, nodding at the Teld champion. He allowed himself a gleeful smile at the thought of what was in store for his brother. 'She has agreed to take you north.'

PEYRE

KINGDOM OF GUIVERGNE

Umbert groaned next to him, holding onto Rab for comfort. They flew through the sky, so high that the trees down below were nothing more than specks of colour. The dog was dealing with the experience far better than Peyre's friend. To be fair, Umbert was still wounded. Peyre resolved not to rib him about it until he was recovered.

Peyre loved it. The wind on his face; through his hair. The thrill he got from the speed and the height started deep in his belly and spread throughout his body. When Kepa began the descent to solid ground, disappointment blanketed him. Back to reality, and all the difficulties that came with it.

He stepped off the roll of carpet, seemingly the only thing that had kept them from falling to the ground. Not that he really thought it was the carpet itself. It was sorcery. He still didn't trust magic, but that experience had warmed him to it a little.

He supported Umbert as his friend got to his feet and hobbled off. Rab pit-pattered off, and his other companions—Gosse, Ida, and Inhan, followed. Gosse staggered for a few steps back on solid ground, then pretended he hadn't, and stared about the group to see if anyone dared say anything.

'Thank you,' Peyre said to the sorceress. 'Quite enjoyed that.'

She tilted her head at him, her violet eyes looking quizzical, not understanding a word. It was quite frustrating. Instead, he put the palms of his hands together and gave a bow.

She nodded at him, as if she understood the gesture. Then she sat down, cross-legged, on her carpet. A gust of wind hit them, and she was rising into the air.

'You know the way back?' he asked her.

Ignoring him, the sorceress from another world took to the sky and shot away, above the trees. Peyre and his friends watched her until she disappeared, while Rab took the opportunity to hunch over and do his business.

Peyre suppressed a sigh and led them northeast. They had to walk, but they had been dropped safely inside Guivergne territory. It was unlikely the enemy had crossed the border, given that so many had been sent into Morbaine.

They connected with a road, which would take them to a town. From there, they could borrow horses, and get to Valennes in good time. There was much that needed doing, and he had left everything to Loysse for too long.

THEY DIDN'T MAKE it to the town. Riders intercepted them not long after they joined the road. A trio of Middians, riding the fine horses of their people. All three of them stared at Peyre and the others, as if they were seeing monsters; or ghosts.

'You are men of Frayne? Jorath, or Cuenin?' he asked them. 'I am Peyre, Duke of Morbaine.'

One of them cleared his throat. 'We know who you are, Duke Peyre. We serve Chieftain Jorath. I am sorry, but we thought you were dead.'

'We've only just made it out of Morbaine. Where are you based? Can you lend us five horses?'

The Middians looked at one another. 'We will ride now and tell

Jorath.' With that, the men moved quickly, and rode back the way they had come, to the east.

'What did you make of that?' Peyre asked.

'Something odd going on,' Gosse said. 'Something they're not telling us, I reckon.'

IT WAS NOT long before the Middians returned. This time, there were a lot more of them.

Jorath led them. He cast his gaze over Peyre and his companions, his lips pressed together. There was something in his demeanour, and that of his warriors, that confirmed something wasn't right. Something between sullenness and anger, Peyre judged.

'You've only just made it out?' the chieftain asked, his tone accusatory.

Peyre felt Gosse stir beside him. He resisted the temptation to move his own hand to his sword hilt. He didn't know what was going on, but it would be better if it didn't descend into a fight. They would lose, for a start. 'Morbaine is taken,' he told the chieftain. 'From south, east, and from the sea. We barely got out. How have things been here?'

'Your people turned on us. We thought we'd be safe here. But they killed Frayne and tried to drive us out. We've had to kill all our animals, save for our warhorses, to keep our families from starving. The Morbainais and Magnians are doing no better,' he said, with a glance Ida's way. 'Maybe worse.'

Peyre didn't understand, frowning in disbelief. What had gone so wrong? He tried to imagine Loysse refusing food to the Morbainais, her own people. He found he couldn't.

'Where are the Magnians?' Ida asked.

'Not far west of here,' Jorath replied. 'I can have some of my men take you,' he said grudgingly.

'Explain what happened,' Peyre said. 'If what you say is remotely true, my sister must have had some cause for her actions.'

'It's not your sister. It's that bastard, Arnoul of Saliers. He's the one your people listen to. He's the one they made king. That's all that needs to be said about the Guivergnais.'

A kernel of icy dread formed in Peyre's chest, while the rest of his body burned with anger. 'Made king?' he asked, not liking the sound of his own voice. 'What do you mean?'

Jorath's expression changed, and an uneasy look came to his face. 'I'm sorry to be the one to tell you, if you didn't know. Ezenachi and the Turned invaded the Empire. Esterel fell, at the god's own hands, so the stories say.'

It was strange. Peyre thought he should have fallen apart at those words. Instead, a clarity of mind settled on him as he filtered out extraneous thoughts and focused on the actions he must take. 'And my sister?'

'I don't know what goes on in Valennes. Lord Russell was captured by Saliers. Since then, we've had to defend ourselves from his forces. All I know is, he rules the kingdom now.'

'My father?' Umbert asked, his voice frail and anxious. 'He still lives?'

Jorath gave an apologetic shrug. 'I know not.'

'Ida,' Peyre said. 'Raise whatever mounted fighters you can from amongst your people. I will do the same amongst the Morbainais. Jorath, you must gather the Middians. We will ride on Valennes immediately.'

'It's not that easy,' Jorath said. 'The entire country is against us. They see us as invaders. Saliers has garrisons in every nearby town. In a few days, they'll have driven us back across the border, into the hands of the Turned. Our warriors are hungry and ill. We're in no condition for battle.'

'I'm not asking you to fight,' Peyre said. 'I'm the King of Guivergne, and I'm marching us to Valennes.'

IT TOOK a day to raise the force of two thousand cavalry. Each warrior travelled lightly and there were no supply carts available. They would have to hurry, and Peyre had every intention of doing just that.

211

Those who couldn't find a horse were left behind, to protect the miserable refugees. Peyre could barely control his anger when he saw the state his people had been left in. Many lacked decent shelter, and all were hungry from food rationing. It would have been even worse in winter. As it was, the people of Morbaine seemed to breathe a collective sigh of relief when Peyre arrived. Their faith in him was humbling. He had to make sure it was deserved.

He led the force of Morbainais north east, connecting with the road that led to Valennes. Behind him, Ida led the Magnians, and Jorath the Middians. He'd learned that those two groups had been the most abused by the Guivergnais, and it made sense to keep them in reserve. The Middians had even, apparently, raided Guivergnais villages to steal food. Jorath hadn't mentioned that. But whatever the truths of who did what first, to whom, he knew Arnoul of Saliers was the man who deserved his wrath. His hatred for the man burned so fiercely it scared him—made him wonder what he would do when he had the man in his grasp.

But he could also acknowledge that a part of his anger was aimed at himself. He'd known the man was a snake, and yet he'd allowed him to do this—left him in a position of strength in the kingdom, where he could carry out his ambitions. *I was stupidly naïve. He manipulated me, making me trust him. I see that now.*

He just had to hope Loysse and his niece, Alienor, were safe. Never mind Lord Russell, and countless other potential victims. He knew he'd never forgive himself if his sister was harmed. *Syele is with her,* he told himself. He wasn't sure what the Barissian woman could do that his sister's husband, with his duchy's soldiers, and a fortress full of armed guards, had failed to do. But he still rested his hopes on her.

Peyre ignored the closest settlements. Part of his strategy was speed, and he didn't have time to divert his force hither and thither. But after two days, they came within sight of their first test.

They approached the town of Laupas. It sat on a major crossroads, guarding the route to the capital. Would they open the gates to Peyre, the rightful ruler of the kingdom? Or had Saliers truly turned Guivergne against his family in a matter of weeks? He would have laughed at the idea a few days ago.

Gosse and Inhan rode with him to the gates, hastily closed at the approach of his force. Peyre had contemplated taking the town by subterfuge. But he needed to know. Would his people acknowledge him?

'Who approaches?' a voice called down.

'Your king!' Gosse boomed up to the fortifications. 'King Peyre!'

'Truly?' the man asked, peering down.

'It is I,' Peyre shouted up.

'Let him in,' the man shouted, and with little ado, one of the wooden gates was unbarred and swung open.

The three of them looked at one another.

'That was easy,' Inhan muttered.

'Maybe too easy,' Gosse said. 'Could be a trap, so be on your guard.'

As Peyre nudged his mount into the courtyard, he saw few soldiers. Once he dismounted, some interested townsfolk edged over, perhaps relieved the force he had brought here wasn't hostile. Meanwhile, the man they had spoken to atop the battlements was barrelling his way down to meet them.

'I am Renild, the mayor here.' He stopped before Peyre, bowed, then—as if worrying that was insufficient—got down on one knee. 'Your Majesty, it is good to see you. There has been such bad news recently, it is a welcome change to see you alive. There have been rumours,' he added, 'that you had succumbed to the Turned.'

'Please, Renild, on your feet. Thank you for your words. But I must ask you. I was told the towns in the south were garrisoned by Arnoul of Saliers. That he has stolen my crown.'

'Correct on both counts, unfortunately. But the garrisons hereabout were recalled north a few days ago.'

'Why?'

'No one informed us at the time, but the reason became clear. The army of Guivergne has returned from Brasingia. They passed through Laupas only yesterday.'

'Led by whom?'

'Led by Queen Liesel. That is to say, the late king's widow. Lord Courion was giving the orders. I am dreadfully sorry about your brother, Your Majesty.'

Peyre nodded absently. 'Thank you. Liesel and Sacha, you say? And they were taking the army to Valennes?'

'Aye. Gone to unseat that brigand, Saliers. Most were men on foot. I am sure you can catch up to them, Your Majesty.'

'Hurrah for King Peyre!' came a shout, and the increasing number of townsfolk who had appeared cheered in response.

Peyre raised a hand, but his thoughts were elsewhere. *Liesel is here.* A great melancholy threatened to unsettle him, as he allowed his thoughts to turn to his brother. *No,* he told himself. *There is no time for grief yet.*

He turned to his two companions. 'Come. We will press on and join the army.' He allowed himself a grim smile. 'Our task of removing that insect from Valennes just got significantly easier.'

* * *

THEY CAUGHT up to the long column of the Guivergnais army, returning home after months spent in Brasingia. Banners depicting the Owl of Guivergne fluttered and snapped. She had protected many of her warriors, but not their king, and Peyre wondered what morale was like among the soldiers. He ordered his cavalry to form the rear-guard, while he and his companions passed the horse-pulled carts, and the weary infantry, who had marched all the way from Essenberg.

It was hard not to deem the campaign in the empire an utter disaster. But that, Peyre knew, was a judgement based on hindsight. He had been all for it. He had persuaded his brother to refuse Inge's peaceful overtures in Coldeberg, and not to rest until they had defeated their enemies. How he wished he could make that decision over again.

The van of the army was a few miles ahead of the main column, moving at pace, but Peyre caught up with them just as the light began to fade.

His arrival caused a stir. Murmurs spread among the mounted

company, passing like a wave from the nearest to the furthest, and soon everyone had pulled their horses to a stop and were staring at him. A little unsure, it seemed, how to react. *They are grieving for Esterel,* he told himself. *I am a poor replacement for my brother.*

The cavalry parted, and the leaders of the force approached. There was Sacha, with Coleta by his side. On his other side was Florent, and next to him, Liesel. *Is this really all that is left of the nobility who went to the empire?*

Peyre avoided eye contact with Coleta. When he looked at Liesel, his emotions became too strong, and he had to look away from her as well. He wondered what she was doing back in Guivergne. The sooner they could talk properly, the better.

'Your Majesty,' Sacha said with a nod and a bow. 'It is good to see you. We heard you were missing and feared the worst.'

Peyre looked for signs of dishonesty in Sacha's words but found none. It sounded more like genuine relief. Their petty rivalry, if one could even call it that, seemed entirely redundant now.

'We have come from Laupas and heard a little of the events here. Any fresh news from Valennes? I am concerned about my sister and niece.'

Liesel turned pale at his words. 'We didn't even know anything was wrong until we entered the kingdom, and probably know no more than you. Saliers has made himself king. Lord Russell is said to be under arrest. We've heard nothing of Loysse. It's pointless trying to interpret anything from that.'

'True. I have brought two thousand mounted warriors with me. Looks like you have substantial numbers, too.'

'Ten thousand,' Sacha said. 'Martras is still in Barissia. Every other lord is here. Saliers has nothing close, even if the soldiers of Famiens are with him.'

'But breaking into Valennes will not be easy. Then there is the Bastion.'

'That is true,' Sacha conceded. 'But we have siege equipment with us.'

'And arbalests,' Liesel added.

'It's surely only a matter of time,' Florent suggested.

Peyre thought about the Turned. They had already reached the border of Guivergne. *We don't have the time for this.*

SACHA DEFERRED to Peyre in decision making. It was his army now. He asked for an early camp to be made. He was desperate to speak with Liesel alone.

They walked away from the noise and prying eyes until they came to a stand of trees. Once they did, Liesel collapsed into him. She was shaking, and he had to hold her up.

'I'm sorry,' she murmured, her head buried in his shoulder.

Sorry for what, he had no clue.

She pulled away from him, rubbing at her eyes with an arm. 'I suppose you want to know how it happened?'

'I could ask someone else.'

'No. You need to hear it from me. The Turned invaded Gotbeck, and he led an army out to meet them. A great army. All for nought, since Ezenachi came before a sword was drawn.' Her voice cracked, and she took a few moments just to breathe and hold it together.

Peyre found it hard to watch, his heart aching, and a lump coming to his throat. This wasn't how Esterel's life was supposed to end.

A small smile came to her face. 'He challenged Ezenachi's champion to a fight. It was Maragin, wielding Bolivar's Sword. You know Esterel. He bested her anyway. That angered Ezenachi. He dragged Esterel towards him, then killed him with the sword.'

Peyre stared at his feet. How apt that his brother went out fighting a duel. He recalled Ezenachi in Magnia, grabbing the sorcerer Rimmon with his magic. His mind's eye replaced Rimmon with Esterel, and tears came at last, sliding down his cheeks and dropping to the ground.

'Ezenachi turned on me next. Idris stopped him. Said he was Esterel's successor. Then swore to obey Ezenachi in everything.'

So, Idris was the emperor now. Peyre found he cared little. At least the man had spoken up. He'd saved Liesel, perhaps, if he understood her words correctly. 'And you came back to Guivergne?' he asked her.

She glanced at him. 'I'm not sure why. I couldn't stay in Essenberg, maybe that's the reason.'

'I'm glad you did.'

'Don't be. It was my fault Esterel died.'

'How could it be your fault, Liesel?'

'I killed Inge. I couldn't stop myself. I was swollen with hatred. Esterel locked me up, but it was too late then. If I hadn't done that, Ezenachi would have let the empire be, and Esterel would still be alive.'

Liesel killed the witch? Esterel had her in a cell? What madness had happened in Essenberg while he was away? 'You and I both know that isn't true. Inge liked to pretend she kept Ezenachi from the empire, but he would have come, anyway. As for the killing, I'd have done the same.'

'But you wouldn't, Peyre, would you? You tried to tell me. A selfish child, you called me. And you were right. All I cared about were my own feelings, and I've brought disaster on us.'

Peyre had a vague memory of an angry conversation in Guslar. *Did I really use such words?* The notion that Liesel believed he thought so little of her tore him up inside. 'I'm sorry. I've never believed that. Liesel, I—' Peyre warned himself to stay quiet. But where had that got him? Gods, she needed to know how he felt. He put a hand on each arm. 'I love you.'

She frowned, incredulous. She took a step backwards. 'You too, Peyre? I thought you were my friend.'

Me too, what? he thought. Alright, it hadn't been the right time to say it. But her reaction was excessive. *She's just lost her husband, Peyre,* he reminded himself.

'I *am* your friend, Liesel. Gods, at least you must know that.'

He stepped towards her, but she raised a hand. He stopped. She looked like she would say more, then she simply walked away.

Peyre watched as she retreated to the camp, then leaned against a tree. His thoughts were erratic, straying from one thing to another, not staying long enough with any. His emotions wouldn't settle. Was he sad, angry, bitter? He didn't know. *Perhaps I am all of those things.*

You are the King of Guivergne, he told himself. But no pleasure came with the title. It seemed all the joy he had once felt as a young man had been taken from him. *Truly, I am become my father. Or worse,* a voice warned him. *Maybe you are Uncle Nicolas, unloved and unloving. Maybe everyone will look at you and wish your brother was king until your dying day.*

SANC

ARBEOST, DUCHY OF MORBAINE

Once Kepa returned, Sanc gathered the champions together.
'We will teleport close to Ezenachi's position. It isn't anything like as far as the journey from Silb. Is everyone ready?'

'My magic is restored,' Temyl said. The russet-haired man considered Sanc with unfriendly eyes. 'But what about this god? Can he see us coming?'

'He can see sorcerers, the same as me.'

'Then there is no chance to take him by surprise?'

'I have learned to hide my presence. If you all lent me some power, I could hide us.'

'But he will see we have vanished from sight,' the Nerisian said, relentless. 'He'll know we're coming.'

'If he looks,' Sanc admitted.

'Seven of us have just arrived in Dalriya. Even if he doesn't realise who we are, my guess is he'll be watching us closely.'

'Temyl is right, Sanc,' Mergildo said, as if speaking to a child. 'We might as well approach in full view. He'll know we're coming. And what of his Turned? How many magic users will he have with him?'

'I can see four sorcerers with him. One, I presume, is Lorant. The champion who wields Madria's staff. He is likely to be the greatest threat of the four. The three others are probably also Caladri. They are easy to spot. They have clawed feet, and they move with a bird-like gait.'

'And the other champions?' the Rasidi asked.

Sanc sighed, recalling the names of the lost heroes Peyre had given him. 'Maragin, a Krykker warrior who wields a powerful sword. Oisin, a Giant with a spear. Jesper, a—an archer. Elfled wears a cloak that allows her to go invisible. Then there is Belwynn, a woman who wields a dagger.'

The champions said nothing. They just looked at him like he was mad.

'Out with it,' Mildrith said, leaping to Sanc's defence. 'You think we can't win? Seven champions defeated Ezenachi all those years ago.'

'But did Ezenachi have followers such as these with him, when our peoples crossed to Silb?' Temyl responded. 'I haven't heard such stories if he did.'

'Then you suggest a different course?' Mildrith asked.

'If we are here to kill him, then no,' Temyl admitted. 'But I am wary of walking into a battle we cannot win.'

'We must all be wary of that,' Sanc agreed.

'Don't worry,' said a voice to the side. Herin scraped a whetstone down both lengths of his blade. 'Ezenachi can't see me coming.'

Temyl looked down his nose at the Magnian.

Don't sneer, Sanc wanted to advise the Nerisian. *I wouldn't advise making an enemy of Herin.*

'Come,' Kepa said. 'We've talked enough. Time to act.'

THEY ARRIVED AT THEIR DESTINATION. Sanc scanned the area for enemies. He felt strong, despite having transported eight people and their mounts. Such a teleportation would once have drained his energy, but he was stronger than he once was.

He had also drawn upon the powers of the other champions. The power they wielded, collectively, gave him the belief they could confront Ezenachi.

Herin had already proven his worth. He provided Sanc with the destination—a spot on the Great Road he had described with remarkable accuracy. Something memorable must have happened here, but when Sanc asked him, all the Magnian offered were some cryptic words about wizards with red eyes, which left Sanc none the wiser.

'Look for him,' Mildrith said, 'while we keep watch.'

Sanc closed his eyes and searched for the lustre that only those with magic gave off. He felt his heart beat faster as he was drawn to the brightest light of all. Ezenachi hadn't moved—he was only a few miles to the east. Surrounding him were many lights but, just as Sanc had seen every time he had looked, only four were sorcerers. 'He's still there,' he said, opening his eyes.

'Now is the test,' Mergildo said. 'Will he retreat?'

'Let's find out,' said Kepa. She allowed her mount to put distance between itself and the lizards—not to mention Mergildo's camel, which seemed to bother the horses just as much as the giant lizards.

The other horse riders—Temyl and Guntram—joined her.

'There's a road that cuts east,' Herin said, pointing the way.

Sanc urged Spike on, and the other lizard riders joined him. They travelled into the Brasingian duchy of Gotbeck. Peyre had been ignorant of developments in the empire, but the evidence Sanc now witnessed looked dire. They passed through a sizeable village, its buildings collected on either side of the road. It was deserted. Indeed, there were no signs of life anywhere. Sanc hoped Ezenachi's presence in Gotbeck meant this was as far as his Turned armies had got in this part of Dalriya. He hoped that meant the rest of his family, and the people he cared about, were safe.

The champions of Silb took in the details. It was strange for Sanc, watching them adjusting to a foreign world just as he had done. It was good they could see this for themselves. Surely, it would reinforce everything he had warned them about.

Sanc checked the location of Ezenachi once more. He hadn't moved. *He must know we are coming*, Sanc told himself. *He is waiting for us.* Soon, his fellow champions would fully understand the threat they faced.

A buzzing sensation made him put a hand to his head.

'I feel it too,' said Mildrith.

They crested a rise. Before them was a wide stretch of farmland, occupied by Ezenachi's host. The Turned were stationed amongst fields to the left and right of the road, the ground they stood on baked dry by days of sunshine. The sky buzzed with winged insects, while others chirped, hidden amongst the crops and meadows. The Turned themselves were silent statues.

'We must ride past them?' Temyl asked. The Nerisian did his best to hide his nerves, but it was not an inviting prospect.

The road ran straight through the farmland, leading to the walls of what looked like a sizeable town. This must be where Ezenachi had based his army. The Turned were mindless servants, but they still needed to be fed, and Sanc knew there must be a sophisticated organisation at work.

He studied the Turned—thousands of them waited, a kaleidoscope of sizes, ages, and races. Some were well armed, others looked defenceless. If they continued down the road before them, the Turned could close in and surround them. But what choice was there? They had come here for Ezenachi. Sanc was not about to turn back.

'Come,' he said, nudging Spike on. Mildrith, Herin, and the Eger Khan followed.

'I could bring a fog to protect us,' Guntram said, sounding as worried as Temyl had. The tall Gadenzian studied the sky doubtfully. The sun had burned away most of the cloud.

'I could bring you moisture on the wind,' Kepa said.

'You could do those things,' Sanc agreed. 'But I suggest saving your magic for when we need it. I don't believe they will attack, at least not now. Ezenachi will talk with us first.'

'And you know that how?' Temyl asked sharply.

Sanc had no answer to that. 'I just do,' he said.

For a moment, it looked like that wasn't enough. But when Kepa urged her horse on, Temyl and Guntram reluctantly followed. Their horses' eyes and nostrils widened, assailed by the smell of so many humans nearby. On Sanc's other side, Mergildo's camel plodded through the grass by the side of the road, seemingly oblivious of the host that waited in such proximity.

The Turned didn't react as they passed by. The further they went, the more Sanc became aware of Ezenachi. He was a presence that threatened to steal his attention from everyone and everything else.

But it was the Giant Sanc saw first.

'Oisin,' Herin muttered beside him.

The King of the Orias, last of his kind. Twice as tall as anyone else. His skin was pale green, and he held his spear, a terrifying weapon that gave him a reach many times longer than anyone else. He stood impassively, just like the rest of the Turned.

As they neared, Sanc made out other individuals from amongst the group who waited for them. Maragin, the Krykker, was armed with the sword of her race. Lorant, a King of the Caladri, and three others of his kind. These were the sorcerers he had detected. Two dark-haired women stood together. The one he didn't know must be Belwynn Godslayer. The one he did was Elfled, Queen of Magnia. She had been so kind to him—he hated to see her like this.

Even worse, though, was seeing the man who held the Jalakh Bow. Jesper. The man who had always looked out for him, who had played the role of father when his own had decided he couldn't. Sanc found his hands shaking with anger at seeing Jesper made a slave.

This group, blessed with powerful weapons, or magic, formed an honour guard in front of their master. Sanc had felt Ezenachi's presence once before, at the Red Keep in Magnia. A fizzing sensation in his mouth and ears, as if the god's presence sickened his body. But now, he saw him for the first time. Or did he? What he saw was a tall, dark-skinned, Lipper man. But that wasn't Ezenachi, merely the god's host. For a moment, he thought he caught sight of a creature much larger, then the vision was gone.

With what sorcery Sanc didn't know, but the god had attached himself to this man. It must have happened many years ago, when he had first arrived in Dalriya. Since then, his power had grown. Slow progress at first, Sanc suspected. Turning one individual at a time, it would have taken patience to infect all the Lippers.

Then his progress had quickened. Whole kingdoms had been enslaved. The people of Dalriya had been slow, or unable, to stop him. Now he had tens of thousands under his command. The most powerful individuals in Dalriya stood with him, meek as sheep, ready to do his bidding.

Perhaps I am the last sorcerer in all Dalriya who withstands him, Sanc considered. *I wouldn't have a chance without the champions of Silb with me.* You don't stand a chance with them, a treacherous part of his mind warned. He was quick to silence it, but the thought had been given life, and it lurked within him.

Sanc pulled on Spike's reins, and the great beast came to a halt. His companions stopped too, and for a while, the two sides stared at one another.

Sanc felt the weight of Ezenachi's attention.

'You are the one who left,' Ezenachi said. His voice echoed like they stood in some vast cavern, a place that hadn't seen the sun or rain in many lifetimes.

'Now I return,' Sanc said. 'I bring with me the champions of Silb.'

'You've come to kill me?' Ezenachi asked. There were hints of emotion in his voice—derision, perhaps.

'If we must. The champions of Silb defeated you many years ago. We can do it again.'

'Strange,' Ezenachi said, his voice grating, as if he spoke inside Sanc's head. 'You dare tell me what happened all those years ago, when I am the only surviving witness? Yes, those murderous invaders defeated me. They took my homeland and made my people their slaves. But you are not them. And I was alone, my people outnumbered by a stronger foe. But look now, Dalriyan. I have an army many thousands strong. I have created champions of my own, to fight by my side. And you come here, the seven of you, thinking you can defeat me?'

The challenge hung in the air. There was a moment of stillness as the two sides watched each other. Sanc couldn't say who was the first aggressor—whether it was someone on his side or Ezenachi's. But as soon as he felt the first crackle of magic, he readied his defences.

The champions on both sides sprang into action.

A gust of wind, and Kepa was vaulting from her horse and flying in the sky, drawing attacks from the Caladri sorcerers. This exposed them, Temyl and Guntram sending heavy bursts of magic their way, the ground underneath the Caladri's feet exploding with the power. Ezenachi was forced to act, forming a barrier that swallowed their magic.

Then Sanc felt that immense power brought to bear. Ezenachi blanketed them with it, the sorcery that had held armies in place, bringing thousands of warriors to their knees.

Sanc fought it, and so did the champions of Silb. He had warned them what to expect, and they were ready. How they fought it off, he wasn't sure. Was their combined power enough, or was there something special about these champions working together? But even if he couldn't explain it, he felt their resistance working. Ezenachi couldn't bully them with his power. Couldn't fix them in place. *He isn't invincible.*

Belief returned to Sanc, pulsing through his body. *We can do this.* From the corner of his eye, he caught movement. Elfled was there one moment, and then gone, using her cloak to go invisible. *Two can play that game*, Sanc decided. He used his magic to create the illusion that he wasn't there, making himself and Spike silent. Elfled's weapon made her dangerous. But if he couldn't see her, at least he could provide the same threat to his enemies.

A crack of noise. Beside him, the Eger Khan's defences flared, only just stopping an arrow that had come for him, lightning fast. The force nearly knocked the boy from his mount, but he managed to roll with the blast, clinging on with his knees and thighs.

Sanc targeted Jesper, aiming a blast of energy at the ground before him. *I can't kill him*, Sanc admitted to himself, knowing it was a weakness. Knowing Jesper wouldn't hesitate. Jesper had no defences, and the impact sent him flying backwards, the bow spinning from his grasp.

But Sanc's attack had revealed his location and Oisin was running for him, the huge spear moving in his hands as he ate up the distance between them. He held his weapon high; ready to strike.

The ground under the giant's feet churned, and he fell, sinking to his knees. Roots shot from the ground where the giant knelt. They twisted about his limbs, holding him in place. They squeezed at his forearm, pulled at his fingers, trying to make him relinquish his weapon.

Maragin arrived. She chopped at the roots with Bolivar's Sword, trying to release her companion from Mildrith's magic.

Sanc built a bolt of magic. *Jesper is off-limits*, he told himself. *But if we are to defeat Ezenachi, I must kill his innocent victims.*

Then the god's voice boomed across the battlefield.

'The killing can start now, if that is what you choose.'

Ezenachi was standing over two prone forms. One, a great green lizard, lay unmoving. The second, a human, struggled weakly on the ground, dark hair spilling over his face.

No, Herin, Sanc despaired. The fool had gone for Ezenachi himself, convinced he could kill him. Alone—his sword against a god. Or maybe he hadn't cared about the consequences should he fail.

'Or you can submit and serve me. You will be well honoured as my champions.'

Herin raised his head a few inches. 'Don't you dare yield on my account,' he bellowed.

Belwynn hovered by the god's side, Toric's Dagger in hand. Waiting for Ezenachi to give her the order.

'Hold!' Kepa shouted from her position above them, palm held up.

Sanc angled Spike to the side, being careful to stay hidden. He didn't have long to think. He was reminded of his last lesson with Rimmon. He'd proved he could produce any magic his teacher asked of him. Then the Haskan had grabbed hold of Rab and asked Sanc to use his magic to save him. *But can you do it with my arm around your dog?* Rimmon had asked. *Or does it defeat you?*

Sanc had not been defeated that day. But now he faced Ezenachi, alert to any attack, and Belwynn with that dagger.

I can make my magic look as I wish it to, Sanc reminded himself. *What if I wish to conceal it?*

He prepared his spell, pouring as much power into it as he could. He unleashed it, and still everyone was oblivious. The blast circled around Herin and struck Ezenachi from the side. Not anticipating it, the god was sent sprawling to the ground.

Kepa reacted quickly, drawing a gust of wind that tugged Herin away.

Belwynn's reaction was slower, chasing after Herin's disappearing body. Kepa guided him towards Mergildo. A Caladri blasted a bolt of magic, but the Rasidi defended the attack with ease.

Suddenly, Sanc was struck. He landed hard on his back in an explosion of pain. He felt himself dragged by some force. Trying to sit up, he saw his assailant. Lorant, the King of the Blood Caladri, had Madria's Staff outstretched and had caught Sanc in a beam of magic. Sanc tried to dislodge himself from his new prison, but was stuck fast.

Mildrith sent a blast at the Caladri, who repulsed her attack.

Released from the Kassite's grip, Oisin burst free of her constraints, his deadly spear still clutched in one hand. It took a concerted attack from Temyl and Guntram before he was forced backwards, Maragin repelling further blasts with her sword.

Sanc fought against the Caladri's pull. With help from Mildrith, he stopped sliding towards his opponent, but still couldn't shake free. A crack of noise and an arrow from the Jalakh Bow shot towards him. With a shout, the Eger Khan redirected the missile back towards Jesper, who had to dive out of the way.

Ezenachi returned to the fray. Kepa was blasted from the sky. The god turned his attention to Temyl and Guntram. At first, they withstood his power. Then their defences collapsed, and they were sent sprawling, Temyl crying out in pain.

A second scream sent a shiver of fear through Sanc. He turned to Mildrith. Blood poured from her neck. Elfled appeared behind her, sharp teeth sunk in. Belwynn drew up next to them, Toric's Dagger horribly close to Mildrith.

'Time to submit,' Ezenachi's voice came, heavy with inevitability. 'Or she will be the first to die.'

Sanc looked around at the sound of marching.

The ranks of the Turned were moving at last. He had led them all to disaster, and there was nothing he could do.

Only submit. Or die.

BELWYNN

DUCHY OF GOTBECK

Belwynn was not in control of her actions. She hadn't been for a long time. For how long, she didn't know. Whenever she tried to focus on specifics, her mind went cloudy.

She knew that days—maybe weeks—would pass at a time, and she had no memory of them. Then, her consciousness would return.

It was a stubborn thing. She had lost control of her mind. She wasn't meant to be here—seeing through these eyes, thinking these thoughts. But this stubborn thing would fight back from time to time. Unwilling to accept it had lost.

She looked at the world through a caliginous fog. Her body moved without her say so. She was nothing but a passive observer, a witness to events over which she had no control.

Yet, when she looked at this man, something deep within her stirred. A sense that, for reasons unknown, she cared.

He rode a creature from nightmares—a giant, green thing—all teeth and claws. Yet his face looked more fearsome than the creature's. It was a face that held her attention. The fog that clouded her vision parted when she looked at him.

He rode straight at her master. *Protect me*, that other voice in her mind instructed her body. Her body obeyed and drew the dagger from her belt.

But her master was powerful and didn't need her protection. She felt his magic as it reached inside the giant beast and stopped its heart. It collapsed, throwing its rider to the ground. He lay there—injured, but still alive.

She looked at her dagger. Ah. She would probably use its thin blade now. To end his life. She didn't want that to happen. *Perhaps I could stop my arm from delivering the strike? There was once a time when I decided what this body did.*

Her master's voice boomed across the battlefield.

'The killing can start now, if that is what you choose.'

Her master's enemies stared at him. They too, Belwynn could tell, didn't want this man to die.

'Or,' her master continued, 'you can submit and serve me. You will be well honoured as my champions.'

The man before her raised his head a few inches. 'Don't you dare yield on my account,' he bellowed.

That feeling inside Belwynn stirred even stronger. The voice, and the words. Was it wrong that she favoured this man over her master? Was it wrong that she hoped his friends would refuse to yield? After all—yield, and they would become like her. She didn't wish that on anyone.

She felt the power of the magic that struck her master, so strong he could not stay on his feet. His enemies took their chance, rescuing the dark-haired man, who was pulled along the ground away from her.

Reluctant to lose him, Belwynn followed. Perhaps it was her master's temporary weakness, or perhaps she had a hidden strength. But Belwynn had regained some control. She moved on wobbly legs, like a babe learning to walk. Her thoughts remained clouded.

Where am I going? What do I hope to achieve? Escape? Not possible.

She chased after the injured man, but was too slow. Then a scream made her stop. One of her master's enemies was under attack by some invisible creature. A deep memory resurfaced, and when the creature appeared, its teeth at the woman's neck, Belwynn wasn't surprised. *Asrai*. A familiar figure, one who had been enslaved, just like her.

Belwynn approached, dagger in hand. Her master told her who he wanted dead. Her purpose was to serve him. Wasn't it?

'Time to submit,' her master warned his enemies. 'Or she will be the first to die.'

A stillness descended on the scene. Her master's enemies turned to a red-eyed man among their number, who cast a look of anguish at the captured woman. A noise made him look behind. Her master's soldiers were marching—thousands of them, completing the trap these people had walked into.

It was over.

No, Belwynn told herself.

She slashed at the Asrai Queen with her dagger. The creature let out a terrible scream of pain. Then it turned on her—hissing; showing its fangs in a face full of fury.

The Asrai's victim, temporarily forgotten, was quick to escape. Roots shot forth in all directions, each one picking up one of her allies, or a mount. As soon as they had grabbed them, the roots drew in, bringing them all together.

Ezenachi released a burst of power at the very place they gathered.

Too late. With a shift almost too fast to see, the god's enemies disappeared.

Her master's soldiers stopped marching. His champions turned to face Belwynn.

'How were you able to defy me?' He demanded.

Belwynn felt Him inside her mind, clawing at her.

His champions closed on her. Spear; sword; bow and arrow; all trained on her. The Caladri used their magic to hold her to the spot.

'It is dangerous to leave you alive,' Ezenachi declared. He was on her, wresting the dagger from her grip.

Belwynn looked at the weapon's thin blade, pointed her way. An object so familiar. She didn't fear it.

Her master punched the dagger into the side of her head.

PART III
RECKONING

677

LIESEL

VALENNES, KINGDOM OF GUIVERGNE

It was Saliers' son, Benoit, who denied them entry into the city. Liesel knew he and Peyre had been close. It only soured Peyre's mood further.

It had been terrible to begin with. He was short and impatient when speaking with everyone. Whether it was Sacha, Gosse, even Umbert, it didn't seem to matter. Coleta was genuinely terrified of him, melting away whenever he was near.

Of course, he was upset about Esterel. But Liesel knew her rejection played its part. Perhaps she could have dealt with it better. But she had felt so let down. Idris and Sacha's proposals had left her feeling nothing more than her titles. To be used to bolster someone else's ambitions.

With Peyre, she had always thought there had been more between them. She had thought their friendship had been genuine—that behind his reserve was someone who really cared. To claim that he loved her so soon after Esterel's death? Maybe men were just different. Everything was a contest—a game to them. Peyre would become king, and then march into Brasingia to claim his brother's empire. She would make a useful tool for such an enterprise, just as she had been for Esterel.

235

The worst of it was that, deep down, she knew the only reason she had returned to Guivergne was for him. She had felt lost and had thought Peyre would save her again. *It's your own stupid fault,* she told herself. But that didn't lessen the hurt she felt. She was here now, for good or ill. Trying to help retake a capital that was no longer hers. *Any sane person would have stayed in Essenberg.*

Peyre gathered his captains for a meeting—out of obligation, it felt, rather than because he wanted to listen to what they had to say.

It was harsh, Liesel knew, to judge him against Esterel. And yet that was exactly what people would do. Esterel had such an easy charisma, making everyone feel he valued their contribution. Peyre needed to learn that. At least, how to pretend.

Sacha outlined what siege weapons they had. Enough to take the city, he reckoned. But they would need to be built, tested, and aimed, and then given time to do their job.

Peyre looked less than enthused.

'We have enough arbalests to drive them from the walls,' she told him, ready to have her say, even if it wasn't welcomed. 'That would cover a direct assault on the gates. It would be quicker than waiting for the trebuchets.'

'Very well,' Peyre said, refusing to look her in the eye. 'Get them into position. Though even that might take too long. If Sanc fails, the Turned could be here in days. If we don't have the Bastion in our hands by then, we're doomed.'

'Sanc?' Liesel asked, scanning the room. Peyre's companions from Morbaine were not surprised by the mention of the name. Sacha and Florent looked as bemused as she felt. 'Your brother? Who left—' She couldn't finish that sentence. It seemed no one truly understood where he had gone.

'Sanc is returned,' Peyre said. 'He has gone to challenge Ezenachi, with sorcerers he has recruited from the world he travelled to. Sorcerers, but not gods. I hope he is successful, but we must prepare for the worst. The last time a similar group of champions tried to stop Ezenachi, he simply turned them to his side.'

Liesel nodded, flicking her eyes around the room again to gauge people's reactions. If Ezenachi strengthened himself by turning these sorcerers to his bidding, the Bastion was hardly going to stop him. But what else could they do? Saliers couldn't be left in place. They had to root him out. Quickly.

LIESEL ORGANISED her arbalests into units, each targeting a different section of the south facing city walls. She knew they could drive Benoit's defenders away, allowing battering rams to force open the gates. But Peyre had not given her such orders.

Instead, he walked alone to the gates.

'We can't allow this,' Liesel hissed at Umbert.

Umbert was watching his friend and monarch with little concern. He had been injured during their escapade in Magnia and Morbaine, and she could tell he wasn't fully recovered. She wondered whether a blow to the head had knocked the sense from him.

'He has the Shield,' Umbert repeated, as if that was a satisfactory explanation.

Peyre had won the prize in Magnia. Liesel knew the stories of Madria's weapons well enough. Even so, there was no reason to put himself in such danger. She wondered if Peyre thought the soldiers who watched him saw it as an act of bravery. She doubted it. Most, like her, would be unsettled by it. It was as if their new king didn't care whether he lived or died. That was not a reassuring message to send out.

Peyre stopped, shouting up at the battlements. She couldn't make out the words, but it was a hectoring voice he used. She could imagine how angry he was with Benoit. How betrayed he felt, and how fearful for his sister. But he needed to control his emotions. Such a public display would not persuade Benoit to change his mind, only harden his resolve.

Atop the walls, Saliers' son was flanked by the Owl of Guivergne and the banner of his house, four silver diamonds on a crimson background. He shouted back at his former mentor, just as loudly, until they were both done.

A silence stretched from the city walls to the thousands who made up the royal army, watching and waiting. Peyre hefted his shield, strapped to his left arm. He wasn't moving, that was clear.

Liesel glanced at the nearest group of arbalests. She could give the order to shoot. It was going against Peyre's orders, but he could punish her afterwards. At least he'd be alive.

A hand, polite but firm, was placed on her forearm. 'He is our king,' Umbert said simply.

Liesel nodded. Yes. It was time for her to respect orders. Esterel might still be alive if she had just accepted his decisions.

A lone voice hollered from the battlements. Muffled by distance when it reached Liesel's ears, it still sounded portentous.

The arrows followed. Too many and too fast to count. They sped towards Peyre from across the length of the battlements.

As each one reached his shield, it was sent back the way it had come. Soldiers lurched away from the missiles, some screaming as they were caught out by the volley. Peyre unleashed a tirade of invective up to the battlements once more.

Whether or not it was Benoit's order, Liesel couldn't tell, but now a catapult released its payload—a great stone, and smaller missiles besides.

This combination arced up and then fell towards Peyre. This time, he met the missiles with a flourish of the Shield. The great stone was redirected towards the gates, gaining speed until it struck them with an almighty crash. Both buckled from the impact, standing askew.

Peyre marched towards the gates. There were a few moments of stunned silence, and then Sacha, Florent, Gosse, King Ida, and the other commanders, were ordering their men to advance. Cheers of delight, mixed with fierce growls of anger, merged to create a sudden cacophony of noise.

Now was the time for Liesel's arbalests to lend their support. She signalled for them to release their bolts. Their missiles soared up to the battlements in waves, the click of the levers adding to the sounds of war. The defenders, already on the back foot, were driven away, hiding behind cover.

A metallic clanging sound reverberated.

Peyre had slammed his shield into one of the gates. Ripped from its hinges, it tottered and fell.

Valennes was open.

WITH THE ROYAL army inside the city, the defenders were unable to put up an adequate resistance. There were too few of them to withstand the thousands of well-armed troops. Some fled north through the city streets. No doubt to the Bastion, where—presumably—Saliers had kept the bulk of his army.

In the fighting, Peyre had got a hold of Benoit, and he wasn't prepared to let go. He dragged him through the city streets like a wayward child, still holding on to the anger that seemed to blaze through him from head to toe.

Leaving Florent and his retinue to hold the prisoners in the city barracks, everyone else followed their king. They marched or led their mounts through the central streets and square, where the people came out to cheer their arrival. Again, it was impossible for Liesel not to compare Peyre with Esterel. Her husband could always show appreciation to an adoring crowd. It was as if Peyre didn't even know they were there, so fixed was he on his target.

Perhaps, she considered, the happy medium is somewhere in between.

Not that Peyre's disregard put the people off. As he led his army away from the city centre, towards the Bastion, the citizens followed. Everyone wanted to witness the next moment in the drama for themselves.

The enemy waited for them. The drawbridge was up, and Arnoul's soldiers manned the fortress walls, densely packed.

Liesel spotted the silver and azure banner of the duchy of Famiens flying, as well as the banner of Saliers. Did that mean Auberi had switched his support to Saliers? They had been allies of old, standing against Peyre's father. The duke had always seemed devoted to his wife, but Liesel had witnessed enough treachery and divided loyalties that the sight didn't shock her.

For all their numbers, and the defensive properties of the fortress, Liesel thought those who had supported Saliers must now be quaking on the inside, even if they refused to show it. The armies of Guivergne and Morbaine numbered in the thousands. Saliers might hold out for a good while, but he couldn't win.

'On your knees,' Peyre demanded of his captive. His voice had a rasp in it from shouting.

A hand on the shoulder from Gosse, and Benoit did as he was told. The young man maintained a defiant air, but there was no sneer or other such provocation.

He is not stupid, Liesel could tell.

'Get Saliers here,' Gosse bellowed up to the battlements.

Jeers and foul-mouthed curses rained down from the Bastion's walls, but there was movement, too.

Saliers appeared. He stared down at the scene, his emotions hidden. Liesel wondered what was going on inside his head. He had heard of Esterel's death, and gambled that Peyre had also been lost to the Turned. But Peyre was very much alive, and his son a captive. Surely, he could see it was over? *But such men rarely do.*

Liesel studied those who accompanied him, but recognised few. No Auberi, or other lords of status. His treason had only worked because the lords and soldiers of Guivergne had been in foreign lands.

'I'm giving you one chance to save his life,' Peyre shouted up to his opponent, once quiet had descended. They were separated by thick stone, and yet the distance between them was only a few feet. He hefted his shield menacingly and gave Arnoul a look so cold and serious that the Lord of Saliers probably approved. 'You will receive a noble death, and he will inherit your estate. If the Bastion isn't surrendered immediately, he dies here and now.' Another flex of his left arm let Saliers understand the threat—Benoit would be battered with the shield in front of all present.

A year or two ago, and those gathered might not have believed Peyre would go through with it. But as she looked at the sombre faces on both sides, Liesel saw no signs of incredulity. She thought the only thing that might stop him was the value of Arnoul's prisoners. She stole a glance at Umbert. It was said his father had been taken prisoner, but no one knew whether he still lived. There was Auberi, also absent. Then there was Loysse, and her daughter, Alienor. They were hostages powerful enough to stay Peyre's hand, surely. Did Saliers have them in his possession?

A single arrow left the battlements. Aimed at Peyre, it flew true. He stopped it with the shield, sending it into the moat.

'Cease!' Saliers bellowed, at last some emotion on his face. 'Disarm that cretin!' he added, glaring balefully at the stretch of battlement where the offender stood. He turned to Peyre, the anger gone as quickly as it had come. 'What guarantees can you offer me?' he asked.

'I give you my word,' Peyre snarled. 'A promise made before everyone present. That is all you need to be certain of my faithfulness.'

Saliers seemed to nod in acknowledgement. 'And those men who have followed my orders?'

'They will be free to leave with your son. Only those guilty of the highest crimes will be punished. You know more than me what atrocities have been committed in your name.'

The fate of Loysse hung between them, unspoken but heavy.

'Less than you might think,' Saliers said, so quietly that Loysse only just caught the words. 'Very well,' he said, his voice louder now, so that it carried to the warriors on both sides. 'King Peyre has returned to Guivergne. I thought him dead, and that mistake led me to commit treason. I am guilty and must pay with my life. The king has agreed to pardon those who followed me. My last order to you is to lay down your arms, open the Bastion to him, and submit to his justice.'

SANC

KINGDOM OF GUIVERGNE

Sanc collapsed to the ground. Exhausted. Feelings of relief and depression battled each other. They had escaped. But only because of Belwynn's intervention. They had been a whisker away from total defeat.

He forced himself to his feet. A look at the other champions told him he was in better shape than most. Kepa and Temyl had serious injuries. Mildrith had been bitten by the creature that had once been Queen Elfled. Herin held one arm with the other and looked as defeated as Sanc had ever seen him.

Mergildo inspected Mildrith's neck. Leaving them to it, Sanc approached the Magnian.

'Are you alright, Herin?' he asked. 'I'm sorry about—your lizard.' Herin had never bothered to name the creature, which made its death feel even more sad.

Herin grunted an acknowledgement. 'What do you think he'll do with Belwynn?' he asked Sanc, eyes rising to meet his.

It was hard to look back. Somehow, she had resisted Ezenachi's control. Harsh reality said there could only be one answer.

'He'll kill her,' Herin said, answering his own question. 'She's already dead.' He bowed his head.

'I'm sorry,' Sanc murmured.

Mergildo had moved on to Kepa, so Sanc left Herin and sat next to Mildrith. 'Well?'

'It'll heal,' Mildrith said. 'I suppose she could have ripped my throat out if she'd wanted.'

'Ezenachi wanted to turn us. He invited us into his trap, and like a fool, I led us there. Next time, he won't wait. He'll kill us as soon as he gets the chance.'

'Next time?' Mildrith questioned.

'What?' Sanc replied, glancing around at the other champions. 'You're not forsaking me, are you? You're the one I rely on.'

'Never,' Mildrith said vehemently. 'But you expect us to go for another fight when we lost that one?'

'Come on,' a voice called over. Temyl. His russet hair hung limp across a pale face. He had been struck by a god's power, and he looked like it. 'Share with the rest of us,' the Nerisian demanded. 'If you two are talking about what next, we all have a right to hear. I don't remember agreeing to you being in charge. And we've all experienced where following this outlander got us.'

Sanc stood. He was weary of it all. He felt as lost as anyone else, he was sure. But he had to fight to keep this group together. Let it fall apart, and everything was over.

'We were defeated,' he admitted, as everyone turned to listen. 'But we stopped him, do you remember? Ezenachi tried to immobilise us; control us, as he's done to entire armies. And we resisted. We have that power when we work together. That is how your ancestors defeated him, I am sure of it. So, how did we lose? He had his champions with him, and an army of thousands. It was too much for us. I admit that. But if we lead an army of Dalriyans, we can beat him.' Sanc forced a confidence into his voice and words that he didn't really feel.

'You think that's possible?' Mergildo asked him. The Rasidi didn't share the antagonism of Temyl. His was a rigorous, logical temperament. In some respects, even harder to deal with. 'From what we've heard and seen, the people of this world are all but defeated.'

'I know it's possible. Morbaine is gone, but my family's kingdom of

Guivergne is greater. The empire of Brasingia is greater even still. Their armies have been stopped by Ezenachi in the past. But now we can protect them.'

'I say this world is doomed,' said Temyl. 'Better to return to Silb, while we can.'

'Better to fight here than in Silb,' Mildrith countered.

Sanc had known where those two would stand. He looked at the other champions. The Rasidi, the Teld, the Gadenzian, and the Eger Khan. His mission hung in the balance.

'Why not,' Guntram said, 'see with our own eyes what kind of army the Dalriyans can muster. Then we can decide our course based on the facts.'

That was an unexpected source of support. Sanc had assumed the Gadenzian would follow the Nerisian's lead. Not this time. He gave the tall warrior a nod of thanks.

Temyl waved a hand, as if too tired to argue. But he must have known he was outnumbered. 'Very well. These Dalriyans must stand and fight if they want to stop Ezenachi. They can't expect us to do all the bleeding.'

* * *

THEY ARRIVED at Valennes in better shape. The injured were healing, and their magical energy, pushed to the brink in the contest against Ezenachi, was restored.

The journey through Guivergne had been eye opening. It had become a land of fear and tension since he had left. It wasn't only the giant lizards he and Mildrith rode north, or their strange companions. Though that hadn't helped their progress. And the presence of the Turned on the border was part of it.

But it was more than that. A sense that trust had broken down. There were signs of conflict in the towns and villages they passed through. New fortifications had appeared, guarded by nervous looking folks who looked like they'd never held a weapon before.

Their relief when they realised he and his companions were merely passing through was palpable.

He was told garbled stories of refugees from the south attacking settlements. Of armies criss-crossing the kingdom, to and from the capital. None of it quite made sense. Peyre had been away, and he'd told Sanc that Esterel had been in Brasingia for months with his army. Still, Sanc was surprised that order had broken down so quickly.

The capital looked almost the same as it always did. Except Sanc could see signs of hasty repairs on the gates. Had the unrest reached as far as Valennes? Certainly, the guards at the gates were out in force, and had hands on hilts at their approach. Again, Spike and Red hardly helped establish a good first impression.

Best to know how things stand. 'Who governs here?' he asked the soldiers.

'King Peyre is in residence,' came the answer.

King Peyre? Two words that knocked the ground from under Sanc's feet. There could only be one reason Peyre was being called king. That bastard Ezenachi had killed Esterel. *I'm sorry, brother. I should have avenged you.*

Herin grabbed his arm, steadying him. 'This is the king's brother. He needs to speak with his majesty.'

There were frowns at that, but some looks of recognition, too. *I've been away so long that I've been all but forgotten.*

'His Highness can enter,' said a man Sanc recognised as a veteran of the military campaigns in Guivergne. 'But who are his companions?'

Herin dug a thumb into Sanc's muscle, waking him from his reverie.

'Don't worry,' Sanc told the man. 'They are with me, and are known to the king. They helped save his life in Morbaine.'

The champions of Silb received some searching looks from the city guards. But perhaps they had been warned of Sanc's arrival, since the veteran waved them all through. 'Keep a leash on those creatures,' he advised. 'Don't want them causing a stir.' He seemed to worry over his words, adding 'Your Highness,' in a show of respect.

245

'Will do,' Sanc confirmed. The respect shown was a little grudging, but the more Sanc thought on it, the very least that was due to him. If Esterel really was dead, he had become the heir to the throne.

It was impossible not to cause a stir, walking through the streets of Valennes with such strange company. Sanc had got used to riding around Silb on Spike, accompanied by an army of lizard riders. Here in Dalriya, they were a complete novelty, and terrifying to many citizens who rushed out of their way. Others simply stared at the sight. The city seemed subdued compared to Sanc's memories. Those who might have approached now looked on with sullen expressions, as if this was only the latest indignity to strike their city. The only exception were the children, who accompanied them on their progress; asking endless, unanswered questions.

A small delegation waited outside the Bastion. Sanc recognised a few faces, first among them Sacha, Esterel's friend, who had risen to a trusted role in the government. He approached the man, handsome as ever, but whose face was grief stricken. It confirmed the answer to his question.

'Is it true?' he asked.

'I'm afraid so, Your Highness. I saw your brother's death myself.'

'Please call me Sanc.'

'Very well. Peyre told us you and your companions went to challenge Ezenachi?'

'We failed to defeat him.'

Sacha nodded, unsurprised. 'But you escaped him, at least. Esterel brought an army against him, and not one of us could even move a muscle without his say so. The fact you survived lends some hope, does it not?'

'I believe it does. Hence, I must speak with the king.'

'Of course. He asked to see you as soon as you returned. He suggests I find your companions suitable rooms?'

Sanc shrugged, then turned to his companions.

'If your brother wants to speak alone for now,' Mildrith said, 'we understand.'

Sanc gave her a little smile, grateful once more for her loyalty. It wasn't the Kassite way of doing things, but she understood things were different here.

No one else, not even Temyl, argued. They all looked tired from their exertions, ready for a safe bed and some proper rest.

They entered the Bastion, and while his companions were found accommodation, he allowed Sacha to lead him to the royal apartments.

Peyre looked relieved to see him. He ushered them both in to his rooms. 'Is it alright if Sacha sits with us?'

'Sure.'

Peyre gestured to two chairs, readied by the fire. A carafe of wine waited for them, and Sanc wasted no time in making himself comfortable.

'Only, Sacha was there, you see. With Esterel. I'd rather you tell Sanc what happened, if you don't mind?'

Sacha took a seat next to Sanc and nodded, though it didn't surprise Sanc to see he didn't relish the task his king had given him.

They all shared their stories. Esterel's confrontation with Ezenachi. Then Sanc told them about his. Finally, Peyre explained what he had found upon returning to Guivergne, and how he had reclaimed the Bastion from the Lord of Saliers.

'Then what of Loysse?' Sanc asked. In that moment, it seemed the only important issue.

'I have sent a team into the east side of the city. Jehan grew up there and knows the places one might hide. Umbert and Gosse are with him. Caisin's agents, as well. If she and Alienor are there—and Lord Caisin assures me that is where they went—they'll find them.'

'I should go,' Sanc said. 'I spent some time there myself, if you recall.'

'I do. And you could locate her?' Peyre asked, suddenly hopeful. 'With your magic?'

Sanc shook his head. 'I can't locate individuals. Only those with magic are more visible than other people.'

'Ah.' Peyre was disappointed. He studied Sanc. 'Unless you think there is something you can do tonight, I suggest you get some rest. You can join in with the search in the morning.'

Sanc found the room Mildrith had been given and lay down next to her. Already asleep, she did little more than grunt at his arrival. But knowing she was next to him helped Sanc give in to sleep.

* * *

HE AWOKE FEELING LITTLE BETTER. It was no surprise his dreams had been troubled, his mind replaying recent events. Elfled with her teeth in Mildrith. Jesper aiming an arrow at Sanc. Ezenachi, killing Esterel with the sword of the Krykkers.

Mildrith shuffled onto her elbows. 'What's today?' she asked, as if fearing the answer.

Sanc could hardly blame her. 'I need to find my sister.'

'I will help. But you should explain everything to the other champions before we go.'

Sanc sighed. She was right.

After checking in with the champions of Silb and ensuring they were being looked after, Sanc, Mildrith, and Herin, who insisted on coming, were ready to begin their search of the east side of the city. In the Grand Foyer of the fortress, they were stopped by a surprisingly cheerful looking Sacha.

'They've found them,' he said, beaming. 'Alive,' he added, unnecessarily.

Sanc felt the stress he carried alleviate. 'Where is she?'

'They're on their way.' Sacha gestured to the edge of the room. 'Please, wait here.'

He hurried off, but soon returned with Peyre, and Lady Liesel. Sanc had learned she had become Esterel's queen while he was away in Silb. She seemed to know who he was, and nodded at him with a shy smile. He grinned back, experiencing a feeling of joy that had been missing for some time.

Then they entered the room. Umbert, Gosse, and the other members of the search party, looking inordinately pleased with themselves. Loysse carried a baby. Sanc's niece, who he had only just learned existed. Next to his sister was the warrior from Barissia, Syele, looking bemused by the fuss. Those waiting in the Foyer began to spontaneously applaud and cheer their arrival.

Loysse gave a little smile, and Sanc could tell she was emotional. Then her eyes caught his and widened in surprise.

'Sanc?'

She rushed over, and they grabbed each other in an embrace.

He felt tears rushing down his face. Loysse was the same, her body wracking with sobs. She pulled away. 'This is Alienor,' she got out.

Their mother's name, of course. He looked at the babe, who looked back at him, a serious expression on her face. 'She's beautiful.'

Loysse smiled, and then Peyre was hugging her, unwilling to wait any longer.

Sanc felt Mildrith's hand at his and he grabbed it, sharing a smile with her. They had lost Esterel, and so many others. But there were still things to be thankful for.

Something made him look up, where the carving of the Owl of Guivergne perched on the balcony above, as if looking over the reunion. It stared down, though its eyes gave nothing away.

THAT EVENING, Peyre hosted his guests at a feast in the main hall. He toasted the champions of Silb, seating them at his table, and passing them the choicest morsels from his plate. It was only common sense for Peyre to want to win them over. After all, the survival of his kingdom and the whole of Dalriya depended on them. But Sanc was pleased that Peyre understood as much, and showed an interest. It wasn't so long ago his brother would have eyed a group of sorcerers with suspicion.

Rab was allowed to attend, and Sanc was pleased to see Peyre had looked after him amid all his other duties. Rab was pleased to see Sanc and Mildrith, but then was soon off bothering the other guests, especially those inclined to pass him a surreptitious treat under the table.

Sanc celebrated as much as anyone—satiating a need to drink and be merry. He enjoyed reuniting with the Dalriyans he had not seen in years. It was pleasing to speak with Umbert and his father, Lord Russell. His father's old friend had aged—no doubt a brief spell as Saliers' prisoner was partly to blame. But the man had always been fair to Sanc—taken an interest in him—and Sanc enjoyed telling him about his adventures in Silb.

Auberi of Famiens was another former prisoner of Saliers'. Sanc was appalled to learn of his blinding by the Brasingians. The duke had refused to go along with Arnoul's treachery and had lost the support of some of his own followers over it. His delight at being reunited with Loysse and Alienor also helped to improve Sanc's opinion of him.

Later, he spoke with Liesel. He counted himself lucky he had spent so much time with Mildrith, otherwise he might have been overawed at talking to such a beauty. Then there was the considerable amount of wine he had imbibed. Which always seemed to help.

They were soon sharing memories of Esterel. Liesel filled in many details of Esterel's life since Sanc had left—including the smaller things which Peyre hadn't bothered to tell. She, in turn, seemed to appreciate Sanc's childhood memories of his brother.

'It is strange,' she said, 'that we share so much in common, and yet have only just met. I feel like I hardly know you, Sanc. Loysse talks about you but Esterel and Peyre—well, their conversation always reverts to swords, and horses, and other dull topics. You know, being men.'

'It's true,' Sanc agreed, 'though it feels like I already knew you before I left. My brother wouldn't stop talking about you.'

She frowned. 'Sanc, Esterel hadn't even met me before you left Dalriya.'

'Not Esterel. Peyre. When he returned from his exile in Barissia.' Sanc smiled at the recollection. He remembered it had seemed like the most romantic thing ever. Peyre, and the emperor's daughter. 'He wasn't talking about swords and horses then, believe me.'

It was only when he noticed Liesel's expression that he realised his mouth had gone before his brain. She didn't know. *Oh gods, Peyre never told her. She married Esterel, and she never knew about Peyre. Except now she does. Because of my drunken stupidity.*

She grabbed his hand, and despite his inebriation, he could feel her squeezing it. Really rather hard. 'Sanc, you're telling me Peyre had feelings for me back then?'

Sanc cast around the hall, desperately looking for Peyre. For anyone who might save him. He knew he had said the wrong thing, but he didn't know what damage he had caused. He didn't know why Peyre had never told her, or what kind of relationship they had. He had been in another world, for the gods' sake. How was he supposed to get out of this?

Liesel's eyes bore into his. They were hazel, with flecks of green, and rather mesmerising. Not as breathtaking as Mildrith's clear blue eyes. Of course not. But still, rather hard to ignore. He could see them thinking, as if realising something she should have already known. Was that good or bad? In his experience, women thinking and realising things was potentially extremely dangerous.

'Sanc, this is important. Peyre has never told me. But I need to know. For his sake as well as mine.'

Sanc gulped. He was trapped. 'He said he fell in love with you. I asked him, did she fall in love with you? He said he was working on that. But then Leopold gave him the scar, and—and you had to escape. That's really all I know.'

Liesel let go of Sanc's hand and closed her eyes. When she opened them, she looked—what? Sorrowful? Rueful? It was hard to say. 'I've been a little stupid, Sanc. As for Peyre. Well. He's been very stupid. Extraordinarily stupid. I see it now. Thank you for opening my eyes.'

PEYRE

VALENNES, KINGDOM OF GUIVERGNE

uberi passed a scrap of parchment across the table. There were six names on it. The first, Arnoul of Saliers. Of course. The second, Robert of Auriac. Peyre grimaced. He was already dead. Loysse had told him the story, and asked him not to share it with her husband.

The third surprised him. 'Firmin? The same man who trades across the realm?' He'd always found him to be polite. Uninterested in politics.

'I've learned a few lessons from the experience, Your Majesty. When authority recedes, others will soon fill it. My understanding is that Firmin was the worst of the lot. Whipped up hatred in the city that led to cruelty, and the death of innocents. Doing Saliers bidding, perhaps. But he revelled in the power he had over people.'

'Very well. And the last three—'

'All men who betrayed me.' Auberi was always calmly spoken, but Peyre could see his brother-in-law's anger bubbling under the surface. 'It wouldn't have happened if I wasn't blind. Saliers was clever enough. He detached me from Loysse. No doubt there were several private conversations with my retainers that I wasn't aware of. Persuading them of his case. He'd have argued they were doing me a favour. Saving the kingdom. Whatever words they needed to hear. But it was treachery, and those three were the ones who took others with them.

'They left me a prisoner, and argued it was necessary. They invited Lord Russell and Chieftain Frayne to a meeting using my name as an assurance, in an underhanded ploy to capture them.'

'I see.' Peyre shared in Auberi's anger. But where that left the duke's authority now, it was hard to assess. The execution of these three would go some way in restoring it, he supposed. But Auberi and Loysse had lost control of the kingdom. Allowed Saliers to take the capital, including the Bastion. *I am king now*, Peyre told himself. *And I cannot hide from the hard choices. Can I trust them again? Or should I take the blame for allowing Saliers to blind me to the threat he posed?*

'What of Benoit?' he asked Auberi. 'Do you think it was foolish of me to spare him?'

'You won back the Bastion without bloodshed,' Auberi reminded him. 'So no, not foolish. But I fear you can never trust him.'

'No. I cannot leave him in Guivergne. That means taking him south with me.'

'So that is the next step? Leaving the kingdom with the army once more?'

'Aye. I have been speaking with my brother and his companions. They believe they can stop Ezenachi. But he has his champions, and thousands of Turned fighters. We need to match his army with one of our own. I wish there was an alternative, but there it is. If we want to survive, we need to be ready to fight.'

'The people are scared and sick of war. They have little appetite for another campaign after what happened to your brother. Remember, the army of Guivergne witnessed it. I've heard the story hundreds of times now, how not even one of them could even lift their sword arm against this foreign god.'

'I know. But I am their king now. I must persuade them.'

* * *

253

WITH INDECENT HASTE, Peyre's coronation was held the day after the executions. He didn't have the time for the grand celebrations of his brother's reign. Not that he really minded.

Recent events in the city impelled him to have the ceremony in the cathedral, as was tradition. Soldiers patrolled the streets, armed and armoured. A show was made of Peyre's guests: King Ida of Magnia; chieftains Cuenin and Jorath of the Midder Steppe; Lord Russell, representing the duchy of Morbaine. The honour guard outside was formed of Cordentine arbalests. It confirmed that a new regime had swept the old away.

Many in Valennes had been quick to lend their support to Saliers. Few had opposed him. That was the reality. Peyre needed to show these people he was in full command of the kingdom. That the interlude of chaos and hatred was over.

The city's bishop led the ceremony. The third time he had done so in four years. Peyre couldn't help recalling the two previous occasions. In this building, his father had hobbled to the chancel. Leaning on his walking stick, he'd come close to falling on his way up the stairs. Esterel's ceremony had taken place in the north of the city, on a platform specially built for the occasion. Peyre recalled it had been so noisy that few had heard his brother's words.

Two very different ceremonies, and two different kings. Peyre felt their loss keenly. But his predecessors on the throne had been his role models, and he resolved to learn from them. To do the best he could.

Even though his parents and brother weren't here to witness his elevation, he wasn't alone. Those people who were important to him were with him. Loysse, who he had feared dead only a few days ago. She sat with Auberi, the highest-ranking nobleman present. Sanc, returned to Dalriya after being away for so long. Umbert and Lord Russell. Liesel sat with them, too. Things were not right between them since he had shared his feelings. But it meant everything that she had come.

Behind them, the rows of seats were filled with the great and good of the kingdom. Then there were Magnians, Middians, and Cordentines. Also invited were six sorcerers, not even of this world. *What would father have thought of that?*

At last, the time had come. Peyre left his seat and walked up to the chancel. To his surprise, he felt no nerves. *Perhaps that means I am ready. Perhaps it's just there is so much else I need to do.*

'I, Peyre, swear to serve the people of Guivergne. I will uphold the commandments of the gods. I forbid all acts of robbery, harm and injustice and will punish all lawbreakers, regardless of their station in life. I will show mercy and strive to remove the burdens on the people. I will recover the lost lands of Morbaine. I will not rest until Ezenachi and his Turned are defeated, and every border of the kingdom is secure. Only then, when Dalriya is at peace, will I find my own peace.'

There. The issue his father had avoided, and his brother had skirted around. The menace that had brought Peyre to the throne. That was what he would strive to achieve, and everyone might as well know it from the outset.

An expectant silence hung over the cathedral after Peyre's words. The bishop of Valennes held aloft the crown of Guivergne, then placed it on Peyre's head.

An almighty roar filled the building. Raw emotion hit him like a wave. He saw the tears on Loysse's face and had to look away. *They're with me*, Peyre realised, as the noise echoed off the walls, rolling over him. Their faith humbled him. *I must honour it.*

THE FEAST, held in the Bastion, was a chance for Peyre to meld his disparate group of allies. The refugees from the south had been cast as the kingdom's enemies by Saliers, and many here had gone along with that. Now Ida, and the last chieftains of the Steppe, sat at the king's table. As did those strangers from Silb. Sanc assured him that such an event was not alien to them, and they seemed at ease. But no one could understand a word they said, except his brother and the Magnian, Herin. Herin's scowl at being given the role of translator grew as each course was presented, and the integration of the outlanders was far from perfect.

The end of the feast was the moment for Peyre to announce his appointments. There were only two vacant fiefs. He made Umbert Duke of Morbaine. He'd thought of warning his friend beforehand, but was rewarded with his stupid look of surprise. Umbert was his most loyal of friends, and could rely on Lord Russell's experience to guide him in government. In one sense, it was an empty title, since not one acre of the duchy was free of the Turned. But it gave Umbert the army of Morbaine, still the best in the kingdom's forces.

The lordship of Corbenay, vacant since Miles was killed in Coldeberg, would revert to his nephew when the boy came of age. But for now, Peyre needed its resources and soldiers. He had considered Gosse first. But Sacha was on friendly terms with the family, and could manage the situation. When he announced this, Sacha looked as surprised as Umbert had—though Sacha did surprised in a dashing way, with none of the gawping and mumbling Umbert had provided. Sacha was an able administrator, and Peyre needed him. With the lordships of Courion and Corbenay, he now had the resources equivalent to a duke.

Then there were the court titles. Peyre kept Caisin on as Lord Chancellor. He was still indispensable to the good government of the kingdom, and he'd remained loyal to Loysse in the face of Saliers' pressure. Brancat remained as castellan—Peyre could hardly remove his old weapons master.

As Royal Steward, he appointed Loysse. There were more than a few raised eyebrows at appointing a woman to government. But she was clever, and she was the one who would stay behind to act as his regent.

He made Gosse Marshal of Guivergne. As a warrior, he had few equals. As a general, time would tell.

'Finally,' he announced, 'a new role at court.' He'd run this one past Sanc first. 'But one borrowed from other kingdoms I have visited. My brother Sanc is appointed Archmage of Guivergne.'

Peyre noted a few in the hall couldn't hide their looks of horror.

'I am honoured, Your Majesty,' Sanc said with a bow.

A small smile played on his brother's lips as he said it. *No doubt he thinks the title beneath him,* Peyre considered. *And of course, it is. Sanc is the most important individual here, not me. But that's not how everyone else thinks. The king is the highest power, apart from the gods. And if Sanc serves me, people can accept him—and his companions. And that is what I need to create. A unity of purpose. That's the only way we win, and we need to have it today, not tomorrow.*

With the formalities over, Peyre's guests were free to mingle. He was pleased when Liesel came to speak to him. There had been an unpleasant distance between them since their reunion.

He suddenly wondered if she had wanted some official position from him. Did she feel a loose part? Guilt gnawed at him. He had thought she had the arbalests. But that was a terrible step down for the woman who had been Queen of Guivergne.

'I've been wanting to talk with you for a while, Your Majesty,' she said. 'I thought I'd wait until now.'

They wandered to the side of the hall, letting others know they wished for some privacy. 'Please, Liesel. Call me Peyre. You allowed me to call you by name when you were queen.'

'Very well. I had the pleasure of speaking with Sanc. Until a few days ago, I had only heard others speak of him.'

'Of course. I'm sorry I didn't introduce you properly.'

'He helped me realise something, Peyre. The other day, when you said you loved me—'

'It's alright,' Peyre interrupted, eager not to return to that conversation.

'No. You need to understand. Please listen. I need to apologise for my reaction. After Esterel died, Idris proposed to me. Then Sacha proposed to me.'

'Sacha?' Peyre repeated, bemused. He turned to look for the Lord of Courion.

'Peyre,' Liesel admonished.

She was one of the few people perfectly happy to tell him off despite the fact he was now king.

'I was hurting, and I felt like I was just a piece of property, to be claimed by anyone with a thirst for power. But you didn't propose, Peyre. You told me you loved me.'

She reached over, taking his hands in hers. A sliver of Peyre's mind wondered what people would make of it. The rest of it didn't care in the slightest.

'It was only after I spoke with Sanc that I realised that,' she continued. 'Then I realised that ever since we first met, you have been looking out for me. Looking after me. Remember when you saved me from Salvinus? Sanc told me you fell in love with me even then. And when I look back on that time, it's like I'm looking at a different person than the one I have become. And of course you loved me. I should have seen it. But that Liesel didn't think anyone loved her. I don't know how no one else noticed.'

'Tegyn did. I begged her not to tell you.'

Liesel shook her head. 'She should have ignored you. Friends don't keep such things from each other.'

'It was too late to tell you.'

'Esterel and I were already married?'

'No. He'd already told me he loved you.'

She shut her eyes for a moment. When she opened them, there were tears. 'You even sacrificed your own happiness for me, Peyre. All that time when you were short with me. I thought I had done something wrong. That you didn't like me. You must have known that, and yet you still kept it to yourself. For me, and for Esterel. I don't deserve you.'

Peyre's heart was thumping in his chest. It had been so long since he had first laid eyes on her. He had lost her before he'd ever had her. He'd got used to the reality of never having her. And now, she was holding his hands, and gazing into his eyes in a way that—what? Made him happy. Could it be that some people lived every day with someone that made them this happy? It didn't seem possible. 'I—I don't know what to say, Liesel.'

'For what it's worth, Peyre. Esterel never loved me. He thought he did. I find it hard to believe you might still want me after all this time. I'm your brother's widow. I couldn't give him a child.'

'Of course I want you, Liesel.'

'Then I'm yours, Peyre. Forever, or as long as you want me.'

'Forever, please.' Peyre looked about the hall at his guests and he was filled with a sense of dread at making small talk into the wee hours. 'And I want to be alone with you. Now.'

'You can't just leave your own coronation celebration.'

'I'm the king, Liesel.' He pulled her closer, and she smiled. His dreams were coming true. 'I'm the blasted king, and I can damn well leave if I want to.'

IDRIS

DUCHY OF LUDERIA

The body of the Bear-man lay sprawled where it had fallen, its back against a giant boulder. Multiple red wounds in its torso were testament to the brutality of its final moments.

Spears were the only effective weapon against the creatures. Idris's gaze ranged from the deadly claws at the end of its muscled arms, capable of crushing any armour, to the powerful jaws protruding from its face. More beast than man, in his opinion.

But then, the Bear-men they fought had been turned by Ezenachi. Who was to say what they had been before? *Gentle and loving, for all I know.* That was a thought. Certainly, since leading the fight back against this new enemy, Idris had learned they rarely operated in packs. This one, like most, had fought and died alone.

He dipped both hands into the freshly made wounds, returning them several times to smear the creature's blood up his arms and across his bare torso.

Footsteps told him his brief moments of tranquility were over.

Turning, he saw it was his sister. That usually meant there was some task he was required for.

Tegyn looked at the smeared blood on his body, already drying brown, with a silent question.

'It cools my skin.'

She shrugged an acknowledgement. 'We've met with the Caladri scouts. Seems we've driven the last of them east.'

It had taken a three-pronged attack to deal with the rampaging Bear-men. Idris had led the Luderians north from Witmar. Duke Jeremias had come from the west with the soldiers of Rotelegen. The Blood Caladri had left their forests and pushed south, led by Queen Hajna. Unable to resist, the Bear-men had either died or retreated east, into the marshes of the Sparewaldi. There, he was assured by his Luderian advisers, the tribesmen would make short work of the creatures.

The maps in the castle library in Witmar all confidently asserted that this quaggy hole in Dalriya was a part of his duchy. Except everyone he asked told him no one went into the marshes. The tribesmen who lived there paid no tax, nor did they recognise his authority in any meaningful way. Any attempt to change this situation, it was stressed, would be the most foolish thing it was possible for a Luderian duke to attempt. Which, of course, made him want to do it all the more. He sighed. Maybe a fun project when this Ezenachi business was over.

'So we will meet with the Caladri?' he asked Tegyn.

'Maybe even their queen.'

'That would be something. Maybe even more fun than wading through a swamp.'

She looked at him like he was mad. 'Come on, Emperor Idris. Time to leave the Bear-man corpse.'

WHEN THEY ARRIVED at the meeting point, a cliff overlooking a bend in a river, Jeremias was already there, in conversation with Queen Hajna. Their entourages stood close by. It seemed the queen had travelled by carriage. The vehicle stood a few yards away, attached to four muscular creatures that looked like giant bulls.

The Caladri were strange to behold—clawed feet, thin-limbed, while their eyes stared just like a bird's. Queen Hajna was the most enticing creature Idris had ever seen. She shared her people's alien looks, and yet seemed to possess a wisdom and grace beyond that of humans. *Perhaps it is just me, but I think she is alluring.*

'Your Majesty,' Tegyn said, taking it upon herself to make the introductions. 'My brother, Emperor Idris.'

'It is an honour to meet you, Queen Hajna.'

'Likewise.' She couldn't help but look at where his skin was puckered and discoloured. But he was used to that. 'Thank for your help in dealing with Ezenachi's invaders. They have been a scourge in our lands. We've had to track each one down through the woodland. It has been easier since we pushed them into the open.'

'We've done all we need to?' Jeremias asked.

'I'm assured by the Luderians that they will not survive the marshland,' Idris told him.

'Agreed,' said the Queen of the Blood Caladri. Hajna looked about them, head twitching from side to side as she examined their location. They had good views in all directions, and the river was at their back. 'We could make a camp here safely?'

'Aye, don't see why not,' Idris said.

'Good. We have allies travelling south down the Great Road. My scouts tell me they will arrive in Rotelegen tomorrow.'

Jeremias frowned. 'Not the Griennese?' he demanded.

All things considered, Idris had found Duke Jeremias to be mild-mannered and easy to work with. Many men in his position might have decided Idris had stolen the imperial title from him. But mention of the Griennese or Trevenzans would instantly change his personality. He would bare his teeth and a look of murderous hatred appear in his eyes. Perhaps it was on account that those people had tried to take his duchy from him, not to mention kill him and his young family.

'No. The Kalinthians have sent a delegation of Knights south.'

'Why would they do that?' Idris asked.

'To help us in our struggle against Ezenachi. They don't have things easy in the north. The Jalakh Khan has a great army, and he is hungry for conquest. But Kalinth has answered my call for help. My husband and king, Lorant, took the staff of our people south to defeat

Ezenachi. He and his companions failed. Ezenachi must be stopped, and my husband saved.'

Recognition dawned on Idris. 'It was your husband who gave me this,' he said, gesturing at the burned flesh on his torso, arm, and shoulder. A sorcerous fire, so hot it still burned him. 'And killed my cousin.'

Hajna studied Idris's injuries. 'I am sorry,' she said, though he could read little emotion on her face. 'But remember, it wasn't really my husband. Ezenachi is a parasite, infecting the minds of his victims. Infecting our world. He must be destroyed.' She shared a look with Jeremias. 'Dalriyans have defeated such an enemy before, in living memory. It is time to do so again.'

* * *

THEY BROKE camp early and travelled west to meet with the Kalinthians.

A thrill ran down Idris's spine when the Knights appeared.

The sun glinted off their armour; the metal polished brighter than he thought possible. Their banners, depicting the Winged Horse of Kalinth, were vibrantly coloured. It made his Luderians look like the meanest of sellswords.

Nor was it just a matter of appearance. Their horses, bred for war over centuries, were formidable looking. It was known the Knights were the greatest cavalry force in Dalriya. Few had come. About five hundred knights, with as many squires. But a single Knight of Kalinth was worth many times more than some of the rabble Idris had led here.

Queen Hajna introduced their leader as Leontios, Grand Master of the Knights. His title was extravagant, but he had come in the same war gear as his soldiers. Muscular, with short blond hair, he gave every impression of knowing how to wield lance and sword. 'I have a message from King Theron,' he said, taking a small parchment from his saddlebag. 'Excuse my reading, I am not a learned man.'

Leontios read the message. He was hesitant and struggled more than once. 'I hereby put my Grand Master and his Knights of Kalinth at the disposal of the Emperor of Brasingia, for as long as is required until Ezenachi is properly defeated. I visited Essenberg in the year 658, at the request of Emperor Baldwin. My kingdom was in dire need of help against the Isharites. I left Brasingia with nothing. The message I received was, in short, *we have our own problems*. Now I am King of Kalinth, I am resolved to not repeat such a message. So it is, despite the ever present threat of the Jalakh horde, I am sending this force south to help our allies. Signed, King Theron.'

Taking his lead from Jeremias and Hajna, Idris murmured his appreciation.

Internally, he felt the Empire had been insulted. *I'm all for sticking the boot into the Kellish*, he assured himself, feeling no personal criticism. *Still. Can't help thinking this Theron sounds a little superior. It's us doing the fighting and the dying here, after all.*

Not that refusing his help crossed his mind for an instant. 'Will you travel with us to Essenberg?' he asked Leontios. 'I would like to host your force in the Imps, our city's barracks.'

'Of course, that would be an honour, Your Majesty. I have a personal favour to ask; though if it is an inconvenience, I would rather you declined.'

Idris frowned. The man was so polite, he felt it would be difficult to refuse anything. *Not a foot rub, though, Leontios. That would be a hard pass.* 'Please, Grand Master, ask away.'

'I would like to pay my respects at Burkhard Castle. To those who fell in its defence.'

It wasn't what Idris had been expecting. A small glance to the side, and he saw Tegyn and Jeremias subtly nodding their encouragement. 'Of course,' he replied. 'It is a minor detour off the Great Road. We can ride there and catch up with the foot soldiers easily enough.'

'Perfect,' Leontios replied. 'I am most grateful.'

. . .

THEY CONNECTED with the Great Road and travelled south. The sun was out, and the heat irritated his skin. But when a breeze came, it felt heavenly.

Idris sent a good half of the Luderians back to their homes. Jeremias also left with his force to Rotelegen, albeit with orders to be on high alert. That meant Idris's remaining soldiers were outnumbered by his strange new allies.

The Caladri and Kalinthians seemed ready to go to war. Idris certainly wasn't. He'd witnessed how that had gone for Esterel and had no intention of repeating the experience. Ezenachi had shaken up the status quo in Dalriya. Somehow—miraculously—that had left Idris on top. He wasn't about to upset the apple cart.

However, a force of Kalinthian Knights and Caladri archers would strengthen his position in Essenberg. He wasn't so naïve to think the Kellish nobility hadn't been conspiring in his absence. No doubt there were many who couldn't sleep as long as Leopold's Atrabian prisoner ruled over them. But any plots they might have concocted won't have included taking on these new foreign allies.

The idea put him in a good mood, giving him the patience to listen to Tegyn's prattle. She wouldn't stop talking about the Kalinthian, Leontios.

'A Grand Master is a grand title in Kalinth, is it not?' she asked him. 'Second only to the king himself, I would say.'

'Wait,' he said, finally cutting through to her point. 'You are talking about a marriage with Leontios?'

Most of Tegyn's talk was, directly or indirectly, about the great question of her marriage. It was an obsession that made his sister, always the sensible sibling, seem not quite right in the head. But although he didn't know exactly how, he realised the obsession was linked to the loss of their father. And so most of the time, especially on good mood days, he was charitable about it.

'Tegyn, you know he is a Knight of Kalinth?'

'Of course I know that.'

'Well,' he added, remaining patient, 'all knights swear a vow of chastity. Including the Grand Master.'

'Oh,' she said, looking crestfallen. 'Now you mention it. I knew about that. I had forgotten.'

Idris struggled to think of something to say. 'Maybe we'll both end up old spinsters, you and I. But at least we'll have each other.'

'Yes, maybe.'

She didn't seem very consoled, and Idris could hardly blame her. But neither could he think of anything comforting to say, so they rode in silence.

BURKHARD CASTLE LOOMED large as their small party approached it. Evening had arrived. It was still warm, but not as oppressive as earlier in the day, and it felt like a pleasant time to visit the site.

Although called a castle, it was actually two huge crags stood side by side. Idris had to crane his neck to look up to the summit. The crags had once been connected by a bridge, with keeps constructed atop each one.

For a long time, it had been celebrated by the Kellish as virtually impregnable. Until Isharite sorcery had unleashed a dragon. Suddenly, the defences had been accessible, each keep destroyed by the creature. The imperial army had evacuated Burkhard, and the Isharite armies had poured into the empire. Even Atrabia, so his father told him, had been days away from falling to them.

'Thank you for accompanying me. I would very much like to go to the top,' Leontios said, gesturing at the winding path that led up the nearest crag. 'I am happy to do so by myself and catch you up.'

Idris and Tegyn shared a grin. 'My sister and I never decline a climb.'

'A Caladri can climb as well as any human,' Hajna said.

Idris thought he detected a sense of humour there, even though the queen's words were said with a straight face.

'Come, then,' Tegyn said. 'It's quite a climb.'

The four of them made their way up. Idris was quick to notice the signs of battle as they walked past. The scrapes of sharp metal on stone. The long stretches where the carved walkway was still blackened from dragon fire. He imagined fighting here against the monstrous Drobax, wearing full armour. Imagined being burned alive in said armour. His skin prickled at the thought. Jeremias had fought here—still a boy, so the stories said. So many must have fallen.

All four of them needed to take a breath at the top. Idris wasn't prepared for the desolation he found. The keep was nothing more than rubble. Wooden defences had been erected where it had stood.

'That must be where the Guivergnais made their camp,' Tegyn said.

Idris nodded his agreement. The ill-fated occupation of Burkhard by the Duke of Famiens. Leopold had told him all about what he had done to the Guivergnais intruders.

Bones were still visible, scattered about the top of the crag. Bleached white after so many years. Some human, some Drobax, no doubt. It wasn't hard for Idris to imagine the last moments of the defenders here. Overrun by Drobax. He glanced across at the second crag. They would have escaped there, across the bridge. He walked to the edge and looked down. He had no fear of heights. But that was a fall that would give you some thinking time before you hit the ground.

'Why has the castle never been restored?' Leontios stood next to him, looking at the same drop.

Idris shrugged. 'That's a question I never asked Leopold, or his advisers. I must admit, it never crossed my mind until now. Most likely, it never crossed his.'

'Even though it was his father who led the defence here?'

'Maybe because of that.'

The comment made him think about his own father's actions in those days. Tegyn and Hajna joined them. Something compelled Idris to speak. 'I wish my father had brought the Atrabians here.'

'What?' Tegyn said, bristling. 'How can you say that? You know how deeply the hate runs for the Kellish, after what they've done to us. Our people would never have come here to fight under their banner.'

'I know that,' Idris conceded. 'But it was a chance to end all that.' He looked around. 'A sacrifice was made here. Something that brought the people of the other duchies together. And we excluded ourselves. It wasn't cowardice, I understand that. But it's no wonder they look at us with suspicion. They made the sacrifice for everyone in Dalriya, including the Atrabians. We weren't here. And we haven't even shown them any gratitude.'

Tegyn curled her lip, refusing to listen. She loved her father too much to accept anything that sounded like criticism.

Leontios and Hajna looked at him, saying nothing. It wasn't for them to comment. But he knew what they wanted. They wanted him to lead the Empire against Ezenachi.

I'd do it, he declared to himself, filled with the emotion of Burkhard Castle. *It's not like I have a tremendous sense of self-preservation. But they haven't felt the power of a god. They don't know what it's like to be so powerless. I know that place too well. I don't plan on returning.*

SANC

VALENNES, KINGDOM OF GUIVERGNE

I don't recall you ever looking this happy,' Sanc told his brother. They were in the royal apartments, just the two of them. 'I don't think it's got much to do with your elevation to the throne, either.'

Peyre smiled. 'No. It's nothing to do with that. Liesel and I spoke the other night. We—shared some feelings.'

He went a little red. Sanc couldn't recall seeing that before, either.

'Ah,' Sanc said, pleased to have his suspicions confirmed. 'So really, you owe me some thanks for putting my foot in it.'

Peyre narrowed his eyes. 'I'll let you off this once, brother. But don't make a habit of it. Anyway, we're here to make plans. The army's ready to march, but we need to decide where we are going and how to defeat him once and for all.'

'Alright. But I'm not the best at tactics.'

'That's where I come in. You and your friends have the sorcery, and I have the army. Now, tell me what happened when you attacked Ezenachi. It should help us develop a strategy.'

So Sanc told him. How they had walked past the Turned and taken on Ezenachi and his champions. How Belwynn's intervention had allowed them to escape. 'We held our own against him for a while. But when the Turned came for us, we were done for. With your army, my hope is we don't have to worry about them. We can focus on defeating Ezenachi.'

Peyre had an astonished look on his face. 'You just walked up to him and started blasting your magic?'

Sanc felt a little embarrassed. 'No. I made sure we were ready to withstand his attempt to immobilise us. And we did.'

Peyre lifted his hands in apology. 'Sorry. I get that. But there are seven of you, all with your own set of powers. Surely you need to work out how best to use them together?'

'It's not that easy, Peyre. Until recently, most of us were enemies. Sorcerers don't let their peers know what they can and can't do. When Mergildo healed Umbert, that was the first I knew what exactly he could do. But you're right. We need to work together more closely.'

Peyre nodded. 'Good. And you can still track his whereabouts?'

Sanc closed his eyes and searched for Ezenachi. He had done it so many times recently that he could find him almost instantly. 'He's still in the Midder Steppe. As are all the champions I can see. Those with magic.'

'He knows you can see him?'

'He must know that.'

'So, he's leaving us guessing. From the Midder Steppe, he could take his forces east into the empire, or north at us. But Liesel says Idris submitted to him. I haven't. So almost certainly, he plans to come here.' Peyre thought about it. 'He can see you and the other sorcerers?'

'Yes.'

'Which means he knows we are allied. He could be waiting to see what we do next, as much as we are studying him. We need a ruse. You and the outlanders are the ones to do it.'

'Alright,' Sanc agreed.

He had wondered what kind of king Peyre would make. But his brother had matured so much since he had left. Accustomed to giving orders and leading armies.

Sanc breathed a little easier. It had felt like he'd been carrying all the responsibility for defeating Ezenachi. Even more since returning to Dalriya, to discover Rimmon was dead. The witch, Inge. Esterel. The list went on.

Peyre was telling him what must be done, and he was grateful for every word.

* * *

SANC WAS a little taken aback that he was allowed to hold his niece. 'What if I drop her?' he had asked, to which Loysse replied, 'Don't.'

'I've only just had the chance to make her acquaintance,' he complained. Alienor had fallen asleep shortly after being passed into Sanc's arms, but she had stared up at him and held his thumb, which he counted as a greeting. 'Now I'm leaving again.'

'There'll be time,' Loysse assured him. 'After it's done.'

She said it as if she had no doubts. But that wasn't possible. Ezenachi had taken too many from them. Even if they somehow bested him, there were no guarantees everyone was coming back.

'I suppose. I'm sorry you're the one staying behind again.'

'I'm used to it. Besides, your feelings change when you have a baby. She's better off here. We weren't on the run for very long, but I constantly feared for her. I'm happy not to go through that again.'

Sanc could understand that. Having a child seemed like a great responsibility. He felt responsible for Alienor's future—for everyone in Dalriya. But it was a different responsibility to that of being a parent, he was sure. He held her a while longer, reluctant to let her go.

Something was on his mind, but he was hesitant about sharing it 'You know, I had a vision, back in Silb. Of our mother.'

'Yes?' Loysse said, gently prompting. No judgement. *How would you know what she looked like*, she could have said to him.

'I had gone to kill the King of Nerisia. Lothar. But she appeared and told me not to. She was right. We won Lothar to our cause in the end. If we hadn't, there wouldn't be seven sorcerers on our side now. Anyway, I was thinking about it. It must have happened at about the same time as Alienor came into the world. Perhaps it was related. Maybe the fact that you named your daughter Alienor, freed mother to appear and guide me? It sounds strange and unlikely when I say it out loud. But do you think it's possible?'

Loysse studied him. 'Maybe. But isn't it also likely that the vision was something you created yourself? Deep down, you knew what was right. And your mind came up with someone you trusted to tell you what to do. If mother appeared to tell me something, I would do it, no questions asked.'

'Yes, I suppose. That's most likely.' *You fool, Sanc. If mother could return, wouldn't she choose to visit her daughter and granddaughter? Not the boy who...the boy she never got to know.*

Sanc gently deposited Alienor into her cot.

Loysse kissed him on the cheek. 'Mother is watching over us, Sanc. And father. And Esterel. You were given your powers for a reason. To defend Dalriya. And that's what you'll do.'

* * *

THEY GATHERED outside the southern walls, where Peyre had smashed his way into the city.

Returning to Valennes had been important. After Ezenachi had defeated them, Sanc had needed to see a route to victory. He had that now, and could communicate it to the other champions.

Despite that, he was eager to leave. It seemed the champions of Silb shared his energy. Rested and restored, it was time to get revenge on the god who had bested them.

There was one last, difficult farewell first.

'You'll look after him, won't you?' he asked Herin.

The Magnian had Rab on a lead, probably the only way to stop him from trying to follow the champions. They would use their magic to move fast, and there was no point in carrying Herin or Rab with them.

'Of course,' Herin said roughly. The old warrior turned to Kepa. 'See you soon,' he said, a lot more tenderness in his voice. Sanc tried not to take offence.

Sanc clambered up to sit on Spike's saddle. The great lizard stretched his legs, as if he too was keen to get moving. Mildrith was on Red, and the Eger Khan on Ripper. They were missing Herin's unnamed mount, the one casualty in their first assault on Ezenachi. Sanc felt the great creature's loss all over again.

Mergildo still had his camel; Temyl, Guntram, and Kepa, their horses. Those on horseback moved off first, their mounts perhaps the most eager of all to get going.

Sanc encouraged Spike to follow on.

Rab gave a little whimper, which tore at Sanc's heart.

'I'll see you soon,' he called over to his companion.

Mildrith gave him a sympathetic look. 'He'll be fine.'

'I wish I could explain it all to him.'

Red pattered off with her quick strides, and Spike lumbered to keep up.

Sanc kept glancing across at Mildrith. He hadn't got to see much of her over the last few days, and it felt good to be adventuring together again. How he wished it were just the two of them. They still had no privacy.

That little smile came to the Kassite's face, when she knew she had his attention. He knew she understood his recent preoccupations. She wasn't jealous. Of all the champions, Mildrith was unconditionally on his side, and that gave him strength.

They followed the roads south through Guivergne. They could have teleported immediately. But their mounts needed the exercise.

More than that, their progress was sure to get Ezenachi's attention, just as the god's movements had grabbed Sanc's. The road they took revealed little about their destination. They could travel to the kingdom's border; to the Empire; to the Steppe; or to Morbaine.

Peyre's stratagems bolstered Sanc's confidence. He enjoyed the thought of Ezenachi wondering what they were up to; how he should respond. The god could see that Sanc and the six champions of Silb were together. But he couldn't know they were alone. He had to prepare for the possibility that they led the army of Guivergne. And their pace—moving at riding speed—suggested just that.

The more Sanc thought about it from Ezenachi's perspective, the more he believed their enemy would funnel soldiers westward to counter their movement. The concept Peyre had introduced to him—of thinking like his enemy—was at once simple and revolutionary.

They made camp at the side of the road. At last, Sanc and Mildrith could stretch their legs and claim some precious time alone.

'So he could be looking at us now?' Mildrith asked after he had shared his thoughts with her. She had a horrified look, which surprised him. Mildrith wasn't easily unnerved.

'Not at *us*. Our consciousness. A sorcerer's is like a light in the darkness.'

'Is that supposed to make me feel better?' she asked, though she looked a little relieved.

'Peyre stressed something else, which makes a lot of sense to me. How we and the other champions need to improve how we fight together. We should learn to complement our powers and work as a team.'

'I suppose he's right. We could do more. Temyl and Guntram have learned to work together over the years. We could start there, ask them for advice.'

Mildrith was willing, if not enthused. That was a start.

'We need to find some way to get the upper hand next time,' Sanc encouraged.

'We need to win!' Mildrith's eyes blazed blue. 'We convinced the others to give this one more try. But don't expect more than that, Sanc. If we can't defeat him, they'll return to Silb. This is our one chance, with the seven of us together.'

Sanc chewed on his lip as the implications of Mildrith's warning struck home. He envisaged a Dalriya where every single person was under Ezenachi's spell. They weren't so far from such an outcome. They would have to win or die trying. Retreating to fight another day was no longer an option.

'Then let's broach the subject with them now. If Peyre's plans are a success, our contest with Ezenachi is only days away.'

LIESEL

VALENNES, KINGDOM OF GUIVERGNE

The Owl of Guivergne observed their parting. It seemed to glare down—as if warning them of the dangers they faced.

Liesel thought none of them needed such a warning. She gave Loysse a farewell hug. 'May the gods protect you and yours,' she whispered.

'I will pray for you, too. And try to look after my brothers, will you?'

Liesel stiffened. There was no malice in Loysse's words. She knew that. But she had done a terrible job of looking after Esterel, and the guilt had lodged deep within her. 'I will do my best.'

They parted, and Peyre said his goodbyes to his sister. He gave Syele a nod. Then he led their small party away.

Liesel looked back once. The owl stood above Loysse, as if ready to defend her. But it was her Barissian protector, Syele, whose presence by her side gave her the most reassurance.

THEY LED their mounts over the Bastion's drawbridge, then rode them through the city. The recent troubles in Valennes had soured Liesel's

275

perception of the city. Its citizens had exhibited a collective weakness, and she wondered at the capital's ability to withstand their enemies. The Cordentine refugees, who had given her and the kingdom so much, had not received the safety she had promised them. It left her with a dark anger.

She had ordered those Cordentine arbalests with family to stay. At least now, under Loysse's command, they would strengthen the authority of Peyre's regents.

Outside the city walls, thousands of troops lined up, ready to march. She and Peyre stopped for a few moments to inspect them.

'Maybe not quite as great as the army Esterel led out,' Peyre said. 'But considering recent events, it will do.'

'It says a lot about the faith your people have, Peyre,' Liesel said. She was aware he needed reassurance now and again. Esterel never had. 'The gloom in the ranks after Esterel's death was tangible. That so many are prepared to leave once again, so soon afterwards, is testament to it.'

'Hmm. Sanc's arrival played no small role in that,' he said gruffly. But she could tell her words pleased him.

Peyre had given Liesel personal command of her arbalests—a small gesture, but one she appreciated. The royal army, the largest single force, was commanded by Gosse, now Peyre's Lord Marshal. Next in size was the army of Morbaine, under its new duke, Umbert. Sacha, Florent, and Benoit of Saliers, each commanded the soldiers of their own fiefs. King Ida led the Magnians. Finally, Cuenin and Jorath led the Middians.

Some of these warriors had been in conflict until recently. Liesel and Peyre had talked long and hard about how best to deal with them. In the end, Peyre wanted them where he could see them, hopeful that his authority—over Saliers, and the Middians, especially—would be enough to dissuade either side from seeking revenge. Even so, when he gave the order to march, he made sure other units separated them.

They hugged the south bank of the Cousel, letting it lead them to the border with the empire. Peyre took care to send scouts in all directions, allaying Liesel's fears. She worried about the Turned. She worried most about Ezenachi coming to take Peyre from her, while Sanc and the sorcerers he had gathered were absent. It was Peyre's plan to have Sanc travel south, then west to Morbaine.

'Ezenachi can see their movements,' Peyre explained to her, understanding her concerns. 'While without Sanc, we are effectively invisible. He has no reason to believe we are taking the army east. We need to keep it like that for as long as possible.'

She could agree with that. 'And what of your plans for when we finally confront Ezenachi?'

'You mean, how will we defeat him? We are reliant on Sanc for that part.'

'I mean, what does victory look like, Peyre? Inge and Leopold offered Esterel a truce. You and I persuaded him to reject it. I can't help wondering where we would be if we had counselled otherwise.'

Peyre gave her a pained look.

'I'm sorry for bringing it up. But this is something you must think about.'

'I know. I am reminded of my father. To bring peace to Guivergne, he showed clemency to his enemies. Raymon of Auriac turned on him, anyway. And Arnoul of Saliers turned on us when we were at our lowest. We'll be safer with Ezenachi dead. That's the undeniable truth.'

'But he's not easy to kill, Peyre. How much more war and death can Dalriyans take? How much longer will Sanc's allies be prepared to fight for a world that isn't even theirs? We might have to accept the next best thing. Defeat him, and impose a peace that both sides can accept.'

'We might have to, Liesel. And I will do that. If I have to.'

Peyre looked like he might say more, then stopped himself. Still, Liesel knew him well enough to see the "however".

However, Ezenachi killed Esterel, and I would have vengeance on him.

The thing was, Liesel dearly wanted the same thing.

But not at any price.

* * *

IT TOOK four days of relentless travel to reach the Kellish border. The weather was changeable; the sun shining one moment, then heavy downpours the next. The worst of the summer heat seemed to have gone, however, and it felt like autumn was around the corner.

The mood amongst the soldiers was solemn. There was little of the bravado and exultation that accompanied Esterel's invasions. But discipline remained strong, and in that sense, the army reflected its leader.

Not long after they crossed the border, they were met with a force totalling about a thousand. The standard bearers of this force carried many flags, including the Owl of Guivergne and the Stag of Brasingia. Two other designs informed Liesel who approached. A gold fess and three stars on purple, for Martras. The green boar of Barissia.

Domard, who had followed Esterel into Brasingia, and now governed Barissia for Idris. He invited Peyre and his generals to his tent, where he had food and drink waiting. When they entered, Domard got straight to his knees.

'Your Majesty.'

'Please, rise, Your Grace,' Peyre said.

Domard got up, one hand on his knee as he did so. Otherwise, little else betrayed the man's age. He had done well for himself amid the chaos, Liesel supposed. Yet she had no argument with the man. He had stood with Esterel whenever asked to, always ready to take the field with the warriors of his duchy.

Inhan was waiting in the tent with the duke. Peyre had sent him ahead of the army to Coldeberg. The only other individual was Ragonde, a stout warrior of Martras. There were no Barissians.

'I am so sorry about Esterel,' the duke said to Peyre. 'He died a hero.' His eyes went to Liesel's, then Sacha's. 'There was nothing any of us could do against that creature.'

Peyre nodded. 'I know. But I would talk of the here and now.'

'Of course.'

'My brother, Sanc, has returned to Dalriya. We have plans to defeat Ezenachi and the Turned, once and for all. We can leave nothing to chance. I need to know where your loyalties stand, Domard.'

'Of course. I am first and foremost a noble of Guivergne, Your Majesty. You have my complete loyalty. That will never change.'

'Good. How are things in Barissia? And how do you stand with Idris?'

'I have kept Barissia on a war footing. We have Turned on our borders, to both east and west. I have not met with Emperor Idris since his coronation. He has given me little direction, except to stress that I must stand with and give every support to Friedrich of Thesse.'

'And how are things there?'

'The Thessians are the most exposed. They have been strengthening their walls, though they have little chance of resisting should the Turned attack. The truce with Ezenachi has held so far. The Thessians are nervous, but their duke stands firm.'

Friedrich, the boyhood friend of Liesel's brother, son of an emperor, was now in an unenviable position. It pleased her to hear Domard speak of him with praise.

'I assume you are marching to Essenberg?' Domard asked into the silence.

'I am. I would have you with me, though I do not wish to strip Barissia of its defenders.'

'Ragonde can govern in my stead,' Domard assured, gesturing at his man. 'What is our goal in Essenberg, if I may ask?'

Peyre gave a little smile. 'I am not come to claim the imperial title, or any such thing.'

Domard nodded in relief.

'I would like the empire to join with me against Ezenachi. What chance do you give me of persuading Idris?'

Domard scrunched up one side of his face. 'Idris was there with the rest of us when—' he paused. 'He witnessed what Ezenachi did to Esterel and wasted no time in submitting. Unless something has changed, I can't see him deciding to fight.'

* * *

NEXT DAY, they continued east. It was still morning when Gosse's scouts warned them of the advance of the imperial army.

'Idris has got wind of our approach,' Peyre said. 'What mood will he be in?'

'He's unlikely to be happy,' Liesel warned. 'And he's unpredictable at the best of times.'

'I'll do my best to avoid conflict. The size of our army should dissuade him.'

'It would dissuade most people. Not Idris.'

He looked at her and recognised she wasn't joking. 'Maybe you're the best person to go speak with him?'

He was probably right. 'Let me go with a small force of my arbalests. Domard should come. And King Ida.'

Peyre raised an eyebrow.

'I want to stress this is about saving Dalriya. Not Guivergne throwing its weight around.'

'Alright. Whatever you think is best.'

THE ARMIES of Kelland and Luderia were arrayed in the fields before them. No Atrabians, or men of Rotelegen, that Liesel could see. But Idris certainly had enough armed warriors to stop Peyre's plans in their tracks. A war with Brasingia at this point would be madness.

Idris arrived with a small entourage. His standard bearers carried the seven-antlered stag, and the insignia of his four duchies. But some of his companions were a surprise and gave Liesel some hope that the encounter might not end in disaster.

Idris leapt from his horse. He radiated energy. As was his custom now, he was bare chested, his scars and burns on full display.

Tegyn, no less of a horsewoman, joined him. Liesel was pleased to see her old friend. She could also have a moderating effect on her brother. There was a Caladri woman, blonde-haired with a stark beauty, and a male warrior, wearing the finest armour Liesel had ever seen.

Liesel approached them, Domard and Ida on either side. She had thought Idris might dwell on her, as he had done so often in the past. But his eyes passed over her and fixed on Domard, staring hard at the duke.

'So, you have put me aside and fallen in with the Guivergnais?'

'Not at all, Your Imperial Majesty. The army of Barissia remains at home, ready to defend the empire. I merely thought King Peyre's proposals would benefit from my attendance.'

Idris looked slightly mollified. He turned to Liesel. 'And you speak for Peyre, I suppose? He is not king, by the way. Your husband promised the throne of Guivergne to me, should he die without issue.'

Liesel pursed her lips, trying to ignore the stupidity of the statement. 'Peyre's brother, Sanc, has returned from his journeys to another world. He has brought with him six champions, with the magical power to withstand Ezenachi. They have already fought him to a standstill once. But they could not fight off his Turned as well. They need our help. Our combined armies are powerful enough to take on the Turned. That would allow them to defeat Ezenachi.'

The Caladri woman made a small, indecipherable noise. 'My husband is imprisoned by Ezenachi, serving as one of his enslaved champions. This news gives me great hope.'

'This is Queen Hajna of the Blood Caladri,' Tegyn said, looking ashamed the introductions hadn't already been made. 'Leontios, Grand Master of the Knights of Kalinth. Both offer the emperor their support against Ezenachi.'

'Duke Domard of Martras,' Liesel said with a gesture. 'And King Ida of Magnia.'

'I, too, am desperate to rescue an enslaved relative,' Ida said. 'My mother, Elfled.' The king didn't hide the pain from his features.

'My heart goes out to you,' said Hajna. 'We must unite and grasp this opportunity to save them.'

'That is exactly what Peyre and Sanc want us to do,' said Liesel. She looked at Idris, and the others, on each side, did the same.

Idris was staring at some invisible, distant point. Only gradually did he realise they were all looking at him.

A grin, a little too manic for Liesel's liking, appeared on his face.

'This is indeed our chance. Come, Liesel. Fetch Peyre. We must return to Essenberg.'

IDRIS

ESSENBERG, DUCHY OF KELLAND

Idris gathered them in Essenberg Cathedral. All of them.

The nobility of Kelland—those men who had found themselves ruled by an Atrabian, much to their chagrin. The Luderian nobility, who had come to accept him. The other rulers in Brasingia: Domard of Martras, who governed Barissia; Jeremias of Rotelegen; Uncle Emlyn. Peyre was here too, with Liesel, and the magnates of Guivergne. The King of the Magnians. The horse lords of the Steppe. The Queen of the Caladri. The Grand Master of the Knights of Kalinth.

Idris couldn't hold back a grim smile at how fate had twisted his life. He had been a prisoner in this city. A laughing stock—his body a plaything for an emperor. Now *he* was emperor, addressing the most powerful rulers in Dalriya.

Perhaps you are also here, father, he wondered. *Still watching over me. I made myself as steel. Strong and sharp. I hope you are proud. I hope you understand what I must do.*

He strode forward and his audience settled. Whatever they thought of him, he at least had their attention. The bare-chested Atrabian emperor, antithetical to the traditions of the empire. *When I die, will they put my body in the crypt below us,* he wondered, *or dump it in a ditch?*

It doesn't matter.

'We are an unusual gathering,' he told them. 'Representing the four corners of Dalriya. In recent times, the peoples of Dalriya have kept to their own affairs, looking inward. But you don't need me to tell you it wasn't so long ago that Dalriyans came together to fight off the Isharites. The great Emperor Baldwin held a conference in Coldeberg, where Magnians, Kalinthians, Caladri, even Krykkers, came to work together with Brasingians. All played their part in defeating our mutual enemy. All suffered.

'My people, the Atrabians, were not represented. Maybe we weren't invited. Maybe we chose not to attend.' He shrugged. 'But later, we *were* invited to Burkhard Castle. Baldwin asked us to fight and bleed for Brasingia. Because of years of warfare, hostility, and animosity, we refused. I say today, that was a mistake.'

As Idris expected, his statement was met with shouting from his audience. From the Kellish and Atrabians, mainly. On different sides for so long, even now one side agreed with him, while the other disputed his words.

He held his hands up to calm his audience. 'I understand the reasons. But there was something bigger at play then, something that should have made us put aside our differences. Today it is the same, is it not? We all know what Ezenachi has done; what he can and will do. We know the Turned are a threat to all Dalriya—they are our collective future unless we can stop their master.

We, too, must put aside our differences, must we not? King Peyre and I must set aside our claims to one another's titles. The Middians and the Guivergnais must set aside their recent hostilities. The Magnians must put aside their feelings of betrayal at the lack of help offered them by the other nations of Dalriya. The Kalinthians and the Rotelegen have experienced the same feelings in recent memory. The Kellish and Atrabians must, at last, put aside their history of conflict. Not forget—I don't ask that. But we must be able to fight together and trust one another. If we can't, Ezenachi has already won.

'We have a chance in the days ahead. Sorcerous allies have come with the power to stand against Ezenachi. It is our one chance of victory. I know we must take it. I am prepared to face Ezenachi, as emperors Coen and Esterel did before me. I am prepared to risk it all to take this one chance. Will you face our enemy with me?'

Idris's audience thundered their response. He'd won them over. But had he talked sense into them, or infected them with his madness?

* * *

THE COMBINED army that set out from Essenberg was the equal to that great force Esterel had led against Ezenachi. Idris prayed they would fare better. *It's my head on the block this time. And I am yet to meet this Sanc, brother of Esterel and Peyre, whom we are pinning our hopes on.*

Their departure left Kelland and his other duchies stripped of warriors, and vulnerable. Tegyn persuaded him to leave a council of noblemen in place, to govern his territories in his absence. With his countrymen's feelings bruised after his speech, appointing Emlyn to head the council at least went some way to assuage Atrabian honour.

Otherwise, every leading figure in Brasingia, Guivergne, and beyond, was in the army that travelled south-west down the road to Coldeberg.

Peyre and Liesel were convinced that Ezenachi, and much of his Turned army, were to the west. They had no firm evidence of this, and Idris had little choice but to put more faith in the pair.

Jeremias led the men of Rotelegen in the van, followed by Idris's own army of three duchies. The fighters of Magnia, the Steppe, the Caladri, and the Knights, formed a unique auxiliary force. Behind came the massed ranks of the Guivergnais. Wagons full of food followed in the rear. Nonetheless, their supplies wouldn't last long. If they failed to bring their enemies to battle soon, this great army would soon disperse.

Jeremias set a hard pace. Those who couldn't keep up were told to return to Essenberg. Warriors who couldn't march had no place taking food from the supplies. They reached the border with Barissia in three days.

When they made camp, a sprawling mass of humanity stretched out in all directions. Many had tents to sleep in; most didn't. There was a chill in the night air—the long, warm nights of summer had come to an end. Everyone shared a sense of urgency. They had a united army; they had powerful sorcerers—according to Peyre, at least. This might be their last chance.

Amidst the noise of camp, a few shouts drew his attention. They were voices familiar to him, raised with urgency. He made his way past soldiers huddling in blankets by cook-fires to find Liesel, Peyre, Tegyn, and a few others, looking about with concerned faces.

'Rab!' Peyre bellowed, a mix of concern and frustration in his voice.

'He pulled free of his lead and ran off,' a warrior was saying. He looked like a veteran whose career went back to the Isharite Wars, though his hair was still jet black. Looked, in Idris's estimation, to be the kind of fellow one doesn't mess with.

'You're looking for a dog?' Idris asked, a little bemused. 'Don't get me wrong, I like dogs. But is that a job for royalty?'

'It's Sanc's dog,' Liesel said. 'Rab.'

'I don't know why he'd run off like that,' Peyre added. 'It's not like him.'

'Trying to find his master?' Idris suggested. 'Did he head west?'

'No,' said the black-haired warrior. 'That way.' He pointed south-east. Gotbeck way. To the land of the Turned.

'Rab!' Idris shouted, suddenly sharing their concern.

'I appreciate the help,' said the warrior. 'But I don't think he's gonna come back. He's a determined so-and-so.' He sighed. 'Sanc's not going to be pleased with me. I'll fetch a horse and ride out, just in case.' He sounded morose and out of hope.

Idris felt a little sorry for the man. 'Perhaps it's fate that he broke free and ran off. Perhaps the gods have given him a mission.'

The warrior gave him a dead-eyed look and stalked off.

Idris raised his hands. 'Just trying to make the man feel better. Who is he, anyway?'

Tegyn smiled. 'That was Herin.'

Idris's eyes widened. 'The man who betrayed the Isharites?' He gave a whistle. That was exactly who they needed in this army. He'd come with the Magnians, perhaps. Yet that didn't explain why he was Sanc's dog walker.

Tegyn caught hold of him just as he set out to follow Herin. 'You may be emperor, brother. But I don't think that will stop him knocking you to the ground if you bother him any more with your talk of fate and divine missions.'

* * *

'Is the king inside?' Idris demanded of the warrior stood guard outside Peyre's tent.

'Aye, Your Majesty,' she said, pulling aside the tent flap.

'We've got problems,' Idris announced loudly as he stalked inside. Peyre and Liesel were standing with three of their companions. 'This pestilence gets worse. Men are dying with it, and it's raging through the ranks. Domard has come down with it now. He's too weak to leave his bed.'

'We are discussing the same thing,' Peyre said. 'There's barely a unit free of the infection.' He glanced at his friend, Umbert, who looked unusually miserable. 'Lord Russell is gravely ill.'

A chill ran down Idris's spine. At first, the outbreak had only affected the lowliest—camp followers, green recruits, men past their prime. Then it spread to the wider soldiery. Now, it was taking hold amongst any rank, seemingly at random. No one knew who would be next. Unease might soon turn into unrest if things got worse.

'Well, how can we stop it?' Idris asked. He'd never experienced anything like it. Much of his army was ill, and the rest were fearful.

'It's spreading from one man to the next in the camp,' Liesel said. 'You must tell your commanders to separate those who are free of it from those with the infection. They must be ruthless about it. And we all must do better with our sanitation.'

'And what is to be done with the sick?' Idris demanded. 'Leave them here?' From the border, they'd travelled half way to Coldeberg. But progress had slowed. Now, too many were too ill to be transported. Moreover, if Liesel was correct, transporting the infected had only served to pass the pestilence on to others.

Peyre sighed. 'It doesn't help that Domard is fallen ill. We need the aid of the Barissians. You are their duke, Idris. Liesel and I will support you.'

Idris knew what Peyre was implying. He had become Duke of Barissia without ever visiting the place. He had little personal authority in the duchy. The Barissians had been ruled by Liesel's uncle Walter before Esterel had taken it. Peyre and Liesel were known here; he wasn't. 'Alright,' he agreed.

'We can't enter Coldeberg,' Liesel said. 'It would be a crime to infect the civilian population there.'

'I recommend picking the nearest town,' said Sacha. Offensively handsome, Esterel's right-hand man had retained his influence at the Guivergnais court. 'Evacuate it completely. Everyone with the illness, however dire or gentle their symptoms, should be sent there to recuperate.'

Recuperate, or die, the Lord of Courion meant.

Idris, Peyre, and Liesel shared a look. It wasn't like they had an alternative plan to consider.

'I'M STAYING!'

Tegyn's eyes blazed, and Idris knew that signal from childhood. She wasn't about to be dissuaded.

'You'll catch it,' he said. He was going through the motions of the argument now, knowing he wouldn't win.

'Some must stay behind and organise the care of the ill. We can't just abandon them.'

Why you, Idris nearly said. But he knew she'd have an answer for him, so he didn't bother. Instead, he turned to Umbert, the Duke of Morbaine. 'You promise me you'll look after her?'

'Of course I will.'

Idris's face screwed up with anger and anxiety. 'I hope you both understand what you're doing.' He stabbed a finger at Umbert. 'You're deserting your best friend when he needs you the most. You should be leading the army of Morbaine.'

'I must stay with my father. Peyre understands. Besides, he can lead the army better than I can. Everyone knows that.'

'And you,' Idris turned on Tegyn. 'Maybe Peyre has other advisers he can lean on, but who do I have to trust in, except for you?'

Tegyn sighed. She looked at him, and her eyes were wet with tears. 'What is it?' he demanded.

She pulled her tunic down and showed him the swellings on her throat.

'Oh. Oh gods, Tegyn, I'm sorry. I feel stupid. And you?' he asked Umbert.

'You don't want to see where I've got them.'

Idris gave him a gentle pat on the shoulder, then turned to his sister.

Tegyn hugged him. For a while, as kids, she'd been taller. Now she only came up to his chest. But she had long been the biggest rock in his life.

'I can't lose you, Tegyn.'

'You won't. Just make sure you help kill that Ezenachi. Listen to Peyre. And his brother. Don't do anything needlessly heroic. And don't tell Liesel or Peyre about us. They have enough to worry about.'

'I won't.'

'Promise me.'

'I promise.'

* * *

THE ARMY LIMPED ON, closing on Coldeberg. They'd shed thousands since leaving Essenberg, to death, disease, and desertion.

Sacha's plan had worked well at staunching their losses. The ill had been left behind, and while fresh cases of pestilence continued to appear in their ranks, they were less frequent. At the first sign of it, the infected were sent away.

They made night camp with the city's high walls visible in the distance. Idris attended a meeting with Peyre. He brought with him Jeremias, Hajna, and Leontios. Each one had fought against terrible odds and survived. He didn't have Tegyn by his side any longer. But they were good allies to have.

They were welcomed into the Guivergnais royal tent. It was busier than usual. Seven newcomers were there, and it took Idris a while to realise who they were.

'You must be Sanc,' he said when it dawned on him.

The red eyes were the giveaway, of course. But he also looked very much like Peyre—brown hair and beard, and broad shouldered. The eyes were arresting. They gave Idris a strange confidence in him. He looked like a sorcerer—looked more than human, and surely that was exactly who they needed.

'Idris, Emperor of Brasingia,' Peyre introduced.

They gripped arms in greeting. Idris looked at the outlanders Sanc had gathered. Ironically, none were as exotic looking as Sanc. Yet, as a collective, they were pleasingly peculiar. One was ancient looking. The older woman had eyes a shade of purple he had never seen before. One was still a child, with an odd shaped head. The young woman had a primitive beauty that stole one's breath. The two men, one of whom was the tallest Idris had ever seen, regarded Idris and everyone else with a flat hostility that suggested they were contemplating unleashing some terrible firestorm on the gathering.

Catching his look, Sanc introduced his six companions. Idris found the only name his brain was interested in committing to memory was the woman's. *Mildrith.* He caught himself staring. She tilted her head, studying his scarred body, and Idris looked away. He introduced his own companions and took some pleasure when Sanc's champions stared at the clawed feet and alien beauty of Queen Hajna.

Sanc spoke, and as he did so, Idris felt the confidence that had drained away over the last few harrowing days, return. Sanc could see —or sense, perhaps—Ezenachi. And he assured them the god was close. He'd taken their bait and travelled west to Morbaine. Sanc's band had then teleported here. All they need do was push the army further west and the showdown would happen. Sanc even reassured them about the state of their army.

'Ezenachi doesn't suspect an army such as this stands in Barissia. Even with the warriors you have lost, it will be enough. Remember, I only ask that you occupy the Turned forces that are with him. It's our job to tackle Ezenachi and his champions. Not yours.'

He made it sound so simple. All Idris need do was lead his warriors against a few Turned. There would be no need for him to get anywhere near Ezenachi. It was a beguiling premise, and Idris would have been tempted to believe it all. If he hadn't made the same promises to his followers. Before leading them against Lizardmen, Caladri sorcerers, and all the rest. A total disaster had only been narrowly averted. He eyed Sanc. For all his power and confidence, he was young. Idris hoped he didn't truly believe his own rosy vision.

Once the talking was done, he made a beeline for the young sorcerer, keen to take his measure. 'I am sorry about your dog.'

Sanc offered a look of pain. 'Thank you. He's never done such a thing before. I shall just have to hope he's alright.'

'You can't use your powers to track him down?'

'No. Only other sorcerers stand out when I search like that. Everyone else is a sea of likeness. And animals, I don't see at all.'

'I'm sorry, then. But perhaps there is a reason. The gods like to play with us.'

Sanc gave him a look of displeasure.

'What? I have said the wrong thing?'

'The only god amongst us is Ezenachi. I hope he is not playing with us.'

Idris shrugged. 'Who says? That he is the only god, I mean. Maybe if I said I was a god, people would believe it?'

Sanc raised an eyebrow. 'Maybe,' he offered, making his doubts clear.

Idris laughed. 'Fair enough. My sister struggles to believe I am an emperor. But, you never know. With the right voice and gravitas, I am sure I could convince a few to believe me a god as well.' He shrugged. 'Sorry, I'm probably making no sense. I tend to do that. Many think me mad.'

'Not at all. Sometimes it's good to look at the world from a different viewpoint.'

'You think so? Well, any time you need it. I'm here.'

PEYRE

COLDEBERG, DUCHY OF BARISSIA

Peyre's forces were the first to break camp and head west. He had the Middians scout ahead. He grieved at the loss of Frayne, the Middian who had come closest to taking on the role of leader of his people. He'd been needlessly and wickedly killed by Saliers. Chieftains Cuenin and Jorath offered no warmth of friendship. He could hardly blame them. They did everything he asked. *At the least, they have learned I am their best chance of reclaiming their lost lands.*

Sanc was another source of information on the enemy. He reported regularly.

'There are significant numbers on the border,' his brother told him.

'You can see them?'

'Imperfectly. But yes.'

'And it costs you energy to do that?'

'Yes, but only a little. I used to have to concentrate and close my eyes to see anything. Now I can do it with my eyes open.'

Peyre considered this. This talk of magic still repelled him, but he was also intrigued. After all, there was a battle coming. He needed to know what Sanc could do. 'So, you are getting more powerful?'

'I think so. I'm certainly getting more used to wielding the magic. That makes it easier.'

'Makes sense.' Peyre's thoughts returned to military affairs. 'How many of them are defending the border?'

'Thousands.'

'I see. And Ezenachi?'

'Hasn't moved.'

According to Sanc, Ezenachi had positioned himself, his champions, and a vast army of Turned in a strategic spot that bordered the Steppe, Morbaine, and Guivergne. Sanc believed he could hide himself and the other champions from Ezenachi's sight. Which meant, as far as the god could tell, they had suddenly vanished in Morbaine.

They couldn't know for sure what conclusions Ezenachi had drawn from that. Perhaps he would believe Sanc and the others had returned to Silb. But the fact that he hadn't moved in days suggested he was conducting a search—making sure they weren't hiding somewhere.

'This game of cat and mouse will end when we reach the Steppe?' Peyre asked his brother.

'Yes. Ezenachi will soon learn about this army. And when he does, he'll know I am here. He'll come for us.'

'So the battle will almost certainly be fought in the Steppe.'

'That makes a difference?' Sanc asked.

Peyre looked at his brother aghast. 'Does it matter whether a battle is fought in fields, by a river, in city or town, in woodland, hilly country, against castle or fort? Surely you know the answer to that?'

Sanc blushed. 'Well, of course. I have enough experience to know that. I meant, is there anything we can do to prepare for it?'

'We know it will be in flat land. Numbers count more in such a battle. Cavalry count double. There is nowhere in the Steppe that offers protection. If we need to, we will have to retreat into Barissia. There is a lot to think about.'

'Retreat?' Sanc asked.

'I have to think about that. Just in case.'

'If you have to retreat, it means Ezenachi has defeated us.'

They shared a wordless look. Peyre knew what Sanc was thinking. If Ezenachi won this battle, it meant Sanc and his champions were dead. There would be no retreat. They would all join the ranks of the Turned, and Dalriya would be defenceless.

* * *

PEYRE MET WITH IDRIS. He tried to keep the numbers at the meeting down. But both armies had become complicated amalgams of forces, and it wasn't possible to deny the leaders of each a place. There were ten of them, drawn from all parts of Dalriya.

'First,' Peyre said, 'Sanc has news. It's not good.'

'Ezenachi has sent a force into Guivergne. It's thousands strong. They've already crossed the border.'

Grim expressions greeted this news. The grimmest, of course, from those who had dependents in the kingdom.

'Thousands of Turned,' Ida said. 'And any wizards? Champions?'

'Two,' Sanc replied. 'Most likely Caladri sorcerers. Ezenachi has kept his champions by his side ever since we returned. This move suggests he is starting to believe we have left Dalriya. That is good for us.'

'Good?' Ida repeated, appalled. 'Sorcerers and Turned carving through Guivergne? Our women and children are there. We must send a force back to stop them. And you,' he said, pointing at Sanc, 'must warn them immediately.'

'They will already know,' Peyre intervened. 'We prepared for this. Riders will be heading to Valennes to warn my sister. The vulnerable will be evacuated.'

'We are here to defeat Ezenachi,' Sanc added. 'That must remain our priority. I cannot afford to waste my powers on anything else, as much as I wish I could.'

'I cannot keep this from my people, or the Middians for that matter. Not after what happened last time.'

Ida stopped himself when Peyre gave him a mute appeal with his eyes. Loysse had taken the blame from many after the damage Saliers had inflicted on Guivergne. Peyre didn't want his sister's name dragged through the mud in front of everyone.

'I cannot stop you from leaving,' Peyre said. 'But you are all needed here. We are about to enter the Steppe and come face to face with a Turned army. As soon as we do, Ezenachi will bring all his strength against us. Who knows, he may even withdraw that army he has sent into Guivergne. We are perhaps a day away from battle. Let us discuss this first, before we make hasty decisions. And after that, if you inform others about the situation, I beg you to do so with care and thought, not wild emotion.'

'Very well,' Ida said.

'I assume you have given our strategy some thought?' Idris asked.

'I have. I have discussed with Sanc at length about how things are likely to unfold. This is what we propose. I march my forces straight for the border, while you circle south with yours. This keeps the presence of the Brasingian army a secret.'

'You can deal with the Turned at the border without our aid?' asked Jeremias of Rotelegen.

Peyre gestured for Sanc to speak.

'Yes. The key is to retain an element of surprise. When Ezenachi hears of the size of the Guivergnais army, I expect him to come straight for it. He won't expect a second army. Four of us will join with your army, Emperor Idris, if that is acceptable. We will keep ourselves hidden. The other three champions will stay with Peyre and reveal themselves. It will encourage Ezenachi to attack them.'

'So the army of Guivergne becomes bait?' Idris asked.

'Exactly,' Sanc said. 'Then we strike once he is committed.'

'All this is really necessary?' Ida asked.

Sanc turned to the King of the Magnians. 'We must take this opportunity. I can't let him escape. This army will dissolve. The champions I have gathered will return home. We are the ones who need to force an encounter. Ezenachi can afford to wait, as he has done so often. Waiting for us to weaken and bend to his will. I can't allow that.'

Peyre could see his brother's words had struck home. Everyone here had suffered, whether from the Turned or other enemies. Everyone understood the stakes, even if they didn't have Sanc's insight on their enemy. He had faith they would see the plan through.

He glanced at his brother. He just had to hope Sanc's plan worked.

* * *

LIESEL FOUND him alone in his tent.

'You're alright?' she asked him.

'Yes. I just wanted a few moments to myself before it begins. Your arbalests are ready?'

'They are. In position, and well supplied. What is that?'

Peyre rotated the wooden carving in his hands. He held it up for her to see. 'A fish. Half out of water.'

'It's very good. Did you whittle it yourself?'

Peyre smiled. He didn't think she was too impressed with it. 'No. It was a gift, of sorts, from one of my soldiers. One of those Barissians I recruited. So long ago now, it seems. He was among the first who died under my command. There have been many since.'

'Never carelessly though, Peyre. You do your best for those who serve you. Everyone knows that. Don't torture yourself with it.'

'I don't keep this to torture myself. It reminds me that everyone in my army, however big a force I command, is an individual. With hopes and passions, unique to them. It makes me ask myself the hard questions. Must I put them in harm's way?'

'I see.' She studied him in silence.

He pocketed his keepsake and looked at her. *Is it possible I will ever take her for granted?* he wondered. He thought it impossible. And yet Esterel had imprisoned her. He struggled to comprehend what had been in his brother's mind in his last days. Had the pressure of facing Ezenachi got to him? Was that why Liesel checked on him so much, looking for signs that he, too, was cracking?

'I'm alright, Liesel. You needn't worry about me.'

After all, he had Sanc to deal with Ezenachi. He wished Sanc had returned from Silb in time to help their brother. Instead, Esterel had put his faith in Inge. She had been his only option.

'Of course I worry about you. That is only natural when you love someone.'

He looked at her, temporarily devoid of speech, then reached out. She moved in and he grasped her, as if she were a raft in a stormy sea. 'I'm not used to you saying that. I suppose I'm not used to being this happy.'

'Then you'd better get used to it. Because I'm not going anywhere. But also, you'd better get out there and lead this army.'

THERE WAS STILL time before the enemy was expected. Peyre met with his captains one last time, though they already had their orders and knew what they were about.

He gave Benoit a nod. 'Your units are in place?'

'They are, Your Majesty.'

Peyre had ordered the men of Saliers to be divided into groups of one hundred and spread amongst Liesel's arbalests. It meant Benoit had limited control over his own force and was about as clear a sign as any that Peyre still didn't trust him. But the young man hid any signs of the anger or humiliation he must feel.

He is skilled at hiding what he thinks, Peyre acknowledged to himself. He allowed himself to wonder what was in Benoit's mind. Did he, like Peyre, recall their previous campaign in the Steppe? They had stopped a Middian revolt in its tracks, that had threatened to undo Esterel's siege of Coldeberg. They had become close in those days, Peyre coming to rely on him. Had any of it been real? Or had Benoit been playing him the whole time? Suddenly, he wished Umbert were here.

'Any last concerns?' he asked, ready to leave them to it.

'We've seen most things it's possible to see on a battlefield,' said Sacha. 'It's magic we know nothing about. What if those champions come against us? Or Ezenachi himself?'

The sorcerer named Temyl muttered at this. The words he spoke were in his foreign tongue, but it suggested the champions of Silb were beginning to understand the Dalriyan language.

'What did he say?' Peyre asked Herin.

'Ezenachi and the champions aren't our concern,' said the Magnian. 'That's for Sanc and these wizards from Silb to deal with.'

'I get that,' said Sacha. 'I'm not planning on charging at a god with my visor down and lance couched. But what do we *do?*'

'We fight,' said Peyre. 'Engage the Turned wherever we see them. Give our champions the freedom to do their job.'

Peyre could see the doubts on Sacha's face. He understood. Sacha had witnessed Esterel, his best friend, killed. He'd been forced to swallow down that bitter taste of Ezenachi's power. 'I've felt his power too, Sacha, remember? In Magnia. I know what it's like to feel unmanned by it. There's nothing wrong with accepting our limits. We have our role. It's secondary to theirs,' he said, with a gesture at the three sorcerers Sanc had assigned him. 'But let's carry it out to the best of our abilities.'

Sacha gave him a smile. It was genuine, as if Peyre's words had given him the purpose he was seeking. 'Of course, Your Majesty. We'll do our best for you.'

With that, they all parted to their places on the battlefield.

Peyre marched over to the army of Morbaine. Accompanying him was the lanky sorcerer of Silb, named Guntram. Even his blond hair was longer than any Peyre has seen before. He towered over Peyre. He towered over everyone, but Peyre found it insulting to his majesty that he be made to feel so small.

They reached the front line of the Morbainais. Inhan had the warriors readied in their ranks, and Peyre gave the young man his thanks. Inhan presented him with the Shield of Persala. Peyre hefted it, fitting his arm to the strap. It always felt good to wield it again. Like an old war ally, the Shield filled him with the confidence he needed for battle.

Guntram stared at the shield and muttered indecipherable words.

'I don't understand.'

'Magic,' he said, his thick accent lingering over the last syllable.

'Yes, it's magic. And it's mine.'

Guntram gave him a wolfish smile. He grabbed a long spear that had been stuck blade first in the ground and twirled the shaft around. He certainly had the reach to make it a fearsome weapon. Peyre got the impression he might be handy in a fight, in addition to his sorcerous powers.

The outlander shook his new weapon. 'Mine magic,' he claimed, then laughed loudly.

Peyre decided to humour him and laughed along.

Inhan raised a doubtful eyebrow.

'Show him your hand, Inhan.'

Inhan raised his metal hand for the sorcerer to see. Then he fixed his shield to it, the curled metal fingers gripping it tight.

Guntram laughed again and patted Inhan on the shoulder.

'I get the impression he likes a scrap,' Peyre said. 'He can fight on my right. He should be safe enough next to the Shield.'

Inhan shrugged, unconcerned with the fine details. It was Peyre's job to worry about those. And of course getting Guntram killed would be distinctly unhelpful.

There was nothing to do but wait now. Their location was flat and featureless, save for a stream that meandered its way through the grassland to his left. Sanc had insisted such a feature was important. From a military perspective, it offered some protection, but Peyre doubted its significance.

Ahead of his position were the groups of arbalests under Liesel's command, mixed with the Viper's units. Liesel had insisted on placing herself there, crossbow in hand. Peyre didn't like it. But he respected it and hadn't argued. Instead, he had assigned Jehan as her bodyguard, who he had told in no uncertain terms that protecting her was his one and only task.

To the right of the Morbainais was the royal army of Guivergne. Gosse commanded this force, equal in size to Peyre's. At the front were Sul and the other warriors from his March Lordship—just the redoubtable fighters one would want in the front line. With Gosse was Temyl. Sanc had told him not to expect either Guntram or Temyl to use magic. All their power had to be saved for the main confrontation.

A few hundred yards behind these huge blocks of infantry, Ida and Herin led the Magnian warriors in reserve. Mergildo, the third sorcerer, was with them. Finally, Sacha and Florent led the cavalry force. They had about a thousand riders each, for while the pestilence had decimated the number of warriors Peyre had, his horses were unaffected. *And it's just as well. It will be no surprise if the enemy we face are Turned Middians, amongst the finest horsemen in Dalriya.*

It was as this thought crossed his mind that the first trumpets blew. The enemy approached. Peyre stared ahead, eager to see with his own eyes.

His Middian allies came into view first. Cuenin and Jorath had led their mounted force west, penetrating the Steppe. Now they retreated, and behind them, the Turned followed.

Peyre had hoped they would. He had his army positioned just as he wanted it. As the Middians streamed past the arbalest positions, the Turned kept coming. Most commanders would have stopped upon seeing the ranks of Peyre's army, reluctant to engage.

But Peyre had learned plenty about the Turned. They had no fear. This was a double-edged sword. It made them a remorseless enemy. But it also meant they would attack, as they did now, when the odds were against them.

There was little attempt on their part to employ tactics. Their cavalry came first, primarily Middian warriors. Behind them, their infantry was a mixture of peoples, genders, ages. Peyre even heard the screams of vossi, who had somehow found their way into this force. For a moment, he was transported back to the forests of Morbaine, being chased by the vicious creatures, their screams getting louder, their darts flying.

But we aren't in the woods this time. Let's see how you do against a Guivergnais shield wall. Let's see how that bark-like skin handles a Cordentine crossbow bolt.

Cuenin and Jorath continued their retreat, using the space between Peyre and Gosse's massed ranks, until they joined with the regular cavalry at the rear.

Peyre wanted to keep them away from the actual fighting. The enemy that approached were Turned Middians, the kith and kin of those Middians who remained free. They were the victims of

Ezenachi, but the battlefield was no place for sympathy or hesitation.

Liesel's arbalests had no such compunctions. A hail of bolts met the Turned cavalry as they came within range. They tore into rider and mount alike, the horses' screams carrying across the battlefield. Next to him, Guntram muttered in what sounded like astonishment. It was perhaps the most devastating use of the weapon Peyre had witnessed. At Essenberg, at least the defenders had been behind stone walls. Here, the enemy had no defences.

Nevertheless, that lack of fear carried the surviving Middian riders on, aware they had a window of time to attack while the arbalests reloaded. But Benoit's warriors did their job, offering a wall of solid shields and bristling spears, a barrier that protected the vulnerable arbalests.

Peyre grinned as his plan was put into effect. The Turned Middians could not break through. The arbalests reloaded. Their second bolts slammed into the Turned. The enemy took the only logical option, retreating until they were out of range.

A cheer rose around him, but Peyre knew they were far from victory.

Rows of Turned infantry, thousands strong, readied themselves. There was clearly planning at work now, as the enemy organised themselves out of range. How they communicated, Peyre couldn't fathom, since it was all done without voice or instrument. The only noise was the screams of the vossi, a relentless sound that grated inside his head, however much he tried to ignore it.

Then, after some unheard order, the Turned were marching in reasonably good order. The arbalests let them come, then released another volley into their ranks. Many fell, but the Turned didn't stop. They ran for the arbalests, numerous enough to overwhelm Liesel and Benoit's forces. Peyre watched with concern as the arbalests released their bolts once more. Then they were moving, retreating from their forward positions. The soldiers of Saliers followed, still facing the enemy.

Now the Turned could get some revenge. Their own archers fired, and the vossi threw their darts. Peyre could see his warriors fall, many picked up by their comrades, and dragged away. The Turned were gaining on them.

'Come on,' Peyre whispered, urging his warriors to get to safety. A sick feeling engulfed him as he imagined Liesel being struck down by an arrow. It wasn't likely—the men of Saliers were taking the brunt of the attack. But it was possible. 'That's it,' he muttered to himself. 'The last time I let her put herself in danger.'

At last, the arbalests reached the gap between his force and Gosse's, two human walls of warriors that represented safety. Peyre strained to catch sight of Liesel amongst them, but he couldn't see her.

The warriors of Saliers came next, the Turned not far behind them. Peyre took a short spear in hand, and many in the front rank followed his lead. He urged them to hold, waiting until the enemy was nearly on them. At last, he judged it the right time. He skipped forwards, from one foot to the other, the spear shaft held behind and angled up, the metal tip just inches from his face. He released, the shaft soaring high before falling, beyond the front rank of the Turned.

Others took their turns, each spear taking its own unique course, many striking a target: killing; wounding; disrupting. Guntram took a turn, his throw landing even farther than Peyre's, before reclaiming his long spear.

Peyre quickly put the Shield of Persala into position. The Turned answered fire, throwing their own missiles, some reusing the very spears that had been thrown at them. Those that came close to Peyre he sent back—darts, stones, arrows, flying into the ranks of the Turned. His soldiers nearby were protected. Beyond the Shield's zone of protection, however, men in the first rank were struck, some already needing to be replaced by those behind.

'Lock!' Inhan shouted, and the warriors of Morbaine interlocked shields. Next to Peyre, Guntram let the wall break, holding his long spear two-handed. But Peyre knew that as inviting as the spot would look to the enemy, the Shield he wielded would protect this part of the line.

'Step!' Inhan bellowed, and the men of Morbaine put their left foot forward, shields in front, weapons at the ready. Save for Guntram, they moved with machine like precision, and Peyre saw a rhythmic beauty in it.

The Turned came onto the shield wall. The Morbainais pushed them back, opening space for sharp steel to prod and strike. The Turned pulled at shields, striking at faces, or down at ankles. The air was thick with grunts and screams.

Next to Peyre, Guntram lashed out with his spear with speed and precision, not allowing the Turned to close on him. With a great strike, his spear blade sank into a vossi chest. The creature grabbed the shaft with a two handed death grip.

The outlander was compromised, and the Turned moved in for the kill. Relying on Inhan to protect him from the other side, Peyre shoved forward with his Shield. When he connected, the enemy went flying. He cleared a space, allowing him to swing his sword with freedom.

With an opening before him, Peyre took it. He pressed forward, leaving the safety of the shield wall. To either side, Guntram and Inhan followed his move, lending him support. He used the Shield to knock aside any resistance, the Turned unable to slow him. Movement to his left caught his eye. Inhan had walked into trouble. Overwhelmed, the young man's shield was ripped apart. A cruel spear strike came for him. Inhan blocked it with his metal hand, turning it aside.

Peyre launched himself at the enemy, his Shield strike sending two of them to the ground. An overhead sword strike dealt with a third. Inhan chopped down a fourth. The Morbainais front line caught up to them, barging their way forward with their shields. They crushed the Turned until their front line couldn't move, trapped against those behind.

The Turned broke apart. Peyre led the Morbainais to the sides, quickly overlapping, getting in behind the enemy. Many armies would have immediately shattered at this, the ripple of the break passing down the line. But the Turned were stubborn. They fought on, despite taking heavy losses.

Peyre heard an unmistakable thundering sound. Peering ahead, he could see the Turned cavalry returning to the fray, aiming to close the hole he had created.

'Form up!' he shouted, and others joined the call, rallying a defensive line as the cavalry attacked.

The Turned Middians thrust down with their spears, using their height to cause the Morbainais problems. Peyre defended with the Shield, neutralising much of their attack. He was exhausted now, raising the great weapon again and again, his efforts depleting his stamina.

A horseman barged into him, buffeting him with his mount. Peyre sprawled backwards. He was caught by those behind, before he landed on the ground. Guntram shoved a spear into the animal's side. It screamed in pain, kicking and bucking, its rider leaping from the mount before he was thrown. Both sides backed away from the injured beast until it saw an opening and ran away.

For a few moments, Peyre stared at his enemy. Dead-eyed hostility looked back. Something in their expression told him they were thinking—still working out how to win. Then, something changed. As one, it seemed, they turned and ran, putting their backs to the Morbainais. Those on horseback raced ahead; the bulk on foot followed behind, not one of them looking back.

Peyre looked left and right.

'There!' Inhan shouted as he gestured, and there was joy in his voice.

From one side came Sacha, the black and gold of House Courion fluttering beside the Owl of Guivergne. From the other, Florent's colours of gold and green. They hounded the retreating Turned, who still ran, unable to offer any resistance.

Peyre let out a breath as he watched. They had won, and the Turned who still lived had nowhere to escape to. Sacha and Florent could chase them for miles if they wished, with complete control over the flat terrain of the Steppe.

The warriors of Guivergne yelped for joy at their victory. Peyre didn't begrudge them their moment. They needed it, after what had happened to Esterel.

The only one who looked more serious was the outlander, Guntram. It was as if this encounter had been his moment of fun. He knew what Peyre knew. This encounter only meant one thing.

Ezenachi was coming.

BELWYNN

DUCHY OF GOTBECK

E zenachi punched Toric's Dagger into the side of her head.
At the same instant that her body died, Belwynn was freed from the god's imprisonment.

As the body of the Jalakh woman slumped to the ground, a hundred thoughts passed through Belwynn's mind. Despair that she and the other champions had been enslaved. Relief that she had helped Herin and his allies escape. Anger that this god from another world had taken *her* dagger.

When the emotion subsided, new questions emerged. The principal one being, *why am I still here?*

She had died twice before. Once, when she had killed the real Belwynn, and in so doing freed her from Madria's grasp. The second time was when Elana's body had become so broken that she had taken the Jalakh woman's as a replacement. This time, there was no vessel to escape to. She reached out for a host but found none.

Why am I not dying? And why, when that dagger entered my skull, was I not obliterated?

She had no answers. She had nothing, not even a body to call her own. No senses with which to experience the world.

Just an amorphous voice that only I can hear. For a long time I appalled myself, some foul shadow living inside a corpse. Now, at last, I feel pity. For I am nothing but a sad ghost, somehow left behind. The uncaring universe has forgotten I exist, and it seems I must spend eternity talking to myself until I go completely mad.

Belwynn had no way to measure time. After an indeterminate span, even the self-pity left her. *Perhaps this is not such a bad way to go. Rather than have it all end with sudden violence, I will gradually fade away. The sun and the rain will wear me down to nothing.*

And yet. A kernel of Belwynn remained and refused to go. It couldn't accept that she had lost, and Ezenachi had won. *Oh, you are one stubborn and unyielding bitch,* she castigated herself.

She called out. She didn't know with what voice or language she called, or who might hear her. But as her latest body began to rot, this last kernel of Belwynn refused to give up, and sent its cry for help into the ether.

* * *

BELWYNN SENSED SOMETHING. She had felt nothing for so long that she reached out hesitantly. It was life. It had a heart that pumped blood around its body. There was a brain, a spine, nerves, bones, muscles, teeth, skin, hair. Her salvation had come.

But something was different.

She reached out again, exploring the creature that had answered her call. It wasn't human. It was a dog.

The choice before her sickened her soul. It wasn't even that she would become an animal. She had descended lower than that already. It was that this creature was alive.

This was the very thing she had taken a stand against. She had refused to allow Madria to control her mind and body. When Ezenachi had come, he had occupied a living, Lipper man. But even worse, he had used his powers to enslave thousands of living people.

Maybe, at first, these gods believed they had good reasons for what they did. The lives they had used were expendable, for the greater good.

But it was a line that should never be crossed.

And here am I, contemplating doing the very same thing. Never mind that it is a dog. Should I treat this creature as subservient to me, just as gods treat humans? Then I, finally, will become just the same as Ezenachi.

She could feel the dog sniff, hear him whine.

You have brought him here, Belwynn, she told herself. *The deed is already done.*

Tentatively at first, she sent her shadow into the creature. She felt his panic as she reached for his mind. *Do it quickly,* she commanded herself.

Belwynn grasped his mind. He only struggled a little before she won control. She reeled at the strangeness of his body. She sent her commands, telling him to walk. She felt herself stumble awkwardly as she used four legs instead of two. But it was only a passing moment of confusion. She adjusted her control over the creature. He knew how to walk. She didn't need to do it for him. She simply had to tell him where to go, and he would obey.

Run, she told him.

Rab bounded away, enjoying the release of his pent-up energy. He would take his new friend to see Sanc.

LOYSSE

VALENNES, KINGDOM OF GUIVERGNE

Loysse had to see for herself.

She sat on her palfrey at the top of a rise. It gave her a view of the road to Valennes. The army of Turned had travelled miles into the kingdom. She had evacuated the local population. Her enemy's destination was clear enough. The capital. It was a force sent to destroy the army of Guivergne. Little did Ezenachi know the army wasn't even here.

That left Loysse with a problem. 'I'm not sure the city walls will hold against them.'

Syele, seated next to her, stared down at the army that would soon reach Valennes. The warrior pursed her lips. 'Maybe not forever. But I reckon they'll keep the enemy busy for a few days. That might be long enough for your brothers to complete their task.'

'There's something nagging at me. If Peyre was here, his army could stop these invaders.'

'Maybe. But he's not.'

'Yet Ezenachi believes he is. So why send a force that might be defeated? Unless there's something else down there,' she pointed at the snaking column on the road, 'that we can't see? Like sorcerers.'

Syele huffed. 'That's cheating. But I suppose it would change things. How can we know, though?'

'We can't. But I must act as if it's true. I can't take any risks. Come, we have work to do.'

* * *

THE WORTHY CITIZENS of Valennes screamed and shouted at Loysse and Auberi, as the Owl of Guivergne looked down from its high perch in the Foyer. She fancied even the owl looked less than pleased at what they'd had to say.

'How dare you betray us? Your job is to protect us!' demanded one merchant.

'Where is the king?' was the refrain of many.

'Someone else needs to be put in charge.'

This was enough for Loysse's husband. At a signal, his soldiers pressed forward, asking the assembled burghers to leave.

'You've been given your orders,' Auberi shouted, visibly angered. 'Get on and do it, or I'll have you thrown in a cell, where you can wait for the Turned to find you.'

'They're all talk,' Loysse murmured to him as the throng left.

'After the last year, I won't miss this city,' Auberi said. 'I'm looking forward to returning to Famiens. I think we'll be quite safe there until this is over.'

Loysse could think of nothing to say to that.

He turned to her, reaching for her hand. She gave it.

'I know,' he said, 'I'm assuming Peyre and Sanc win. If not, it doesn't really matter where we are.'

She smiled. 'True enough. You are happy to lead the main column north? It will be full of these disgruntled fools...'

'Of course. But I don't want you hanging around here any longer than necessary.'

'Brancat assures me it won't take long.'

'I don't see why the man can't deal with things himself.'

'He's old-fashioned, Auberi. He's going to be forcing the obstinate

JAMIE EDMUNDSON

few to leave their homes and businesses. I have the authority to do that and he doesn't. He just wants me there. Besides, I'll be with his best guardsmen. You know I'll be safe, don't you?'

'I trust Brancat, of course. I just don't like the idea of you hanging around in the city longer than you have to.'

'I know, husband. I promise I won't.'

'Very well.'

Auberi had his soldiers lead him off to make final preparations. The citizens of Valennes, their numbers swelled by refugees from the south, would be led north by Auberi. Many he would take all the way to his own duchy of Famiens. The rest would head to other safe locations. It would become a waiting game. They had to hope Sanc could defeat Ezenachi before the whole realm was lost.

Syele approached Loysse as Auberi was escorted away. 'How do you think he will feel when he finds out you have deceived him?'

'I am sure he will hate me forever. But Alienor will have one parent alive. That's all I really care about.'

LOYSSE HID her emotions as she said her goodbyes to those she loved. Alienor had Brayda and Cebelia to look after her. Even when she tore herself away from her daughter, there were so many others leaving Valennes for whom she felt a deep pity.

At times, Coleta had looked broken since Esterel's death. Now, she was looking after Ida of Magnia's siblings—still children. They had lost their parents and their homeland under the most horrific circumstances. Valennes had not turned out to be the place of safety they needed. They were retreating ever further north, through foreign lands.

Lord Caisin approached her. 'I wish you well in your endeavour. You are sure about it?'

Loysse had confided in the Lord Chancellor, his loyalty to her proven beyond doubt in the last few months. 'I am.'

'Then I have a parting gift.' He gestured to one side, where his henchmen, Ernst and Gernot, lurked. 'They've offered their services to you. Who knew I had two such heroes in my employ?'

Loysse allowed herself a grin. 'More likely they see a chance to crack heads and stay the right side of the law.'

'Maybe so. But they have a fierce loyalty. Not to you or I, so much as to this city. It's strange what can motivate people.' He shrugged. 'Anyway. The best of luck to you, Your Grace.'

Auberi led his flock out through the north gates of the city.

When the great column of refugees was out of sight and sound, Loysse turned a circle, taking in the empty city. It was strange. Already, the absence of people gave Valennes an eerie atmosphere, as if monsters lurked in the shadows.

'Come,' she called out to Ernst and Gernot. 'Help me bar these gates.'

* * *

LOYSSE LOOKED out from the city's southern battlements. The Turned army, the same she had seen on the march a few days ago, had arrived at Valennes.

She cast a nervous glance at the sky. Night was coming earlier these days, but there were still hours of daylight left. She didn't want to lose the city today. A day might make a significant difference in the final reckoning.

There were two hundred volunteers on the walls of Valennes. Whether they were all strictly volunteers, she had her doubts. They were mostly guards of the Bastion or city watch, whom Brancat had persuaded to stay behind. She didn't need to know his methods.

The old weapons master turned to her now. 'Time for you to leave, Your Grace.'

She gave him an incredulous look. 'I'm not leaving! You think I will retreat to the Bastion by myself, and watch the rest of you man the walls?'

'That's exactly what you shall be doing. No one needs to worry about your safety when we have ladders against the walls.'

'I certainly shall not.'

'Why is it you refuse every reasonable request I make?'

'Lord Brancat, I thought we had the perfect relationship. We come at a problem from different perspectives, argue, and end up with the best outcome.' She saw Syele smirking. 'It is Syele's job to worry about my safety, not anyone else's.'

Brancat shook his head, defeated. 'I truly wonder what your father would make of it.'

For a moment, Loysse tried to imagine. But this was so beyond her father's world that she couldn't.

'Everyone in position,' Brancat bellowed. 'I need to see you with a bow in hand, manning a machine, or at a rock station.'

Two hundred, Brancat had told her, was the minimum required to make it look like the city walls were properly manned. They all had orders to retreat to the Bastion at the first sign of trouble. But if the Turned believed they were besieging an occupied city, with a full garrison defending it, they would behave accordingly. If they knew the truth, they could barge through the gates in no time.

Sitting with Syele next to a bucket of rocks, above the west gate, she watched the Turned make their preparations. First, they encircled the city.

'Most armies would do the same,' Syele said lazily, chewing at hard bread. They had one thing in their favour, at least. More food and ammunition than they would need.

Loysse kept flicking her attention back to the sky. The sun was refusing to set, still casting plenty of light for an assault. She could see the Turned making ready for it. Wheeled catapults, battering rams, and ladders, were being carried to the front. Whenever they threatened to get close, an arrow or two would sail from the walls, letting them know the defenders were watching.

'But the Turned especially,' Syele added.

'Why them especially?'

'They want to catch those inside the walls, don't they?'

A shiver ran down Loysse's spine. It hadn't crossed her mind until now. She'd made peace with the idea she might end up dead. But if she became one of them? It horrified her.

'Don't worry,' Syele said. 'I'll slit your throat before that happens.'

'Is that supposed to be funny?'

'Sorry. Soldier's humour. Tends to get grim before a battle.'

'It's not funny, though, is it?'

'S'pose not.'

'Besides. They'd be no one left to slit yours. We'll have to do it simultaneously.'

Syele grinned. 'Deal. Eh up,' she said, turning serious. 'They're coming.'

It seemed the Turned were forgoing the use of catapults. Groups of them wheeled rams or carried ladders. From what Loysse could see, they were attacking every section of wall simultaneously.

'Do you think they know?' she asked. 'How few we are?'

'Could be. Could just be testing our defences.' Syele returned her bread to her pack, a sure sign things had become serious.

Wordlessly, they each grabbed a rock. Arrows fired down at the ram, thudding into its covering of hides. Then the archers changed targets to those carrying ladders—a more immediate threat.

The ram reached the west gate. The Turned who manned it launched the log beam, building a steady rhythm.

Loysse's first rock bounced harmlessly off the top, as did Syele's. They chose a larger one, so heavy they had to carry it between them.

'Steady,' Syele grunted. 'We want this one to hit. Alright. Now.'

They tipped it over the side and it gathered pace, landing on the front corner of the ram with a bang. Peering down, Loysse could see the protective covering of wood and hides had been smashed, exposing those inside. After a few moments, however, the pounding resumed.

Meanwhile, Loysse could see ladders landing against the city walls. The Turned scampered up, unconcerned with their personal safety. It became a race to stop them. The defenders took axes to the tops of the ladders. They threw rocks, or heated sand, down at the attackers.

A thunderous crack drew Loysse's attention. A ballista, mounted on the corner where the south walls met west, was targeting the ram she and Syele had struck. It fired long bolts at the machine, aiming for the gap Loysse and Syele had made. After the second bolt struck, the beam stopped once more. Looking down, she could see significant damage had been done, perhaps even making the machine inoperable.

But Loysse had no time for celebration. Balls of fire rose towards the city walls from where the mass of Turned waited in their lines. They targeted the ballista. The guards ran, just in time. The flames struck the machine, again and again, engulfing it in fire.

'There's our answer to whether they have sorcerers,' she said, looking for the source of the fire. She identified a group of horsemen. They were a mixture of different races, and she couldn't work out which was the sorcerer. Logic dictated it was a Caladri. 'How can we target them from this distance?'

'I don't think we can,' said Syele. 'In fact, I think it's time we got out of here.'

Loysse made to argue. But she heard shouts of alarm coming from more than one location. She saw Turned climbing ladders. She digested the fact that there was a fire flinging sorcerer amongst the besiegers. At least one.

'Alright,' she relented.

Syele didn't hesitate, making for the stairs that led down from the battlements.

Loysse ran after her. This had always been the plan. Head for the Bastion as soon as danger appeared. For the Bastion was their best chance of holding out. Not miles of city walls.

Syele's descent was rapid, and when she hit the ground, she kept running. Her pace encouraged Loysse to go just as fast. They couldn't be caught in the streets. They wouldn't stand a chance.

They ran through the city, turning up one street and along the next. North, then east, then north again, making for the Bastion. Loysse imagined Turned in every building they passed and she kept her pace going.

Her lungs burned. *We need to rest. At least walk for a bit*, she told herself. An almighty crash sounded behind her. Loysse found a second wind, running after Syele once more.

The Bastion appeared up ahead. The Turned had not yet reached the fortress. *We'll make it.* The question of how the Bastion might stop a sorcerer arose in her head and she pushed it aside. She had no answers.

They were among the first to arrive, making their way across the lowered drawbridge. There they waited, watching as the guards from the other sections of wall streamed their way. More crossed the drawbridge, and Loysse began counting. She reckoned about a hundred had made it. The flow had slowed now. A few more arrived, in ones or twos, the gap between each arrival getting longer. Loysse felt a tremendous sense of relief when Brancat appeared, bringing up the rear.

'The duchess?' he demanded.

'Here,' she shouted. 'I'm safe. You think any more might come?'

'I may be the last, but we'll hold a while longer. The Turned have breached the walls, but they're not chasing us through the streets.' He grimaced. 'They don't know the entire city is empty.'

Loysse nodded. The Turned would begin searching every building for enemies. Ambushes. Only gradually would they realise they had already won the city.

One more straggler appeared. Brancat waited a good while longer before ordering the drawbridge raised. The portcullis was lowered, and the gates shut and barred.

Syele blew a sigh of relief before noticing Loysse's expression. 'What ails you?'

'Ernst and Gernot didn't make it.'

'Huh. More 'n likely they fled when they saw how things were going. Gotta say, probably the sensible choice.'

SANC

THE MIDDER STEPPE

Sanc accompanied the army of Brasingia. It entered the Steppe several miles south of Peyre's army. The land they marched through was empty, its occupants drawn north to fight Peyre's incursion.

Sanc had enough information to know his brother's invasion had been a success. A tiny light that represented each individual allowed him to follow the course of the battle. He had seen the Turned repelled and driven off.

He'd seen many individual's lights blink out of existence. His three allies—Temyl, Guntram, and Mergildo—still lived. Their light was stronger than anyone else's. Beyond that, he had no more idea about individuals. Those he cared about the most—Peyre, Liesel, Herin—he simply had to hope had survived the bloodshed unharmed.

Idris swung his army north. Sanc rode next to the Atrabian, directing him.

'You can still see him?' Idris asked. Again.

'I see him.'

Sanc could see all three armies as they marched towards their confrontation. He didn't have to close his eyes anymore. He hid his own presence, and that of the other sorcerers with Idris's army.

Sanc's power had grown since returning to Dalriya. His progress had slowed in Silb. It developed much faster upon returning home. He couldn't be sure why that might be the case. But his power gave him newfound confidence. Kepa flew above the army, looking out for any surprises that Sanc's vision might miss. But he didn't think even that was necessary.

'He's heading straight for Peyre's position,' he assured the emperor. Idris's nerves were understandable. He couldn't see or feel what Sanc did. 'He still doesn't know we're here.'

'And the numbers with him?'

'More than you and Peyre have combined. But how many will be ordinary men and women? He must have sent many of his best warriors north to Guivergne.'

Sanc was not really so confident. But he sensed the emperor, for all his outward bravado, needed reassurance.

The ruse he and Peyre agreed on had worked. Ezenachi's forces were divided, and he had lost the initiative. It meant the disease that had ravaged the Guivergnais and Brasingian forces was not so damaging as Peyre and Idris feared.

As they approached the moment of truth, Sanc had little time for nerves. It became a question of timing. They didn't want to get too close and alert Ezenachi to their arrival. However, hang back too far, and Peyre would face Ezenachi alone. That couldn't happen. The three champions with his brother had no chance of holding off the god. They would be swiftly overwhelmed and destroyed.

As Sanc discussed the problem with his allies, it became clear they would have to divide their force. Only those on horseback had the speed to catch up in time. Idris asked Duke Jeremias to lead the Brasingian infantry, who would take longer to arrive. The Blood Caladri, too, had no better option than to march on foot.

Sanc rode next to Mildrith and the Eger Khan, their giant lizards bounding ahead. Above them was Kepa. Behind them, Idris had the cavalry of Brasingia, while Leontios led the Knights of Kalinth. Kepa called down when the Turned came into view.

Sanc let out a breath of relief. This was exactly what he'd wanted. Attack the enemy from the rear and sow confusion. Ezenachi would have to halt his advance and face them. Then Peyre could come from the other direction and close the trap.

'Give us the honour of leading the charge,' Grand Master Leontios requested.

No one argued. The few hundred knights he had brought with him were the finest looking horsemen Sanc had ever seen. Encased in armour, with pages carrying their lances, everyone knew their legend as an attacking force. Their horses were even more impressive—bred for war, they were tall and powerful, with their own heavy barding to protect them.

Leontios ordered his men into a gallop, tall lances pointing to the sky. Sanc followed on Spike. His job was to get to Ezenachi as fast as possible. Behind, Idris was ready to capitalise on the initial strike of the Kalinthians.

The Knights picked up speed as they closed on the Turned. Spike couldn't keep up, and the knights pulled away. Mildrith and the Eger Khan joined him, their mounts fleeter of foot than poor old Spike.

Only now did the Turned notice what was coming. Some stopped, turning to defend against the fast approaching, metal clad riders. Others kept going or were caught between the two options. It was hardly the kind of organised response that might stop the Kalinthians.

The Knights lowered their lances and formed a wedge shape, transforming into a spear made of horse flesh and metal. They charged, pounding into the nearest Turned. A shockwave hit the enemy, who could do nothing to stop them. The nearest were flattened, the Knights barely slowing as they rode over them. Some Turned were hurled into the sky by the impact, their bodies turning somersaults.

Sanc continued to give chase. The Knights were opening a path straight to Ezenachi. As the sheer number of Turned slowed them down, they struck out with their lances, their reach far superior.

Those who lost their lance drew longswords from their belts and continued the slaughter.

Spike began to catch up, reaching the bloody ground where the Knights had first struck. Ezenachi's army was finally dealing with the surprise attack. Thousands of Turned were marching back the way they had come. Leontios had done his job. He needed to extricate his force before they were surrounded.

The ranks of Turned parted. *Ezenachi*, Sanc thought. *But surely I would sense him.*

He froze at the sight. They were black with a green tinge. Large and powerfully built, they moved frighteningly fast. 'Lizardmen,' he said, realising they must be the creatures Idris had warned about.

Their twitchy movement reminded him of the giant lizards of the Egers. 'Don't get any ideas, Spike,' he warned. 'They're not on our side.'

Long spears, including three-pronged tridents, were their weapon of choice. They ran on foot, straight for the Knights, and without fear. Then they were jumping, far higher than a human was capable. They landed on the horses of the Kalinthians. Some knights skewered them as they descended. Others, caught by surprise, failed to prevent them from finding purchase. The advance was halted as Knights and Lizardmen tumbled to the ground, and horses shrieked in fear and pain.

Sanc looked behind. Idris's cavalry was on its way. The infantry wouldn't arrive for some time.

'We can't afford to wait,' Mildrith shouted at him, reading his mind.

She was right. Their whole plan depended on getting the first strike in. But leaving their allies to do the fighting was easier in theory than practice.

Mildrith pushed Red ahead, through the fighting, into the oncoming Lizardmen. Sanc followed.

Red skipped past one threat, then the next. Spike, less agile, didn't have that option. He butted the first Lizardman to get in his way, his bony spikes slamming into his victim with crushing force.

The next, he sliced open with his long talons, tearing his victim in two.

Then Sanc felt a tug of air. It was time. 'Take care, Spike,' he said, removing his feet from the stirrups.

Above, Kepa was gathering funnels of wind. He floated upwards alongside Mildrith and the Eger Khan. They sailed above the Turned, avoiding the fray. As they rose, Sanc could at last get a clear view of the battlefield ahead. A great mass of Turned remained before them. Beyond, he could see the army of Guivergne. Peyre's cavalry came first, his infantry marching behind. The Turned, faced with this second attack, were lining up in long ranks to face his brother's warriors.

A sensation Sanc recognised crept up on him. Nausea, and a fizzing sensation in the mouth. A yearning to submit; to obey; to push oneself into the dirt before the power that manifested itself. He resisted and used his own power to search Ezenachi out.

'There!' he cried, a pulsing light pinpointing the god's position. He was embedded amongst his Turned slaves, his champions by his side. Ordinarily, he would be invincible. But Sanc had brought the champions of Silb, and between them they could resist Ezenachi's might. Sanc had brought two armies, and they were enough to deal with the Turned.

He hoped.

Kepa manoeuvred the four of them together as they glided towards their target. Wordlessly, Sanc, Mildrith, and the Eger Khan leant the Teld their power. Sanc searched for the others. He spotted them emerging from the front rank of the cavalry. The rest of Peyre's army had been stopped by Ezenachi's command. But two horses and a camel kept walking, their riders resisting the magic that assaulted them.

Three more made seven—a sacred number. Relief, more than any other emotion, hit Sanc. The most complex part of the plan had been executed. Now it was time to see if the rest of it would work.

A deep rumbling from underground signalled it was time. Kepa intensified her magic until a windstorm blew. The wind whipped at them, and he sensed Mildrith tightening the binds of magic that held them together. A blast of magic lanced towards Kepa from the ground, but Sanc returned it with ease. From his right, a mist appeared. Sanc could see it rising from the ground, its grey tendrils stretching into the sky. Another blast of magic, this time aimed at Guntram, was deflected by Temyl.

The mist met the wind, and a roiling grey funnel grew above Ezenachi's position. Perhaps the god could have stopped them. But at that moment an explosion sounded deep below the surface where he stood. At first, nothing happened. Sanc stared, transfixed, ignoring the wind and rain that buffeted him.

Then Ezenachi was falling. A wide circle of earth, containing the god and his champions, and as many as a thousand Turned, sank. It fell fast, causing those caught in the circle to lose their footing. As this plot was torn free of the land that surrounded it, huge chunks of earth fell from above, smashing onto those below. Some Turned, unfortunate enough to be standing where the rent occurred, lost their footing and fell over the edge.

Kepa took yet more of his energy. The funnel of air and water snapped and turned, diving for the crater. As the sunken, broken earth slowed and settled, it was bombarded by a fierce squall. Chunks of earth and bodies were sent flying into the sky, crashing together, as they were hit by the devastating power. A whirlwind spun about, carrying its victims with it. Some bodies caught in it were shot so far they were sent back up to the land above.

Kepa released her storm and the air slowly cleared, revealing a scene of devastation. She lowered them down into the crater until they were back on their feet.

Movement caught his eye. A large pile of earth, pale bodies visible amongst it, shifted. The top of the pile slid to the ground, and Sanc saw the telltale signs of a large magical shield flicker away.

The Giant, Oisin, was the first to emerge, clearing a path through which the others followed. Ezenachi, still occupying the body of a Lipper warlord. Maragin the Krykker and Lorant the Caladri, were at his side. Sanc's heart twisted in his chest as Jesper was the last to exit.

Sanc was desperate to talk with his old friend. Instead, Jesper gave him a dead-eyed snarl, and put an arrow to the Jalakh Bow.

Was that all there was? Perhaps Ezenachi had positioned his Turned sorcerers elsewhere on the battlefield, leading his warriors.

The cold and sickly feeling of apprehension grabbed at Sanc. If that were true, he had left the warriors he had brought here defenceless.

Mildrith interrupted his thoughts. 'Don't forget the one with the Cloak will be out there.'

Sanc had forgotten Queen Elfled. He searched for a light amongst the debris, aware she was likely hiding somewhere. 'I can't see her,' he warned. 'Perhaps that Cloak even hides her from my sight.'

'A great expenditure of power,' Ezenachi taunted them, his voice echoing around the crater, as if it belonged in such a place. 'With little to show for it.'

'Little to show?' Sanc mocked back. 'You have no slaves to defend you now, save for these few wretches. You are surrounded. This is where we destroy you.'

'You have only succeeded in isolating yourselves. There are four of you for me to deal with. Once I kill you, I will shackle your army. In that moment, Dalriya will be mine.'

LIESEL

THE MIDDER STEPPE

Liesel gawked as the land sunk, forming a giant depression in the middle of the battlefield. Dirt was catapulted into the atmosphere. The squall of wind and water leapt down from the sky, blasting the crater.

Ezenachi's hold over her was relinquished. *Is he dead?* she allowed herself to wonder. *No, Liesel. It's not going to be that easy.*

She thought she heard Peyre's voice, giving orders to the ranks of cavalry. He had gathered the best horsemen they had, from Guivergne, Magnia, and the Steppe. She watched them set off, long rows transforming into the wedge shape, designed to break through enemy ranks. She knew Peyre would put himself at the tip of that wedge and she worried for him. But he had to get those three sorcerers to that crater as soon as possible.

They were soon galloping into the distance, and Gosse was shouting his own orders, repeated by his lieutenant, Sul. The Marshal had his warriors about him in the centre of the line. Liesel was to his right, a group of arbalests with her. They had been divided and placed at different points within the infantry, protected by spears, swords, and shields.

By Liesel's side was Jehan, the young guard given the dubious honour of keeping her alive. He wore a serious expression, and was wont to look at her as if she were a hatchling, who might snap at any moment. Liesel did her best not to get irritated, understanding his anxiety.

The infantry marched, Gosse urging them to go at pace. Their role was to occupy the ranks of Turned warriors who remained. With Gosse's force bearing down on them, they had no time to stop Peyre's advance—no time to rescue Ezenachi from the seven champions who had come to kill him.

The distance between the two armies closed frighteningly fast. Liesel realised the Turned were marching for them, too. The front ranks of the enemy were exclusively made up of fierce looking Lipper warriors. These looked like the elite of Ezenachi's army, placed at the front to break the army of Guivergne.

Gosse was shouting again. 'Quiet, fools!' he demanded, as some soldiers had begun shouting challenges at the approaching enemy.

'Quiet, fools!' Sul repeated.

Most closed their mouths, not willing to get on the wrong side of the fur clad marshal. The Turned who approached were deathly quiet, and so when Gosse gave his next orders, Liesel heard them clearly enough.

'Slow...and halt!'

'Slow...and halt!'

The infantry stopped. Ahead, the Turned kept coming. Liesel could make out dead-eyed faces now, full of hostile snarls.

'Arbalests, ready!' she shouted.

Liesel unhooked her crossbow, then got on one knee.

Unbidden, Jehan joined her, protecting her with his shield.

'Shoot!' she shouted. She lined up her own target, steadying her breathing, locking her arms against the weight of the weapon. She pulled the trigger, holding her position for a moment. Then, she put her foot against the prod, putting her weight on it, and pulled the string back onto the catch.

The volley had disrupted the Turned advance. She had enough time left. She loaded another bolt and got off a second shot.

The Turned weren't far off now, and Gosse was giving the order for the shield wall.

'Back!' Liesel shouted, leading her arbalests away from the front rank, allowing others to take her place.

In front of her, men lined up shields, readied their spears, short swords, and maces. Gosse gave the order to attack, and the Guivergnais moved forward to meet the Turned. There was a thud of wood, a shiver of steel, and the first screams rang out.

The two sides heaved against one another. It was a steaming scrum of flesh, with barely the space to breathe, let alone swing a weapon. Neither side gave way.

Liesel had half expected the Turned to concede ground. For they were up against the fighting men of Morbaine and Guivergne, who had marched across Dalriya and won many victories.

Now, she conceded, she had been over confident. It wasn't just that the Lippers they faced were the elite of Ezenachi's army—warriors who had been there from the beginning, with their own long list of victories. There was the pestilence. Many warriors were missing, and of those who were here, a good proportion had suffered from illness in recent days.

Most of their leaders were absent, deployed with Peyre's cavalry force with the task of breaking through to Ezenachi. Peyre, of course, being the greatest absence. Men fought twice as hard for their king.

Even more important that I step up, then, Liesel told herself.

She reloaded her crossbow and approached the rear rank. Raising her weapon high, she looked for a target.

'Are you sure that's wise?' asked a nervous Jehan beside her. 'You may hit one of ours by accident.'

'If there's any danger of that, I won't release,' she told him.

Liesel closed one eye and aimed. No one was moving very much. On the other hand, the gaps between bodies were so small she couldn't find a clear shot.

She waited patiently, knowing that a shot might open up at any moment. The crossbow was so light there was little strain on her body, unlike holding a longbow string taut. Finally, the press shifted enough for her to get a full view of an enemy Lipper warrior's head. She focused on her breathing, not willing to press the trigger until she was sure of the result. The warrior wore a metal helmet, but it was open, revealing his face. Aim too high, she'd strike the helmet. Too low and it would enter his cheek, causing minimal damage.

Liesel pulled the trigger. The bolt snapped into his eye socket. The Lipper's head slammed back. He was dead, but his body didn't fall, still jammed tight amongst the press.

Liesel turned away. She bent over and vomited onto the ground. Tears streamed down her face.

'Are you alright, my lady?' Jehan asked.

She wiped a sleeve across her face and stood tall. 'I just want this suffering to be over, Jehan.'

'Of course. So do we all.'

Liesel stared across the battlefield. 'Please, Sanc,' she prayed.

SANC

THE MIDDER STEPPE

Once I kill you, I will shackle your army. In that moment, Dalriya will be mine.' Ezenachi withdrew a dagger from his belt. *Toric's Dagger.*

Sanc wasn't sure what extra power the weapon might give the god. But he knew it meant Belwynn was dead. He made two fists, letting his anger fuel him. He launched a strike on Ezenachi, a lance of green magic. *I am here to kill him, after all.*

Ezenachi didn't defend it. He released his own blast of power, a blaze of purples and yellows. The two strikes met at a point between them. Here, the magic crackled as they fought to get the upper hand. Sanc had to pour more power into his attack, just to maintain parity.

Ezenachi's champions leapt into action. Maragin and Oisin ran for Sanc, sword and spear ready to cut him down. Mildrith sent a blast at them. Maragin used Bolivar's Sword to block it. Doubt threatened Sanc's mind. If that sword could negate their magic, they were in trouble.

Kepa intervened, whipping a sudden gust of wind that sent both Giant and Krykker flying backwards.

Sanc first heard the crack that sounded like thunder. Then the

Teld's scream. Still holding off Ezenachi, he glanced over. Kepa was on the ground, an arrow protruding from her chest.

King Lorant used Onella's Staff to deliver the finishing blow. Pulses of enhanced blue light streamed towards Kepa.

The Eger Khan stepped in front of Kepa's prone body. He stopped one pulse, then the next. Each time, Sanc thought the boy's defences would be breached. Somehow, he held on.

Ribbons of grass sprouted through the broken earth of the crater. They wrapped around the Caladri, pinning his arms to his body, denying him the use of the staff.

Another thunderclap. Jesper sent a second arrow at Mildrith. She redirected it, the speed of the return forcing the Halvian to dive out of the way.

Ezenachi poured more power into his attack. The purple and yellow pushed Sanc's green lance back, the crackling of their union getting closer. Sanc concentrated all his efforts, sweat pouring, his body shaking with effort. It wasn't enough. Ezenachi was getting closer. In moments, he would reach Sanc and it would be over.

Sanc stopped his own attack, instead creating a defensive shield around himself. Ezenachi's blast struck, but his shield protected him.

One of my first lessons, Sanc acknowledged. *Defence is easier than attack. Thank you, Rimmon.*

Ezenachi strode towards him. His magic pummelled at Sanc's shield. It might crack at any moment. Sanc thought he could hear Mildrith shouting. But he didn't dare lose focus on his defence. He could feel Ezenachi grasping for him.

'Don't despair at your defeat,' Ezenachi said. Sanc could have sworn there was genuine sympathy in his voice. 'You don't have to die. You could be the first among my champions. You can rule Dalriya for me.'

I can't lose, Sanc told himself. *But if I do, I'd rather die. Like Rimmon.*

So close to death, memories surfaced, one after the other, pushing their way into his consciousness. The first was his teacher, Rimmon, discussing his predecessor, Pentas. *'Were your eyes a sign that you were*

Madria's new servant? Had She passed on some sort of power to you on his death?'

Sanc remembered Ezenachi's arrival at the Red Fort. He had transported hundreds of Magnians to safety, surprising his teacher with his power.

He recalled, in Silb, how easy it had been to get into a Nerisian fort and kill Count Erstein. How he'd stared into the blade of his knife and asked himself, *Am I a monster?*

He'd lifted the King of Nerisia, Lothar, from his horse. Reached for his heart, as Ezenachi now reached for his. Then he'd stopped himself. His mother had visited him. *There is another way,* she'd told him. Or had she? Loysse's voice filled his ears. *'But isn't it also likely that the vision was something you created yourself? Deep down, you knew what was right.'*

He remembered his insistence on visiting the Temple of Peramo, where the seven gods of Silb lay in their stone sarcophagi. He saw himself pushing aside the tombstones and looking inside. But hadn't he already known what he would find? Human remains. Nothing more or less than that.

Idris had said something to him only a few days ago. *'Who says? That he is the only god, I mean. Maybe if I said I was a god, people would believe it?'*

And finally, Sanc understood. *I am not a servant of a god. Neither am I a monster. I am human; and I am a god. Because what is a god? Only someone who has given themselves the title. Well, I am the god of Dalriya. This world is not Ezenachi's. It is mine.*

'I will rule Dalriya,' he said to Ezenachi.

Ezenachi's power wavered. The hand that grasped for Sanc's heart disappeared, replaced with an invitation. To submit. To obey. *Tempting,* Sanc supposed, *to surrender to a higher power.*

'But not for you.'

Sanc discharged his shield. A renewed power surged through his veins. His magic flared, and he struck out.

He drove Ezenachi backwards.

LOYSSE

VALENNES, KINGDOM OF GUIVERGNE

It took the Turned the rest of the evening to secure the city. In the Bastion, they had an uneasy night, taking turns to keep lookout. An attack might come at any moment, and no one could sleep for long.

The Turned waited until first light before they arrived, streaming towards the fortress in their thousands.

'Peyre told me they need to sleep,' Loysse murmured, as she watched from one of the sharp-angled Bastion walls. Two hundred defenders were posted around the fortress walls. It was better than it had been on the city walls, but still too sparse to be effective. 'Perhaps that's why they have waited until now.'

'I'm sure they do,' Syele said, a sour look on her face as the scale of the threat became visible. 'No doubt they slept like babies and are fully refreshed for a day's carnage. While we've endured a sleepless night.'

Syele had become a rock in Loysse's life. But she didn't always appreciate the straight talking. Sometimes, positivity could go a long way.

The warrior seemed to catch her thoughts from her expression.

'Still,' she attempted gamely, 'that's given more time for your brothers to do their work. They might kill Ezenachi at any moment.'

'It's unlikely,' Loysse admitted. 'Still, one must have hope. To keep fighting.'

'Whatever tickles your pickle. Now then. Something's happening out there.'

The Turned repeated their methods from yesterday, first encircling the Bastion, then bringing forward their siege weapons. They also carried rubble, gathered from pulling down nearby buildings. They made great piles of it.

'To fill in the moat?' Loysse asked.

'That would be my guess,' Syele said. 'Though there'll be a massacre, if that's truly their plan.'

Liesel had leant Loysse a squadron of arbalests to defend the Bastion's walls, and they taught the Turned a lesson about the crossbow. Any who came within range were struck by the bolts, both deadly and accurate. Even so, fifty arbalests were too few to stop a full-scale attack.

The Turned advanced from all positions. Those in the front held aloft shields, while those behind held strips of wood or piles of rock.

The arbalests on the walls held their aim until they found an opening. They hit their targets with impressive regularity. Then there was a wait while they reloaded. Brancat's archers kept up a steady rate of fire, making life difficult for the attackers. But the Turned reached the moat, unloading their debris into the water.

From her position, it took Loysse a while to notice what was happening on the neighbouring section of wall. 'Over there!' she shouted, pointing due south.

Two Caladri sorcerers were sending blasts of magic up to the walls, targeting arbalests. A bolt was sent straight for the female sorcerer, its aim true. With a causal flick of a wrist, the sorcerer stopped the missile in midair. The male sorcerer blasted the arbalest responsible.

'What can we do?' Loysse asked Syele.

'I'm not sure,' the warrior admitted. 'Sending more arbalests over is just going to get them killed. Oh no. What foul play is this?'

The sorcerers, having cleared the southern walls of arbalests, had moved onto their next phase. The piles of rubble began to move, floating through the air, then fusing together. Loysse could see what they were making. A path, beginning near the Caladri's position, and leading up to the walls of the Bastion. The Turned could simply march straight into the fortress. She cursed, as the fortress's defences were neutralised before her eyes. It seemed there was nothing they could do. The enemy had sorcerers, and they didn't.

'Look there,' Syele said, pointing.

Loysse squinted. Two figures were shuffling towards the sorcerers. There was something familiar about them. Ernst and Gernot! A unit of Turned warriors, gathered around the sorcerers, noticed the intruders, rushing them. Pulling aside their cloaks, Caisin's thugs aimed their crossbows and released.

The two sorcerers turned towards the threat at the last moment. One bolt was stopped, but the second struck its target in the neck. The male sorcerer fell backwards, hitting the ground. He didn't get up. The path they had been constructing collapsed.

The female Caladri released a fiery blast at Ernst and Gernot. The flames restricted Loysse's sight of them. Then, the Turned warriors were on them. Loysse had to look away.

Syele puffed out a breath. 'Well done,' she said, honouring the men's sacrifice. 'If we could just take out that last sorcerer, the Bastion might hold off the rest of them.'

'You think so?' Loysse asked her. The moat was still intact, and it prevented the Turned from getting to the walls and placing ladders. But there were so many of them.

'I do,' the warrior said, and the certainty in her voice gave Loysse some belief.

'Go fetch Brancat,' Syele said. 'Tell him we need to defend this spot, with archers and arbalests. Enough to stop that sorcerer.'

Loysse didn't waste time. She had to zigzag along the star-shaped walls, running as fast as she could to the other side of the fortress, where Brancat had positioned himself.

She glanced at the space around the fortress. Bodies littered the ground, but plenty of Turned were still making it to the moat. Still, she knew Syele was right. It would take them hours, maybe even days, before they could get inside. If the Caladri sorcerer rebuilt that path, the Bastion would be breached in moments. Unbidden, she pictured what would happen next—what their last moments would be.

When she reached Brancat, she forced herself to speak calmly, not to blurt it all out like a scared child. She saw Brancat's eyes widen in alarm when she talked of the path. To her relief, he took charge, shouting out orders. He stripped the other sections of wall to the bare minimum, and he and Loysse led the reinforcements to the southern sector. Already, the Caladri sorcerer was rebuilding the path.

Brancat cursed and began organising his guards.

Loysse looked about wildly. Syele wasn't where she had left her. An object caught her eye, and as she went over, she saw it was a dagger. One of Syele's. Why would she leave it here? Had she fallen off the wall?

Loysse picked it up. The blade had grit on it. She glanced at the wall where the dagger had been left. There was a crude carving, clearly done in a hurry.

DEFEND WALL

Loysse knew instantly. *No. She's gone to kill the sorcerer.* Loysse wanted to scream. *I need you by my side, Syele. Now more than ever.* But what would her warriors make of such an outburst?

Brancat ordered his archers and arbalests to fire in unison. Bolts and arrows flew towards the Caladri sorcerer. She encased herself in a magical shell. Not even one got through her defence. Even worse, she held the path in place.

Brancat looked over. For a heartbeat, he revealed what he was thinking.

What do we do now?

IDRIS

THE MIDDER STEPPE

After all the strategy and marching, it felt good to be riding into battle.

Until the Lizardmen came. *Not these bastards again*, Idris thought, as the trident-wielding enemy launched themselves at the Knights of Kalinth. Many a knight was dragged to the ground, while behind the lizard folk, the Turned infantry marched to join the fray.

Meanwhile, in the sky, Sanc and his sorcerer friends disappeared from the scene. 'Thanks a lot,' Idris muttered dryly. He drew his sword, holding it aloft, looking left then right along the line of Brasingian cavalry he commanded. There were Atrabians, Luderians, Kellish, and warriors of Rotelegen with him. Not a full imperial host. Not by any stretch, when one considered those who had fallen to the pestilence; or their infantry still labouring to rejoin them. But these riders would fight with him, and that was good enough.

'Let's do this,' he shouted, urging his warhorse into a gallop. *Perhaps not the most precise of commands*, he had to admit. *But really, what else are we going to do, except crack heads and chop limbs?*

They rode through a hail of arrows and other missiles. Then Idris led them into a murderous melee. Lizardmen and Knights grappled in desperate one-on-one contests. Some Knights struck out from horseback; others, unseated, fought on foot. In amongst it all, riderless horses kicked and bit, or tried to escape the slaughter.

All the Brasingians could do was target the Lizardmen. Idris swept his blade left and right, feeling the battle frenzy build within him. The Lizardmen were terrifying. It was true. But they wore little armour, and after their initial onslaught, they were vulnerable to a sharp blade. Idris and his cavalry pushed them back, giving the Knights a chance to retreat and carry their wounded from the field.

The Lizardmen were stubborn enough, but in the end they ran for the safety of the ranks of the Turned infantry. Who were closing fast. Here, Idris could see a mix of enslaved peoples—Cordentines, Sea Caladri, Brasingians, Magnians, the peoples of the Confederacy, and more. Men and women—some well-equipped warriors—others just ordinary folk with improvised weapons and armour. Not the most fearsome of opponents. But there were just so many of them.

He couldn't help looking behind, hoping to see his own infantry arriving in the nick of time. Nothing, except the injured making their slow escape west. *Our job is to keep them occupied*, he reminded himself. *And we are doing that. We don't have to die in the process.*

'Withdraw!' he shouted, backing his mount up.

The surrounding riders followed his orders. The Turned kept coming, but Idris's cavalry had the speed to keep them at a safe distance.

Then, to his left, the sound of combat. An entire unit of cavalry had either not heard or ignored his order, engaging the enemy.

'Damned Kellish!' Idris exploded out loud. *Probably looked at the opposition and fancied a go.*

His warriors looked at him for leadership. He had no real option. Hiding his reluctance, he pointed his blade at the enemy. 'For Brasingia!' he shouted.

With his warriors repeating his battle cry, he led the charge. As he approached the front line, a Confederate woman lunged at his mount with her long spear. He pulled up just in time, avoiding the strike. Then he was buffeted from behind, his warriors too eager to join the battle. His horse was pushed forwards. It was all he could do to lean

337

forward, one hand around his mount's neck, and steer the spear aside. His mount continued its momentum, then rose onto its hind legs and kicked the woman, felling her.

Idris struggled to stay in the saddle, pushing down on his stirrups and squeezing with his knees. Then, someone grabbed his sword arm, and dragged him from his horse.

Idris landed on his side. The wind was knocked from him. A Turned still had hold of his arm, and he fought desperately to keep hold of his sword. A figure loomed over him. Idris put up his left arm to defend himself and was rewarded with a hammer blow on his forearm. His vambrace took the blow, and yet the pain was excruciating. A numbness shot up and down his arm, from fingertips to shoulder.

With his left arm useless, Idris was forced to let go of his sword. Knowing another blow could come at any moment, he could do nothing except roll over onto his knees. One arm hung limp. He bent down, his elbow on the ground and his right hand instinctively placed above his head. All he could do was hope that the killing blow didn't come.

The fighting surged around him. He shouted in pain when a horse stood on his boot. The killing blow never came, and yet it didn't feel safe to move.

A series of screams. A body toppled over him. Something was happening. Idris got to his knees. He came face to face with a giant blue lizard. A horn on the end of its nose was mere inches from his face. Around it was a pile of Turned, their bodies ripped open. The lizard gave him an angry hiss.

'Either you're going to kill me,' Idris said, 'or you're inviting me for a ride.'

Gingerly, he got to his feet. 'Well. I've always been an optimist.' Taking care to make no sudden moves, he took the beast's leather reins in his good hand and hauled himself into the saddle.

His new mount had created a bit of space on the battlefield for him. But elsewhere, the Brasingian cavalry were still engaged in a furious fight with the Turned. 'Come, Spike,' he said, recalling the name of Sanc's prickly friend. 'Let's do this.'

SANC

THE MIDDER STEPPE

Sanc rejected Ezenachi's offer of submission, pushing him away with his magic.

'Kill them!' Ezenachi commanded his champions, a snarl of anger on the Lipper's face.

Oisin and Maragin came for Mildrith, weapons at the ready. Lorant's staff glowed with its pale blue light. Behind them, Jesper prowled to the side. He held the Jalakh Bow loose, waiting for an opening.

On the other side of Mildrith, Kepa was still prone. The Eger Khan defended her, but he could only do so much.

Mildrith can't hold them off, Sanc realised.

But before he could come up with a solution, Ezenachi was at him. The god held one hand out, magic pulsing around it. In the other was Toric's Dagger.

The weapon made to kill a god. A chill ran up Sanc's spine. *Does he know what I am? Did he know before me?*

Something—maybe Brancat's training—made him draw his own knife. It was pitiful, really, to hold such a lowly thing against a weapon of Madria. *But my father gave this to me. Told me I was a man. Surely that means something?*

Sanc blocked a blast of magic. Then Ezenachi was close, stabbing at him. Sanc twisted out of the way. But Ezenachi moved fast, closing in once more. Sanc lashed out. Their blades met. Sanc felt a pulse of magic and his knife shattered into pieces.

Ezenachi swung for his head.

As he ducked, Sanc made himself invisible. He hurled himself out of the way, rolled, and came up on his knees. In an instant, he took in the situation. Mildrith was shielding herself, while Lorant poured his magic through Onella's Staff, sending a blue beam that might force an opening in her defences at any moment. Oisin and Maragin slashed with their weapons, sparks flaring in Mildrith's shield. Jesper released an arrow. It was deflected away from Mildrith by the Eger Khan.

Sanc hurled his magic at Lorant. The force of it sent the Caladri spinning through the air. But he had revealed his location.

Ezenachi launched a heavy blast of magic at him. Sanc put up a defence, but the power sent him sprawling onto his back.

I can't believe we lost, Sanc had time to think.

Then Ezenachi was struck by two blasts of magic, forcing him to back off and raise a shield. He let out a cry of frustration at coming so close to ending Sanc.

Hearing his enemy's anguish gave Sanc renewed vigour. *He fears me,* he realised, getting to his feet.

Their allies had arrived just in time. Temyl and Guntram pummelled Ezenachi, keeping him on the defensive. Mergildo struck Oisin from behind, sending him sailing through the air until he crashed into the edge of the crater. The force of the impact dislodged a section of earth that tumbled onto the Giant, burying him.

Mergildo's second strike was aimed at Maragin. Forewarned, the Krykker used Bolivar's Sword to block it. But Sanc breathed a sigh of relief as Mildrith escaped, running over to the Eger Khan and Kepa.

The enemy counterattacked. One crack after another sounded as Jesper loosed his arrows at Mergildo. Lorant attacked Temyl and Guntram, his staff giving him enough power to occupy them both.

With Ezenachi freed, Sanc had no choice but to fight the god again. He sent a blast of magic at him. Ezenachi blocked, then sent his own. Sanc met it with his blast. Just as before, the two strikes crackled with intensity where they met. *This time, I win,* Sanc insisted.

But from the corner of his eye, he could see Maragin coming for him. The Krykker stopped, held in place by the Eger Khan.

Sanc renewed his efforts. He poured everything he had into it, and he could feel Ezenachi doing the same.

'Watch out!' Mildrith screamed.

Some instinct made Sanc crouch down. He felt, rather than saw, a body topple over him.

Elfled.

Fear gripped him. Still invisible, she came for him again. He had no choice but to reach out to stop her. He grabbed the Cloak. She was on him, clawing at his hand. He felt her breath on his neck as she tried to reach him with her teeth. He had to get rid of her. Redirecting his magic, he opened the hand that held her and blasted, driving her away.

Why aren't I dead?

He looked at Ezenachi. The god's arm was held tight by strands of grass. He strained, desperate to blast Sanc while he was unprotected, but Mildrith held firm. With a howl of fury, he threw Toric's Dagger into the sky. It sailed away, as if it might reach the heavens.

His hand freed, Ezenachi turned on Mildrith, launching an attack. She defended, and the Eger Khan leant his support.

Sanc got to his feet, readying himself. Ezenachi had his back to him. Surely, this was his chance.

Maragin intervened, defending her master. She held Bolivar's Sword ahead of her. Remembering Rimmon's training, Sanc sent a blast of magic that curved around, avoiding the weapon, striking her down from behind.

A pile of earth erupted, and Oisin exploded out. He ran for Sanc. With a sigh of frustration, Sanc blasted the Giant back where he had come from.

Sanc readied to strike Ezenachi.

Shouts of alarm sounded from the other side of the crater. Turning, Sanc saw Mergildo, arms outstretched, eyes wide in surprise. A blade erupted from his neck. Toric's Dagger passed straight through.

The Rasidi sorcerer collapsed to the ground.

Toric's Dagger didn't stop. It soared around the crater, a roving blade that might strike at any moment.

And Sanc heard a deep, ugly sound come from Ezenachi. He was laughing.

PEYRE

THE MIDDER STEPPE

Peyre used the Shield of Persala to smash the last of the Turned out of his way.

He reached the edge of a giant crater, right in the middle of the battlefield. It was a scene of devastation, but amongst the broken earth, he saw figures moving. Two beams of magic—one green, the other a mix of purple and yellow—clashed against one another. He knew one was Sanc, and the other Ezenachi. It filled him with awe and pride that his little brother was down there, fighting a god.

The three champions wasted no time. They slipped from their mounts and slid down the side of the crater, using their magic to manoeuvre themselves.

Just in time, I reckon, Peyre thought. Sanc and his allies looked to be on the back foot. Surely the arrival of three more sorcerers would even the balance?

But Peyre had his own problems to deal with. He'd led his cavalry in a charge, smashing their way through the ranks of Turned to get those sorcerers to Ezenachi. It was a vital part of the plan. But now his cavalry was surrounded—the crater at his back the only place that offered protection.

It wasn't just their compromised position on the battlefield. Somewhere out to the north was the Turned cavalry. They were free to strike anywhere on the battlefield so long as his horsemen were stuck like this.

The Turned crowded them. They had his cavalry trapped.

'This way!' he shouted. He pushed into the Turned, keeping the crater to his left. It meant he could strike out freely with his sword arm. He hacked down with his sword. Strapped to his arm, the Shield of Persala was a second weapon, repelling anything that struck it.

With him came the finest horsemen in his army. Florent of Auriac forced his way alongside Peyre. His mount was a dun colour and slimmer than most warhorses. But it was a ferocious thing, snapping at the Turned ahead of it, more like a dog than a horse. They made progress into the ranks of the Turned, carving a path. A bit farther, and they could break through to the flank of the enemy and escape.

More horsemen battered their way next to Florent, widening the line. Sacha of Courion flicked out with his sword blade, making his opponents look slow and clumsy. None could withstand him for long. King Ida and Herin joined them. Inhan. Then, Cuenin and Jorath arrived with the Middians. The most natural horsemen in the entire army, they sliced through the Turned with ease.

To his left, a flash of metal caught his attention. He couldn't help but be distracted, slowing his advance to look at it. A dagger. Ancient looking. It sailed through the air like a bird, whipping past him.

He followed its path as it dove towards the crater. Towards Mergildo.

No. He shouted a warning. But it was useless, the din and clash of the fighting around him making it impossible for those below to hear.

Helpless, he watched the blade come at the sorcerer from behind. The outlander had no chance. It tore through the back of his neck and came out the other side, still flying, twisting one way, then the next. A devilish enchantment was on it, and of course, Ezenachi must be behind it.

Ahead of him, his companions had slowed, casting anxious glances his way.

'What is it?' Sacha yelled at him.

'I have to go down there.' He patted the Shield of Persala in explanation. *This weapon is needed to help Sanc*, he realised.

Sacha nodded in understanding. 'We will do the rest,' he shouted. 'Good luck.'

Peyre sheathed his sword and dismounted. Florent waited with him, taking the reins of his horse, as the others renewed their attack on the Turned.

'Thank you,' Peyre said, then turned towards the steep side of the crater. He had no magic to help him get down there. *Or do I?* He unstrapped the shield, studying it briefly. *Will you protect me?* he wondered.

There was only one way to find out. Gripping the shield tight, and holding it out before him, he launched himself off the edge. *This will either look glorious or witless*, he had time to think, before the shield met the ruptured ground of the crater. It protected him from the impact and he sprung back into the air, landing on his feet.

He took in several individual combats, as the champions on each side deployed magic or weapons against one another. It was hard to keep track of—hard to assess where he should help. He looked up instead, scanning the sky for that damned dagger.

There. It was circling around the crater, above the action. It travelled towards the opposite side, where Peyre could see Sanc engaged with Ezenachi. He wasted no time running in that direction. He passed close to Temyl and Guntram, who were holding their own against a staff-wielding Caladri.

Glancing to the right, he was just in time to see Jesper aiming for him. Their eyes met briefly, and he wondered whether there was any recognition there. The arrow came with shocking speed, and he only just raised the Shield in time. A crack echoed around the crater, then a second one, as the arrow struck the Shield and returned towards the forester. With a snarl of frustration, Jesper dived out of the way of his own missile.

For a desperate few moments, Peyre tried to catch the flight of the dagger once more. There. It had flown past Sanc and was heading for a group of three champions. He ran towards them, shouting a warning. But at that moment, a twelve-foot tall, green Giant roared a challenge and ran for them, his huge spear held in one hand. They didn't hear Peyre.

He sprinted, eyeing the dagger all the time. Mildrith sent a blast of magic at the Giant. It leapt, jumping over the blast, and came down with the long blade of the spear aimed at her. Somehow, she shielded herself from the strike, but Peyre could see the pain and exhaustion in her face.

The dagger gathered speed, aiming for the young boy. Unaware, the lad sent a blast of magic at the Giant, trying to protect Mildrith.

I'm not going to reach it in time, Peyre realised. Three more steps and he launched himself into the air.

At the last moment, the lad saw him coming, turning in shock.

Peyre clattered into him. With his arm outstretched, he slammed the shield into the dagger. The weapon spun away and landed, blade first, in the crater floor.

LIESEL

THE MIDDER STEPPE

The front ranks grudgingly pulled apart, neither having gained ground. The dead and injured on both sides were dragged away. Liesel couldn't help looking, identifying those she knew. She found it hard to even get angry. It wasn't as if she could truly blame the Lippers they fought. They were the first of Ezenachi's victims.

'Arbalests!' she shouted, doing her best to keep the melancholy from her voice. She led her unit forward. She would take no pleasure in it. But for every Turned warrior they took out of the battle, they were reducing the losses on their own side.

'Ready!'

Those arbalests with her readied their weapons. Scattered elsewhere amongst the infantry, more would do the same. The enemy did their best to hide behind shields or cover their heads.

'Shoot!'

The bolts flew towards the enemy. Then stopped. They spun around and came back.

Liesel was so taken aback, she didn't move. Her bolt was stopped by Jehan, placing his shield in front of her. Many of her arbalests weren't so fortunate, crying out in pain as they were struck.

Liesel scanned the ranks of the Turned. A Lipper woman. There was something in the way she raised her hands that told Liesel. She had witnessed enough magic to know.

'That's her!' she screamed, gesturing at the woman. She looked down the line until she met eyes with Gosse. 'A sorcerer!' Liesel shouted at him. 'We have to stop her!'

Understanding dawned on Gosse. The Lippers had a sorcerer with them. They had none.

The Turned stared in silence, not even celebrating the intervention of the woman. The sorcerer herself gave Liesel a flat look, knowing she had been identified. Her hand raised higher, and she unleashed a blast of magic.

'No!' Liesel shouted, reaching out a hand.

Too late. Jehan put himself in harm's way, his shield in place to block the magic.

But, of course, it didn't.

Jehan was hurled backwards. Liesel caught him as he fell, the impact sending her sprawling to the ground.

She heard Gosse give the order to charge; heard Sul repeat it. Booted feet rushed past her. She turned Jehan onto his side. He wasn't conscious. She put a hand to his neck. She was shaking so much she couldn't tell. *Control yourself, Liesel*, she commanded. She touched him again; found a pulse. That was something. She looked elsewhere. His left arm and hand were red raw. Perhaps the shield had protected him to an extent, because she could find no other signs of physical injury.

She crawled on her hands and knees to retrieve her crossbow. Her breath came quick. She moved slowly, as if through invisible mud. She pulled the string back and fitted another bolt. Then she sat on the ground next to Jehan, unsure what to do next. Her mind and body weren't responding properly.

She heard the clash as the two sides fought again.

Get up, she told herself.

She refused.

An arbalest staggered towards her, still holding her crossbow. She was pretty—a redhead, face full of freckles. What was she doing here?

348

She's here because you brought her here, Liesel reminded herself. The woman clutched at a bolt embedded in her shoulder.

Shame made Liesel get to her feet. 'You can walk?'

'Aye, Your Majesty.'

'Then get yourself straight to camp. We have doctors there who can help.'

The woman pointed at Jehan. 'I can help you with him, my lady.'

'No. I can do it. You need to go straight away. You're losing blood and may soon feel much weaker.'

'I'm alright.'

Liesel sighed, staring at Jehan. She could hold him under the arms and drag him. But he would be a dead weight in his armour. 'Then help me get him up.'

Liesel discarded her crossbow and went down on one knee. Between them, they manhandled Jehan over her shoulder. She needed the woman's help to get to her feet. Even though that was a tiny victory, she wasn't sure she could walk with him. One step, then another. Slow and painful, but if she focused on one step at a time, she would make it.

Her companion accompanied her. They weren't the only ones staggering away from the battlefield. The injured supported one another, helping those who couldn't walk themselves. It was hard to process. *If we lose,* Liesel told herself, unable to stop the thought from appearing, *these might be the lucky ones.*

The camp was a long way back towards the border with Barissia. Dark thoughts plagued her. If they *were* to lose this battle—and how could she know one way or another—the remnants of the army might make it to Coldeberg. The city had sturdy walls and a castle.

The shouts of combat continued behind her. They hadn't got far when she realised the shouts were getting louder. She turned, still hefting Jehan's weight.

The infantry of Guivergne was in retreat. Not a full-blooded flight —enough soldiers were still in formation, giving way to the Lippers who pressed them. But in places, the line was ragged and broken.

They had held against their enemy at first, but now it seemed they were second best. Perhaps that sorcerer had swung it for Ezenachi.

We can't run, Liesel reminded herself. *Our job is to occupy the Turned. If we allow them to, they will turn around and go help Ezenachi.*

'Help me,' she said. They placed Jehan onto the ground, as gently as they were able.

The first soldiers reached them. They walked backwards, arms stretched out, supporting the rank in front.

'We must hold!' she told them.

But all they gave her were apologetic looks. They had to move at the pace of those in front.

'Careful!' she shouted, pushing the next rank out of the way before they trod on Jehan.

It wasn't until the front rank reached her that Liesel got anywhere. 'Hold here!' she told them.

The warriors gave her wild-eyed looks, as the Lippers prodded at them with spears, looking for an opening. But they did as she asked.

Along the line, she glimpsed Gosse. She pushed her way through to reach him. He was backing away from the enemy, one arm around his friend, Sul. She could see scorch marks on them both, the same as Jehan had.

'We need to hold here,' she told him.

'Hold!' Gosse bellowed, and the surrounding soldiers dug in, linking shields and readying weapons.

'Put him down,' she said, then helped Gosse get Sul to the ground.

Sul looked bad—his injuries worse than Jehan's. He was barely conscious. Gosse's men pulled him to a safer position.

'We got the sorcerer,' Gosse said with grim pride. 'Sul put his spear in her. But she left her mark.'

The big man's beard was singed; his face and neck were red and weeping; his armour blackened. Liesel wondered how bad his injuries might be beneath it.

'We can't run,' she said simply. 'We must give Sanc and Peyre more time.'

'Aye,' he said. 'Form up, lads,' he commanded.

The Lippers eyed them warily, not yet prepared to engage. Liesel had stopped their rout, but many soldiers were still leaving the battlefield. She worked quickly with the time available. She had a standard-bearer plant the Owl of Guivergne in the soil. Beside it, she gathered Sul, Jehan, and the other wounded.

'Look after them,' she told her arbalest.

'Here, Majesty,' said the woman, handing over her crossbow. 'I can't pull the string with this shoulder.' She took a short sword from Sul's belt, holding it with her good hand. 'This'll do me.'

'Thank you.'

Liesel had done her best. They had enough warriors for a last stand, at least. Enough to occupy the Turned a little longer.

Then a noise like thunder made her turn to the north. It was the sound of the Turned cavalry. They were heading for their right flank. She studied their numbers. Not the entire cavalry. But enough—more than enough—to swing the battle against them.

The Guivergnais infantry moved into position, readying spears and shields to defend against the new arrivals.

Liesel decided to lend them her support, trusting Gosse to hold off the Lipper infantry. Some of her arbalests—those few who were still able—accompanied her. They arrived in time to release their bolts at the front rank of the charging cavalry.

Then, the cavalry were hacking at the Guivergnais shield wall. The infantry held them off long enough for Liesel to release another bolt. Then another. But the pressure was unrelenting. Liesel realised this was a flaw in their plan. Their infantry was weakened, and it faced the best of Ezenachi's troops.

The shield wall broke, and the Turned cavalry isolated and killed pockets of infantry. There was a ragged retreat. Liesel was part of it, desperately trying to keep her feet. She shouted to the warriors she fought with, telling them to make for the standard she had erected. Few could hear her above the gruesome sounds of battle.

They were driven backwards, like sheep. The Turned cavalry were manoeuvring around to their rear. They would soon cut off their escape route back to camp; back to Barissia. Liesel knew what the

Turned were up to. Once the killing was over, they would capture the survivors and hand them over to Ezenachi.

The less experienced warriors looked at her nervously. But Liesel had no more experience to draw on than they did. Apart from Gosse, lending his strength to the front rank, they had few leaders with the authority to offer solutions. The responsibility weighed on her. She suddenly wished Tegyn was with her.

'There!' one of the younger men said, pointing east, where the Turned were close to completing their encirclement.

Liesel hid her relief. A unit of infantry, half a thousand strong, was marching for their position, standards hoisted. The Owl of Guivergne…and four silver diamonds on a crimson background.

'The Viper,' someone said, then spat.

'Benoit of Saliers,' warriors declared, unhappy.

Few wanted to be saved by a traitor. But Liesel was willing to accept the help. Peyre had pardoned Arnoul's son, a decision many disliked. Yet here he was, bringing his followers into the fray, when he could have slunk away. As they came, his soldiers stopped small groups of retreating soldiers. Most turned about and joined Benoit's force.

It left the Turned in a quandary. So close to surrounding Liesel's force, they now backed away.

As the reinforcements closed, Liesel caught sight of the young lord leading his troops. He had his father's dark colouring. Where Arnoul rarely revealed what he was thinking, Benoit had a hungry, violent look in his eyes.

He held sword and shield, and his whole body seemed to throb with murderous intent. He was fearsome, and Liesel had no shame in admitting it was a joyous sight. His confidence spread to those who walked with him, many his own age or even younger. Liesel was reminded of the contests Esterel had held to celebrate their wedding. Benoit had given a good account of himself there, only losing out to Peyre. Even if most Guivergnais hated his family, his followers believed in him.

Benoit marched to his right, facing off against the Turned cavalry.

The warriors with Liesel joined up, until Benoit's force was linked with Liesel's, and Liesel's, to Gosse's. It was only a few hundred more warriors, but the resolve of the Guivergnais strengthened. Men banged their weapons against shields.

The Turned cavalry stopped backing off. Now they advanced, making for Benoit's position.

Liesel glanced over to where Gosse stood with his fur-clad followers. There was no change of expression or mood amongst the Lipper infantry who opposed them. They remained silent, only the occasional snarl revealing anything that might be called emotion. Their advance began shortly after the cavalry. They marched towards the Guivergnais position, moving as one. They linked shields and readied spears.

'For King Peyre!' Gosse bellowed as they came. 'For Guivergne!'

SANC

THE MIDDER STEPPE

Ezenachi laughed.

Anger and bile rose within Sanc. He fed on it. His power was draining away. He could feel there wasn't much left to give. *Even a god has limits*, he reminded himself. *That is why Ezenachi always retreats to rest after an attack. And that's why we cornered him here. I have to finish this.*

He launched another attack.

But Ezenachi knew it was coming. He turned his attention from Mildrith back to Sanc, defending against his strike. Then nothing. They stared at one another. Amusement still seemed to play across the god's face.

'I can defend against you for as long as I need to. I'll outlast you,' Ezenachi said, his dry voice sounding inevitable. 'You know that.'

Suspicion filled Sanc's mind. It was a nothing statement. Was he playing for time? His hackles rose. Was Elfled coming for a second go? Then he glanced across and saw Peyre running—saw Toric's Dagger, on its way to the Eger Khan.

He sent a blast of magic to stop the weapon. But Ezenachi blocked it, a knowing smile on his face.

354

Somehow, Peyre got to the dagger just in time. His shield knocked it away.

Sanc ran for the dagger. Something told him it still held the key to victory. Ezenachi blasted him. He was forced to stop and defend himself.

Maragin advanced on Mildrith, Bolivar's Sword negating the Kassite's attempts to hold her off. The Eger Khan screamed as an invisible force pulled him along the ground by one foot. Kepa, still prone on the ground, an arrow in her chest, sent a blast of wind. For a moment, the boy rose into the air. Then he fell to the ground, freed of Elfled's clutches.

Peyre got to his feet. He looked at the dagger, its hilt sticking from the ground. He met eyes with King Oisin and they both ran for it. Peyre was closer, but Oisin was faster, and they came against each other before they could claim it. Spear met shield. The impact sent his brother flying backwards. In other circumstances, Peyre's confused face might have looked comical. The shield clearly didn't work as normal against the spear.

Oisin didn't pause, snatching the dagger. Mildrith fixed Maragin's feet to the ground and her blast struck the Giant. But as he tumbled over, he threw the dagger. It sailed towards Ezenachi.

Sanc sent a blast to stop it, but Ezenachi deflected it with one hand, catching the dagger with his other.

Ezenachi smiled, as if victory was his.

'You are powerful,' he told Sanc. 'But you should have escaped Dalriya when you had the chance.'

He advanced, Toric's Dagger in hand.

There was a brown blur, and the dagger was gone.

Sanc followed the blur. 'Rab!?' he said, unbelieving.

His dog turned, the weapon held in its mouth. He dodged an arrow and ran for Sanc. Sanc blocked Ezenachi's strike and held out a hand as Rab ran past him.

Got it.

He faced Ezenachi. He sensed the change in the atmosphere.

Suddenly, Ezenachi's champions were running to protect him, everything else forgotten.

Arrows whistled in at Sanc, one after the other. So fast, and so powerful, that he was forced to defend himself with a magic shield.

Lorant sent a blast from Onella's Staff. But Guntram blocked it, and then Temyl caught the Caladri with a blast of his own. Mildrith and the Eger Khan faced off against Oisin.

Look out for that Asrai, Mildrith, Sanc pleaded.

Maragin got in front of Ezenachi, challenging Sanc to get past Bolivar's Sword. Ezenachi readied his magic.

Jesper's arrows stopped, Temyl and Guntram occupying both bow and staff.

Sanc advanced, his knuckles white as he gripped Toric's Dagger.

Maragin was in a fighter's stance.

I'm no fighter, Sanc admitted. *And that sword is a lot longer than this dagger.*

Then Peyre was on her. He took the blow from her sword on his shield. He braced against her strike, then swung low with his sword, forcing her backwards.

Sanc's path to Ezenachi was open.

IDRIS

THE MIDDER STEPPE

It was a desperate fight. The outnumbered Brasingian cavalry were falling to the Turned. Those who extricated themselves pulled away from the melee, a decision Idris had tried to take earlier, before the damned Kellish ignored him.

He knew full well he would be dead if Spike hadn't rescued him. He gave the lizard freedom to pick its fights, holding on to the reins with one hand. His other arm still hung limp and useless, though he was gradually getting the feeling back in it. All that got him was a jarring pain up and down the limb every time his mount twisted and turned.

The creature had tough skin almost everywhere; anywhere it didn't, it had bony spikes. The Turned seemed unable to find a weak point. Meanwhile, its great claws tore into the enemy, ripping through anything but the strongest armour.

Even so, Idris could feel Spike tiring. The beast was fighting a rear-guard action, virtually alone at this point. He gently encouraged him away from the lines of Turned, joining those few horsemen, Brasingians and Kalinthians, still unscathed.

The Turned didn't give up, marching towards them. Enslaved by Ezenachi, they would never stop.

Idris looked nervously beyond the front ranks. They had to keep the pressure on. If Idris and his fighters were dismissed as no threat, some of the Turned would go to their master, aiding him against Sanc. That simply couldn't happen.

The sound of horses at full gallop made Idris swing Spike around. A score of knights were heading for him, pulling up as they got close. With relief, he identified Grand Master Leontios among them, having feared the knight had fallen in the fighting. It looked like he had grabbed a fresh horse, and his lance, too, looked new.

'The infantry draw near,' Leontios said.

Idris felt some of his tension ease. 'Leontios, I could kiss you.'

The knight raised an eyebrow. 'Please don't. Bring your riders with us. We can move to the flank now.'

Idris shouted the order to his warriors and followed Leontios. The knight led them south, away from the Turned.

As they departed, the first of the infantry arrived. The Caladri came at speed, their clawed feet propelling them towards the Turned. They moved in silence, and yet there was something terrifying about them. Hajna led them, and Idris thought he had never seen such a magnificent sight as the Queen of the Caladri leading her people into battle.

She raised an arm and her warriors stopped instantly. Most took longbows in hand, stringing their weapons and nocking arrows with their mechanical way of moving. No order was shouted, and yet they released as one. A blizzard of arrows struck the Turned, causing terrible damage.

The Turned released some missiles of their own, but it was a feeble response. The Caladri kept firing, each archer fully stocked with missiles, using bows with impressive range and power.

Better even than Atrabian archers, Idris had to admit.

The Turned had no choice but to charge, making up the distance between them as quickly as possible to steal time from the Caladri. Another arm gesture from Hajna, and the Caladri backed away.

Behind them, the imperial infantry appeared at last. Jeremias led the rank and file of the army into battle. *They've had to do a lot of walking*, Idris admitted. *But they're fresher than the rest of us.*

Idris turned away and followed Leontios, who led their cavalry away from the battle, across the grassland of the Steppe. A stream ahead of them formed a natural edge to the battlefield, and they swung around, facing the lines of infantry.

'What's the plan?' he asked the knight. Leontios' war experience was second to none, and he was one of the few soldiers Idris was happy to follow.

'We wait for the infantry forces to engage one another, then attack the Turned on their flank.' The Grand Master stared at the lines of warriors closing on one another. 'We might just get the upper hand here.' He looked across to the far side of the battlefield. 'I see no Turned cavalry to stop us.'

'Why's that?'

'I suspect Ezenachi put his best troops at the front. The Guivergnais will have to deal with them.'

'Well, they've the army for it,' Idris said, detecting a strand of jealousy in his own words. The army of Guivergne had humiliated Brasingia. All well and good when Leopold was their target. Not so good now he was emperor.

'I hope that's the case,' Leontios said.

It might not be so bad if the Guivergnais took a mauling, Idris considered. What was that to him? Then he remembered Liesel was with them, and changed his mind.

LIESEL

THE MIDDER STEPPE

The Turned battered them. Ezenachi's veterans were unyielding, free of exhaustion or pain. His horsemen were fresh, able to use their height advantage.

The warriors of Guivergne had proven themselves masters of war in the last few years. But they were only human. They buckled under the relentless pressure.

Liesel fired her bolts into the enemy, making sure each one counted. When she was out, she grabbed a spear and jabbed it at their ankles, trying to lame them.

Those warriors around Gosse and Benoit held. Elsewhere, their lines bent, as warriors died or gave way before the onslaught. The Turned outflanked them once more, and the army of Guivergne lost its shape, their ranks collapsing.

The Turned were everywhere—in front and behind—and everywhere Liesel looked, she saw men dying. She discarded the spear and drew her short sword.

A Lipper came at her with a spear. The shaft had been snapped in half, so his reach was the same as hers. She defended against his attacks, using the small skills she had picked up. He seemed wary of her blade, content to wear her down rather than over commit. Amidst the cut and thrust, Liesel had no fear. It was do or die, and there was no time to think of anything else.

Without warning, a great sword came down on the Lipper's head. A bear-like figure grabbed her and half-carried her away.

'To the flag!' Gosse shouted.

Before she knew it, he had deposited her unceremoniously amongst the bodies that lay scattered around the Owl.

'Stay down!' he shouted, before returning to the fray.

Sul and Jehan lay where she had left them. A few feet away, she spotted a fan of red hair in the dirt. She moved over to the body of her arbalest, turning her over. Her pretty face was battered beyond recognition. Tears came unbidden at that, and Liesel had no strength left to stop them.

The Turned surrounded them. Liesel forced herself to her feet, blinking away her tears. She stood over Jehan, holding her sword in front of her. There were only a dozen defenders left around the flag now.

Gosse roared as a mighty Turned warrior grabbed his sword arm. He was rushed, trying to fend off multiple strikes.

Liesel swung at his attackers. A punch sent her spinning to the ground. She tried to shake off her daze. A body landed on top of her. She couldn't shift it. *Gosse*, she realised.

She wondered if she should hide like that.

Then Gosse's heavy frame was moving, and hands were lifting her up.

Benoit and a dozen of his warriors stood there, panting, their blades dripping with gore. The corpses of the Turned attackers lay about them.

Gosse was sitting hunched over, his eyes rolling in his head.

Plenty of Turned still surrounded them, though they too seemed to draw breath for the final fight.

Liesel met Benoit's eyes. A fire still burned there. 'If you survive,' he said, 'tell Peyre what I did.'

Then he was gone, throwing himself at the enemy.

SANC

THE MIDDER STEPPE

Sanc's path to Ezenachi was open.

He took it.

The god unleashed his magic, enough to destroy anyone else. But Sanc withstood it. What was more, he kept moving, one step at a time —Toric's Dagger now in range.

'This is my world,' he said.

Ezenachi's eyes widened. The god had no choice but to shield himself, stopping Sanc's dagger slash from reaching him.

'I can outlast you,' Ezenachi said.

Sanc gave it everything, pushing as hard as he could. But his teacher, Rimmon, had been right. Even if he had become more powerful than Ezenachi, defence was easier than attack. Killing a god was near impossible.

He began to wonder about the alternative—a truce, or peace. Forcing the god of Silb to give up some of his conquests in Dalriya. But that only opened the door to endless years of war, and Sanc wasn't prepared to accept that.

There had to be a way to break through Ezenachi's defences.

He backed away, giving himself precious moments of thinking time. To his right, Peyre and Maragin were engaged in a fearsome combat. Then it came to him. There were other sorcerers in this crater. He had to use their magic, just as he and Rimmon had leant one another their power at crucial moments.

But he had a problem. Each of his allies was engaged in their own life and death struggle. Taking someone's magic from them would most likely see them killed.

Ezenachi, sensing weakness, converted his defence to attack, forcing Sanc to shield himself. He used his power of sight to survey the sorcerers in the crater, each one of them a bright light burning with power. There was one easy starting point.

Sanc reached out to Kepa. He felt her—in terrible pain, the arrow in her chest causing so much damage that anyone else would have died. Somehow, she was able to use her control of air to keep herself breathing. Ashamed to do it, he pulled at her. Sensing him, Kepa spared what she could, sending her magic through the air to support him. It wasn't enough. He needed more.

'Peyre,' he shouted, gritting his teeth against Ezenachi's attack. 'I need your help.'

PEYRE

THE MIDDER STEPPE

It was sword against shield—and they negated one another. When the two weapons came together, the shield protected him, but failed to repel the sword.

Maragin was a relentless opponent in any situation; as a Turned, she didn't tire or experience doubt. She simply kept coming. She swung at Peyre's sword arm and he withdrew his weapon, fearing what would happen to his blade should it meet Bolivar's Sword.

Striving for patience, Peyre at last got past her defence. He whipped in a strike—but it struck the Krykker's tough skin, and he wondered whether she felt even an ounce of pain.

'Peyre,' Sanc shouted over. 'I need your help.'

I'll have to try something different.

Peyre retreated before the Krykker. *Maybe having no doubt can be a weakness.* It was a risky tactic, but Peyre began to slow.

He blocked the Krykker's strikes at the last moment, encouraging her to believe he was tiring. She came on even faster, aiming to land a blow before he could react. He dropped his shield a few inches, and she went for the opening, a high strike aimed at his neck. He anticipated it, shoving his shield up to meet the sword at the beginning of the swing, knocking her off balance.

Peyre lunged forward, swinging his sword around to hit the back of her ankles, putting all his strength into it.

With her upper body pushed back and her legs jarred forwards, Maragin lost her footing and tumbled over.

With his shield still blocking Bolivar's Sword, Peyre leapt after her. He grunted as he pushed off on his tired legs, but they didn't buckle. As the Krykker hit the ground, Peyre's blade followed, skewering through her neck.

Peyre didn't have time to take in what he had done—didn't have the luxury of emotion. He dropped his weapon, took Bolivar's Sword from Maragin's lifeless grip, and turned on Ezenachi.

Pulling in a lungful of air, he launched himself at the god. This was his chance. With Sanc occupying Ezenachi, he could finish it.

He led with the Shield, using it to deflect the god's magic. He felt the power of Bolivar's Sword surge within him, as if he was born to wield the weapon.

Before he could close in and use it, Ezenachi used his magic. The Shield absorbed much of the power, but still he was knocked backwards, sliding through the dirt of the crater floor.

'The Giant,' Sanc shouted at him.

Peyre frowned, gripping the hilt of Bolivar's Sword. He was the one who would destroy Ezenachi. He was king. He didn't take orders from his little brother.

Peyre shook his head, freeing himself of such thoughts. Sanc was the one with magic. He had to trust that his brother knew what to do. Turning away from Ezenachi, he made for the King of the Giants.

He hadn't got far when Rab let out a low warning growl. Peyre stopped in his tracks, and Rab ran past him, leaping into thin air. Except it wasn't thin air. For a few heartbeats, the dog was suspended in midair, his powerful jaw clamped onto something invisible. Elfled.

Peyre wasted no time, running for Oisin and launching his attack. This time, when the Spear struck his Shield, Peyre withstood the heavy blow. He twisted inside, thrusting forward.

And the tip of his blade still didn't reach the Giant. The difference in reach between himself and Oisin was laughable.

Peyre skipped aside as the Giant swung his spear in a wide arc. This was not going to be easy.

SANC

THE MIDDER STEPPE

With relief, Sanc watched his brother turn and make his way over to where Mildrith and the Eger Khan held off King Oisin. Peyre carried both sword and shield now. At last, the battle was turning in their favour.

Sanc renewed his attack on Ezenachi, using Kepa's help to force the god to raise his magic shield again. He still didn't have the strength to penetrate the god's defences. He needed his brother to turn the tide.

He heard Rab's bark and watched as his dog was hurled through the air. But as soon as he landed, Rab was back on the attack, barking and snapping at the ankles of the invisible Asrai. He allowed himself a moment to wonder what Rab was doing here, and how he was intervening in the combat at vital moments.

When Peyre launched his attack on Oisin, Sanc wasted no time in drawing on Mildrith and the Eger Khan. They added their power to the flow coming from Kepa.

Sanc tried to break through Ezenachi's defences. His hand shook as he pressed Toric's Dagger home. The support of the other sorcerers strengthened him.

Ezenachi's face constricted in rage and pain as he threw all his power into stopping Sanc.

It was so close. Agonisingly close. Sanc was pouring everything he had into it. A hollow feeling grew within him. He was past caring if he was using too much power. Sacrificing himself to kill Ezenachi seemed more than reasonable. But still, Ezenachi held him off. *What more can I do?* Sanc wondered, trying to fight off despair.

'Finish it.' Mildrith was next to him. She grabbed his spare hand, channelling her magic into him in a purer, stronger form.

Toric's Dagger slid into the Lipper's heart.

Ezenachi stared at them in disbelief as the body he occupied gave out and collapsed to the ground.

An ethereal form issued from the body, ghostly and vaporous. Ezenachi's true form, deprived of the body he had inhabited.

Moving as one, Sanc and Mildrith shot their arms forward, palms out. Finding a last drop of energy from somewhere, they blasted him.

Gossamer thin, the spirit before them burst, evaporating into the air.

LOYSSE

VALENNES, KINGDOM OF GUIVERGNE

Neither the arbalests nor the archers could break through the Caladri sorcerer's magic defence. Meanwhile, she completed her construction of the bridge. It reached from the ground to above the walls of the Bastion. The Turned began to make their way along it, holding shields in front of them.

Brancat ordered the archers to transfer their target from the sorcerer to the line of attackers. Some were struck, the accuracy of the arbalests proving deadly. But they were simply replaced by more Turned. There were thousands of them, and they had no fear. They only obeyed their master.

Loysse knew it was only a matter of time before the Turned were inside the Bastion. Killing that sorcerer was the key. That was where Syele had gone, she was sure.

She made her mind up, deserting the Bastion walls and its defenders. She descended the stone steps of the tower, spiralling around into the depths of the fortress. This tower was famous in her family. Esterel and Peyre had escaped the Bastion from it, swimming the moat and then exiting the city.

Loysse allowed herself a bittersweet smile at the memories of her brothers recounting the episode—Esterel embellishing the tale; Peyre deadly serious. *Now I'll have a story of my own. I pray I live to tell it.*

She entered the ground floor room. The secret exit from the tower was a window, only small enough for one person to wriggle through at a time. The wooden board that covered it had been unbolted. That was when she knew for certain that this was where Syele had gone.

Loysse wasted no time in pulling open the board and climbing out. She closed it behind her and got her bearings. She was in the kill zone, a thin stretch of ground outside the walls of the Bastion. Beyond it lay the water moat. Above her, casting a shadow on the ground, was the rubble path the Caladri sorcerer had constructed. Turned warriors made their way up. One of them fell, a bolt embedded in his chest. He landed in the water with a splash, then sank and disappeared.

Loysse moved to the edge of the water, peering ahead. She saw movement underneath the makeshift bridge. Right at the far end, where it started, a figure crouched. Syele. She'd found her.

She wasted no time entering the water. She had to fight to stop herself from gasping and revealing her position.

She swam, staying hidden beneath the bridge.

Ahead, she saw Syele circling around the bottom of the path, peering toward the Turned sorcerer. She held the blade of a dagger in her hand. It suddenly occurred to Loysse that if she threw that weapon and killed the sorcerer, the bridge above her would collapse back into its constituent parts and fall on her head. She moved out from under its protection, heading across to the bank.

When she got there, she scrabbled at the ditch, trying for a hand-hold that would bear her weight. She grabbed at a patch of grass, but when she pulled on it, it came away in her hands. She hoped the splash that followed wouldn't be noticed. But a figure loomed above her.

Syele knelt by the ditch, offering a hand. She looked furious, and Loysse felt like nothing more than a child facing a stern parent as she was hauled out of the moat.

'What do you think you are doing?' the warrior hissed. 'I told you to defend the walls.'

'What good am I up there?'

'What good are you here?'

That hurt. 'None, I suppose.' She felt a burst of anger. 'You're my bodyguard. I never gave you permission to leave me.'

'So you followed me?'

'Yes.'

Syele's eyes widened, disbelieving. 'I must kill that sorcerer. There are too many lives at stake.'

'I know.'

'You're likely going to die with me. What kind of bodyguard brings their lady into a situation like this?'

A crash sounded behind them. Turning, Loysse saw the bridge collapse into the moat, waves spreading out from the impact.

But that wasn't what grabbed Loysse's attention, like a hand to the throat.

It was the Turned who had fallen into the water. They were screaming and shouting. Calling for help.

Realisation dawned on her. 'Here!' she shouted to them. 'Swim over here and we'll haul you out.'

Syele looked at her, dumbfounded. 'What's happening, Loysse?'

Loysse got to her knees. 'Get down here and help me,' she said, reaching out to the nearest figure. Tears began to stream down her face, and she smiled despite them. 'He did it, Syele. Sanc did it.'

IDRIS

THE MIDDER STEPPE

The small band of cavalry watched as the Brasingian infantry met the Turned. Jeremias had the warriors of Rotelegen with him, the standard of the Rooster held aloft in the centre of the line. Elsewhere, Kellish, Luderian, and Atrabian soldiers joined the fray. Behind, the imperial archers mixed with Hajna's Caladri, aiming over their comrades, their missiles falling on the rear ranks of the Turned.

Idris observed the horrors of war from a distance—the ordeal of the shield wall; the fickleness of Death, choosing who would receive an arrow in the face, a spear thrust in the gut. And yet a strange part of him itched to join in. Spike grunted, which was more than likely his way of saying the same thing.

Leontios waited until their infantry had got the upper hand, then ordered the canter. A thrill rose in Idris. This was as close as he'd ever get to being a Knight of Kalinth. And what boy had never dreamed of such a thing?

Leontios didn't order the famous Kalinthian charge. Only a fraction of them carried lances or had the training for such a thing. Instead, they maintained a medium pace and engaged the flank of the Turned. They forced the Turned to break formation to defend themselves from lance and sword; from Kalinthian charger and giant lizard. Spike, having rested, attacked the enemy with renewed vigour. Idris merely held on, though his left hand could grip the reins now, making life a little more comfortable.

There was no great shattering of the Turned's lines. But, assailed by infantry and cavalry, they were rolled backwards, conceding ground to the Brasingians.

Suddenly, something changed amongst the Turned. Idris yanked at Spike's reins, pulling the lizard away.

The Turned were wailing. Many sank to their knees, reminding Idris of the power Ezenachi had exerted over the Brasingian army. He caught words and phrases from mouths—prayers, questions, expressions of grief and deliverance.

'Withdraw!' he bellowed, anxious to stop his warriors from continuing their attack.

For Idris realised the wretches before him were no longer the Turned.

LIESEL

THE MIDDER STEPPE

Liesel experienced true exhaustion. She had no energy left for emotion. She had just enough to stand without falling; just enough to grip the hilt of her sword without her hand going slack and letting the weapon fall to the ground.

Benoit and his brethren fought and killed; fought and fell; until not one of them was left standing. Liesel supposed Arnoul's son had redeemed himself. It would have been nice if someone could have survived, and told Peyre about the Viper's last moments.

The Lippers closed on the Owl of Guivergne. Jehan and Sul lay by the standard. Gosse sat with them, unable to get to his feet, unwilling to lie down. Only half a dozen stood with Liesel to protect them. Like her, their faces were as blank as the expressions of the Turned. They were breathing their last breaths, and there was nothing else to it.

A lone horseman, detached from the cavalry engagement to the north, approached. The Turned paused, observing him.

Herin slid from his mount. He drew a longsword, which he held two-handed. As he walked towards them, he swung it around his shoulders, as if warming up before a session on the training field.

'Help me up,' Gosse muttered.

Liesel offered a hand, but didn't have the strength. She dropped her weapon, gripping him by elbow and hand, and somehow raised him to his feet. Gosse grabbed his sword, gazing at it as if it were some alien object he had never encountered before.

Herin began his bloody work. He used his sword as defence and attack. He blocked a blow from one assailant, then hacked at another. Each swing was precise and swift—faster, perhaps, than any other swordsman she had seen. There was a brutality to his work—some deep hatred burned within him, fuelling his progress. He cut a path towards the Guivergnais standard. But he was just one man. First one blow, on his arm—then another, on his hip—slowed him.

Wordlessly, Gosse and Liesel moved towards the encounter. The big man swung his blade, as if responding to Herin's deeds. Not nearly as refined, his blows had an agricultural simplicity to them. Liesel supported him, doing her best to defend where he left himself open.

It was enough to complicate things for the Lippers. A moment of thought, of hesitation, was all Herin needed. His boot slammed into a knee; his hilt into a face; his ricasso deflected a slash; his edge sliced through a wrist.

The three of them met and put their backs to one another.

The Turned around them stumbled away or bled out.

More replaced them.

All Liesel could hear was Herin and Gosse's breathing—desperate gulps of air into their lungs, so that they might raise their sword arms again.

Then, the whole battlefield exploded in noise. Wails and cries carried to where Liesel stood.

The Lippers who surrounded them reacted differently. They howled with pain and fury. They shouted to the heavens. And there were words. Words in the Lipper tongue that Liesel didn't understand. But she knew what they meant.

Ezenachi was dead.

PEYRE

THE MIDDER STEPPE

Peyre changed tactics, leading with Bolivar's Sword, ready to strike with the Shield of Persala.

Oisin harried him with the Spear, each strike aimed at a different location, coming from a different angle. It was all Peyre could do to keep him at bay. *One wrong move and I'm in trouble.* That spear blade was the same length as his sword. Combined with the Giant's strength, it could slice him in two, or skewer him.

Not really fair, since I have two weapons to his one, Peyre mused. But Oisin's greater height nullified any advantage Peyre's weapons gave him.

He was grateful when Oisin backed off, though wary of what the Giant would do next. Focusing on his opponent's footwork, it took a while for him to notice the Giant's expression. A look of relief faded to sorrow. More emotion than Peyre had ever seen in a Turned.

Barely daring to hope, he looked across at Sanc. He and Mildrith stood over the body of the Lipper. Peyre had seen enough corpses. This one looked like any other. He didn't know what a dead god should look like. Just not like that.

'He's dead?' he asked.

Sanc looked at him as if he had just woken from a dream. 'Yes.'

376

His brother had just destroyed a god, but he sounded fragile; devoid of the elation one might expect. Peyre knew nothing of magic, but he suspected Sanc had given everything he had to get the upper hand.

Around the crater, those who had been in the midst of battle tentatively came together. They inspected the fallen. The outlander sorcerer Mergildo was, of course, pronounced dead. Peyre had witnessed that.

Jesper's face was full of grief as he staggered over to inspect the sorceress, his arrow still in her. Kepa still lived; she assured them she could stay that way for the time being, before her injury was properly treated. It was only then that Peyre recalled Mergildo had been the one with the healing powers. None of his companions looked like they could help her. It was Jesper and Lorant, King of the Caladri, who knelt beside the woman and worked on her wound. They tied strips of cloth around the injury to stem the bleeding.

A short distance away, Oisin and Elfled knelt next to Maragin. Peyre, guilt-ridden, joined them.

Elfled smoothed Maragin's hair from her face, a curiously gentle reaction. Oisin wept openly for his old ally. He held one of her hands in his massive ones, making her look like a child.

'I'm sorry,' Peyre said. It sounded inadequate, but he couldn't find the words to say more.

Elfled studied him with her dark eyes. The old queen of Magnia would have had some appropriate words, he was sure. But the Asrai simply stared in silence.

'You must not blame yourself,' Oisin told him. In the king's eyes, Peyre got a glimpse of the age and wisdom he had accrued. 'I knew Maragin more than anyone here. And in your shoes, she would have done exactly the same. Believe me.'

'I only got to know her a little,' Peyre said. 'But I believe you. I suppose that makes it a little easier to take.'

From the battlefield above the crater, cries and wails could be heard, a crescendo of silenced voices now freed. Their collective lament only got louder.

'There are thousands of stories such as Maragin's,' Oisin intoned. 'People who have lost loved ones. People who have been forced to do terrible things; to make terrible choices. Both those enslaved by Ezenachi, and those who remained free. It will take a long time for Dalriya to heal.'

SANC

THE MIDDER STEPPE

E zenachi was dead.

The world kept moving, but Sanc couldn't move with it. Ever since Rimmon had set him the impossible task of defeating the god who had invaded Dalriya, he had been striving to achieve just that. Now it was done, he didn't know what to do.

Of course, he was exhausted. Physically, mentally and emotionally —not to mention he had drained his magic until it was empty. Then he'd drawn more. It might never come back, but he was alive, and that felt like a miracle.

Mildrith stood with him, no doubt experiencing a similar feeling. They watched as Kepa was treated, then glanced across at Rab, who had planted himself next to Maragin.

'Come here, boy,' he said. But the dog ignored him.

'Is he waiting for her to wake?' Mildrith asked.

'Perhaps.' Sanc wracked his tired brain. 'But I don't recall Rab ever getting to know Maragin.' His hound had been acting strangely recently, that was for sure.

When she was ready, Oisin gently lifted Kepa into his arms.

'Now we need to find a way out of here,' Mildrith said. 'Unfortunately, Kepa is the one who could have done it with no trouble. And I have nothing left to help you teleport.'

'Same,' Sanc said. The thought of using magic made him queasy, as if his body was reacting against the damage it would cause him. He had no ideas to offer, his mind refusing to think. He just knew that somehow, they would get out of here. He would drag himself away from this place until he could lie down to sleep.

Led by Oisin, the small group of former allies and enemies approached him. Sanc caught sight of Jesper's face, and at last some emotion tugged at him. His oldest friend had a look of sorrow on his face. No wonder, given what had happened to him since Sanc left for Silb. But there was pride there, as well. Pride in what Sanc had done, and that was what broke through his emptiness.

Jesper's expression suddenly changed, replaced with a look of horror. 'Watch out!' he shouted.

Sanc attempted to move, but a fist to the jaw drove him to the ground. A second blow, and he saw Mildrith land close by. He tried to move—tried to resist the iron fingers that prised open his grip and took Toric's Dagger from him. But he had nothing left to give.

The dagger was at his throat. 'Stop!' came a warning voice in his ear. Maragin's voice. But how was that possible?

Jesper and the others stopped in mid stride, appalled looks on their faces.

'Maragin, we thought you dead!' Oisin said. 'What are you doing?'

'Not Maragin. She *is* dead. It's Belwynn.'

'How?' Lorant asked, the Caladri looking as confused as everyone else.

Sanc turned to look for Rab, but Belwynn pressed the blade to his neck, cutting him. 'Move again and I will finish you.'

'Rab,' Jesper said. 'She came here with Rab.'

Mildrith picked herself up from the ground. 'Let Sanc go.'

'Let him go, Belwynn,' Oisin repeated, almost chiding. 'We've all suffered. You more than most. But don't do this.'

'You don't get it, do you?' Belwynn asked. 'Ezenachi is gone, but what about this one? Think about what he has done. Travelled back and forth to other worlds. Teleported all over Dalriya. Made himself invisible. And killed Ezenachi, virtually by himself. Let him live, and we are simply allowing a new god to take his place.'

Everyone looked from Belwynn to Sanc, assessing him. Resignation blanketed him. Belwynn wasn't wrong. If he knew anything about her, he knew she would go through with it. He didn't have the power to stop her.

Even Peyre seemed to look at his brother anew. 'But Sanc hasn't enslaved people or killed innocents. He doesn't make people worship him, or command others. He's the one who stopped Ezenachi.'

'He hasn't,' Belwynn agreed. 'Yet. But the amount of power he has will corrupt him. It's only a matter of time. Dalriya is not safe with him alive.'

'Wait!' Jesper said, reaching out a hand. 'At least let Sanc speak. What gives you the right to act as judge and executioner?'

'Alright,' Belwynn said. 'Do you deny it, Sanc? Do you deny you have the powers of a god?'

'I can't deny the powers I have. Everyone has seen them. Do they make me a god? Maybe so.' Sanc saw Mildrith shake her head and go pale. 'But what about you, Belwynn? You have killed two gods. You were struck by Ezenachi with Toric's Dagger and survived. You put your spirit inside a dog. By your own logic, you should also be killed.'

'I'm already dead,' Belwynn said. 'If anyone can find a way to destroy me, I won't stand in their way.'

'I'll do it if you harm him,' said Mildrith.

'You know what I mean, Belwynn,' Sanc pursued. 'By your own logic, you are as much a threat to Dalriya as I am. In Silb, the first champions were worshipped as gods. These sorcerers who I brought here can control the very elements around us. Does that make them gods?'

'And him,' Peyre said, pointing at Oisin, who still held Kepa in his arms. 'Hundreds of years old. And look at the size of him.'

'Is there a point, Sanc?' King Lorant asked. 'Dalriya has been devastated by two gods in two generations. It's only right that we are cautious about you. You are the saviour today, but what about tomorrow?'

'That *is* my point. Diis came to Dalriya from another world. So did Ezenachi. Do you believe it will never happen again? How do we prepare for it if it does? Not by killing our most powerful sorcerers. We need them to defend us. Belwynn, you fear one figure becoming all powerful. Then we must guard against that. I am not so powerful that I can overwhelm everyone else here combined.'

Sanc watched carefully as the others digested his words. What he couldn't know was how Belwynn reacted. But Toric's Dagger was not pressed quite so close to his neck as before.

'Like a league?' Oisin asked. 'A league of gods, or champions, or whatever we call ourselves. We come together to deal with a threat. And we make sure each other never gets too powerful.'

'And we agree to an alliance,' Sanc suggested. 'The champions of Silb and of Dalriya. If one world is threatened, the other comes to its defence. Just like we have done here.'

Belwynn withdrew Toric's Dagger. Sanc turned and looked into her eyes. Except they were not hers, they were Maragin's. For all his magic and insight, he couldn't read her. Couldn't tell how sane she was. Couldn't tell *what* she was. She had no light that revealed her presence. 'You agree to tolerate my existence?' he asked her. 'As I will tolerate yours?'

'I can barely tolerate my own. But yes. A league, as Oisin puts it. I will keep watch. And the rest of you can keep watch on me. That's as it should be.'

'The League of Watchers,' Oisin said.

Sanc thought it had a ring to it.

PEYRE

THE MIDDER STEPPE

On the south side of the crater, enterprising Brasingians hung a couple of ropes that reached down. Oisin got Kepa out first, then a few figures climbed down, desperate to know what had happened.

Hajna, Queen of the Blood Caladri, wept with joy when she found her husband alive and freed from Ezenachi's grip.

Emperor Idris and Leontios, the Kalinthian, wanted chapter and verse on what had happened.

Peyre stared at the east side of the crater where his army had been fighting. No one appeared, and he began to worry.

Idris caught his look. 'The fighting may have been worse over there,' he suggested. 'And it was bad enough on our side.'

'Help me get out, will you?'

Idris and Leontios gave him a shove up and then Peyre pulled himself up, one hand on each rope, feet walking up the wall of earth. Pulling himself over the edge, he had to wait on hands and knees while he regained his breath. The exhaustion of the battle had caught up with him, and his body was demanding rest. But he had to find Liesel. The more he thought about it, the more he came to believe something had gone wrong. He had left his infantry without cavalry support for a crucial period. Weakened from the pestilence, lacking leadership—had he made a terrible mistake with his tactics?

He made his way east. Around the crater, the former Turned huddled together. Many seemed in shock, bereft of purpose. Some spoke together, others sat alone, staring into the distance.

Soon, however, there was a gap on the battlefield, empty of the living or the dead. It told him much. The Turned must have advanced on the Guivergnais, not the other way around. His fears grew, and he ran, desperate to discover what had happened. A lone horseman approached from the other direction. With relief, he recognised Ida.

The King of Magnia pulled up. 'Ezenachi is truly dead?'

'Yes,' Peyre answered, no interest in celebrating victory. 'Liesel?'

'They are looking for her,' Ida said, taking in Peyre's haunted expression. 'We broke out and engaged their cavalry. It was hard going. But the damage had already been done. It's a bloodbath, Peyre. Bodies from both sides lie heaped. But they'll find her. Inhan, Sacha, Cuenin and Jorath—they're all looking.'

Ordinarily, Peyre would have found pleasure in the list of names who had survived. But at this moment, he was only interested in one name. If Liesel was dead, and it was his fault—he knew he'd never forgive himself. Would never find joy again. He thought of his father after the death of his mother, and a creeping dread gripped him.

'My mother?' Ida asked.

'Sorry,' Peyre said, shaking himself. He needed to get control. He was the King of Guivergne and had to carry himself as such. 'She lives, Ida. She is free of Ezenachi's spell and not seriously injured. When I left, she was still in the crater. There are ropes you can climb down,' he added, gesturing back to where he had come from.

Ida sighed with relief. 'Thank you. Here,' he said, dismounting. 'Take him.'

'You're sure?'

'Of course. I pray you find her alive and well. I'm sure Gosse will have done everything in his power to protect her.'

Peyre hauled himself into the saddle and set off without a backward glance. Soon, he was passing clumps of bodies where the two forces had first met. There had been a brutal clash between the two infantry forces, an even contest with severe losses on both sides. He glanced to his left. If the enemy cavalry had hit, the Guivergnais would have been overrun. He cursed himself for allowing it to happen and pressed on.

The picture changed, with evidence of chaotic fighting and a retreat by his army. He looked about the flat terrain, unsure which direction to take. He could see small groups of horsemen riding about the battlefield. Looking for Liesel on Sacha's orders, he hoped, rather than looting. He heard a groan from the ground nearby. He didn't want to look, or care. But he saw a Turned—former Turned—soldier, lying in the mud. The side of his face was caved in, but he reached out with one hand.

'Your Majesty!' came a shout. Three riders approached, wearing the red pall on white of Morbaine. Inhan was calling him. 'We've found her, Your Majesty! She's alive!'

Relief flooded Peyre. 'Take me, will you Inhan?' He gestured at the Turned on the ground. 'Please take him back to our camp,' he ordered Inhan's companions.

He followed Inhan across the ground, still littered with the fallen. Ahead, the standard of Guivergne had been planted in the dirt. A ring of dead lay around it. About forty people had gathered there. As Peyre neared, he saw they were still treating warriors. He saw Jehan being placed onto a makeshift litter. Guilt stabbed at him.

Liesel stood by his litter, concern written on her face.

He dismounted, and made his way over to her, as if walking through a dream.

His soldiers cheered when they saw him. Some were shouting questions, but all his attention was directed at Liesel.

She looked spent, but she smiled at him as he put his arms around her, desperate to hold her and reassure himself that she was real. 'I'm sorry,' he whispered in her ear, 'I got it wrong. I didn't mean for this to happen.'

She put a hand to his head, as if it was her job to reassure him. 'It's alright, Peyre. We're alive, and Ezenachi is dead. You did it. You won.'

PART IV
EPILOGUE

678

BELWYNN

SAMIR DURG, THE JALAKH EMPIRE

In the throne room of Samir Durg, Belwynn presented Khan Gansukh with the bow of his people. If he was surprised, or pleased, to see the weapon returned, he didn't show it. Instead, he feigned boredom. His mother, Bolormaa, sat to one side, head in her knitting.

'You look different,' he commented.

'The Jalakh body I took was broken beyond repair. This is my original body. I dug it from its resting place in a graveyard in Heractus. It's strange to look the same as I did all those years ago. But that's magic. I've witnessed it all my life, yet I still don't understand it. I've met many who claim understanding; I don't think anyone really does.'

'Huh. And Ezenachi is really dead?'

'He is. Another god destroyed. They have been replaced by a new system. Watchers. There are many of us instead of one, each monitoring the others. It is the safest system. It ensures no one person can become all powerful.' She brushed her fingers across the hilt of Toric's Dagger.

Gansukh sneered. 'You think I care about this system?'

'I wasn't telling you.'

. . .

Leontios had insisted on accompanying her all the way to Samir Durg, with an entourage of knights. Now they set a route for Kalinth. Belwynn found she didn't mind the company.

'You're really returning to Heractus?' he asked her, sounding excited, and she remembered the boyish young knight whose sword she had once blessed all those years ago.

'I am the Watcher of the North.' She gave him a look. 'Self-appointed, of course.'

'And you don't mind shaking things up in the kingdom? When people see you. You're not worried about how Theron will react? And Lyssa?'

She thought about it. 'Yes. I am worried. But that's not such a bad thing. It means you care. I haven't cared about much in a long while.'

She reflected on the people in her life she had loved and lost. So many, it seemed. But there were a few she still cared about, and that was a blessing.

'It will be hard at first,' she admitted. 'But it feels like I'm going home.'

JESPER

LANDS OF THE KRYKKERS

Hundreds of ships nestled in the harbour belonging to clan Swarten.

Years ago, all but a few score Krykkers had evacuated across the Lantinen to Halvia. This time, it would be permanent, and no one would be left behind. It wasn't only the Krykkers. The remnants of the Grand Caladri also boarded the departing ships. Many of the ships belonged to the Sea Caladri. Ravaged by their enslavement under Ezenachi, they too had decided to leave Dalriya.

'Let the humans have it,' Darda, one of their warriors, said dismissively. She and Jesper stood with Oisin and Stenk, supervising the migration.

'But Dalriya has always been your people's home,' Jesper said, not fully understanding the reasons.

'We have been stuck in the far corner of the continent for generations,' she said, 'watching as the humans multiply. The result is inevitable, especially now. Better to take destiny into our own hands. While we still can.'

It was a damning verdict on his own people, but Jesper didn't argue. It was clear he would not change any minds. 'The Blood Caladri will stay in Dalriya?'

'They have the Staff of Onella, remember,' Darda said, as if that explained the difference. But Jesper thought the Blood Caladri had always trodden a different path, even before they had the staff.

'What are your plans, Jesper?' Stenk asked him.

The Krykker chieftain had ended up with Bolivar's Sword on his belt once more, after the death of Maragin. He had always been uneasy with the burden. Her passing had led to the Krykker people's decision. It was as if there was no one with the determination or authority to replace her. Instead, their lands would lie empty for a while, then no doubt be colonised by the more intrepid humans of the region.

'I haven't seen my family in a long time,' Jesper explained. 'Now I am free of all responsibility, I intend to travel to the far west and find them. After that, I'm not sure.'

'You are always welcome to visit us, friend Jesper,' Oisin rumbled.

'Thank you. But don't mistake my feelings. I'm not sure what I will do, and that feels exciting.'

'I see,' Oisin replied. 'For my part, I know exactly what I will do. Return to my wife and son and never leave them again. For the King of the Orias is not the last of his kind any longer.'

Jesper smiled. 'Thank you for heeding our call once more. I am sorry about how things worked out. If I could have done things differently...' He gave a helpless shrug.

'Release that burden,' Oisin advised. 'You did your best. And remember, we have made progress for the future. The Watchers will protect our world from now on. We are safer than we've ever been. The Spear and Sword will protect the people of Halvia.'

Stenk sighed, staring down at Bolivar's Sword as if it might bite him. 'Then we must find someone with the stature to wield the weapon of our ancestors.' The Krykker looked at Jesper for a moment. Then he drew the sword from its scabbard and offered Jesper the hilt.

IDRIS

ESSENBERG, DUCHY OF KELLAND

I n his private rooms in Essenberg Castle, Idris met with the other dukes of Brasingia. There were only two of them: Jeremias of Rotelegen, and Friedrich of Thesse. It certainly made ruling the empire a lot easier than in the old days.

'So, we are agreed?' he asked them. 'Otto is given the archbishopric of Gotbeck. But Gotbeck is subordinate to Thesse.'

Both men nodded. Friedrich, of course, looked most satisfied.

Gotbeck was in a much weakened condition since Ezenachi's invasion. It made sense to give Thesse control, and it was a nice reward for Friedrich, doubling his estate.

'I've heard from Zared of Persala. He thanks us for the return of the Shield. He also makes encouraging noises about our solution to the problem of Grienna and Trevenza.'

It was the turn of Jeremias to look pleased. The Griennese and Trevenzans had long been a thorn in his side, siding with Leopold against him. It would be a simple enough matter to add Grienna to the duchy of Rotelegen. If Zared was happy with taking Trevenza, there was little those states could do to stop them.

Enriching Jeremias and Friedrich was the most politic thing to do. He had four duchies. Domard's death from the pestilence meant he

393

now ruled Barissia directly. It would have been enough to cause jealousy amongst his peers if they weren't given something as well.

Idris took a great deal of pleasure in imagining what Leopold, Inge, and Salvinus would have made of it. It was their collective dream, after all, to dominate the empire in such a way. Multiple duchies made Idris the true ruler of Brasingia, like no other emperor before. The rest of Dalriya had better watch out. Never mind sorcerers, champions, Watchers, or whatever else. He would make the empire so powerful, none would dare threaten his people again.

'There's one more thing,' he said, the map of Dalriya unfurling in his mind's eye, full of possibilities. 'The Confederate kingdoms of Ritherys, Corieltes, and Doica are struggling, even to feed their people. They are reliant on our aid. I have received overtures from them to formalise the relationship. Imagine if we added this territory to the empire?' he said, excited at the prospect.

And why stop there? He asked himself. *The Sea Caladri are leaving their lands. The empire might stretch all the way to the south coast.*

Jeremias and Friedrich were far less enthusiastic than he was. It would, of course, make him even more powerful.

But let's be realistic. What can they do to stop me?

'You've been very busy, Your Majesty,' Jeremias said at last.

'You're right. I have. But I will have some time off in a few days. I've been invited to a wedding.'

LOYSSE

VALENNES, KINGDOM OF GUIVERGNE

Syele shut the doors of the council chamber and nodded to Loysse.

'Let's bring this meeting to order,' Loysse said, and the chat around the table quietened.

She was once more tasked with governing in Peyre's absence. Not that she minded. She was happy in Famiens, but it was remote. Meeting up with old friends was a pleasure.

She saw familiar faces amongst her colleagues, but some titles had changed. Gosse was now Duke of Martras. His lordship of the March had been passed to Sul, who also joined them. Loysse was a little dubious as to his worth, since the man had a tendency to agree with everything Gosse said. Inhan was now Lord of Saliers, and was doing a good job of pacifying that rebellious part of the country.

Florent's title hadn't changed. He shared some duties of government with Lord Caisin. But Caisin's mind was as sharp as ever. He sat with ink and parchment, controlling the record of the meeting. Peyre had certainly left behind enough advisers for Loysse to delegate as many duties as she wished.

'Before we get down to business,' she said, 'I want to raise the matter of Brancat. He's informed me he intends to retire to Morbaine when the king returns.'

'We need to decide who will replace him?' Gosse asked.

'Brancat has recommended Jehan, and I don't think many will argue with that.'

'O' course not,' Gosse said. 'Best man for the job.'

'Best man,' Sul agreed.

'I was thinking he should have a send off. Maybe not a party. He won't want a fuss. Maybe a feast in his honour.'

'Of course,' said Caisin. 'The man deserves no less for his work in Valennes. And all those years in Morbaine. Think of the great warriors he trained.'

Naturally enough, Loysse's thoughts turned to Esterel. The pain was still there, if slightly less raw. She caught Florent's expression, who seemed to be thinking the very same. Her brother was a ghost who hovered over them, impossible to forget for any length of time. But she liked to think he watched them all with a stupid grin on his face; proud of their achievements; laughing when they laughed.

'Has Brayda come down with you from Famiens?' Gosse asked.

'She has,' Loysse said, no idea of how it might be relevant.

The duke smiled broadly. 'Then maybe she can make some of her pastries for the feast.'

'I'm sure she will,' Loysse said, in the indulgent voice she sometimes used with Alienor. 'Anyway, we need to discuss the emigration of subjects north, into the—'

Gosse cleared his throat. 'Sorry for interrupting, Your Grace.' He jabbed a digit at Caisin. 'Lord Chancellor, can you make a note of that? Brayda. Pastries.'

PEYRE AND LIESEL

ARBEOST, DUCHY OF MORBAINE

When you know a place so well, it's easy to forget how beautiful it is. Peyre felt like he was seeing his old home through fresh eyes.

Arbeost had been done up. Boughs and garlands of flowers adorned the buildings. The chateau bulged with food and drink. The training grounds had been taken over by marquees to shelter the guests. But they weren't needed. The sun had decided to grace the event with its presence. Children played on the grass, all the way down to the riverbank. Everyone had a smile on their face.

Peyre mingled with the guests. Alliances still had to be bolstered, after all. He talked with the Midder lords, Cuenin and Jorath. He let them tell him how their efforts at rebuilding were going; what resources he could provide to help. He didn't push them on the future of the Steppe. Better to let things take their course naturally, without interfering.

Excusing himself, he moved on to King Ida. 'I got your report on the treaty with the Lippers. Things are still going well in the south?'

'Aye. The border is respected. But it is not such a hard border as it used to be. Magnian and Lipper merchants regularly cross it with goods to sell. Out of necessity, mainly. There are a lot of hungry folks in both realms. But the difference compared to my father's reign is remarkable.'

Mention of Edgar encouraged Peyre to ask the question he was most interested in. 'And Elfled? Have you seen her since?'

Emotion filled Ida's eyes. 'I have taken to walking along the beach. Sometimes, she will appear in the waves. As if she knows I am coming. We'll look at each other. There is still a bond there. What she's thinking, I can't say.'

'It can't be easy,' Peyre said. 'But then, losing my mother wasn't easy. At least you can still see her. And who knows what the future will bring? She's alive, so there's always hope.'

'I'll never give up hope, Peyre.'

Ida looked down at the stream. Coleta was there, playing with his siblings. It seemed a strong bond had been formed between them during those hard times of the Magnian exile. 'She is extraordinarily pretty,' Ida said. 'Don't you think?'

Peyre looked at him sharply, wondering if he knew of his own relationship with Coleta. But it didn't seem so. Instead, Ida gave him a quizzical look, wondering why he didn't answer.

'Coleta? I suppose she is.' Peyre gestured over to where Sacha and Idris stood talking with a group of Morbainais noblemen. 'She just looks so similar to her brother.'

Ida raised his eyebrows at the odd comment, and Peyre felt a fool. 'Well, I don't have that...obstacle. I think she's beautiful. Inside and out.'

* * *

THEY WAITED in the ducal rooms in the chateau. They had done their hair, their skin, their nails, and sewn each other into their dresses.

'You look beautiful,' Liesel told Tegyn.

'Not as beautiful as you.'

'More beautiful than me.'

'Hardly.'

'Shut up.'

They embraced.

'Stop it,' Tegyn told her. 'If I cry, my eyeliner will run.'

A knock at the door.

'Enter!' Tegyn called.

Lord Russell came alone. He still looked older than he used to—he was taking longer to recover from the pestilence that had laid so many low. But he beamed with happiness when he clasped eyes on Tegyn.

'You look lovely, Tegyn. I hope you don't mind me coming to see you. I was worried you might come to your senses and escape before you went through with marrying my son.'

'Don't be silly, father. I love Umbert too much. Besides,' she said, with a mischievous look at Liesel. 'I'm not getting any younger. I'm ready. Maybe you can start getting everyone into the church?'

* * *

LORD RUSSELL CALLED them into the church.

Peyre made a beeline for Umbert. 'You're sure you want to go through with this?'

Umbert made a face at him. 'You think there's any chance of escape at this point?'

'No. Tegyn would hunt you down and kill you.'

'I know. You've got the rings?'

'Of course.' Peyre checked his pockets until he found the rings. 'Seriously, I'm thrilled for you, you know that? I wondered if you'd ever settle down. How did you know Tegyn was the one?'

Umbert thought about it. 'She told me she was.'

That sounded about right. Peyre grabbed his arm. 'Come, Your Grace. Time to get married.'

* * *

Idris led Tegyn down the aisle and Liesel fought off tears as she observed her two friends. He'd not even needed persuading to wear a long-sleeved coat over his scars.

She walked behind them, holding up Tegyn's long dress, even though fresh rushes had been placed on the floor.

When Tegyn was in place, she stood to one side, next to Peyre.

'Hello you,' he whispered.

'Hello you. I had turned my mind against it. But now I wonder if I might like to do this again. One day. With you, I mean.'

'Whatever you want. So long as I get to keep you forever, I don't care.'

SANC

MOURNAI, KINGDOM OF NERISIA

It was probably the most populous city in Silb. When he thought of all the places he'd been on this continent, it was strange that this was his first time in Mournai. And yet, his convoluted path through Silb—full of doubt and questions—had worked. He'd done what Rimmon had sent him to do. Whenever he reminded himself of that, a feeling close to peace would settle on him.

King Lothar was feasting the rulers and champions of Silb in his palace. It seemed peace had come to this world, too. After their time in Dalriya, it was hard to see Temyl and Guntram as enemies any longer. Sanc thought they felt the same. Guntram, certainly. Temyl, he was less sure.

Kepa and the Eger Khan had become the closest of allies. The young ruler of the Egers had wasted no time in making his feelings plain to Lothar and King Ordono of the Rasidi. The Telds should have some of their lands returned, if justice and peace were to be restored to Silb. Herin's murderous looks reinforced the argument. Negotiations wouldn't be easy. But the balance of power had shifted in Silb. Sanc knew Kepa and the Eger Khan would get their way. They didn't really need his support, though they had it.

Sanc could almost taste the freedom that lay before him. That great weight of responsibility eased.

'I must speak to the Scorgians,' he said to Mildrith. 'I don't suppose you'll be coming with me?'

'No thanks,' she said. Some things clearly hadn't changed. Mildrith's dislike of Lenzo seemed permanent. 'But I think you should go and sort that out,' she gestured with a look of distaste.

Sanc looked over to see Rab getting petted by Lenzo, Gaida, and Atto. All three men were patting the dog at once, in a rather intense silence. Rab stood still, perhaps enjoying the attention, but it was hard to tell. It was an odd-looking sight.

'They're not used to dogs,' Sanc said, excusing them.

'I know, but by the Irgasil, what made them think that was normal? Have they ever seen anyone else do it?'

Sanc headed over straight away. To his relief, the Scorgians gave Rab a break when Sanc took a seat at their table.

'He's a good boy,' Lenzo observed of Rab.

'Yes,' Sanc said. He didn't have the heart to say anything. He knew Mildrith would have come right out with something rude. 'He helped me to defeat Ezenachi,' he reminded them. In his recounting, he hadn't mentioned that Rab had been possessed by Belwynn. Some things were too difficult to explain.

'He took the dagger and gave it to you,' Duke Atto said. 'Who's a clever boy?' he asked Rab. Sanc feared he was waiting for a response from the hound. If so, he'd be waiting a long time.

'I'd like to offer you and Mildrith Arvena,' King Lenzo said to him, a sparkle in his eye. 'It's a beautiful city, and I shall miss it. But I am stuck in Irpino all the time these days. I could come and visit with you a couple of times a year. And if I can't have the pleasure of living there any longer, I'd like you to.'

'That's very kind, Your Majesty. But I don't think Mildrith and I will have the time for it, either. We are heading for the Kassite lands after this. There is much rebuilding work to be done there.'

'You said as much earlier. But I can't understand why you would want to go to those barbarous lands instead of Arvena. I mean, you had to live with them long enough. You haven't forgotten the smell, and the mud? And the terrible people who live there?'

'They're not terrible, Your Majesty. Besides, the Kassite lands need our help. Arvena doesn't. That city can run itself.'

'I honestly don't get it. You'd rather go live in the place that's depressingly poor and needs your endless help, than a place full of comfort and culture that will leave you alone?' He frowned at Gaida, looking for help.

Gaida shrugged, equally bemused. 'I've never thought the lad was right in the head.'

'He's in love,' Atto said with a grin. 'He'd do anything to please his woman. I wonder how long that will last?'

Sanc grinned at the ribbing he was getting. 'Anyway, Mildrith and I will travel between Silb and Dalriya for the foreseeable future. Peace needs to be worked at. I need to make sure the two worlds don't forget each other.'

Lenzo puffed out a breath. 'Sounds like you're deliberately making your life as hard as possible. You won, Sanc. You're still young. It's time to celebrate.'

Sanc reflected on that. 'Even you have responsibilities now, Your Majesty. You said so yourself. Compared to what I once faced, what lies ahead of me doesn't seem so bad at all. The last few years have been difficult. Tragic, when you stop to think about it. I want to make sure something like that never happens again.'

WITH TREATIES OF PEACE SIGNED, the delegates of Mournai said their farewells and left the city.

A small, odd-looking group left via the north gate. Sanc rode Spike, and Mildrith rode Red. Rab padded along beside them. Kepa and Herin went on foot. But the Teld champion held a rug, which Sanc knew would carry her and Herin west.

'Farewell, Herin,' Sanc said, feeling emotional. 'I'll visit whenever I can.'

Herin grunted. 'I won't. I intend to get to those mountains and never leave. I've done my share of roaming around this world and that.'

'Well, you deserve your retirement.'

'I don't deserve it at all. I've simply been lucky. But I've lived long enough to learn a few things. If you strike gold, don't throw it away.' He looked at Kepa. 'I don't intend to.' Then he glanced at Mildrith. 'I suggest you don't either.'

'I won't.'

'And then there's the rest that Herin forgot to say,' Kepa said with a flinty look at her companion. 'About how proud your parents, brother, and Rimmon, would be of what you've done.'

Sanc smiled. Once, such words would have caused heartache. But his sense of peace extended to those he had lost. 'I know,' he said.

He raised a hand in farewell, then he and Mildrith began their journey north.

Confident he knew the destination, Rab loped ahead.

Sanc couldn't stop staring at the Kassite riding next to him. Did he really get to spend the rest of his life with her? Like this? It was like he'd been holding his breath, waiting for the next obstacle to appear. But it hadn't come. He released that last breath and he smiled.

He took in her leather clad body, her braided blonde hair. He waited patiently for her to turn her head so he could look into those blue eyes.

Mildrith knew he was watching her and conceded the ghost of a smile.

ABOUT

Thank you for taking the time to read *A Reckoning of Storm and Shadow*. If you enjoyed it, please consider telling your friends or posting a short review. Word of mouth is an author's best friend and much appreciated. Thank you, again. Jamie

Sign up to Jamie's newsletter and get a free digital copy of his short story collection, *Mercs & Magi*
subscribe.jamieedmundson.com

f facebook.com/JamieEdmundsonWriter
BB bookbub.com/authors/jamie-edmundson
g goodreads.com/Jamie_Edmundson

Printed by Amazon Italia Logistica S.r.l.
Torrazza Piemonte (TO), Italy

56594990R00242